LUCIFER'S FLOOD

THE DELIVERER

LINDA RIOS BROOK

REALMS
A STRANG COMPANY

LUCIFER'S FLOOD

LINDA RIOS BROOK

REALMS
A STRANG COMPANY

A NOTE TO THE READER

This book is fantasy. It is not intended to be regarded as a theological treatise. Having said that, allow me to share why I wrote it.

I believe, as do many lettered scholars and ministers, that there was a span of time of unknown length between Genesis 1:1 and Genesis 1:2. The possible mistranslation of a single word holds the potential to shift our paradigm in understanding the war in heaven, the creation of the earth, and the exile of Lucifer. "And the earth was without form, and void; and darkness was upon the face of the deep" (Gen. 1:2, KJV).

Many theologians argue that the word *was* should have been translated "had become." Known as the gap theory, this position assumes that a cataclysmic event may have occurred on the earth before the Spirit of God hovered over the chaotic deep and restored creation. *The Chumash: The Stone Edition* (Jewish commentary on the Torah) translates Genesis 1:1–2 in this way: "In the beginning of God's creating the heavens and the earth, the earth had become a confused, desolate, empty place, a wilderness."

If this translation is accurate, what happened to the earth to bring it to such devastation? Our understanding of the Genesis account may be likened to arriving late at the theater, only in time to see the start of the second act of the drama. We don't know what the first act was about, or even that there was a first act. Even if we presuppose a traditional interpretation of Genesis to be the full account of a finite creation in need of no further investigation, it still does not satisfactorily address what an infinite God might have been doing before creating the heavens and the earth.

While this story is fiction and should not be interpreted any other way, in weaving the tale, I—and the editors—have taken great care not to mishandle the biblical accounts contained herein. Jewish commentary (mentioned above) and *Dictionary of Jewish Lore and Legend* (Thames & Hudson LTD, London) have influenced the treatment of the men and women of Genesis. If their characterizations cause them to appear too "human," it is intentional. My desire is not to persuade believers to any other point of view, but to challenge the assumptions of those who do not believe but desperately wish they could.

This is a story about rebellion and consequences. It is about demonic strategy to disrupt and destroy the people of God. But ultimately, it is a story about the unrelenting love, grace, mercy, and determination of a sovereign God in pursuit of His errant children.

—LINDA RIOS BROOK

J ERUSALEM WAS MYSTICAL at night. Samantha Yale stood at her office window. She never tired of the view of the golden dome reflecting the pure light of a full moon. Her days started early and ended late, but she never failed to take a minute at the end of it all to appreciate the majesty and beauty of the most intriguing city on the earth. Tonight was different though. She was waiting for someone.

She had learned to be cautious about strangers. The nature of her work tended to attract two kinds of people: the serious scholars, those interested in communication forms of prehistoric races; and the not-to-be-taken-seriously kind. These were the ones who would waste her time if she let them. On first contact with an unknown person it wasn't easy to tell which tribe he or she represented. She had learned to weed them out quickly. When the conversation turned to aliens, UFO abduction, or government conspiracy, she quickly ended the meeting, ushering them out the door with a promise to pass the information on to others.

"I need to get a life," she said as she watched for some sign of her expected visitor. The street below was empty. She assumed he would park in the visitor's space right in front of the building, but no beams from oncoming headlights announced an approaching car. A glance at her watch told her he was not late yet. She continued to watch and wait.

Stealthily as a cat, a man in a trench coat stepped through the ground fog and hesitated beneath the pale light of the street lamp. "Where did he come from?" she asked herself as she watched him look around as if checking to see if someone followed him. He seemed uncomfortable with the large satchel under his arm, shifting it from one side of his body to the other as if expecting it to be snatched from him by some thief hiding in the shadows. A dog barked in the distance; he jumped, almost dropping the satchel.

She watched him as he turned in circles, apparently unsure of which way to go. Hoping this wasn't whom she was waiting for, she was beginning to get a sense of the tribe he belonged to. "Please, God, don't let that be him."

Finally making up his mind which way to go, the man made for the steps leading into the building of the university and rang the entry bell for after-hours visitors.

"I knew it." She groaned. "It's him. He probably doesn't have a car. He's probably not an archaeologist either. I shouldn't have agreed to this."

Samantha moved toward the door, took a deep breath, and turned the knob as soon as she heard the first tap. The man looked like he had slept in his clothes. He was disheveled and seemed confused that she had opened the door before he completed knocking on it. Academics were often careless with their appearance. She had known more than a few who couldn't be bothered with pressed pants and combed hair. His persona was not really that different from many of the older rabbis and professors who roamed the hallways of the university. Still, something about him was unsettling.

"Mr. Eman, I assume." She opened the door a little wider.

"Yes, Dr. Yale." He paused and did a visual sweep of her office before stepping in. "Thank you for seeing me on such short notice." Samantha knew good manners meant offering to take his coat, but she did not want him to feel comfortable enough to prolong his visit.

"Please sit down." She motioned toward a wingback chair in front of her antique desk. He waited until she sat on the other side of the desk before sitting himself.

"What can I do for you, Mr. Eman?" She glanced at her watch again.

"Dr. Yale, I read in the *Jerusalem Post* about your work," he paused waiting for her response. She gave none. "About the Torah codes."

"Yes, I know, Mr. Eman. You mentioned that on the phone. How can I help you?"

He shifted his eyes from side to side then down to the bottom of her desk as if he had suddenly forgotten why he was there.

"How can I help you?" she repeated.

He jumped as if startled. "I'm sorry," he paused. "Languages of antiquity—that is your expertise, isn't it?"

She nodded.

"Then I have something to show you."

"You said that when we talked. Is it in your bag?" She looked at the satchel he held firmly in his lap.

"Yes," he said making no movement to open it.

"Mr. Eman, you said you had scrolls you wanted me to see. Are they in your bag?"

"Yes, I have them right here," he spoke in a low, secretive tone. "I want to know if you know what they are." He carefully unlocked the bag and removed a rolled parchment, laying it on her desk.

Her archaeology training restrained her from picking up what was obviously a very old document. "Where did you get it?" she asked, rummaging in her desk drawer for a magnifying glass.

"What do you mean?" he asked.

"I mean where did you get it?" She laid the glass down on her desk, folded her hands, and leaned forward. "No trick questions, Mr. Eman. I simply want to know where you got it. I cannot help you if you won't tell me where this came from."

"I found it—them. There's more than one." He pointed to the open satchel. "I have more of them right here."

"Where did you find them?" she tried again.

"In a cave near Hebron."

She thought about asking him what he was doing in such a cave but thought better of it. "Better not to draw this out just yet," she thought.

"Are you going to unroll it?" He seemed anxious.

"I'm afraid to do that." She held her magnifying glass over the scroll, looking for any evidence of a hoax. "I don't know how old it is or what it is. Opening it might cause damage."

"No, it's OK," he answered quickly. "I unrolled it once already."

Her suspicion was proving to be true. Obviously he had no specialized archaeological training. She sighed at the carelessness of nonspecialists who were forever destroying important evidence with their careless treatment of ancient objects.

"You might have destroyed it."

"I didn't. You'll see. Open it." He pushed the scroll a little closer to her.

Her suspicions grew as the idea of a hoax seemed more and more likely. "Why did you bring this to me, Mr. Eman?"

"Because of your work with the Torah codes."

"I see." She was becoming more convinced he was one of the UFO tribe.

He became nervous when she said nothing more. Pushing the scroll slightly toward her again, his tone seemed almost urgent. "Please open it, Dr. Yale. This is older than the Torah."

"What?" she had not expected such a comment. "Very unlikely, sir, but even if it were, how could you possibly know?"

Unsure of her motivation, her natural curiosity as a scientist or his escalating anxiety, she carefully untied the leather string that held the scroll and gently rolled it open. Feeling no fragility of a document that might crumble beneath her fingers, she unrolled it a little more.

"What kind of material is this?" she asked, never looking up from the scroll.

"Parchment, I suppose," he answered.

"No, it's not."

"No? Are you sure, Dr. Yale?"

"I'm sure it's not parchment." Gently she rubbed the material between her fingers. "If it were parchment it would have cracked and turned to dust with the careless handling you've displayed here. That alone argues against it being as old as the Torah. I'm afraid it isn't a genuine relic, Mr. Eman. Sorry."

"No, I mean, yes, it is," He shifted to the edge of his chair, causing her to sit back slightly in hers. "Look at it. It has writing on it."

Reluctantly, she picked up her glass and examined the inscription. She leaned closer to the scroll, seeing for the first time the faded but clearly visible markings that suggested writing. It was not the work of an amateur forger. After several minutes, he broke her concentration.

"It is writing, isn't it?" he pressed.

"It's more than an alphabet," she responded leaning back in her chair and pressing her fingers together. "It's cuneiform, Mr. Eman. Do you know what that is?"

He shook his head.

"Cuneiform comes from two Latin words: *cunaus*, meaning wedge; and *forma*, meaning shape. Individual words, like this one..." Without touching the document, she pointed with the tip of her pen at a rectangular shape, "...are called pictographs because the word looks like what it means." Moving the pen across the scroll, she continued. "These wedges and hooks are called ideographs, which also represent words. This line of characters is an ideogram, which represents a concept." She paused to see if he understood her explanation. Assuming from his silence that he didn't, she tried an analogy.

"Think of it like this: Consider this desk we're sitting at. If I said to you, 'This desk cost me an arm and a leg,' what do you think I mean?"

"The desk cost a lot of money."

"Exactly. You would not have thought I had cut off my arm and leg in exchange for it. That's how an ideogram works. It takes words that mean one thing and strings them together until they present a different concept altogether. To translate cuneiform into a modern language means mastering a large syllabic alphabet as well as a large number of ideograms, which also means very few people alive today can do it."

"But you can," Eman looked intently into her eyes.

Tapping her fingers together as if measuring out her words, she said, "Yes, Mr. Eman. I suppose I could. There's only one problem. Parchment was unknown when cuneiform was used. It was etched into clay tablets. How do you suppose it came to be written on this strange material?"

"Will you do it?" he asked, ignoring her question.

She stood and walked to a nearby table and poured a glass of water. He waved his hand to decline the one she offered him.

"I won't do it until you tell me more about where you got them."

"I can't." His voice was distraught. Standing up to face her, he continued. "Look at me, Dr. Yale. I promise you I didn't steal them. And I know you've figured out that I'm not capable of creating this caliber of forgery."

"Why are you so desperate to have them translated?"

Eman slumped back down in his chair. Putting his head in his hands, he shook it from side to side. "Because it's a diary."

She suppressed a smile. "A diary? Whose diary?"

"Please, Dr. Yale. I can't tell you anything more. Just translate the first scroll. Just one, then you'll see."

Her training and experience shouted, "Fakery!" into her brain. Whoever he was and whatever he had were bound to be part of a con game she had not yet figured out. "I should have thrown him out," she thought as she watched him with his head resting in his hands. But there was something pathetic about him. He didn't seem capable of a complicated plot.

"One scroll," she agreed, overriding training and experience with a gut-level intuition that told her to pay attention to what was before her.

"Thank you, thank you, Dr. Yale." He jumped to his feet and reached for her hand and shook it fervently. "You'll see. When can you do it?"

"I'm not sure. I'll get to it as soon as I can. Give me your card and I'll call you."

His face fell. "I don't have a card or a phone. I'll have to call you." Leaving the scroll on the desk and fastening his satchel, he hurried to leave.

"No phone? Not even a cell phone?"

"No, no." He stumbled as he caught the satchel strap on the arm of the chair almost turning it over. "I'll call you. In twenty-four hours I'll call you." He moved to the door.

"Impossible," she began, but before she could protest or ask any more questions, he was gone.

Samantha was still standing when at last she shook her head as if reviving from a trance. "What happened here?" She surveyed the empty room, confused as to how this strange man could have disappeared so quickly. She carefully opened the heavy oak door and peered out to see if he might be lurking in the hallway. Satisfied the corridor was empty, she closed and locked the door and returned to her desk. Staring at the scroll and trying to decide what to do, she became aware of the strange disquiet she felt toward it.

Through her open window she could hear the chiming of a faraway clock. "I shouldn't do anything with this until tomorrow." Half rising from her seat, she abruptly sat back down as if an invisible hand had rested on her shoulder, compelling her to stay where she was. Fingering the scroll, but reluctant to open it, she attempted to reconcile her uneasiness with the excited curiosity of an explorer rising up within her.

"You don't need this distraction, Samantha Yale," she said aloud, as if hearing her own voice would convince her that whatever it was, tomorrow was soon enough to find out. "Thou shalt not kid thyself, Sam. You know you wouldn't sleep anyway."

It had always been like that for her—captivated from her youth by the intrigue of the past. "What is, *was*," her mentor had insisted. "What was, *is*." She closed her eyes to remember the wisdom in his eyes as he taught her. "You cannot understand the end, Samantha, until you understand the beginning."

But where was the beginning? How far back could the human mind go in search of it? Gently unfurling the ancient document, she took it captive, placing paperweights at each corner to forbid its escape until it gave up its secrets. With the magnifying glass in hand, she looked intently at each marking as words emerged and came alive with the voice of someone long ago who beckoned her to listen.

CHAPTER 2

ALL RIGHT," she said as she gave in to the lure of antiquity. "Talk to me." Taking her pen in hand, she began a careful translation.

It's not like I didn't try to fight. I swung the sword with all my might, but Rafael did not even duck. He ripped the blade from my grasp and wielded it right back at me as if it were nothing and I was less. If utter terror had not propelled me to jump much higher than I was able under normal circumstances, well, that would have been the end of me right there. Some of us were warriors, and some of us were not. I was among the "nots." No sane person would confuse me with a warrior. That's why Rafael lost interest in me so quickly and went after a more worthy opponent. He realized I was neither a threat nor a trophy.

I may not have a lot of courage, but I do have common sense. I quickly began looking for someplace to hide. The safest place for me would be the throne room—if I could make it there. Not a chance. From a distance I could see it was so heavily guarded that it would be certain destruction to try to break through that line.

I was afraid to stand up and run lest I get in the way of those flashing swords. Abandoning any pretension of pride I might have once had, I dropped on my belly and crawled like a worm until I found an unguarded rock where I curled in a ball and tried to make myself as small as possible. The lightning flashes from the swords were so terrifying that I got a cramp trying to force myself lower still behind the rock that couldn't possibly protect me anyway. With my eyes shut tight, I waited for it to be over.

That's why I didn't see what happened. I was too afraid to look until the thunderous crashing around me became so horrible that what I couldn't see scared me more than what I could. Sensing a pause in the action, and hoping I wouldn't make my situation worse, I opened one eye to see if I could get away before the fighting started up again.

When I looked up and saw Michael the archangel and captain of the host not three feet from where I was hiding, I squealed as if I had been sliced in half. Michael's eyes flamed, and his bulging muscles pulsed as he swung his sword in my direction. I fell over and pretended to be dead.

With my eyes closed again, I didn't move a feather as I listened to the sounds of war around me. Michael never missed, so I knew I was not his target, but it didn't take long to figure out who was. It was Damon, the platoon leader, who had met the might of Michael's sword. I swallowed the scream rising up in my throat and continued to play dead.

I was desperate to find out how badly Damon might have been hurt. If it wasn't too bad, maybe he would give me cover while I ran away. I cracked my eye again in time to see Damon's severed head roll across the ground and land right on top of my left foot. Playing dead was no longer working for me.

I nudged Damon's head away with my toe, then jumped up and ran, flew, stumbled, and tumbled back toward the throne room, babbling all the way. I knew I must get through somehow. What would I say? I would plead for mercy. I would plead insanity. I would grovel at the feet of the guarding angels. Call me a traitor or call me a coward, I did not care. I was working out my plea in my head as I ran along the streets of gold, dodging the lightning bolts bursting forth from both sides.

I was almost there, but I was too late. A thundering silence settled in like a fog over the city of God. As quickly as it had begun, the war in heaven was suddenly over.

CHAPTER 3

S AMANTHA LOOKED IN the mirror over the lavatory of her private bath—one of the few perks she had as a fellow at the university. With her tousled black hair and faded makeup from the day before, she knew she was fast beginning to resemble the absent-minded rabbis and professors who slept in their clothes. She remembered how her mother had told her as a teenager that African American girls like her had naturally beautiful skin and didn't need costly cosmetics like her friends painted on their faces. "Mama, you were so wrong," she thought as she tried to freshen her tired face with a splash of water.

She had not left her office in more than twenty-four hours. A lone cookie from a box lunch days before was all she had eaten since beginning the translation. Now she waited eagerly for Wonk Eman's phone call.

Pacing the length of her office and occasionally looking out the window for some sign of him, her mind raced through the possible implications if the scrolls were authentic. At last the phone rang. She picked it up and waited before speaking.

"Is it you, Dr. Yale?" asked the whispering voice on the other end.

"Yes, Mr. Eman, it's me."

"Please call me 'Wonk.' I am so uncomfortable with Mr. Eman."

"As you wish." She did not suggest he call her "Samantha."

"Did you read it?" he asked anxiously.

"Yes, I did. When can I get the other scrolls?"

Silence.

"Are you still there, Mr.…uh…Wonk?" she wondered if the connection had been lost.

"I'm still here." He paused again. "I'm sorry, Dr. Yale. I hadn't thought this far ahead. I wasn't sure you would translate the scroll. Now that you have, I'm not sure what to do next."

"The first thing you must do is bring me the other scrolls." She hoped she did not seem overbearing; he was such a nervous type, and she did not want to scare him away.

Silence.

Intentionally using her softest tone, she prodded him. "Wonk, I cannot translate the scrolls if I don't have them. You do want them translated, don't you?"

"Yes, of course," he replied. "They must be translated."

"Can you bring them to me—today?" she gently pressed.

"I will have them delivered to you. I can't come myself. Someone could be watching me. There could be consequences."

"Now, listen, Wonk," she struggled to keep her tone soft. "You assured me the scrolls had not been stolen. If they're contraband, I can't touch them."

"No, no, nothing like that. They belong to me."

"Then bring them to me yourself. You should be careful about sending them by messenger. If you must, then use a delivery service like FedEx—or an agency that issues a tracking number so they can't disappear."

"I will do it. By tomorrow I will have them to you. But you must be in your office to receive them. They can't be left to anyone else."

"Don't worry, Wonk. I will stay in my office tomorrow until they are delivered."

"Yes." His voice seemed unconnected to his thoughts. "Yes, of course, they must be translated. I know it must be done."

Samantha attempted to reassure him. "It is the right thing to do. I need to see all of them to ascertain the true historical value of such a discovery." She paused; hearing no response, she continued to affirm his decision. "After all, I know you are anxious to know what they will reveal."

"I already know, Dr. Yale."

Chapter 4

SAMANTHA ARRIVED AT her office much earlier than usual. Although the package would not be delivered until 10:00 a.m., she took no chances on missing an early delivery. No matter how many times she looked at her watch, the minutes passed at the same speed. Finally, she heard a knock on her door.

"Dr. Samantha Yale?" asked the delivery man in a blue uniform. She nodded.

"Sign here." Giving her a copy of the delivery confirmation, he carried the box into her office and set it down on the small conference table. "This OK?"

"Yes, right there is fine. Thank you very much." She quickly ushered him out the door.

Taking a letter opener and a pair of scissors from her desk drawer, she began the task of cutting through the tape that bound the box on all sides. Lifting the lid and removing the bubble wrap, she paused a moment to consider how she should remove the scrolls. She hoped they were in some kind of order.

The scrolls had been carefully arranged in layers of four across. Assuming this to be the chronological order, she took them out one by one and laid them cautiously across the rectangular table. "How will I keep them in order if I have to move them?" Looking around her office for a solution, she spied a pad of Post-it notes on her desk.

"Why not?" She took the pages from the pad, numbered them, and attached one to each scroll. "Twenty-first-century bookmarks meet antiquity."

She carried the first scroll to her desk and carefully rolled it out. She paused for a moment to consider the task she was about to undertake. Looking intently at the markings on the strange parchment, she thought, "If this is a hoax, it is artfully done."

Taking her pen in hand, she began to unravel the secrets of—she wasn't exactly sure of what. An angel? A deranged person of long ago? Her anticipation escalated as she set about the search for the elusive writer.

I have a name. But no one has called me by name for a long, long time, so I don't suppose it matters much what it is. No one could understand what happened to me on that awful day. It was not my fault, but I was blamed and punished as if I were as guilty as the rest. Let me remain hidden in the shadow of anonymity. At first, I dared to hope there might be some restitution if I just had the chance to explain how such a disaster came about—as if confessing would somehow bring redemption for the foolish and tragic thing I did that, let me be clear, was not my fault. If any modicum of redemption were available to me, I would risk anything to attain it. But it is not so. Redemption is not possible for me. It was not only a terrible mistake, but also an eternal one.

None of what happened is fair to me. Why should redemption be available to humans and no one else? What makes humans more worthy than I am? I have feelings. I tried my best. I made one mistake—just one— ever. Shouldn't I be entitled to a second chance? When I tell you what happened, you will see it was not my fault.

You can only understand the lunacy of the rebellion if you first know about Him. Everything begins and ends with Him, so I shall try to tell you what He is like. He is called the Ancient of Days, Elohim, Yahweh, Jehovah, I Am, and God. He is without beginning and without end. He did not come to be; He was, He is, and He will always be. His existence defies the limitations of the finite minds that He has created. His creation would call His name by what they saw Him do. And we, those who are like me, saw Him do marvelous things. Indeed, we were some of the earliest part of His creation. I don't know when we came to be or how we came to be, but suddenly we *were*, and it was as if we had always been. And so we knew Him as the Creator God who existed in three persons: Yahweh (the Father), Adonai (His Son), and Ruah Ha Kadosh (whoever He was because no one was ever sure). Three distinct beings and yet in such perfect oneness with one another that it never occurred to any of us that an outsider might be perplexed as to how such a thing could be. This is how it was; how it always was. Not one of us questioned how or why. They were One, and we were the host of heaven.

Adonai, His Son, was forever making things. I often wondered where He got His ideas. (Some thought He really didn't have any ideas of His own. They were His Father's wishes, and He just carried them out.) Whatever the case, one could never be sure what He was going to make next. For example, He would make a useful thing one day and the next make something that seemed to have no purpose at all. Like the planets—what was He thinking? After taking a look at a few of them, it was obvious to me He had truly not thought through what He planned to do with them before He started. As far as I could see, all but one were duds. Still, He kept on making them until a good part of the universe was cluttered with them. To me it seemed He just could not get the formula right.

The stars, on the other hand, were a good idea. We could see that right away. If nothing else, it gave Him a place to put the useless planets. Earth was the only one you would take out of the closet to show company.

I remember the awe in all of us the first time we really looked at Earth. It was beautiful. The blue and green oceans were teeming with life we had never imagined. The seas alone could have been a universe unto themselves. There in the depths of the waters were caverns so massive that they could have swallowed up any canyon on the surface of Earth. The mountain ranges deep beneath the surface dwarfed the magnificent ranges that spiraled above the land itself.

And let me tell you about the fish. Keep in mind that none of us had seen one before. To be sure, Adonai made many other life forms far more complex and interesting to look at. None of us truly appreciated the complicated engineering required to make a working model from fins, scales, and gills. He made it look simple, so naturally, we thought it was.

As far as I was concerned, this displayed an aspect of Adonai's character that defied understanding. He made thousands of them. Big, little, beautiful, funny looking, ferocious looking—every kind of fish you might imagine was there in the pristine waters of Earth. But that wasn't what fascinated me as much as the tiny ones that lived near the ocean's floor.

I couldn't believe the detail that went into making these little bitty creatures. No bigger than two or three inches at most, they lived in the coldest depths of the water, where humans would never go. Miniature works of art, painted with iridescent colors of chartreuse, aqua, green, blue, and yellow, and many of them with funny little headdresses that looked like hats made of fine feathers. Now here's why I marveled at these particular fish: Who was going to see them? Who would know they were there?

Nothing that lived above the waters could have descended to those depths. Not for eons could that happen, and then only in specialized craft much like what would eventually penetrate outer space. What was the point of putting so much creativity and beauty into something that no one would ever see?

Then I figured it out. He created them for Himself. He delighted in them whether any other living thing knew about the fish or not. He made them for His own pleasure.

Adonai liked the idea of fish so much that He did something I have rarely seen either He or His Father do. For the sake of the fish, He would defy one of the natural laws He had set in place to govern this new world. As nearly as I could tell, He did it solely to protect His fish.

Simply stated, here is how this law works: objects denser than water will sink in water. Ice is denser than water and should sink, but it does not. It floats.

Why? He must have been thinking about the parts of Earth where the waters would be so cold they turned to ice. Instead of sinking to the bottom, as, say, a rock would have, the ice stays on the top of the water. He wanted to protect His fish. The ice floats on top, and the fish continue to swim about in the waters below completely unaware of the amazing thing that has happened on their behalf.

Everyone in heaven came to the show when the comets were about. They looked like balls of fire shooting through the blackness of space at enormous speeds, dragging a tail of ice behind. It was breathtaking to watch. To be candid, the first time I saw a comet, I thought Adonai must have created it as a toy. I tell you there was no limit to His flair. For example, who would have thought of making a blue sky to match the seas? Skies were black, at least the ones we had seen before.

Then one day, He got an idea for something entirely different—and totally disruptive, I might add. How can I describe it? A rift? An interruption? Out of eternity where everything had been "now," He separated "now" into "past" and "present" and "future" and named it "time." Time had a beginning and passages and an end. Then He stepped out on the edge of time with His Father, and They observed what He had made. They liked the concept so much, They made everything else They created obedient to time. Even the universes and the stars and planets became governed by time. But the Godhead—the three of Them—were neither in time nor subject to time. And neither were we.

Time was to move forward, never backward, and at a steady pace with no sudden surges. It was then when He decided to put life on Earth. It was not going to be like anything They had done before. I don't know that we ever saw the three of Them as excited about any project as They were about this one.

We angels were not that interested in a new life form—especially if it were on one of the planets, even if it was the pretty one. That is until we found out the new life form would definitely be inferior to us and that He intended to set us as guardians over it.

Considering how things turned out, if He could do it over again, I'm pretty sure He would have made a different decision. It's His own fault that He couldn't have a do-over. If He hadn't made that law about the passing of time and that everything in time must pass with it, He could have reversed things and no one would have known the difference. But I digress.

Up until that day, we in the angelic realm never considered the notion that we could rule over anything. But once we did think about it, it made perfect sense. After all, we had beauty, strength, gifting, personality, intelligence, and free will. Why shouldn't we rule something—in the proper order, of course? The three made the decisions about the affairs of Earth, and we would carry them out. At first, we never thought to do it any other way.

And why would we? Our place in the universe was exalted, inferior to no other created thing, and our purpose was to do His bidding. In all of creation we were created the closest to the hearts of Yahweh and Adonai. The third member of their being, Ruah Ha Kadosh, did not actually interact with us. In fact, most times we were not really sure when He was around. He was not visible in the same ways the Father and the Son were visible. I suppose that sounds strange, but I don't mind telling you He *was* strange—mysterious even. At least it appeared so to us. It was easier to see the evidence that He had indeed been *somewhere* than to identify precisely where that *somewhere* might be. In other words, we could better point out where He *was* than explain where He *is*. But when anything important happened, He was always there.

Knowing humanity as I do, I'm certain that it's impossible for you to imagine what life was like for us before that tragic day. One of the design errors in human makeup is that history is completely wasted on you. You humans amaze us with your unquestioned belief that nothing grander than yourselves ever existed or that anything important ever happened before you came along. You really have no idea how it was.

It was much more majestic than you have imagined eternity and paradise to be. In fact, humans have such an impoverished view of what heaven is like that it amazes me that so many of you hope to go there when you die. If paradise were no more than you seem to think it is— cloud sitting, strumming harps, and singing hymns—I can't imagine why anyone would hope to spend eternity there. Why does that idea hold so much appeal for you, then, when nothing of the sort appeals to you now? It must be that you desire paradise only as an alternative to hell, but you are not really eager for it. Oh, but if you knew what it was really like, well, you would long for it as I most painfully do now. Neither your language nor mine is sufficient to describe heaven, so I shall not try. It is unspeakable. It is marvelous. I desperately long for the way it was when I was there with Them. But it is quite lost to me.

I wish I could explain what transpired in our hearts that dreadful day. I don't know how or why we began to change, but I do know when. From the first day we were set as celestial guardians over Earth, we were never the same. Lucifer pointed out to us that we had never before been allowed to realize our full potential, but now we were finally finding our true place. We liked being in *charge* of something. Not me, of course. No, thank you. I didn't want the responsibility of ruling over anything, but for some of the others, it was a different thrill altogether. I won't name names, of course, but let me tell you, some of them were absolutely giddy with the taste of power. It was embarrassing. That's when they began to believe a terrible thing. I will admit that hearing them talk about the possibilities did give one a bit of a tingle—even me. Lucifer helped us imagine ourselves in lofty ways completely contrary to our nature.

"Perhaps we were made to rule," he proposed.

"Lucifer's right," someone quipped. "Why should there be only one ruler?"

"Why shouldn't we rule ourselves? What in creation is more magnificent than us?"

The more they talked, the more they began to desire more than heaven. I began to wonder if we had somehow missed out on something. It wasn't long until we developed such pride in our own extraordinary selves that we started to consider how we could leave our sphere and its confinement. Lucifer was right.

"Why should there be limits for us? And who should decide what they are?" he asked.

Angels cannot handle ambition. Until Lucifer introduced us to the concept, our entire purpose for being was to carry out the plans of God; we never thought about doing anything else. Of all God had made, we were the most like Him. The heart of God was love, and He lavishly loved us. Perhaps that's why we were so foolish as to think our actions had no consequences. We had never disobeyed before. It had never been in anyone's imagination to do such a thing.

And that's how things would have remained if it hadn't been for Lucifer. It was entirely his fault. As one of the highest-ranking archangels, he had access to the throne room—something that none of the rest of us had. That's why we attached so much weight to what he said. Lucifer caused us to think about how exciting things might be if he were in charge. I don't know why, but I have to tell you there was a strange exhilaration about the idea. I found myself being swept along with the others in the excitement. Did we never once think there might be consequences for disobedience? Oh, yes, we did. But not really.

We were convinced that God's love for us was so great that it would not allow Him to bring punishment against us. Nonetheless, I was nervous.

"What if God isn't amused by Lucifer's political ideas? What if He thinks self-rule for us is rebellion?" I asked. "Will He just overlook it like nothing happened?"

"He can do nothing else. He is all about love, and He cannot deny His own nature," Lucifer assured us.

"Then are we safe to insist on our own way?" asked another. Lucifer nodded confidently, so we agreed that it must be true.

It was our knowledge of the depth of God's love for us that makes our betrayal all the more despicable. Oh, I know you think that you know about Lucifer. There was a time when we thought we did too. Believe me, you know nothing. You do not know his cunning or his hatred for all that lives on Earth. You do not know the extent of his willingness to corrupt, destroy, and steal. Perhaps that is the true reason I have decided to tell you what I saw happen. Lucifer is the source of my misery. If I seem bitter at times as I recount the events that forever changed heaven and Earth, well, it is because I most certainly am. It began with the rebellion of Lucifer.

Yahweh Himself would say Lucifer was the seal of perfection. He was wise, perfect, and beautiful. He glittered like a star when he moved about. He was clearly God's favorite. This is why none of us could have imagined what was about to happen. Even when the summons came, we were not alarmed. We were called to assembly in the high court of heaven, but that had happened before. God often called us to assembly when He had something new to share. He wasn't looking for our input, of course. I think He liked the looks on our faces when He amazed us with His inexhaustible creativity.

"What's the meeting about?" someone asked, but no one seemed to know.

We mused out loud as to what might be in store until the Ancient of Days took His place on the judgment seat of heaven. The atmosphere changed instantly. The angel next to me whispered, "Something is wrong."

"Wrong?" I whispered back. "How can anything be wrong in heaven?"

No one dared say anything more. Without being told to do so, we fell to our knees and folded our wings at the weight of His presence.

But something really was wrong. We had not seen Him like this before. The only word I can use to describe Him is *somber*. But how could that be? He was never somber. What was there to be somber about in heaven? We looked to Adonai for a clue, but His eyes betrayed nothing of what His Father was about to say.

Following God's gaze, I realized that Lucifer was standing alone among the kneeling angels. I nudged the angel next to me. "Tell him to bow down."

"He doesn't have to," he answered back.

"Do you see God's eyes?" I asked as quietly as possible.

The angel raised his head and saw the eyes of God sweeping across the legions bowed down before Him. Ducking back down, he quickly tapped the wing of the angel next to him, starting a moving line of nudges and whispers for Lucifer to bow down, but he would not.

"He isn't going to do it," the angel answered.

"Make him," I blurted out.

"Make him?" he asked incredulously, as if I had suggested some ridiculous thing, which, I suppose I had. Certainly none of us could make an archangel do anything.

"Then tell him to go stand by himself." I eked out the words and lowered my head as the cherubim who went before God ceased moving and lay flat on their faces as Omnipotence rose from His seat. Peering directly into Lucifer's eyes, as if no one else were in the room, God the Father opened His mouth to speak. The tone in His voice was heavy beyond bearing as He said to the arch-angel, "From the day of your creation, you were sheer perfection. Now look at what you have become. Evil has been found in you."

The pillars of the courtroom trembled at His words, and smoke rose above as the atmosphere became unstable. No one dared stand.

"What did God say?" The muttering swept through the kneeling angels.

"Evil? In Lucifer?" The accusation telegraphed through the whispers of the gathered host.

"Wait a minute," I interrupted. "What does God mean by *evil*? We don't know anything about *evil*."

For a moment the telegraphing stopped as the others realized what I said was true. Although it was clear from God's words that something was definitely wrong, no one in heaven could possibly have understood something that until now had not existed. Before Lucifer's rebellion, there was no concept of evil, so how could we possibly be sure what it was?

"It has to be about Lucifer's intent to rule," one of the others said.

I hunkered down a little more and tried to imagine what I would do right that minute had I been in Lucifer's place. I would be apologizing, groveling on the floor, and working on a plea. To this day I don't know why Lucifer risked it. He must have known he had picked a fight he could not possibly win. He should have backed down. That's what I would have done. The accusations against Lucifer began among the still kneeling, anxious angels.

"Why did we let him get this far?"

"Why wasn't his position enough?"

"Lucifer was cherished and denied nothing. Now look at what he's done?"

"He shouldn't have involved us. We haven't done anything."

"We're guilty by association; that's all. We don't deserve any punishment."

The angel next to me tugged on my wing and asked, "What did God think was going to happen? Is He going to take some responsibility for this?"

"What are you saying?"

"He spoiled him, overindulged his every whim. This really is partly God's fault, you know."

"God's fault?" I was unnerved at the utterance, though I had privately thought the same thing.

"Didn't God know that if He gave us the ability to defy Him, it would only be a matter of time until one of us thought to try it?" By now others were finding their tongues.

"He must have known it would happen in the right circumstances. Maybe Lucifer was tricked. It could have been one of us," came a voice from behind.

I said nothing more but began to think about Lucifer's defense. It was a bad idea on God's part to put both power and free will into the same being. If there were a better control system of checks and balances, none of this would be happening.

Not that it matters now, but I believe that in the beginning Lucifer truly loved God, but somewhere along the way, his love turned inward and decayed into a yearning for a power that was denied him. It happened after Earth was hung in space. Lucifer rebelled against the boundaries he had been given concerning Earth, whatever those boundaries might have been.

That's the thing you need to know about God. He sets boundaries. But here is where it gets fuzzy. If we wanted to do so, we could cross the line we were not supposed to go beyond. How's that for mixed signals? Why would

God make us able to do something we were not allowed to do? I've never understood that about God.

It was obvious to me that Lucifer was in trouble because he had crossed some kind of boundary concerning Earth, though no one knew what it was. God, who created and loved him, must now do one of three things: move the boundary, indulge him, or destroy him. I could see that nobody was going to win this one.

All of heaven could feel the heaviness in God's voice when He confronted Lucifer. When the rest of us realized God's favorite was not getting a pass, we got really quiet and waited to see how he would respond. Lucifer was outraged.

"Objection! Out of order! There is no legal precedent for this. How can this be?" he demanded of God, the court, and anyone else who might be listening. His voice trailed off as he began muttering gibberish as if Yahweh would know what he was talking about. None of us did.

Lucifer shamelessly began to accuse God right there in front of us.

I shuddered at how far he went as he ranted against the goodness of God.

"You are an imposter, God. It is Your power and not Your love that brings about Your will." Lucifer bellowed to the heavenly host that Yahweh was not a God of love at all.

Then he turned toward us. "He is a God of manipulation who creates free will and then denies it." Lucifer tore his hair and stomped his feet. He contorted with rage. His eyes were filled with fire and hatred. Like one gone mad, he spun to confront the other archangels who stood at their posts.

"Listen to me," Lucifer sputtered, "or you're next. Can't you see what is happening? This jealous God cannot be trusted."

"What does he mean, we could be next?" someone whispered from the ranks. The angels looked at each other as if the thought of such a thing had never been in anyone's imagination. Lucifer did not miss the uneasy glances exchanged between them. He pressed in harder.

"None of you are safe. See how He will destroy anyone who does not obey His every whim. Why do you think He has turned against me? He is jealous of His own creation."

I raised my eyes carefully to look at Michael's face. How long would this tirade against the Most High God be allowed to continue? I didn't know what would happen next or which way I would run when it did.

Nobody tried to stop him, so Lucifer continued to make it worse. "Only I of all the heavenly host dare to speak the truth. The rest of you are cowards."

Lucifer drew his sword from his belt and brandished it about so furiously, some stepped back from him in fear of losing a wing. I found myself cringing at every swipe and secretly wondered why someone hadn't taken that thing away from him as a precaution. Weapons are a bad idea in a courtroom. I wondered whether the consequences of Lucifer's fit might fall on the rest of us.

I really blame God for not putting an end to the foolishness right there. If only He had, the whole thing would have been over before the court of angels began to divide. "Surely they aren't choosing sides?" I thought. "Who would choose to side with a deranged archangel and against the Most High God?"

If there was going to be a fight, I wanted to get away before it started. I began thinking about the consequences if I stood in the wrong place. Some of the host moved close behind Lucifer as he condemned the cherubim, God's holiest angels, for their obedience to God. He accused them of pretending that their allegiance to the Ancient of Days was based upon love when in truth they were terrified of His absolute power and demands for unquestioned loyalty.

Lucifer jeered at them. "This God you bow down to would rather destroy my beauty and cast me down than admit that the creation has become more desirable than the Creator." Lucifer blistered the air as he whirled about with the flaming sword, ranting like one gone completely mad. "I will raise my throne above the throne of this misguided God. Choose whom you will follow, or die."

My eyes were twitching in terror, but God did not blink. It seemed for a moment like He might not do anything. Confusion grew as the angels asked, "What if it's true?"

Some of the neutral angels listened and believed Lucifer's claims and moved toward his side. Now, here's something you need to know about him. He is the prince of lies, but he doesn't lie all the time. He has no qualms about taking something that *might* be true and concocting a believable and persuasive fabrication that is completely wrong.

Once you hear one of his exquisitely constructed part-truth lies, you will find yourself thinking about it. Pretty soon, you will be wondering how it *could* be true. That's what happened to me.

I'm ashamed to admit it, but I found myself seeing things from Lucifer's point of view. He brought up an extraordinarily important question with repercussions for everyone. If God were willing to expel the prince of the archangels, His favorite, what might He do to any of the rest of us if we displeased Him?

"Ridiculous," I said to myself. "It would not happen. It could not happen. The whole idea was preposterous."

My last nerve was about to unravel when I realized that sides were being chosen for a fight, and no one would be allowed to sit it out. I zigzagged back and forth across the room, fretting about where to stand. If

I stood with Michael's warriors and they lost, Lucifer would destroy me for disloyalty. I had that clearly figured out. If I stood with Lucifer's side—way in the back, of course—and they lost, Michael might simply overlook me since he never seemed to notice me before anyway. It was possible. It was at least worth a try.

Then Adonai stood up—a bad sign for us all. Standing meant judgment was about to be unleashed. The Son of God pronounced the sentence on Lucifer. "You corrupted your splendor by your sin. You corrupted My Father's glory by your ambition. Depart, and be cast down to Earth," His voice thundered.

I could barely take in what I was hearing. Lucifer cast out? Cast out to where? To what place is an archangel exiled?

"God can't really banish an archangel, can He?" whispered someone whom I could not identify.

"Of course not," I muttered to myself, but I did not convince myself in the least.

Lucifer so miscalculated the nature of God; he truly believed God would not—could not—destroy what He loved. I can look back and see why this strategy never had any possibility of working. Lucifer failed to take into account that the *holiness* of God was as great as His *love*. God would not allow His holiness to be profaned among His creation, even for the sake of His love.

At Adonai's command, Michael unleashed his powerful army as war broke out in heaven. Lucifer fought back with all of his power, and one-third of the heavenly host fought with him.

The offense within Lucifer blazed and consumed his heavenly nature. "Thrown out? Expelled from heaven? Cast from the presence of the One who created me? No!" he raged. "You will never do it."

But God most certainly did. The war in heaven was on.

Lucifer raged against the judgment of the Most High God and lost not only his place in heaven but also his name. He would no longer be called "Lucifer the light bearer." He would be called "Satan the accuser," because he accused God and the other angels who remained faithful to Him.

Following Michael's orders, Rafael, Ariel, Gabriel, and the other archangels brandished their flaming swords with great skill and precision. They seemed to grow taller, enormous even, right before our eyes as we actually diminished before them. I could feel myself shrinking and my wings wilting before their wrath. That's when I realized I had been standing in the wrong place.

"Oh, no." I protested, scurrying toward the other camp. "I didn't choose sides yet. I was thinking it over." But it was too late.

One of the rebellious angels forced a sword into my hands, and I swung the best I could but hit nothing. I knew I looked foolish. Suddenly the atmosphere became suffocating and heavy. It was as if someone had removed the pillars that held heaven in place and unleashed an invisible force upon us. We staggered under the weight of what we could not see. Pressed down, barely able to stand, we felt a strong wind that came from nowhere and from everywhere at once. We rolled back and forth as we lost our footing. I felt dizzy beyond description.

"Oh, no," I thought as I tried to find somewhere to sit and hold my head steady until it stopped spinning. "Ruah Ha Kadosh has entered the fight."

Trying hard to stay out of the path of the clashing swords, I stood up as best I could and looked around for Michael or Gabriel or anyone who might be in charge and who would help me. I planned to grovel and beg for mercy for a chance to correct my incredible lapse in judgment. I threw the sword down and stumbled all over myself, getting to the rock where I hid until Michael came and cut off Damon's head. As Michael turned away, I shook my feathers out, rolled the dead demon's head off my foot, and practiced saying the words I would use to explain what happened. I would say how I had been standing in the wrong place and inadvertently appeared to be following Lucifer. I would crawl on my knees to Michael. I would explain how I'd been confused lately and frequently had trouble making important decisions.

Now, praise God, my mind had returned to me, but while it was gone, it appeared I had joined the wrong side of the war, which I never intended to do. When I realized my mistake, I fully repented and came over to the righteous side where I'd always intended to be before my mind left.

I could almost touch the hem of His garment. But I was not fast enough or close enough. Before I could offer a single word of repentance, with a mighty gush of breath, Ruah Ha Kadosh executed the word of God. Satan and one-third of the heavenly host were cast out of heaven and thrown to Earth.

Sadly, I fell with them.

Chapter 5

THE SENSATION OF falling was terrifying. We flailed about like unstrung puppets caught in a hurricane. We had no control over our movement and no frame of reference for what was happening. We tumbled out of the realm of the heavenly light into perpetual darkness unlike anything we had seen before—not like this anyway. We had known the absence of light, but we did not know that there could be such a pulsating void of suffocating nothingness. We were falling through a realm where the gloom was so thick that it could be felt. It was a terrifying and strange place, and yet there was something eerily familiar about it.

It was like an odor one has smelled before but now cannot quite remember where or when. We had not realized that we were careening through second heaven, which existed far below third heaven, where we had lived with God. We didn't have long to ponder what this dominion might be like, because we continued to fall until we crashed through another border and reached another realm. When we regained our equilibrium, we knew that we had arrived on Earth.

Perhaps you wonder, "Why Earth?" Surely there were other planets more suitable as a penal colony for our rebellion. Planets where there was no life—desolate, barren, frozen, or parched. Surely Earth had not been created for us. Satan certainly knew about Earth. After all, he had longed to be given special charge over its affairs, but now, it was his prison.

I can tell you I realized right away our fate could have been much worse. At first one might argue that this was hardly banishment. Earth was more beautiful in those days than it is now. This fragile and delicate planet hanging alone in space had obviously been created for something important. It was not designed for rebels like us. Satan never really valued the beauty of Earth anyway, so its exquisiteness was completely wasted on him. From the day it was made, all of heaven knew how much God particularly favored Earth. So when I realized where we were, I thought there had been some mistake.

None of it made sense. Why were we alive? Why had we not been utterly destroyed as lawbreakers? What would we do on the most beautiful of the worlds God had created?

"Is this really Earth?" we asked each other.

"It must be," someone responded. "This is not so bad."

The others agreed; it could have been much worse. We could have landed on one of those horrendously hot planets.

"Must have been a mistake," someone else offered.

None of us had an answer, but I knew God did not make mistakes. We were here for a purpose, but only He knew what it was.

We wandered aimlessly about Earth for several days—I don't know how many. We were still outside the realm of time, so it was hard to know how long we had been there. While the others were arguing over territory, I found myself thinking about God.

How was He feeling about those of us who had betrayed Him? He had certainly loved us. I wondered if He missed us at all. As much as He loved us, we all felt that He loved Lucifer even more. We never knew whether it was true, but in the end, we didn't really mind. I've often wondered whether or not God ceased to love him because he behaved like an overindulged child. Did his rebellion truly change the affection of God toward him—or us for that matter? After all, God is so above the presumption and foolishness of His petulant creation. I wondered if God regretted His decision to cast us out without giving us a second chance.

No longer the light bearer of heaven, Satan the accuser and we whom he had mesmerized tried to figure out why we were on Earth. Satan really seemed to be as perplexed about it as the rest of us. Although, of course, he would never say so.

I also found myself thinking about the host who had remained in heaven and wondered if they were watching us. We used to do things like that, you know. We would stand on the edge of heaven and speculate about Earth. Knowing the angelic realm as I do and the angels' penchant for gossip, I could just imagine what they might be talking about.

"Why didn't Yahweh destroy the rebels?" they must have mused.

That's what I would have been asking. It's too simple to say that it was because God loved us so much He could not bear to destroy us. No one who knew the slightest thing about His holiness would consider such sentimentality. Perhaps simply being cast from His presence satisfied the demand of His holiness and His justice, but I doubted it. There had to be another reason.

Now as I look back on how things turned out, I wonder whether or not God regretted that He had not destroyed us right then and been done with it. Why didn't He use His might, indignation, strength, and power to utterly crush Satan and the rest of us? If He had, no one would have thought twice about His right to do so. He should have completely eradicated any memory of us. I daresay no one in heaven or on Earth would know that we had existed. It would have been as though we never *were* at all. Heaven could have gone on carrying out God's ideas like we never happened. We would have been obliterated from its history. No one would have known or wondered about us. If you ask me, God missed a fantastic opportunity to clean the whole mess up and be done with it.

Instead of ending it neatly and completely, as He probably would have if He had only thought it through a little more, God permitted the righteous anger in Michael to rise up. There was no doubt about who the players were. Michael and his angels utterly conquered us and drove us out of heaven.

"Is this Michael's fight?" the gossiping angels must have asked one another. "Why doesn't God seize the moment to demonstrate His omnipotence?"

Certainly the heavenly host was aware that the weight of His glory could destroy anything that opposed it. If you ask me, God left Himself wide open for unhealthy speculation among the remaining angels when He let Michael take the credit for the war. The utter destruction of the rebels by His hand would have forevermore insured that there would be no further rebellions. Why did He not show Himself forth in His unlimited might and authority? He must have known how history would record that it was Michael and his angels who overcame Satan. Was God even a little worried that this might go to Michael's head? After all, if Satan could be corrupted, then no one was exempt.

Perhaps it was because the power of God was never in doubt. I suppose He did not consider it necessary to demonstrate a power of which every one of us was certain.

At first I could not see why it seemed more important to prove His restraint and compassion where we were concerned rather than settling once and for all what could happen to anyone who thought he could outwrestle God. It took me awhile, but I think I finally figured it out. God would allow Satan to show the futility of existence apart from His presence. Heaven was watching, and heaven would learn.

If it were possible that a created being should have been able to muster his gifts and abilities (which Satan was permitted to retain) to be victorious, independent from God's presence, surely Satan was that one who could do it. And if Satan could do it, then others, as we had done, would follow. I thought God was taking a big risk to allow Satan the opportunity to realize his ambitions. He was given domain to rule just as he wanted. With no strings attached, this rebellious angel would be allowed to rule apart from the presence of the One who had created him. He would be permitted to establish his own throne and his own kingdom, but not in the heaven where God was.

All of heaven would be standing by, watching to see what he would do. With all of our powers and abilities and corrupted nobility, we found ourselves in a beautiful place crafted by the very hand of God but with no idea as to why. Having no further recourse to God and not willing to challenge him for control, we pledged our allegiance to Satan the accuser of our brethren.

But we did not pledge our devotion. We had known devotion only to God. We pledged allegiance to Satan out of fear and a lust for his power. We never doubted for a moment that Satan loved anything but himself.

I knew that all of heaven would be standing on the edge of eternity to watch and see what Satan would do with unrestrained power.

I could have told them.

CHAPTER 6

I WONDER IF IT is possible for the human mind to understand the horror of banishment. I doubt it. Perhaps you could try to imagine what it would be like to be suddenly disowned and thrust from Earth into space and sentenced to remain alive forever on another planet. How long would it take before the awareness of total abandonment and separation from everything that caused you to be who and what you are began to birth sheer terror into your very soul? It is not death, but it is everything you fear death to be.

I have observed human ways for a very long time, and I marvel at the extremes to which you people will resort to avoid death. It's not the idea of being dead that troubles you. Some might find death to be a welcome escape if only one could be assured that it were nothing more than an endless, dreamless sleep. As a matter of fact, even to me the notion doesn't seem that bad. What people fear about death is that it is nothing like that at all. You fear being awakened, regaining consciousness, and realizing there's been a terrible mistake: you're not dead at all. You're still alive but far removed from your home and familiar surroundings and cast into another dimension where you are entirely alone.

You fear death because the unthinkable hides in your imagination. What if death is only a door through which you are forced to pass, only to find that you have remained exactly the same person? You retain your consciousness, your talents, ambition, emotions, and every aspect of aliveness that gives meaning to your existence. But the world in which these things have meaning and relationship is suddenly closed off to you.

Your life on Earth was worthwhile only in so much as it had purpose, definition, and meaning to the world around you. You pass through the door called death, and the world you have known is gone. Your meaning and purpose are gone. There is no longer the possibility of a God to whom you can cry out. You are completely alone.

It was something like that for us to find ourselves suddenly on Earth with no way to return. We were angels, more glorious than you can possibly imagine and created to live eternally in heaven, not on Earth, no matter how pretty it was.

When I came to my senses after the crash, I was appalled at what had happened to Satan. At first I wasn't sure it was really him. How could he change so drastically? He was no longer the light bearer—or anything close to it. He was ghastly. The grandness of all that he had been was horribly changed. The light that emanated from him was completely gone. He was gray and thin— so thin I could almost see right through him. It became so apparent that his beauty and glory had only been real because of his relationship to God. His beauty, talent, and charm were real and meaningful only as he reflected the attributes of the God who made him. Disconnected from God, He became unspeakably ugly.

How can I explain the change in him? Imagine a Christmas tree decorated with ornaments and set aglow by hundreds of lights. You behold the beautiful tree in its halo of lights and exclaim how glorious it is. You don't take notice that its brilliance is completely dependent upon the hidden electric cord that winds itself silently from bulb to bulb until it is at last plugged into the electrical outlet where the power is. You don't become aware of it until the cord is unplugged and the tree becomes suddenly dark and loses its beauty. The ornaments are still there, as are the light bulbs and sockets, but the glory that is a Christmas tree is gone. That tree once so admired and set in a place of honor to be the center of your home is suddenly lifeless, dull, and dry. What was once a Christmas tree, full of promise, is now only a dead plant with meaningless ornaments and fake icicles that are too much trouble to remove. I have watched as you dragged it to the curb to be carried off by the garbage truck.

It was like that for Satan. All of the ornaments and reminders of his existence when he was the light bearer still hung on his being. But the relationship to God that had given him meaning and purpose was completely gone.

As it was for Satan, so it was for the rest of us who had fallen with him. It was stunning to see how our feet had become hooves. Even our wings were changed. Most of our beautiful feathers had been replaced with slimy scales. The others were like Satan, the essence of ugly. I had not found a way to look at myself, so I held out hope that somehow I might look a little better. In stunned disbelief at what had happened to us, we staggered about Earth as one who has consumed too much alcohol staggers about in his surroundings. He is not sure where he is. He is unsure of what has happened to cause such pain in his body. He is disoriented and tries to remember how he came to be in such a state. Yet at the same time, he is afraid to remember. Had he really done this to himself? Surely there was someone else to blame for his condition.

Regret and remorse are the most bitter of companions. At least that's how it was for me.

Once we realized the finality of this new reality, panic overtook our common sense, and we began to blame one another. Someone must be held responsible for what had happened to us. Finally, someone dared to say it.

"It was Satan's fault. He misled us."

"That's right. We would never have rebelled on our own," said someone else.

"How could we have been so foolish?" another added.

Then as one angry mob, they turned on him. I knew this to be an extraordinarily dangerous move. I knew they were underestimating Satan's wrath. I tried to tell them, but I couldn't get a word in, so I kept to the back of the group and waited to see which way things might go.

Of course, I was right, and things went bad quickly. I cannot begin to tell you what an ill-conceived idea it was to try to overthrow Satan. God had not destroyed us, but Satan almost did. Everyone had underestimated his strength, his power, and his capacity for ruthlessness. He obliterated the first line of attack against him, and I'm quite sure he would have annihilated the rest of us had it not been for one thing. We were all he had left. Whatever he planned to do, he would need us to carry it out. Make no mistake; we would remain alive only as long as he had use for us.

When we realized we could not match him in strength or power, we did the next most illogical thing.

We turned on each other. Well, everyone except for me. I hid behind a tree. As if we hadn't learned one thing from the futility of the war in heaven, we proceeded to wage war on Earth. If I could not fight in heaven, where I knew my way around, then I surely wasn't about to chance getting hurt and lost on Earth, having no idea where anything was.

They raged and fought against one another in an attempt to secure a position near Satan. After the failed coup, each one was anxious to prove a newfound loyalty to the fallen prince. I suppose they thought being near him might be the best place for protection, though protection against what, I don't know, since there was nothing on Earth more fearsome than them. Perhaps they thought Satan would reward those who were the closest to him. I think some naïvely held out the hope that Satan might rule them like God had. Not a chance.

I've concluded that angels, in their natural state, are not strategic thinkers. Perhaps it was because in heaven we never needed to evaluate cause and effect. God caused all things, and the effect was never in question. I'm pretty sure it never crossed anyone's mind that if they destroyed Earth, there would be absolutely no place for us to go. I thought about pointing it out, but I changed my mind. The enraged angels were intent on making things worse and looking for a target. It wasn't going to be me. Earth would have to fend for itself.

God's favorite planet reeled at the violence of the war between the fallen angels. As the human body reacts by spontaneously ejecting an object that can bring about its destruction, so Earth reacted to the devastation the warring angels wreaked upon it.

Earth itself began to fight back, but things only got worse. In their fury, rage, and horror at God and at each other, the angels unleashed their devastating powers upon Earth, never mind they were about to destroy the only place left for us to exist. The angry angels tortured and ravaged every beautiful thing God had placed upon this planet. All that did not perish immediately became defiled, injured, and hostile.

It seemed as though Earth had lost its balance, as the seas boiled from the pollution of the raging angels. The waters were black and ominous and began to overtake the land as if trying to escape its domain. Finally, the dark water overtook and drowned every point of light and beauty on the injured planet. That was the first flood upon Earth. It was Lucifer's flood, caused by his wrath, and it destroyed all the wonder God had created on this delicate blue and green bauble.

Earth could take no more. It jolted and spun off its course. It reeled and retched until it expelled us completely. It was as if we had been vomited from the mouth of Earth into yet another realm far above its surface. I knew we were in danger of being forever flung into nothingness. I thought we should apologize to Earth, make up with it if you know what I mean.

"Look, this could work," I told the others as we hung temporarily suspended between the planet and oblivion. "We can adapt and live sensibly upon Earth."

"And do what? Exist in the floodwaters? Nothing else is left," someone pointed out.

That's when Satan had his second bad idea.

"We will make our way back to heaven," he said as he began flapping his wings in an attempt to get traction.

"Why didn't we think of that?" came a facetious voice that could not be identified. "I'm sure God has gotten over the rebellion by now."

Futile as it was, we decided to try it. Everyone flapped for all he was worth. Some climbed on top of each other, as if getting tall enough would enable us to reach something. Satan climbed on top of everyone else, then he and some of the other strong ones were able to lift off and get a foothold into the kingdom of the air: second heaven. It was the same realm through which we had fallen when we were thrown out. It was not third heaven, mind you, or anything remotely close to it. It was dark and empty of all the glory that heaven is. It was a discarded part of eternity, but eternity nonetheless.

"This is close enough," Satan announced.

No one was going to argue. We knew if by some miracle we had made it all the way back to third heaven, the angelic guard would have been waiting for us, and who knew what might happen to us then?

That's how Satan's kingdom came to be established in second heaven. It was terrible. It was dank and cold. It would be some time before I learned that the awful smell was sulfa. Because God made all things, He must have made this place as well, but I couldn't imagine why. Since we had fallen through it when we were cast out, I knew it hung somewhere between third heaven and Earth. We had been able to climb from Earth to this place, so I wondered if there might be a back door leading to third heaven. I desperately searched for one but did not find it. An ironlike ceiling above and floor below contained this new abode. It had three closed sides like a cave and a ledge from which we could see Earth and the emptiness of space.

That's when Satan decided he needed an army.

"What will he do with an army?" I said to myself. "We lost the war in heaven, and we lost the fight with Earth. What else is there?"

I suppose he was looking for something else to attack, so an army it was, and, of course, a pecking order had to be established. He assigned us our place according to our aspects, which are particular talents held by some and not others. I didn't know exactly what kind of assignment I would have, but I was pretty sure it would be out of everyone else's way.

Satan declared that we were now an army of demons whose purpose was to serve him. That's what we were now—demons. Don't ask me why. We had become more like a street gang than a heavenly host.

The strongest ones he divided into categories of powers, princes, thrones, and principalities. Satan stirred them up by telling them they would have their revenge and rule again over Earth in due time. I was assigned to be the watcher with no real authority over anything. My job was to watch Earth and report what I saw.

"Total waste of time," I would have told him if he'd asked me, which he didn't. Satan couldn't seem to get a grip on the fact that he had lost Earth. If he wanted me to watch it, then watch it I would. I found myself a rocky perch on the edge of second heaven, where I set up my post.

The first thing I noticed was that some who had fallen with us were unable to rise above the chaos to reach the kingdom of the air. Some were too weak. They were more like angel-ettes, created without the multidimensions given to the stronger angels. Their personalities were limited to only one aspect, which made them, more correctly, spirits, not angels.

The spirits were created by God to be rapid messengers to carry out His will in heaven. Each spirit had been fashioned with an aspect of the nature of the Lord. I don't know why they were on Earth at all. They were not equipped with the same personality complexities that would have allowed them to choose to follow anyone, especially Satan. But there they were: cast-offs of heaven and now trapped on Earth. My guess is they were cast out with the rest for the same reason as me. They were probably standing in the wrong place at the wrong moment and got swept up in the hullabaloo.

When in heaven, a spirit was a useful delivery system for God. They could be dispatched quickly from His throne to impart His aspect, something of the nature of the Lord, when and where it was needed in any part of the universe. These spirits were named according to their purpose. One was a spirit of peace; another, a spirit of joy; yet another was a spirit of love. They would race to and fro and carry the aspect of God's nature wherever a piece of God needed to be. Their purpose was good and noble.

In one way the spirits were like me: never intended for battle. Battered and beaten, they were trampled upon by the stronger demons in the hasty retreat from Earth. The spirits were sacrificed and used as shields, hostages, and steppingstones by the raging demonic angels.

I could see they were in terrible condition. Their aspects were damaged and distorted. The angel who had once been Peace became Fear. Love became Hate. Joy became Despair. When they realized they had been abandoned on Earth, they panicked. By itself, a spirit with only one aspect would be at the mercy of any entity that could do more than one thing at a time. Left alone upon Earth they quickly learned they must cluster together to survive. Each groped about for another spirit with whom he could unite for protection, though against what I'm sure they did not know.

"We are cut off. We are cut off," they wailed as they realized there was no escape from the dank floodwaters suffocating Earth.

They sought one another out and clung to each other. Rejection and Fear of Abandonment would stay together. Envy, Greed, and Lust would hover together. Abuse, Anger, and Violence would enable one another. Shame, Self-Loathing, and Sexual Dysfunction would hide together in the shadows. They agonized, not knowing if they would remain in captivity to the angry sea or simply cease to exist. There was nowhere for them to hide, no vehicle, no habitation in which their aspects could function. They wailed and sank deep into the angry waters to which they had been abandoned.

They did not know a worse fate awaited them.

Chapter 7

FROM MY PERCH I was able to see the entire planet at one time. I had not fully realized the extent of the devastation, but now I could see how terrible it really was. It had been so beautiful and full of light and color before we arrived. But now, it was a catastrophe: dark, void, and empty; covered by Lucifer's flood; and nothing at all like it was when God made it. I wondered if He had the heart to look at what it had become.

The battered Earth was exhibit A in proving that Satan's rule did not include creating or preserving anything. The delicate blue planet in space was now nothing more than a swamp. Really, that is what it looked like. The whole place was little more than a cesspool where nothing but the formless spirits tried to hide. The dark waters churned savagely with the flailing about of the frantic phantoms fighting desperately to escape their watery prison. The dank and the dark covered the face of Earth. Nothing was left.

That is why I couldn't figure out Satan's continued obsession with it. Not a day passed when he didn't grill me about what was happening on Earth.

"Nothing is happening," I said. "Let me watch something else for a little while."

"No," he replied. "Let nothing escape your watch."

You know, you can look at swamp water for just so long before your mind starts to wander. Mine wandered off more than it should, especially when I would think about the unfairness of why I was condemned to such monotony in the first place. I wondered how I could go about appealing my sentence. Since no one was around, no one heard me calling to God and insisting that He review the evidence against me. He could have heard me if He wanted to. He sees and hears everything that happens in the universe, no matter how slight it might be. He didn't hear because He had dismissed me. I was a closed case as far as He was concerned.

The more tedious it became watching nothing happen on Earth, the more I forgot to watch at all. I spent my time thinking about my case and what I would say if I got a hearing in God's court. Fortunately, on that particular day I had collected my wits, was in possession of most of my mind, and was doing the job to which I been assigned: watching Earth do nothing. If I had as much as blinked an eyelash (which I really don't have), the whole thing would have escaped my notice. It was that fast. Something was happening in the water.

When I think how easily I could have missed it, I shudder at what the consequences would have been. It was so small, if I had looked away for a moment, I might not have seen it at all.

What I saw *happen* was in actuality what I saw *not* happening. There in the deepest part of the sea-turned-swamp, where the water had churned continuously for as many eons as I had been on guard, in a space no bigger than a clenched human fist, the water had stopped its relentless roil. It was perfectly calm.

"Now what do you suppose is causing that?" I asked myself. I stood as tall as I could on my perch and strained to see if there was something strange in the water—at least stranger than the frantic spirits I knew to be in there. How one understands "strange" is relative to his neighborhood. I blinked hard, then looked one more time.

There was no doubt about it. The calm spot began to ripple out and was growing in size at an alarming speed. At the same time the center from where it began became clear. My thoughts were running in a dozen different directions. I was really sorry I had left them unbridled for so long. I tried to gather them in long enough to formulate a coherent response to a rapidly changing reality. All the while the mirrorlike phenomenon was spreading quickly over the enlarging calmness.

I wondered what I should do. Should I report it? How would I explain it?

"Lord Satan, I wish to report nothing happening in the center of the sea."

I would have to do better than that, so I strained to look more closely. I tried to remember the cleanup operations I had seen, but I could not think of a single one that could cause those dank waters to become clear. The truth is, I could have flown out there for a better look, but I couldn't get myself going. There was something out there that caused what few remaining feathers I had to stand on end, and I couldn't do a thing with them.

At first it was hard to look, but then I could not look away. I knew I had to run or fly to tell one of the others what was happening, but I could get neither a foot nor a feather to cooperate. I flapped for all I was worth without going anywhere. Flying is not as easy as you might think, even for an angel. It requires a good deal of concentration. For example, if you only get one wing to flap, you can't really go anywhere, so you end up hopping around in a circle looking ridiculous. By now my concentration had shattered into little pieces, each locked on thousands of gently rolling waves, one after the other, full of clear water subduing the dark waters that had been there only moments before. The crashing anger of the sea was settling down as if it had become a gigantic pond.

"It cannot be. It cannot be." I must have said it to myself a dozen times. I gave up flapping and hopping and just stood there for a moment, completely mesmerized and undone by the miracle taking place before me and wondering how I was going to find the nerve to tell Satan that his nightmare had arrived.

Ruah Ha Kadosh was hovering over the waters of Earth.

Chapter 8

HUMANS HAVE NO concept of true fear. I have watched and listened to you for centuries as you speak of being afraid, as if you understood the meaning of the word.

"I'm afraid of heights. I'm afraid of the dark. I'm afraid of sickness. I'm afraid of being alone."

Humanity in its entirety consists of whiners—always has. How is it you humans have never understood that what you call "fear" is a warning system that God set within you for your protection? You fear heights, and so you do not teeter recklessly on the edge of a high cliff. You fear the dark, which experientially if no other way you must know is total nonsense. The dark is no match for the weakest human being. No matter the depth of the blackness, when a human appears with the smallest glimmer of light, do you people not see how the darkness flees?

You fear sickness, and so you take care of your physical bodies and disease has no entry point. You fear being alone and so are careful to behave in a civilized way so that others like you will want to be where you are.

This is not fear. It is a guidance system that God put within you to warn you when you are too close to areas of danger. Misunderstanding the point altogether and disliking the feeling you call fear, you humans take immediate action to alleviate the feeling. The fear you disdain is your protection, but most of you are too simpleminded to know it.

Shall I tell you about fear? I know it very well. When we first fell from heaven, only two of our emotions were in working order: fear and hatred. Some had so much hatred that they knew no fear. I was so afraid I didn't have the nerve to hate anything. I didn't know if our other emotions would ever function again. I wondered if I would miss the other feelings I used to know. We had them all, you know: love, joy, sorrow, sympathy, gratitude—all of them, same as you.

I especially missed sorrow. You likely cannot imagine what I mean since humanity exhausts itself trying to avoid feeling badly about anything. But I sometimes think that if I could only feel grief again, it would lessen the fear. If I could have conjured up a good cry, I just knew I'd feel better.

If only I could weep or feel remorse, perhaps that would hold the escalating terror within me in check. If I could feel one bit of compassion for the devastation we brought upon Earth, then perhaps the ravages of fear that consume me could be contained.

Here is how we differ, you and me. When you are afraid, you respond to the thing that is making you afraid. You turn on the light, move away from the edge, and take your medicine, and the fear subsides. You may even feel better than you did before the fear came upon you. When you do something about your fear, you overcome it and become its master.

Now here's how fear is an enigma for humans. The more fear you deal with, the less fear you have. Fear responds to humans in the same way that the darkness responds to humans. It knows humanity is its master. Fear knows that God has made it subordinate to mankind and that it must obey. It is so obvious. I marvel that you people can't figure it out.

It is not so with us. There is no limit to our capacity for fear. When we reach a new level of fear, that mark moves higher yet again. We can go deeper into fear, but we can never retreat from it. Do you wonder what we fear?

For the most part, we fear each other. We dare not break rank or our mutual destruction is assured. More than anything else, we fear Satan.

He's become much worse, you know. When we first fell, I really believe he was as confused as anyone else by what had happened. It took him some time before he realized our fallen condition was going to be eternal. As he processed that reality, his confusion lessened, and his hatred grew. His hatred is without repentance, and we worry his hatred will overcome his sense of survival, and if it did, he would unleash his wrath against us.

It is strange that we never feared God. Although His power was without limit, so much more so than Satan, He could have destroyed us with a glance, yet we never feared that He might do so. God's strength and omnipotence were never frightening to us. In fact, we were comforted by it because we knew He was our protector.

Not so with Satan. He would destroy us in a moment if it advanced his purpose the slightest bit. We know that. He doesn't do so because he needs us. He cannot carry out his horrible vengeance without us. Satan is not omnipresent, as God is. He cannot create, as God can. If he destroys one of us, he has diminished his army, and his army is all he has.

Nonetheless, we know that if we fail him in our assignments, his rage will overtake his cunning, and he will destroy the one who failed him. We must be victorious in our assignments or be destroyed, and yet victory in our conquests does not relieve our fear in the least. Victory itself creates more fear in us, and of a far worse kind.

You probably think that when we were expelled from heaven, that was as bad as it could get for us. Perhaps you think we will be forever contained in a sort of spiritual limbo, occasionally interrupting the affairs of humans. Oh, that it could be that way. But no, we have a future just as you have. A terrible, terrible day awaits us, far worse than anything we have experienced before. The more victorious Satan is, the worse the judgment that awaits us.

As I trudged back to the place where Satan had set his throne, I don't know which I feared the most. Was it what I had seen happening over the seas? Or was it the fact that I would be the one who had to tell him? I knew I must tell Satan what I had witnessed out there: Ruah Ha Kadosh hovering over the wasteland that had become Earth. Somehow or another, this would end up being my fault. I just knew it.

"Lord Satan," I stammered.

He didn't acknowledge me with words, just a glare that meant I was bothering him.

"I have a report," I continued. He interrupted me before I could finish my sentence.

"What? Don't lie," he snapped.

"There's a disturbance on Earth." I paused to check out how he took the first part. So far, so good. I tried to select my words carefully. "Now, I could be wrong about this, but I'm almost certain, well, not that certain, but as certain as one could be without getting any closer, which I didn't. It looks as if…"

He slapped me out of my *careful* mode right into *blurt-it-all-out* mode.

"Ruah Ha Kadosh is hovering over Earth. End of report," and I fell to my knees.

At least he didn't take the time to swing at me again or to blame me for something that was not my fault. He spun around and sped off for the edge of second heaven.

"No, no, no," he bellowed, sideswiping any demon along the way who made the mistake of getting in his path.

He came to such a sudden stop that he almost flipped right over and off the edge. "No!" he screamed into the vastness of space. "You cannot have it, God. It is mine. Earth is mine. Leave it alone."

As he railed against God, the darkness over the earth began to swirl and dissipate. Things moved quickly after that. The rest of the demons raced behind Satan and stood near the edge to see what was going on. It was thrilling and horrifying at the same time. Not since we fell from heaven had we heard the voice of God, but there it was, perfectly clear as His words pierced the atmosphere, and we fell on our faces as if dead.

He said, "Let there be light," and there was light.

You cannot begin to imagine what it was like. Let me try to explain so that you can understand our mounting fear. Illumination beyond what any eyes could bear penetrated the darkness and banished it from the face of Earth. All of the misery, destruction, ignorance, sorrow, and wickedness that had made up the "darkness" started to disappear. It was not light as you have experienced it. It did not come from a star or fire. It came from God Himself. It was blinding, without shadow, and there was no hiding from it. It was painful to us. It was as if our entire being were one great eye that had been in total darkness now suddenly thrust into glaring sunlight. That is what it felt like, only worse. One can close an eye that has been assaulted by bright light, but there was nothing we could do to shield ourselves.

Satan howled as he slunk back, seeking refuge in the deeper darkness of second heaven. We pulled back into the blackest cave with him, trying to hide and waiting to see what God would do next.

Then God said, "Let there be sky between the waters to separate them."

Every one of us was transfixed and unable to move. I had forgotten what it was like to hear Him speak and bring order out of chaos with just His word. How can

I describe what it was like to hear His voice again? It was like delicate bells and peals of thunder all coming together in beauty and majesty.

Everything within me yearned to jump up and cry out to Him, "Here I am, God. Please take me back. Let me come home with You." Instead, I rolled into a ball and bit my tail so I could not speak. I could not chance it.

Then God said, "Let the water under the sky be gathered to one place, and let dry ground appear."

It wasn't so much that God was creating something that never existed before. It was more like He was calling Earth back into its original order before our fury had been unleashed upon it. Not being subject to time ourselves, I can't really say how long it took us to scandalize and pillage Earth into the travesty it became, but for Earth, it was a painful and slow process. Now God was speaking, and the elements of Earth came into perfect order before the words were completely out of His mouth. Seconds—that's all it took for Him to restore Earth and cancel everything Satan had done to it.

That's when it first occurred to me that this was a very strange thing for God to do. Think about it. What was the point? Why would He send Ruah Ha Kadosh to call the chaos back into order? Didn't God know that it would happen all over again? At least that would be the case if He allowed Satan to retain any access to Earth. Since He had not yet destroyed any of us, I presumed that He wouldn't. But it made no sense to me to restore Earth unless He planned to banish Satan once and for all. I wondered if He had really thought this through. I wasn't the only one perplexed by this strange action of God.

"Why is He fixing it?" a demon near the door of the cave asked.

"He must plan to destroy Satan—and us," someone else whispered.

"He can't. He won't. It isn't time." I was relieved that someone besides me could confirm that such an action would indeed be outside the rules.

"He must be planning to send Satan somewhere else—and us with him," the first demon replied.

I didn't dare contradict an already nervous demon, but I knew that wasn't going to happen. He sent Satan to Earth for a purpose, and although I couldn't figure out what it was, it had to be for some other reason than tearing the place to shreds. God must have a plan that included restoring Earth, but what could it be, and why now?

Unless God intended to confine Satan in some way from being able to engage Earth, He would have to know history would quickly repeat itself, and Earth would again be reduced to shambles. Satan doesn't improve with experience. He can't be rehabilitated. If Satan could not rule Earth without destroying it the first time, the second time would only be worse.

The more I thought about it, the less logical it seemed. The only possible explanation was the obvious one. God jumped the gun, simple as that. He got ahead of Himself. In His desire to see His favorite planet restored, He completely overlooked the fact that He had yet to deal definitively with Satan. So God went right on restoring as if everything were going to work out just fine.

Then God said, "Let the land produce vegetation: seed-bearing plants and trees on the land that bear fruit with seed in it." And, *poof,* just like that, it was there.

"That's a waste of time," said the demon with the best view. "What on Earth needs fruits and seeds?"

Good question. There was no living thing on Earth now, except for the plants that just popped into existence a few minutes ago.

Satan stood up and walked in silence to the edge of second heaven. Saying not a word, he stood there, staring at what was happening, as if anticipating something. But what? He knew God better than any of us. If anyone could make a good guess at what God might do, it would be Satan. We watched him carefully to see if his countenance betrayed his thoughts.

"Is he trembling?" someone whispered.

"Shut up," another hissed, slapping at the stupid one who dared say such a thing where Satan might overhear it.

I dared not look at him directly, but curiosity got the better of me, and I had to chance a peek. I swear it was true. No doubt about it, he was trembling—not like I would be doing, of course. He did not convulse or hyperventilate, but there was definitely a quiver there. Satan afraid? But of what? What could be scarier than him? It couldn't be fear of God. God had sent no signals that He might be thinking about doing something to Satan at this point. The former prince of angels was almost pitiful as he shuddered and stood silently by, unable to prevent what he saw happening on Earth.

It was after God set the sun and moon in place and set the celestial clock for the passing of seasons that we finally realized He was indeed up to something. He was about to create some sort of life on Earth. Of course, that was the purpose of the vegetation.

I didn't know what God had in mind, but whatever life He intended to make had better be a superior model to Satan. Otherwise, Satan would have it for lunch before the first season was over. All of us were thinking the same thing. We watched with curiosity as He filled the seas, the skies, and the garden with living things. It was lovely and all that but, so far, it was nothing Satan would care anything about.

Perhaps if I had paid more attention to God's words rather than being so caught up in watching Satan quake, I might have figured out what was about to take place. I should have remembered that every word God speaks means something. Each of His words "cause" and then there is an "effect." No exceptions. I had missed the importance of the small words because I had long forgotten how to listen to God's voice. The little words, had I been paying attention, contained the key that could have explained everything and at least given us a warning. I should have known better, but I had not practiced my listening skills since I was thrown out of paradise with the real rebels. A person gets rusty.

You can only understand what a paradigm-shifting big deal was about to occur if you first understand the concept of eternity.

Eternity "is." Everything in eternity is "now." There is no progression of chronological or linear time as humans understand it to be. And so, when God labeled His work as the "first day," "the second day," and so on, I thought nothing about it. None of us could have imagined what He was about to do with that new dimension I mentioned earlier, the one He called "time." Even if I had realized what He was doing, I would not have guessed that it had anything to do with us. Earth might be subject to time, but not angels—or demons. We could observe it, but we were outside its boundaries. We were eternal beings, after all.

There was no warning whatsoever. When the pillars started shaking and collapsing and the floor shifted under us, we still did not get it. Then there came a loud rushing sound that almost deafened us and sent us tumbling until I thought we were falling out of heaven all over again.

When the tossing and rumbling finally subsided, I wasn't sure where we were. It seemed as though we were still in second heaven, but something was drastically different. We might never have really figured it out on our own had Satan not whirled to face us with wrath and rage and fear spilling from his eyes and his mouth.

"We have been sucked into time," he growled.

And that is exactly what happened. God set a clock for us. He introduced time into eternity. Seconds, minutes, hours, and days passing and not returning and not repeating. It was undeniable that we were being pulled forward in time, but toward what?

How can I describe it so that you can understand? Consider how you and everything upon Earth are subject to a law, a force that you know as gravity. It is a consistent and unchanging law that God ordained. You do not think about it because it has always been there. It is everywhere, and all things on Earth or coming near

Earth are subject to the law of gravity and will obey it—
except for us.

We angels cannot see the force per se, although we
can easily observe what it does, but we ourselves are not
subject to its effect. There is no up or down for us; we
just "are." If we were suddenly made subject to gravita-
tional pull, it would be an unnatural shift in our sense
of being. It would mean that we were part of Earth's
destiny. It would mean that we had become anchored
to its purpose. We would be forced to adjust to a new
reality. For one thing, we would have to learn the limitations of direction.

Time had begun for us. Time was moving forward,
and it was pulling us along. If it had "begun," did that
mean it would also "end"? I had a million questions and
no one to ask. What was the purpose of time where we
were concerned? What could it possibly mean?

The others staggered about, each trying to find his
equilibrium in this strange new reality, so no one was
interested in discussing the philosophy of it with me.

Perhaps it is because we now had a reference point in
time that what happened next seemed so startling. If it
had occurred in heaven, third heaven where God lived,
it would have been ordinary. No one would have noticed.

After all, they were always together in paradise.
The three of Them—Yahweh, Adonai, and Ruah Ha
Kadosh—the Godhead. But suddenly, there They were

on Earth. I was sure we had never known them to leave heaven.

"What is happening?" the demon voices murmured to each other.

"Look, there!" another voice shouted.

We looked up and saw Michael's warring angels gathered at the perimeter of this new expanse called "sky." I just knew they were there to hunt us down and finish us off.

"Run, run, run," I stammered pulling on the wings of the demons, trying to make them see the good sense of getting away. One brushed me away so hard that I lost my balance and fell, where I decided to stay. Looking through the group of standing demons, I could see the mighty guards of heaven with their fiery swords drawn and at the ready, but for what purpose if not to wipe us out?

Suddenly, everything and everyone became eerily still. A reverent silence descended around us. It was as if everything in heaven and Earth had stopped for a moment—even time. The winds pulled back in complete stillness. No sound interrupted the unmistakable sanctity of the moment. Something unprecedented was about to happen on Earth. I myself had chills.

Satan knew it also, and he paced back and forth feverishly trying to anticipate what the Holy Trinity was about to do. I had to see what was going on, so I convinced myself the warring angels weren't interested in me, and I slowly stood and joined the others. I could see the Holy Trinity clearly as they moved together as in a dance over the surface of the newly restored planet. In such perfect harmony, it was difficult to be sure who was doing what, but I dared not go any closer. Ruah Ha Kadosh hovered as Yahweh (or was it Adonai? I cannot be certain—it was just God) stood upon the face of Earth.

Then God said, "Let Us make mankind exactly in our image, male and female. Let them rule over the fish of the sea and the birds of the air, over the livestock, over all the earth, and over all the creatures that move along the ground."

It was impossible to distinguish among them as the Trinity. God touched the earth, scooped mud into His hands, and spat into it, forming a kind of clay. Right there in front of us He made a human being and named him Adam. Then, Yahweh or Adonai or both—what does it matter anyway—kissed Adam, and Ruah Ha Kadosh entered his nostrils, and Adam came to life.

CHAPTER 9

I WILL CONFESS TO being stunned by Adam's appearance. He was the spitting image of God, if you will pardon the pun. There was only one of him (we wouldn't figure out the male and female part until later), and beyond a doubt, he encompassed the essence of the triune God. I believe that may have been the moment when Satan slipped over the edge into complete madness. There is no other explanation for his behavior. His wrath exploded into bleating howls that he bawled and growled into the expanse above as he threw aside every demon unfortunate enough to be near him.

At the time, I could not think of any reason for such unrestrained rage. "No, God!" Satan spewed the words as he burst out from the edge of second heaven. "This creature will not have You."

Satan was behaving like a scorned lover who was bent on destroying not only a rival but also himself in the process.

With nary a thought to the consequences, and fueled with passion and jealousy, Satan flew with force toward Adam to destroy him. In less time than a flash can occur, Michael and the warring angels descended around Adam with their swords drawn for battle and the certainty of victory on their faces. I was scared half to death, but I don't think Adam had a clue as to the danger he was in. He stood there not appreciating the scale of warfare about to breakout over him.

Of course Satan could not pass the angelic line of defense. As he drew near them and saw their flaming swords, he came to his senses and realized they would destroy him with pleasure. They only needed an excuse. The bruised archdemon regained his sense of self-preservation and whimpered back out of their reach. We dropped our gaze to the ground and pretended not to have seen anything.

He should have known Michael would stop him. Maybe his jealous fit had short-circuited his thought-processing ability. That might explain some of his faulty reasoning. Because he had once held a position of authority in heaven, perhaps he thought he still had influence where the angelic guard was concerned. Of course, it was not remotely true. Although he ruled over us, fallen as we were, he retained nothing of the majesty and power of the faithful angels. Compared to them, Satan had become, well, *wimpy* is a good word (although, please, don't attribute it to me). The heavenly host could have destroyed him easily. I wondered why they didn't just go ahead and get it over with.

Humiliated to his core, Satan limped back to the precipice of our domain and glared at those of us who had witnessed his meltdown. We stretched our wings, shuffled our hooves, hummed a little tune, and pretended like we hadn't seen a thing. We absolutely had not seen Satan rebuked and mortified by the warring legion of the heavenly army. As far as we were concerned, it never happened.

Like a child in a temper tantrum, Satan did everything but hold his breath and turn blue. With his claws clenched tightly together, he continued to watch what was happening upon Earth. Some of the other demons and myself moved away from where he stood, hoping his preoccupation with Earth would prevent him from hearing us.

"Did you see what happened back there?" the first demon ventured.

"Did you see how he reacted to that clay man God made?"

"Why couldn't we have seen this earlier?" another asked.

"If we had, none of us would be here now. It was embarrassing. He acted more like a spurned lover than the prince of power he calls himself," another voice interjected.

"It was a lie," another whispered. "God was never jealous of Satan. Satan was and is jealous of God's affection toward anyone else."

"I knew it all along," a voice came from the side.

"Knew what?" asked a chorus of voices.

"I knew about his jealousy for God. That's why he hated Adonai."

Gaping mouths and wide eyes is about all we could muster in response.

"What do you mean he hated Adonai?" several asked at once.

"Couldn't you see it when we were in heaven? No one was closer to the Father than Lucifer—Satan—except for the Son. Lucifer never wanted to be the Father; he wanted to be the Son. How could you not have seen it? It's always been about his jealousy of Adonai."

"But he said he would raise his throne above God's. We heard him say it," another demon reminded us.

"No. You assumed he meant Yahweh's throne. That was never the case. He wanted Adonai's throne."

I covered my ears with my wings and refused to listen to anything more. I knew I would never be good under Satan's intense questioning, and I didn't want him to pull such gossip out of me. I couldn't tell what I hadn't heard, and I'd already heard far more than I wanted to.

I knew it was dangerous, but I ventured back toward the edge of second heaven to get a closer look at how things were coming on Earth. What was this "mankind" that God had made? It probably meant something terrible for us; at least Satan thought so. Otherwise he wouldn't have had such a public fit about it.

Satan saw me as I started to slink away, but he insisted I stay on guard with him to hear and record every word God might speak to Adam. Of course, I obeyed, although most of what was going on with Adam was not that interesting. God had to tell him every little thing to do. This new life form couldn't figure out a thing for himself. It was boring for both of us, but then think about our frame of reference. Once a person has stood in heaven and watched God create universes and solar systems from nothing, watching a clay imitation of God name animals was not that exciting. But it wasn't long before things got a lot more intriguing.

God said to Adam, "Multiply and subdue Earth, and take dominion over every living thing upon it."

"Multiply?" I said aloud. "What does God mean by that?"

I puzzled over what God could have meant by such a strange command. Adam was not like the animals. He was much more like God Himself. They, the Trinity, do not multiply. They just *are*. I was very confused and wondered if Satan knew what He meant. Before I could ask the question, he grabbed me by my tail and swung me around till I was facing him. He yelled into my face so that I had to close my eyes at the heat from his words.

"Adam will not rule over anything. Earth is mine." He seethed at me as if daring me to disagree, which was the absolute last thing I intended to do. Oddly, Satan did not seem at all fascinated by the "multiply" idea but latched right on to the "rule over everything" part.

"This will not stand." He threatened, cursed, and paced, but he also knew the truth. As long as the warring angels stood guard around the sky's perimeter, watching over this new creation, Satan would not be able to come near Adam to see what he was about. It would be his certain destruction.

Bored with it all by now, Satan turned and trudged back toward his throne in the center of second heaven, and I tried to follow. Before he could get comfortable on his seat, the sound of a great rushing wind and a pillar of white fire appeared before him and split the darkness that had been his refuge. Satan grasped the arms of his throne and sat frozen in place.

I jumped backwards and wrapped myself around my perch and held on for all I was worth. I knew what was happening and who was making it happen, although I could not look upon Him. Ruah Ha Kadosh had opened the heavens, and there before us stood God, the Ancient of Days. He was magnificent. His hair was like wool, His eyes flame, and He roared over the heavens, the earth, and everything that was or would be. All of us except Satan collapsed before His splendor, unable to move and hoping to die quickly rather than face His wrath. The wrath of Satan cannot be spoken in the same language used to describe the wrath of the Ancient of Days.

"Where can I hide?" I cried before I got hold of myself and realized that there was nowhere to go to be out of His sight. Surely it would be over very soon. He would destroy us. I knew it.

Still wrapped around my perch, I tucked my tail under, shut my eyes, and waited to die. And still I waited. (This new time thing must not be working properly. Obviously it had stopped.) What was happening? Nothing.

I chewed on my tail to relieve the stress. Still nothing. I opened one eye. Yes, I was still present. My tail would never look the same, but I was still alive, which meant that Satan and the others must still be alive too. I dared not try to open my other eye because I could feel that the glory of God was still somewhere about.

Then the Ancient of Days spoke to Satan. "Do you see what I have made on Earth?" Satan did not respond.

The voice of God continued, "I have created Adam to redeem and restore what you have attempted to destroy.

They will reign with Us in the place that you coveted and lost by your rebellion."

Why did God keep referring to Adam as "they"? I wanted to ask someone, but I decided then was not a good time to bring it up.

Heaven and Earth hung suspended together as if in a fragile balance altogether, all at once and all at the same time. Physics would have to explain it; I could not. At first there was silence as Satan glared past God directly at Adam, who, in my opinion wasn't coming close to grasping the seriousness of this situation.

Satan found his voice and managed to growl out what I thought was a very good question. "What is this man that you are mindful of him? What has he done either good or bad that You would make him ruler over Earth?"

"This Earth is mine, and I will not give it up," he continued. "Will You steal it from me? Why don't You just destroy me now in the presence of witnesses? Show Yourself for the tyrant God that You are."

I did not expect God to answer at all, much less to answer as He did.

"Adam will obey Me, and they will accomplish all that I have purposed. I will love them with an everlasting love. They will love Me and follow Me completely."

Satan shot back, "They will not. If they have free will, they will not obey You. Will You leave the warring host to guard them so that their affection for You cannot be tested? That is no contest."

I desperately hoped Satan would stop talking. I didn't know how much more God was willing to take from this rebel.

"Is that what you call love?" he taunted God. "Let them freely choose between You and me. It will be as it was with the angels whom You despised because of their devotion to me. Adam will laugh at you. They will defy You. They will follow me. Unless you force them to obey, they will choose my ways over Yours. They will hand Earth back to me."

From where I crouched in fear, I could see both the angelic guard on the edge of the sky and the faces of the fallen demons who poked their heads out of hiding to hear how God might answer Satan's accusation. As I looked at the perplexed faces in both camps, I realized how much God was willing to risk on this untested prototype of humanity. Both sides had something to win or lose on the basis of how well Adam functioned.

God replied, "I have given Adam complete free will, just as I gave you. If they obey me, I will do all that they ask."

What was I hearing? I was so confused by what God said that I lost concentration, and I am uncertain what happened next. The blackness had returned, and the glory of God had departed. That much I knew, but it was all I knew.

It was not like God to make a wager, and yet that appeared to be what He did. He must be trying to make a point, but what could it possibly be? He was allowing a contest with consequences all of heaven would regard as unthinkable. If Satan had not obeyed God, why did God think that this much-inferior model—Adam—would or could obey?

When things settled down, I unwound myself and moved closer to the edge and looked down upon Earth. I wanted to get a better look at this race God had created. Adam was not that impressive. He had a physical body. That right there was the first mistake God made with him. How could Adam fight against a supernatural foe when he was confined to a body of flesh that could be injured, perhaps even destroyed? An obvious design flaw.

He did not seem to have any particular talent. He could not fly. I suppose he was beautiful, but hardly a match for any of us, at least how beautiful we used to be. His physical body had to be fed. It had to sleep, a concept I could not relate to, although I admit it did have a certain appeal for me. (From time to time I've actually closed my eyes and tried to do it, but I cannot seem to get the hang of it.)

Angry as I was at God for never giving me a chance to plead my case before Him, at that moment I felt sorry for Him. This was never going to work out as He hoped. That free will thing was the fatal flaw. I couldn't imagine Satan would take Adam seriously. I turned to leave when my eyes caught sight of my evil master staring at Adam. I shall never be able to erase from my memory the ghoulish thing I saw in his contorted face. He stood salivating after the man.

CHAPTER 10

S ATAN WENT BACK to his den, and I returned to my post to watch Earth. I had to admit it was a lot more interesting now that it had been reordered and mankind created. I was curious to see how it would turn out.

God made a fabulous home for Adam in a garden personally designed for him. God named the garden Eden, and it was lush—full of every kind of tree and plant that would ever be needed by humans or animals.

There were many trees in Eden, but only two that mattered: the tree of life and the tree of the knowledge of good and evil. God told Adam, "You are free to eat from any tree in the garden, but you must not eat from the tree of the knowledge of good and evil. For when you eat of it, you will surely die."

Considering the consequences of the cosmic rebellion, surely someone in heaven must have tried, albeit unsuccessfully, to convince God that His insistence in giving Adam the ability to choose between one thing and another was a terrible idea that had no possibility of ending well. If God couldn't be talked out of the free will idea, He should have at least let Adam practice a little on something that had no consequences. Let him choose between an apple and a kumquat. Don't let a novice's first choice be one that could alter the balance of the whole world.

The choice to obey or not is far too dangerous to be experimented with. It should be banned from every universe. I could be the poster child for why free will is an eventual disaster for anyone who has it. The ability to defy God is the cause of all my misery. Lucifer decided he could rebel against God. One-third of the angels chose to follow Lucifer. And what did it gain for us? Loss of everything we once held dear—loss of our home with God; loss of our purpose for being; loss of our high place; nothing but loss with regret, despair, fear, and hatred becoming our destiny.

Why does God insist on imposing free will on creatures who cannot possibly use it correctly? He knows what is best for everything He creates. We would be so much better off if He just eliminated the choices. I would not be wasting my existence sitting on a perch in the service of a tyrant if God had only restricted Satan's ability to defy Him.

It is that part of God's nature I cannot understand. He created all there is and all there will be, and He made it perfect. Then, for no reason anyone can explain, He programmed in a fatal flaw. Into every intelligent life form, God deposited the ability to defy its Creator. Can someone help me understand why this was a good idea?

Believe me, I know the company line: God wants those who love Him to do so of their free will. He will coax. He will woo. He will implore. But He will not force His creation to obey, though He could easily do so. How much trouble would He have saved Himself and how much devastation and misery could have been avoided if the rebellion in heaven had never taken place?

I can attest to the fact that we who were cast out of heaven would be so much better off today if God were only willing to be a benevolent dictator. Suppose that we had not chosen to rebel because the choice was not available to us. What if we had been slaves in obedience to Him? Certainly we would still be in paradise and never have known the difference.

Then assume that we annoyed Him in some way and in His anger He cast us out of heaven anyway. If it had happened like that, we would be in the same place where we are right now. And yet, I daresay we would be so much better off. If our destiny would have been the same, what difference would it make *how* we were thrown out? I know I would feel better if I could blame this on God's will and not mine.

When God said He would give free will to Adam, I wanted to shout, "Don't do it, God! Look at us. Look at what it does to those who are less wise than You." But I dared not say a word. It would have been the end of me. When Satan realized that Adam would indeed have the ability to choose, his excitement at what this might mean could not be contained.

Adam's job description was not that hard. He was given ruling authority over the garden, and if he obeyed and worshiped God, he could count on living happily ever after. How hard was that? As I understood his assignment, Adam was to push the boundaries of the garden further and further into the unsettled land until Eden covered Earth. Should have been a piece of cake for someone created in the image of God.

That is very well how it might have ended up if God had not given Adam the option of choosing between those two trees. By far, that was God's worst mistake with Adam. But it wasn't His only one. Let me tell you about God's second greatest lapse in judgment.

CHAPTER 11

G OD DECIDED TO separate them.

She was always in there. I'm not sure why God kept her hidden at first, but whatever she was, she was not an afterthought. It may have been because Adam was an experiential learner. If God had surprised him with the concept of a partner before showing him what a partner was for, I'm pretty sure Adam would have missed the point entirely. God was always patient to walk him through the practical application of a great idea before turning him loose with it. God knew He had to lead Adam to the point of wanting a partner before springing the woman on him.

It was brilliant how God went about it. He gave the man the task of naming the animals. This meant he had to really look at the animals to know what they were before he named them. In doing this work, I believe that he immediately latched on to the comfort that two animals, male and female, provided for each other. It also allowed him to figure out there was no suitable partner for him among the animals. That may seem obvious, but in all honesty, Adam was not that quick on the uptake. It took him forever to name the animals. I thought he would never get around to broaching the subject with God, but one day he did. He asked for a partner.

Eager to give her to him, God told Adam to lie down and go to sleep. While he was sleeping, God took one of his ribs and then closed up the place with flesh. Out of that one bone, God revealed Eve. When Adam woke up, there she was, and she was gorgeous.

We angels were familiar with every living thing in the universe. We have seen about all there is that is beautiful, but I have to tell you, she was a showstopper. We were somewhat dazzled by this new creation. Until God took Eve out of Adam, we had never had a frame of reference for anything female. The angels were all male. Adam was male, or so we thought, but apparently not entirely. We couldn't figure out what she was for. She was like Adam, smaller though, but with a lot of upgraded features. I found myself strangely attracted to her, especially her long hair that flowed and shimmered like strands of gold. In terms of beauty, God really outdid Himself with Eve. Clearly, she had been part of Adam from the beginning, but now, she would be distinct from him. I wondered if that meant that she would also have free will.

They were amazing to watch. They loved and trusted one another right from the beginning. I suppose it might have been something like the affection and trust they held for God Himself. There was no envy, no struggle for power, no suspicion between them. The demons could have learned something about teamwork by watching them, but, of course, you cannot teach a demon anything.

The man and woman worked together at the task of the garden hand in hand, each helping and submitting to the other. Adam had more physical strength and wanted to protect her. Protect her from what I don't know, since we weren't allowed in the garden yet, but it was quaint to watch them. She did not seem to mind the difference in their body mass and his obviously greater physical ability.

I remembered how I once felt that way about God. I did not feel diminished because His power was so much greater than mine. At least, I didn't feel that way until Satan pointed it out to me. Between Adam and Eve there was intimacy and trust I had not seen since we lost paradise. Unfortunately for them, Satan saw it too. Naturally, that would be the first thing he would try to destroy.

As I watched them, I began to appreciate how God had created them equal but interdependent on one another. Adam won out in the brawn category, but without a doubt, Eve was the thinker. Adam could do amazing things, but it was Eve who figured out what things were worth doing.

Had Eve never come along, the flaw in Adam's ability to communicate with another human might never have come to light. When God was the only person Adam had to talk with, it didn't matter that much how good he was at detail. After all, Adam could not possibly tell God something He did not already know. I'm certain God must have been aware of Adam's proclivity to speak in headlines: no paragraphs, no fine print, no sidebar articles. So why did God leave it to Adam to tell Eve what the rules were? Adam was sure to leave out something important.

Every evening God came down and walked through the garden with Adam and Eve. I listened carefully because Satan wanted a full report on every word. Each night, before the presence of God ascended from Eden, I would find myself wanting to call after Him.

"God, wait. Tell her about the rule. Tell her about the two trees. Don't leave it to Adam. It's Your only rule. He's sure to forget something."

Of course, I never did any such thing. I would not have dared, and God would not have listened.

As I knew would happen, the day came when Eve asked Adam about the two trees in the garden. I was afraid he would gloss over the importance of what God said about the trees and leave out some important detail. I worried about the wrong thing. He left nothing out. In fact, he added to it.

CHAPTER 12

S ATAN BECAME POSITIVELY obsessed with the new dimension of time. It didn't mean much to the rest of us since we didn't feel its passing anyway. We might have forgotten about it completely were it not for the fact that Satan kept saying we hadn't much time or we would soon be running out of time. I wondered, how would one go about doing that? If we ran very fast, did it mean that we would run past it? And if we did, what of it? We had always been outside of time before.

He watched Adam and Eve intently now, studying their every move. I thought he might try to approach them soon after God's departure from the garden, but he didn't. He just watched them. He paid attention to everything they did. He shied away from his watching post in the evening when God appeared in the garden and walked its paths with the two of them. Satan did not want to be seen by God (as if line of sight were necessary for God to know what was taking place). He knew. He always knows.

We were surprised when Satan called us together to tell us his plan. He never consulted us about anything. I guess I'm not really sure he ever had plans before. He simply set about to do whatever was on his mind at the moment. He certainly never weighed consequences, nor was he concerned about what any of us might think. The fact that he was thinking this through and waiting, watching, and planning must certainly mean the stakes were high. Whatever his plan might be, it would be certain to include the destruction of Adam and Eve. Satan could never corule with anyone. We obediently lined up to hear what he had to say.

"I have a plan to reclaim Earth," Satan announced. "I will tempt Adam and Eve to disobey God."

The demons who were out of Satan's view rolled their eyes and nudged one another until the one at the end of the line ventured a response.

"Uh huh," he said. "Now that is an interesting idea."

More glances and firmer nudging until someone else dared comment.

"Has lord Satan thought about what it might take to tempt people who already have everything they could possibly want?"

That is exactly what I would have asked if I had the nerve. What could he possibly use to tempt someone who lived in a virtual paradise where they lacked nothing?

"I will convince them God has withheld something valuable and I alone can offer it," Satan smirked.

Murmurs of approval circulated among the demons. No one could guess what it might be that God had not provided, so it was a normal question when someone asked, "What is it you will offer them?"

In a serious voice, Satan responded, "I will tempt them with a piece of fruit."

I bent down, stuffed my hoof into my mouth, and bit down hard. "Chomp, bite, choke, swallow your hoof, but do not chortle. Do not even grin," I warned myself.

The murmuring and nudging started up again. Finally, the demon at the end of the line stepped forward and spoke up. "Fruit, is it? You're going to tempt them with fruit. I see, well that could work."

"That could work," echoed the other demons in mock approval.

"But I wonder, my lord," the demon continued, "did you notice that the garden is full of fruit trees? Of course I don't know anything about it, but fruit as an enticement to disobey God? Do you really think so, Master?" He groveled away before Satan could swing at him.

"Imbecile," Satan roared. "Of course, it is not ordinary fruit. I will offer them fruit from that which is forbidden to them—fruit from the tree of the knowledge of good and evil."

"They might be curious about it," I mused silently, "but that couldn't possibly be enough to entice them to defy their Creator. How good can fruit be?"

Satan must have been able to read the doubt on our faces when he said, "Watch and see what I will do."

Just that fast, he was flying toward Earth. We crowded up to the edge of second heaven. I was amazed when I saw what he was up to. I had no idea he could do such a thing. As easy as you please, Satan took on the form of a serpent right there at the entrance to Eden.

"Did you know he could shape-shift?" someone asked.

"I didn't know that," came the answer.

"Neither did I," said someone else.

I myself was stunned Satan could assume the form of some other living thing God had made. When could he have learned to do it? He'd been with us the whole time. Amazing! Just when you think you know a person. I must admit that it was very clever to choose an animal as beautiful as the serpent. I secretly wondered if any of the rest of us had such talent and couldn't wait for an opportunity to try it myself.

I realize that you have no idea how beautiful the serpent was when God made it. It walked upright and had arms and legs like many other animals. It did not have a forked tongue, nor was its bite poisonous. What the serpent was then and what it is now is an object lesson in why one does not want to be the object of God's curse.

We watched as the serpent positioned himself against the tree of the knowledge of good and evil, as if it were an ordinary tree. He made it look easy and safe. Nothing bad happened to him as he sat on a low-hanging branch and plucked a piece of fruit from it. His being able to do this was a critical marker as far as I was concerned. If Satan were able to come in contact with the tree with nothing happening to him, it seemed less likely there was any real danger for the humans either. I wondered why God had made this such a big deal.

Adam and Eve were both working in the garden that day. Satan waited until Adam was some distance away and then called out to Eve. When Eve saw him, she was completely disarmed by how comfortable he was languishing on the tree branch that held so much fear for her.

I think Satan intentionally waited until he could talk to Eve alone, out of earshot from Adam. There was no doubt he was fascinated by her beauty and how different she was from Adam. I must say she was captivating. After their separation into two beings, Satan rarely looked at Adam anymore. But I would often find him leaning over the edge of second heaven staring at Eve.

"Did God really say not to eat of this tree?" he asked.

Clever of him to do that. Satan did not really accuse God of anything right then, not taking the chance of putting her on the defensive. He merely asked a question. And a very good question it was. Then Adam returned to see what was going on, but he said nothing. He did not seem that concerned that the serpent was talking to Eve. After all, at that time all animals could talk. One of them was always talking to Eve, her being the much better conversationalist of the two. The animals lost their language after the curse, but I'm getting ahead of myself.

Ignoring Adam, who was distracted by a bee flitting about his head, the serpent jumped from the branch and sauntered around the trunk of the tree, pulling off some of its leaves to Eve's complete astonishment. In a soft voice, the serpent said to Eve again, "Did God tell you not to eat from this beautiful tree?"

"Yes. He said we could not eat from it or we would die."

"Now why would God say that? You can see it's harmless, can't you?" He reached for another ripe piece of fruit and extended his hand to offer it to Eve. Eve took a step back and gasped at such an action.

"No. We cannot eat the fruit. We cannot even touch the tree or we will die."

"Oh, no," I cried. "I knew it! I predicted this would happen!" I ranted in a rare display of emotion as I stomped back and forth behind the line of demons. "I knew Adam would never get it right! Why did God leave it to him to tell her about the rules of the trees?" The other demons had no idea what I was talking about and ignored me completely.

Adam, never one for detail, had obviously told Eve not to eat from or touch the tree. God said nothing about touching anything. One rule in the entire universe, and it gets misinterpreted in its very first use.

The serpent grinned and continued to dangle the fruit in front of Eve, who stepped further back, being careful not to accidentally brush up against the fruit. Adam reached out and took her by the arm.

"Uh, Eve," Adam found his voice. "I'm not sure that's what God said."

"What do you mean you're not sure?" she asked. "We are not to eat from the tree or even touch it. That *is* what God said, right?"

"He probably didn't say anything about touching," Adam said as he swatted at the bee.

"Adam, pay attention," said Eve as she grabbed his swatting hand and brought him face-to-face. "You need to be very sure about this."

"Yeah, yeah, well, I'm pretty sure. He didn't say anything about touching."

Eve turned away and looked like she might cry. Adam took her by the shoulders and gently turned her around.

"Don't be upset. So much was going on that day. I could have heard God wrong." Adam strained as if trying to remember as he looked at the serpent pulling leaves off the tree. "I guess God must not have said anything about touching, or the serpent would be dead."

Eve did not seem convinced. She said nothing in response and looked at the serpent sheepishly.

The serpent moved slowly toward her, saying, "The tree is right here in your garden. Why would God care if you ate from it or not?"

Both of them folded their arms, shifted their weight from foot to foot, and looked uncomfortably at each other, then at the serpent, but neither had an answer.

"There can only be one reason," said the serpent as he pulled off more leaves and crushed them between his fingers. "There's a power in the tree God doesn't want you to know about."

"What kind of power?" Adam asked.

"The power to know good and evil. If you eat the fruit from this tree, you will be like God. You will know everything and will never die."

Adam and Eve stepped away and whispered quietly with their backs to the serpent. I listened intently as they talked themselves right into what Satan had wanted them to believe all along: nothing was forbidden. If God had said it was forbidden, then He must have an ulterior motive. Very clever, indeed, I must say. They walked back to where the serpent was, and Eve extended her hand.

"Don't do it!" I shouted into the air, but I knew they were going to do it anyway. The other demons looked at me as if I were addled, but they weren't interested enough to find out why.

The serpent gave Eve the fruit; she took a bite and then gave it to Adam. I would come to be amazed, as history unfurled, how humans got the idea this was Eve's fault. I was there, watching and listening from the first day God gave the rule to Adam while Eve was still a rib. It had to be Adam who gave Eve the information about the tree. How could she have known any other way? No one else heard, so no one can be sure what he said to her.

Maybe Adam did it with good intentions. I've seen other humans do the same sort of thing when warning someone they care about of possible danger. I've heard them overstate the consequences without the slightest hesitation. For example, a parent warns a child not to touch an electrical socket because if he does, he will get electrocuted. Of course, that wouldn't happen from touching a socket. It seems to me it is human nature to embellish when someone's safety is at stake.

"That a girl," Satan said as Eve took a bite of the fruit and gave the rest to Adam. "See?" he chided. "Nothing happened."

Eve looked embarrassed, and I could tell she wondered if Adam could be trusted to hear from God. Their relationship had already changed. She would have never have thought such a thing before the fruit.

The show was over as far as the other demons were concerned. They turned and headed back to Satan's den, slapping one another on the back and celebrating how easy it was for Satan to get Earth back. I knew things weren't over yet, so I stayed around to see what would happen when God showed up, as He was sure to do.

I climbed up on my perch and tried to figure out what the real problem was with what Adam and Eve had done. To be candid, I expected God might think it over and give them a pass. A rational mind would have to conclude this episode did not merit changing the destiny of Earth. Adam and Eve wanted to know the difference between good and evil. So who doesn't? Later on I would hear God tell people a thousand times to flee from evil. How does one flee from evil if he doesn't know what evil looks like?

They wanted to be like God; again, who doesn't? As time passed, I would hear humans sing about wanting to be more like God, with God liking every note of it. Why is it fine for future generations to want to be like God, but not them?

Was any of what Satan said to them true? Not really. Their eyes were opened to things they hadn't paid attention to before, but those things had always been there. The first thing they saw was their nakedness. They had never been anything but naked. They just hadn't noticed. I don't know how they saw themselves prior to this, but being naked was apparently a big surprise to them. They sewed fig leaves together and made coverings for themselves. With this new knowledge Satan had promised them, they somehow connected being naked with knowing good and evil. Who knows?

When they heard the rustling of the trees and felt the coolness of the air, they both took off in different directions and nose-dived into the underbrush. God had arrived.

God called, "Adam, where are you?"

Adam crouched down and did not say a word. I knew how he felt as he hid behind a palm tree, hoping God would not find him. I found myself remembering the sorrow, fear, and self-loathing that overwhelmed me when I realized that by my own ambivalence, I had disobeyed God and separated myself from Him forever. Why did I listen to Lucifer?

As I heard God call for Adam again, I began to feel sad, hurt, and angry about it. God was actually seeking after this disobedient creature. God had never searched or called out to me after the rebellion. I hadn't really done anything wrong, not like Adam anyway. Adam knew the rule and intentionally disobeyed. I was a victim of circumstances. If God had cared the slightest thing about me, He should have realized it and given me a second chance.

At God's third call, Adam sheepishly stepped from behind the tree. He looked like a tree himself, decked out in his new leaf clothing.

"Adam," God said, "why didn't you come when I called?"

Adam didn't work very hard on his answer. "I heard You in the garden, and I was afraid because I was naked, so I hid."

Then God replied, "Who said you were naked? Did you eat from the forbidden tree?"

Adam looked around for Eve and, not seeing her, leaned in and whispered to God, "Yes, but it wasn't my fault. The woman You put here with me made me do it. She gave me some fruit from the tree and insisted I eat it."

Satan blew his cover as a snake when he roared with delight as he heard what Adam said.

Right then Eve stepped out into the clearing and stood behind Adam. Unaware she was there, Adam continued to explain to God how this was Eve's fault. I could see her face clearly as she listened to Adam accuse her. I'm quite sure that if I had been capable of pity, I would have had it for Eve that day. She was crushed and horrified. She could barely assimilate the idea that this man upon whom she had depended, believed, and loved was now willing to sacrifice her to the certain wrath of God.

An awful thing happened in that moment for humanity. A breach occurred between men and women that has never been successfully mended. Satan would nest forever in that breach. Both of them were truly horrified when they realized that their enticer ridiculed them in the presence of God.

"Kill them," Satan ranted to God. "They defied You like I told You they would. Destroy them for their ambition. Just like You did it to me, now do it to them."

God's eyes blazed as He turned from Adam and Eve and faced Satan, who stopped ranting and fell down under the weight of His gaze, laying still on the ground in front of Him.

When I saw the wrath in God's eyes, I was too terrified to continue watching. I tucked my head under my wing and pretended I hadn't seen a thing.

CHAPTER 13

I TRIED HUMMING A tune so I would not hear what God said to the serpent. "Hmm..."

Humming is not a natural skill for angels, and I had a little trouble getting a rhythm for it. Finally I ran out of breath and gave up. I did not want to hear because I had no desire to be the only witness to Satan's further humiliation. When I couldn't hum any longer, I couldn't help myself. I heard every word.

God told the serpent, "Because you've done this, you're cursed beyond all cattle and wild animals, cursed to slink on your belly and eat dirt all your life."

It was amazing to see. The serpent began a meltdown before them. His legs and arms contracted, and he turned into the serpent you humans are familiar with: long, full of scales, and when he tried to speak, he could only hiss.

His teeth became fangs filled with poison—a bad idea if you ask me. The serpent wriggled violently, and I knew it was Satan trying to escape the serpent's body, but God would not let him go. He held him captive inside the snake until He finished speaking.

OK, I know I said earlier that Satan shape-shifted. It made sense at the moment, but hearing the curse made me rethink things. Maybe it was not shape-shifting I saw, but a kind of possession.

Until God spoke the curse, it had not occurred to me whether the serpent might have been complicit in some way with Satan's scheme. Otherwise, why curse a helpless animal? Before Satan seduced Adam and Eve, my guess is he first charmed the serpent to allow him to use his body.

Shape-shifting or animal possession—it doesn't really matter. The deed had been done. I thought about asking Satan about it but gave up the idea. The answer would not be worth the beating.

God continued, "I'm declaring war between you and the woman, between your offspring and hers. He'll crush your head, and you'll wound his heel."

I had already figured out that offspring had something to do with that multiply and subdue commandment from earlier. But what could God have possibly meant when He said Satan was going to have offspring? How was that going to happen? Not wanting to miss a word, I hung as far over the ledge as I dared without falling off.

I couldn't believe Satan didn't jump on that idea right away. He didn't seem one bit mystified or interested in the offspring comment as it pertained to him. God released Satan from the serpent that slithered away very quickly. Satan pulled himself together as best he could and more or less slumped over. Unable to stand upright before God, Satan must have been truly terrified, thinking this time He would certainly destroy him completely. Otherwise, I'm sure he would have insisted on more clarity on the bizarre notion of offspring.

God surprised me when He allowed Satan to escape the garden unscathed. One might have thought the enemy of both man and God would be feeling victorious after his bloodless coup, stealing Earth from Adam and Eve. Instead, when he summoned me to his den, he seemed nervous. He demanded I recount all that happened in the garden encounter with God. I was afraid when I realized he knew I had listened to the whole thing.

I tried to explain. "I wasn't paying that much attention. I barely heard anything."

"Liar," he shouted at me rising from his seat. I assumed the groveling position and he sat back down.

"Tell me exactly what He said. Don't change any of the words," he demanded.

I raised my head a little. "I wasn't eavesdropping, sir," I wanted to be sure he didn't think I was spying on him.

"Don't grovel, imbecile."

"Right, I just thought I should explain why I happened to overhear..."

He cut me off. "Do not think. Watch and report, nothing more."

"Yes, of course, not a problem," I quickly agreed. Then I sat very still waiting for his reply.

"Then tell me what He said, you idiot!" Clenching his claws and grinding his teeth, he shouted at me loud enough for all creation to hear. I was terribly embarrassed by it, but that did not quell his rudeness the slightest little bit. He continued, "How long must I endure your ineptitude? Just tell me what you heard Him say."

"Right, well, it was something like this," I began. "Cursed is the ground—"

He interrupted. "Not that part, after that."

"Right," I jumped ahead, "and cursed are you above the livestock—"

"After that," he interrupted again.

"You will crawl on your belly—" before I could finish the sentence, he threw a stone right at me.

"After that, toward the end," he dropped his head to rest on his claw and waved me on with the other one.

"Oh, right, I know what part you mean." Obviously, God's comment about offspring had not gone right by him after all.

"God said He was declaring war between your offspring and the offspring of the woman." I stopped right there, thinking that was the intriguing part. But, he waved me to go still further.

"The last line, give me the last line." He sighed as if weary of the whole ordeal.

"God said something about you striking the heel of her offspring and then her offspring would stomp on your head and crush it to dust." He glared at me.

"God said He would stomp on my head?" he demanded.

"More or less," I realized I shouldn't have added my own translation. His eyes shot fire at me. I tried to amend what I said. "Actually, now as I recall, maybe it wasn't quite that." He glared at me more fiercely, and I backed up more trying not to trip over my tail.

"Now I remember," I managed to get the words out. "It was more like her offspring will crush your head, but I'm sure He did not mean it literally."

Satan drew back and sat down on his throne, saying nothing more. I didn't know what to do, so I stood there. He went deep into his own thoughts, and when I was sure he was no longer aware of whether I was in the room or not, I crept out as quickly and quietly as possible.

I went back to my perch to see if anyone was still in the garden. I wondered if God had destroyed Adam or Eve or both of them for their disobedience. Instead, I saw God was talking to the woman. Adam stood by; both of them looked ashamed about the whole thing, but he said nothing. I strained to listen to God's soft voice and then could not believe what I was hearing.

"Eve," God said in the most tender tone. "You sinned against Me. Why?"

"The serpent beguiled me, and I believed him," Eve whispered, her eyes full of sorrow at what she had done.

Then God turned to Adam. "Adam, you sinned against Me, knowing full well what you were doing. Then you hid from Me and blamed Eve for your actions." God's voice was quiet but stern.

Adam shuffled his feet in the leaves and shifted his weight uncomfortably, but he did not reply.

God continued to speak to the man. "Your intentional, unrepentant sin prevents you from remaining in Eden. I told you to obey Me in just one thing. Was that too much to ask? " I could tell God was grieved by the judgment He was about to pronounce on Adam. "You must leave. You cannot stay in Eden."

Then God turned back to Eve. "Eve, because you were deceived, your sin is not as onerous to me as that of Adam. Do you want to stay in the garden without Adam?"

"What did He say?" I blurted out to no one at all as I tripped over myself, trying to get to the edge of second heaven to hear better. I could not be hearing God correctly.

God continued, "You may stay here, and I will watch over you, or you may go into exile with your husband."

Eve looked over to Adam, who pleaded with her with his eyes not to abandon him, although, in my mind, he had been perfectly willing to do that to her. God saw the pain and sympathy in Eve's eyes as she looked back at Adam.

"If you go with him," God spoke softly, "then your desire will be to please him. He will misinterpret your love for weakness and he will rule over you."

Adam did not dare say a word, but his eyes said it all. "I won't, I promise. I'll take care of you. I'll love you." It was all right there in the tears welling up and spilling over his cheeks. Eve was distressed as she looked first to God then to Adam.

I could not stand it anymore. I leaned over the edge and shouted at Eve, not caring who in heaven or Earth might hear me.

"Eve! Listen to me. Don't do it. Adam is not worth it. Stay in the garden with God. Nothing is worth being separated from Him."

When I heard her say she would go with Adam, I collapsed in a heap of emotional exhaustion. I did not have the energy to climb back on my perch. I sprawled there on the rim with one claw and half my tail hanging precariously over the edge of the abyss. I didn't know whether God was as distressed with her choice as I was, but if He was, He did nothing to show it. I thought He would leave them right then, but He didn't. In fact, He did something completely unexpected, and, dare I say, out of character. He made garments of skin for Adam and Eve.

"Why does He think they need more clothing?" I muttered. "If He thinks they need apparel, why not let them keep the coverings of leaves?"

That would have made much more sense since the garden was quite warm and much better suited to grass skirts than wool and fur. They were going to be conspicuously overdressed for their surroundings.

That by itself was not the "out-of-character" part I mentioned earlier. In order to make clothes of skins for them, God had to kill one of His wonderful animals and shed its blood. Now think about that for a moment. To God, the giver of life, all life is precious. He did not destroy the rebellious angels, some of whom most certainly needed to be destroyed; yet here He was sacrificing the life of an innocent animal.

"For what?" I asked myself, "So Adam and Eve could have more useless clothes, which they did not need to start with?"

I have pondered this question for a very long time, and until now I haven't figured it out. It had to have something to do with the blood, but what?

So the Lord God exiled Adam and Eve from the Garden of Eden to work and sweat over the ground from which they had been made. After He drove them out, He placed cherubim on the east side of the garden where they stood vigilant with their flaming swords flashing back and forth to guard the way to the tree of life.

Having chosen the tree of the knowledge of good and evil, Adam and Eve were banished from their home and never allowed to return.

I knew just how they felt.

CHAPTER 14

THE MORE I thought about Adam and Eve's meltdown in the garden, the more I found myself annoyed with God about how He handled it. They committed intentional sin, and yet their entire punishment consisted of being moved outside the garden to another perfectly acceptable place on the planet. Furthermore, contrary to what I thought would happen and what *should have* happened, God continued to watch over them. I sinned against God by accident, and look what happened to me—thrown out of paradise to a foreign place with no chance to appeal my sentence.

Why should humans and nobody else get a pass— or at least a second chance—when it comes to sin? I've now chronicled humanity through several generations of Adam and Eve's kids, and I can tell you there has not been any noticeable improvement in any of them. For someone with the responsibility for worlds and universes beyond the scope of earthly imagination, God was spending way too much time trying to fix humans. He does so until this day. Why does He keep trying to make you people into something you cannot be? He gives you much more credit for using your intelligence than you deserve. Mankind falls into such a predictable pattern of behavior, it isn't entertaining to watch anymore.

Act one: God gives people a choice between obedience and rebellion. Act two: they always rebel. Act three: He finds a loophole in the law and forgives them. End of play. Then the cycle starts again. Humanity does not learn a thing from experience. That's why I cannot understand why He didn't save Himself millennia of grief by canceling the mandate to Adam and Eve to multiply.

"Cut your losses," I would have told Him. "Start with a fresh batch of clay and forget the free will thing altogether."

Surely He must have known that any offspring born of Adam and Eve would be just like them. And indeed that is what happened.

God was right when He warned Eve that her childbearing would come through great pain. Cain came screaming from Eve, who was in writhing pain and all alone because Adam had passed out at the first glimpse of Cain's bloody head emerging. I don't know how Adam thought he was going to get any kids, but I'm confident this was nowhere in his thinking. One can hardly blame him, though. His only experience with new life was when he took a nap, woke up, and there was Eve—all cleaned up and pretty, fully functional and able to take care of herself from day one. He probably thought it was always going to be like that.

Eve was mostly on her own in birthing the baby. It made me nervous to watch. In my mind, no other human experience would more clearly define the difference between man and woman than childbirth. Man will endure pain for what is to be gained by it. Woman will endure pain for what is to be loved, with no guarantee that she will be loved in return.

Eve loved her children so intently before they were born that she endured her own body splitting apart to give them life. Adam liked the kids once he got used to them, but I can tell you that if it had been up to him to give birth, the entire human population would have stopped at three. In fact, when Eve told him she was going to have another baby, Adam told her to figure out what was causing it and quit doing it.

Although Adam and Eve would live the rest of their lives with the consequences of their sin, God was still incredibly kind to them. They knew He was helping them, though He never dropped by for a walk anymore. They wanted their children to know about Him, so they were forever telling stories about God and how He continued to take care of them and teach them. My opinion is they were trying to find ways to make up for what they had done in the garden. As a matter of fact, the whole idea of humans offering something back to God from their earthly labor started with the two of them. I thought it was silly. God is in need of nothing that His creation could offer Him. Surely they must have known that.

Yet, they were sacrificing food or whatever to Him as if they thought He must have to eat like they did. You can imagine my surprise when I realized God Himself was the One who gave them the idea to do it.

If true justice prevailed, they were supposed to be living under a curse and deprived of any special consideration from God. Now, I ask you, how would a reasonable person understand a curse? A curse, in my mind, means no supernatural intervention—none at all. That's what I got; no sympathy whatsoever. Throw them out and let them make it on their own, I say.

But here was God coming up with a scheme by which He could get around His own rules and give them whatever they needed. By giving some of the fruit of their labor back to the Lord, He now had a legal method to bless their work and their obedience. I no longer had any compassion for them at all. They taught their children to do the same in returning part of their earnings to God. Before long, I could see how offering God the first portion of something He didn't need to start with was a form of interaction, communion you might say, with God. So much for living under a curse.

Cain, the first son, went into agriculture. He thought the offering ritual was silly and that God couldn't possibly need the crop as badly as he did. Cain went along with it because it was easier to do it than argue all day long with his parents about it. Nonetheless, Cain was always looking for a way to minimize his losses. When it was time for the offering, Cain would present God with a plant that looked like it was going to die anyway. Then he would make a big show out of offering it up. The Lord, as I knew would be the case, was unimpressed, so much so that He blew the smoke of the offering right back in Cain's face.

Abel, the second boy, got the hang of giving first-fruits right away. He made his living tending the flocks because he was good with animals. He never seemed to begrudge the offering ritual in the least. It seemed he rather looked forward to it. He would take the best part of the animal, dedicate it to God, and then burn it up right there before Him on an altar. Then Abel would take the rest for himself.

Until this happened, Satan had not paid that much attention to Adam and Eve's kids. But when he heard the rest of us talking about the petulant Cain, he sparked to immediate attention. He walked to the edge of second heaven and watched intently to see if there would be a further exchange between Cain and God. And, of course, you know there was.

God let Cain stew in his pity for a while and then spoke to him. "Why are you angry, Cain? What's the matter with you?"

Cain did not answer. He put his hands in his pockets and kicked some leaves around with his foot.

"You must do what is right," God went on. "If you persist in offense, sin will overtake you. Cain, start now. You must master it." God almost pleaded with him

The dawn of understanding cracked open for me when I heard that. A lot of things I had been unable to comprehend suddenly became clear. I should have seen it before. Satan is going to need human beings if he wants to get anything done on Earth. If God restricted Himself to work through mankind, Satan would have to do the same.

Satan hurried back to his lair and summoned one of the most loathsome of our kind to his private chambers. His name was Murder. Satan assigned Murder to go down to Earth and shadow Cain. When Cain thought about how God had embarrassed him, Murder was to affirm his feelings by entering into the conversation Cain was having with himself. Ever so seductively, Murder crept into Cain's mind.

Murder reminded Cain of every childhood incident where Abel was favored. He would tell him Abel plotted to make Cain's offering look meager.

"Why would Abel offer such an extravagant sacrifice if not to shame your efforts?" Murder whispered.

As Cain's offense grew against Abel, Murder was to watch for the moment when Cain's self-pity swallowed up his common sense so that he blamed God for His unfairness. When it happened, and it did, Murder sailed through the open door into Cain's soul.

One might think Cain would have lost his ability to make choices after more or less becoming a slave to Murder's orders. Not so. Cain's spirit warred against the intrusion of Murder into his soul. Two out of three wins, so it would be Cain's flesh that would choose between the desires of the soul and the demands of the spirit. The design flaw in humanity's makeup could never have been more evident than at that moment.

I make no pretense to be smarter than God, but even I would have known not to use flesh and blood as building materials in creating a reasoning life form. Flesh is fickle, inferior, and completely unreliable in a crisis. Its demands are never satisfied, and it's in need of constant maintenance. It is easily enticed, manipulated, and bargains for very little. The souls of men would not have near the casualties if it were not for their skin, blood, and bones.

Things might have turned out quite differently if it had not been for Cain's soulish desires. I feel certain his mind would have overcome his emotions had it not been for the pleasure of revenge, which caused his skin to tingle in anticipation. Cain was probably still thinking it over when he asked Abel to go for a walk with him.

Cain found his brother with the cows. "Let's go out to the field."

Abel tried to engage him in friendly chitchat, but Cain was not much of a conversationalist that day. His mind was consumed with listening to Murder speak into his inner ear.

"Do you want to know why your brother deliberately made you look foolish in front of your parents?" Murder whispered.

Cain was listening, and as he did so, Murder slipped deeper into Cain's consciousness and unleashed a power into Cain that exhilarated him beyond anything he had ever felt.

Murder continued, "It's about the inheritance. You're out of the will now. When they die they will leave everything to Abel. He will drive you away."

"I'll be destitute to wander Earth with no place to live," Cain said in his own mind.

Murder didn't have to say another word. Cain's mind took over at that point, and as the demonic power surged within him, he talked himself into fratricide.

"Abel has tried to turn my parents against me all my life. He won't get away with it," Cain assured himself.

Ecstatic with the demon's power coursing through his soul, and lusting for revenge, Cain picked up a stone and attacked his brother and killed him.

For less than an instant, Cain was thrilled by his power over life. The adrenaline surge satisfied his need for revenge. But he had only a moment to revel in his sense of invincibility; as quickly as Murder had seized Cain, he left, taking his power with him. Cain fought to retain the ecstasy that bled out of his soul, but he could not. He slumped over, weak, mortified, and full of fear.

Murder couldn't fly fast enough to get back to Satan's lair to brag about his success.

"Just like his old man," Murder laughed, "dumber than dirt." Satan roared and slapped Murder on the back with his claw in that silly way we males have of congratulating each other.

Cain looked at his slain brother on the ground before him and became horribly afraid.

"What have I done?" He dropped to his knees and tried to revive his slain brother. Cain lifted the bleeding head of Abel and tried to remember why he had hated him so. He dropped Abel's head and jumped to his feet as if trying to grasp something that was no longer there. Where was the awesome power that he felt moments before? Where had it gone, and why was he now in such deep despair?

Satan roared with satisfaction at the whimpering Cain who had been so easily seduced by Murder. In fear of being discovered, Cain dug a shallow grave and buried Abel. Then he ran as far as he could until the weight of God's presence bore down upon him, driving him to his knees.

God said, "Where is your brother Abel?"

"I don't know," he replied. "Am I my brother's keeper?"

I wanted to shout out, "Bad answer, Cain," but, of course, I did not for fear of being overheard by you-know-who. Oh, but if I could have advised him, I knew I could have gotten him a lighter sentence. I've watched God and humans long enough to know God's soft spot.

"Cain," I would have said. "Lose the machismo. Repent. Beg for forgiveness. Grovel. I know God. He loves that stuff. Trust me, it will work." But, of course, I said nothing.

God said, "What have you done? Your brother's blood cries to Me from the ground where you buried him. You've brought a curse on the land. From now on you'll get nothing but failed crops. This won't be your home any longer, and you'll be a restless wanderer on Earth."

Cain got the very thing he so feared—the curse he had only a day before pronounced upon himself. Still on his knees, Cain whimpered to God, "This is not fair. This punishment is more than I can stand."

I was disgusted with the whole charade. "Cain," I shouted, no longer caring who heard me, "can you be more of a wimp? Banished from your land? You call that punishment? Let me tell you about punishment. How about if God expelled you from the planet? How about being left alone to float endlessly in space? You are still alive and on the same earth where you were born, and yet you whine like a sniveling coward?"

When I thought he could not get any more pathetic, he whined some more.

Cain said to God, "My punishment is too much. I can't take it! You've thrown me off the land, and I can never again face You. I'm a homeless wanderer on Earth, and whoever finds me will kill me."

Then God said to him, "Not so. If anyone kills you, he will suffer vengeance seven times over." Then God put a mark on Cain's head so that no one who found him would harm him. God went home, and Cain went on to live happily ever after in the land of Nod, east of Eden.

I simply could not believe it had happened again; another pass for humanity. I wanted to fly after God and demand a hearing. "God, if you are going to punish those who sin against You, at least be consistent. Where do You get off letting a murderer go free? Is that what You call punishment? Why does he get another chance? Why didn't I?"

I slouched back to my perch, covered my head with my wings, and groused at the unfairness of it all.

Cain got married and had many children. Adam and Eve conceived again, and Seth was born. He too married and had many children, and the whole population of Earth grew. While this went on for decades, Satan remained somewhat passive as far as humans were concerned. Ages came and went, and while the demons were allowed to vex the humans from time to time, Satan seemed oddly disengaged with the whole thing.

Then one day, he turned his attention to the ruling principalities over Earth. They had been in place since Earth was created and were the very powerful angels who had authority to govern the affairs of Earth before Satan stole it. The fact they remained at their posts and the fact that Satan thought he needed an army meant there was sure to be a fight at some point. I stayed away from them myself, not knowing where their loyalties might be in light of the Fall, humans, and all that.

When I saw Satan flying toward them, I knew he had a plan. Another kind of war was about to be unleashed upon Earth.

CHAPTER 15

I COULD NEVER HAVE been a member of the elite angel league, of course, but many others were chosen, hundreds of them. God had a lot of ideas about the countries and continents mankind would discover on Earth, but He also knew humanity would have no idea where to start. To help humans get the hang of managing the many challenges in bringing order and stability to their growing society, God appointed protectors from the mightiest of the angelic guard and set them in government over each of the divisions of the planet. As it always was with Him, when He gave power and authority, it was an irrevocable gift.

By now, can you figure out what a wretchedly bad idea that was? How could anyone who hoped to maintain peace and devotion to oneself ever suppose that the combination of irreversible power, authority, supernatural ability, and free will might be a good idea? Someone on the council should have warned God about what could happen in a setup like that.

That is how it came to be that these mighty ones were established in provincial reign over Earth, helping humanity learn to manage the planet. But before these angels were assigned to Earth, they were in third heaven. Like all the angels, they were under the authority of the archangels, the chief among them being Lucifer.

Because most of them had been trained under Lucifer before he went bad and became Satan, they recognized him immediately when he approached, in spite of the fact that he now looked like the last three days of a misspent life. The mighty ones had not followed him into rebellion, but their prior familiarity with him and the natural curiosity that we angels have left open an unfortunate door that God should have thought about and closed off at once.

I would never have had the nerve to do it, but Satan was not even a trifle reluctant about approaching the awesome angelic brigade. Knowing how sly and disarming he can be, I would have expected them to have their guard up when they saw him coming. Perhaps they thought there was little to fear from this battle-scarred old archangel. Or maybe they were simply curious and wanted to hear Satan's side of the story for themselves. More likely they had forgotten how cunning and crafty he really is.

Every one of the demons in second heaven gathered on the ledge and tittered nervously among themselves like schoolgirls at a sock hop as they watched Satan approach the prince of Persia. I was apprehensive, but I stood by as well and hoped they wouldn't come after us.

"Hail, mighty one, son of God," Satan called out to the prince as he bowed low before the surprised angel.

Although he tried to appear nonchalant about it, one could not miss the twinkle in the prince's eyes that betrayed his pride at receiving such a greeting from his former superior. I wished I could have been a voice of reason in the prince's ear. I would have warned him of what was sure to happen.

"You do not know what Lucifer has become," I would have whispered. "He isn't here to chat with you. Run! Run like the wind. If he is talking, he is lying. He will flatter you, and you will believe him, and then you will want to hear more."

The mighty prince of Persia puffed up like a toasted marshmallow as Satan lavished him with praise. No doubt he would have drawn his sword and lopped Satan's claw off if he had only known how many times his former mentor had derided him before God. When Lucifer, as he was known then, learned of his judgment, he slandered all of the other heavenly beings, especially the mighty ones who ruled Earth. Now here he was, fairly groveling as he bowed down before the prince and flattered him with all sorts of unbelievable adulation. By the time Satan set the trap, this "mighty" one stepped right in.

Satan did what he does best. He asked a question, "Have you considered the daughters of men?"

For a moment, I was paralyzed by the horror at what I knew was coming next. Someone must stop him. I tapped and tugged at the leering demons there on the ledge, trying to get someone to listen to me.

"Stop him! Stop him before it's too late," I pleaded.

They rebuffed me and pushed me away from where they stood.

"He knows what he's doing," one said.

"We don't need your opinion," another added, "Get to the back of the line and leave us alone."

"No, you must listen to me," I begged as I tried to wiggle my way in among them again. "God will not stand for it. I know what I'm talking about. You must listen to me."

But they would not. They kept watching and sneering with delight at the transaction under way between Satan and the prince. I had to try again.

"Don't you see what is happening?" I screamed at their lustful faces. "If he succeeds in tempting the mighty ones to breach the forbidden zone, it will be the end of us all. God will not hold back. He will not show mercy."

"Mercy?" the ugly one snarled. "What mercy did we ever receive? We were banished, thrown out, discarded as if we had never mattered."

I shot back, "You are still alive, you fool. God let you live. He let us live instead of turning us to ash, as He could have. If Satan does this thing, we will be cast forevermore to Tartaroo."

He drew back for a moment at my words. We knew about Tartaroo, the deepest part of hell reserved for rebellious angels.

"Then we will reign there," he bragged.

"Is there no limit to your stupidity? For once in your pitiful existence, just try to think five minutes ahead. Are you so thick-skulled that eternal damnation means nothing to you?"

Demons do not respond well to constructive criticism.

When I regained consciousness, I tried desperately to remember what happened to cause me to be hanging upside down by my tail over the jagged edge of the cliff that rimmed second heaven. I was bewildered and completely helpless, dangling over the abyss below. One of my wings was broken, and my eyes were swollen shut. I could feel several loose teeth. When I opened my mouth to moan in pain, one actually fell out and tumbled into the blackness below. Everything about me hurt: my hooves, my claws, my scales, and my other wing had a tear in it.

It was awhile before I could recollect what I had done to get myself into such a fix. I hung there in the darkness for the longest time, trying to get my fragmented memory back together. When the image of Satan and the prince came crashing back into my consciousness, I was terrified. I had to get down. I swung myself back and forth in hopes that my tail would break off and I would at last fall into the bottomless darkness below me. Whatever was down there would not be as bad as the wrath I knew would soon be loosed from third heaven.

"Perhaps the abyss won't be that bad," I said to my quaking self. "Perhaps I will fall forever and simply cease to exist."

I swung harder, but my tail did not break off; it only hurt more.

"Limbo," I muttered, "I'm caught in limbo. I can't go down and I can't get up. Help! Help! Help!" I shouted to a demonic horde that was no longer there and would not have responded even if they had been.

I should have known no one was going to help me the least little bit. I flapped my working wing for all it was worth until I was able to levitate upward to the edge of the cliff. I grabbed hold with my good claw and pulled myself up until I could rest my cracked head and broken appendage on the ledge. I unwound my tail from the protruded stone below where I had hung for who knows how long. Somehow I was able to pull the rest of me up until I lay on the rim, exhausted and wishing I were dead. After a while, I crawled back to my perch and waited to see what would happen next.

I felt the sound before I heard it. I cringed into a ball at the blood-curdling screams coming from the women of Earth. For all the horror we had wrought upon Earth, there had never been a sound of despair like this. The floor of second heaven reverberated as the cries from the women went up and up and up until it was only a matter of moments until they would pierce through this realm and reach third heaven. Soon God would respond to the terrible thing that had happened on Earth.

The sanctity of mankind had been breached. The mighty ones, incited to indulge their lust by the deceitfulness of Satan, transgressed their own nature to violate the daughters of men. The holy angels surrendered to sexual immorality and went after the forbidden flesh of human women, condemning themselves to suffer His vengeance in eternal fire.

Satan danced and laughed from the safety of second heaven as Earth reeled at the rape of the women. Freaks and giants would soon be born, and many mothers would die in agony in their birthing. In their lust, some of the mighty ones went after the human men and the men became insane from the violation and in turn deposited their seed into the animals. The gene pool of all human and animal life was degraded beyond redemption.

"How do you like it now, God?" Satan jeered toward heaven.

And for a moment, it seemed as if Satan had finally won, his revenge accomplished against the mighty angelic guard, who had remained faithful to God in the cosmic rebellion and now plunged into the unquenchable fire of His wrath for degrading His most prized creation.

"Woe to Earth," I moaned. A species God did not create was now in the midst of mankind.

The Nephilim were upon the earth.

CHAPTER 16

IT WAS HORRIBLE. They were awful. A half-breed demon turned out to be far worse than a demon in its natural state, and much more dangerous. A regular garden-variety demon, as all of us were, had limitations when it came to our ability to interact with humans. We who were part of the fall could create circumstances that would cause humans to do terrible things to each other, but we ourselves could not actually touch any of them. God left a gaping hole in security when He failed to anticipate that the faithful angels might at some point rebel, because He neglected to place the same prohibition on them.

I suppose it never crossed God's mind that His elite force might think to be anything but helpful to mankind. They would never have dared be any other way to this new life form God seemed to favor so much. That is surely the reason God's wrath was unleashed upon them so ferociously. They weren't condemned to a fallen state in second heaven as we were. Much worse, they were judged right there on the spot and thrown down to the dreaded Tartaroo. Let me tell you, our punishment had been but a swat on the backside compared to their complete banishment.

It seemed that Satan had won in that regard as well. The faithful elite guard who failed to follow him in the cosmic rebellion ended up being caught in yet another of his webs of deception. Satan's revenge on the heavenly host was now satisfied.

I don't know why, but it was unsettling to me that God had not anticipated something like the Nephilim. As a result, they carried a human gene, and it gave them legal access to afflict humans directly. No seduction, clever ruses, or half-truths were necessary. If a Nephilim wanted to devour a human, it just took one.

Satan wanted to throw a party to celebrate his triumph over heaven and Earth, so he released upon the Nephilim all of the spirits of lust he had held in captivity. They went wild. The demons in second heaven danced around, vicariously participating in the revelry and gloating as if they held some great victory in their hands. I really wanted to join in. It gets tiresome being the only one who sees the cloud behind every silver lining. I couldn't get in the mood when I knew the celebrating was premature. How could they have forgotten what God was like?

Maybe I should have tried to warn them again.

"Better yet," I said to myself, "maybe not."

After all, I was still feeling the beating I had endured at their claws when I tried to reason with them before, only to be left hanging upside down over the abyss for my trouble. My equilibrium had not righted itself either, and I was fearful of tipping over and giving them something else to ridicule. I picked up my injured tail and slunk off to find a place to lie down.

"Fools," I was tempted to shout at the reveling demons. "Don't you know God is brooding over Earth this very minute? No matter how it looks at the moment, this is not going to end well."

Instead, I said nothing. It wasn't worth another pounding from them just to be proven right later on.

"We've won! We've won!" they shouted in their drunken delight as the lustful Nephilim ravaged every living thing upon Earth.

And I have to admit, the longer it went on, the more it looked as if they might be right. After all, God imposed upon Himself the rules of engagement over Earth. If mankind could not redeem it, then Earth would be Satan's possession forever. Not only had Adam and Eve failed miserably, but now the whole gene pool of man and beast was corrupted beyond redemption. God would have to scrap it and start over with a new batch if He wanted to continue trying to make the humanity thing work. There was no way I could see for God to get around having to destroy the whole Earth and everything in it. Satan saw it as well. He was delirious with anticipation.

The whole demonic horde was irrepressible in their glee at the seeming certainty of having Earth back to do as they pleased. Since God had restored it so marvelously from the devastation of Lucifer's flood (in preparation for Adam, of course), it was in great shape. All of them were excited to have it back to rule over again without interference.

As the mayhem continued and God seemed to be doing nothing but stalling for time, I started to feel a little less nervous about a terrible retribution. God simply could not fix this and stay within the rules, so I wondered if He had decided to accept the inevitable— Earth was lost to Him.

Although things looked bad for God, somehow I knew it wasn't over. That's why I continued to watch Earth, just in case. I wanted to go inside to get away from the tremors, which were making me queasy. It had been happening for days now. The atmosphere shuddered under the weight of God's eyes as He searched to and fro about Earth. He was looking for something I suppose, but for what, I could not guess.

After a while, it looked like it might finally be over. I was about to give it up and go party with the others when company came. I should say came and went. He rocketed past me faster than a lightning bolt, singed my injured wing, and knocked me over as He passed through second heaven without slowing down. Nothing was left in His wake but the clashing of thunder as the air He had split crashed back together. Oh, I knew who it was all right. It was Him—Ruah Ha Kadosh—racing to Earth below.

"Why is He going down there this late in the game?" I wondered. I moved back to the edge and followed the trail of light that flowed after Him, enabling me to track His movements. Tracking Him may be a bit of an overstatement since I could not actually see where He was but only where He had been.

I was about to be proven right again. When I was sure of what He was doing down there, I left my post and went inside with the revelers to give Satan the news. I tried sauntering into the party room as I had seen Satan do when he wanted to pretend that he wasn't really worried. Sauntering was apparently not in my skill set. The partying stopped short and every eye darted my way as if I had walked into the room with an off switch that abruptly stopped the festivities.

Satan saw my expression and glared at me as if daring me to bring bad news. "You saw something. What was it?" he growled.

"They missed one, sir," I stammered. "The Nephilim— they missed one."

"One what?" Satan demanded.

"A human being, your majesty; they missed him, one uncorrupted man. He must have gotten away during the raids," I explained.

Satan spun rapidly and pointed his claw at one of the largest demons.

"Get down there! Find out who it is." Satan yelled as if the demon were off in another dimension instead of five feet away.

"No, wait," I blurted out before my mind caught up with my mouth. "It's too late."

"Too late?" Satan snarled, daring me to tell him something he did not want to hear.

"Ruah Ha Kadosh—He's already there. He found a man named Noah."

I tucked my tail and hunkered down just in case, but to my surprise, Satan did not swing at me as he usually did when he had nothing else to do with his frustration. The look in his eyes was not so much anger as shock. He didn't say or do anything at all right then. He dropped his noisemaker by his side; the party was over. He walked out to my perch, climbed up on it, and looked down at Earth. He sat there for a long time and then began to mumble to himself.

"The Nephilim are hunters; how did they miss him? Where was he hiding?" As he walked back toward his den, he snapped at me. "Listen to every word. Let nothing happen that I don't hear about before it happens."

So I hopped back on my perch, and I listened.

This is where it gets hard to explain what I saw. Ruah Ha Kadosh was clearly talking to Noah; I heard Him. But because no one can really *see* where He is at any given moment, only where He's been, it looked like Noah was talking to the thin air.

"Noah, you are a righteous man and have found favor with God," the voice said.

Noah was a righteous man. That's what I heard Him say.

But what exactly did He mean by "righteous"? Satan would want to know. Certainly neither Noah nor his family had copulated with the mighty ones, but to be honest about it, he was not the only one on Earth who could say that. Maybe Noah had not broken any of God's rules.

"No," I reasoned. "That cannot be it. God hasn't made any more rules since that incident with the trees in Eden." Mankind had only one rule to obey, and look what happened. God was not about to make things worse by giving him any more. Whatever it was that had made Noah righteous, it was not about *not* doing something God had forbidden.

I looked over my left wing to see if the party had resumed, but it hadn't. It was eerily quiet. The other demons had gone back to their common lair. I had a clear line of sight to Satan's throne, where he sat staring at nothing.

He had not anticipated Noah. Now he had to regroup.

CHAPTER 17

M Y ASSIGNMENT WAS to stay on guard and watch how things developed with Noah. Satan wanted to know if God's declaration about him being righteous might have a loophole in it somewhere.

"I hope so," I thought. "Maybe I can improve my standing with the group if I can report how I've found a legal technicality that might void the whole deal."

God continued to talk to Noah. "I am going to put an end to all people because Earth has become a sewer filled with violence and degradation. I am surely going to destroy every living thing. So make yourself an ark of cypress wood with rooms in it, and coat it with pitch inside and out."

Noah did not answer God. But if he had, by the look on his face, the whole of his reply would have been, "OK, whatever." Noah did not come close to grasping the enormity of what God had said. God announced an extinction-level event, yet Noah failed to emit the slightest gasp. I wondered if God was a little disappointed in Noah's lack of enthusiasm.

I have a theory about how God wired humans. It's like He put a genetic code in their central nervous system to link them with their ancestors and descendants through a corporate memory, so to speak. The code and memory somehow keep them linked to one another across the centuries. That's why it's not uncommon for a person to look like or behave like a distant relative who lived long before. No doubt about it, Noah was from the same gene pool as Adam and Eve.

Think about it. Suppose God Almighty Himself stopped in your backyard one day to talk with you. Then suppose He told you He was about to destroy the whole neighborhood and save you and yours. Suppose He assigned you to do something you did not understand, and when you finally grasped it, it would be completely ridiculous. Wouldn't you have a few questions?

That is exactly what happened to Noah, minus the questions part. God talked to him about the end of the world, and Noah just stood there, nodding obediently at every word as if he understood everything being said to him. I could stand no more.

"Noah!" I shouted across the expanse, knowing full well no one would hear me. "This would be a good time to ask Him about the fine print. Get a little detail. Define some terms. Let me help you out. Let's start with the obvious, what do you say?"

I paced back and forth on my perch as I tried to coach Noah from afar. "Ask God what an ark is. Start right at the beginning."

If I didn't know what an ark was, which I did not, I was dead certain Noah did not have a clue; but did he ask for clarity? Not one bit. Noah stood there with no more understanding of what God was saying than if He had told him to build a barbeque pit for a neighborhood get-together.

Then God said to Noah, "I'm going to bring a flood on Earth that will destroy everything alive under heaven. Total destruction."

"Here's your chance, Noah," I coached from my perch. "Impress God with your intellectual curiosity. Ask Him what a flood is. He knows you have no idea what He's talking about. You've never even seen it rain."

God continued, "I'm going to establish a covenant with you. You will board the ship, and your sons, your wife, and your sons' wives will come on board with you. You are also to take two of every living creature, a male and a female, to preserve their lives with you: two of every species of bird, mammal, and reptile; two of everything so as to preserve their lives along with yours. Also, get the food you'll need, and store it up for you and them."

Several alarms should have gone off in Noah's head right then, but nary a ding-dong sounded. God's plan failed to consider the personalities involved. Noah should have pointed out a few things to Him. He should have said, "God, You haven't really been down here in quite a while. Things have changed. You can't imagine how complicated these people You've made have now become, especially the women.

"Let me explain the downside of this plan and what You're about to unleash if You put these people on an ark together. An ark must be a boat of some kind, right? A mother-in-law and her three daughters-in-law in one boat, full of wild animals?"

"And with no one to help out but Adam's grandsons," I would have added.

Noah should have waved his arms at this point for effect. "I mean really, Your Majesty, stop and think this through for a minute. Who is going to be in charge of what? Who gets kitchen duty versus potty patrol? Who is going to referee? It's not that I'm worried about the water, you understand. I am sure that I could survive Your flood if that's what You've got in mind for me. Believe me, I'm grateful, but You've got to know it's tenuous at best as to whether or not any of the men can survive the boat ride."

Noah had nothing close to the training needed to go into the boat-building business. Maybe that's why it took him so long to get it done. He should have asked God from the get-go how long this project was supposed to take. Once he began, it seemed to take forever. To be sure, people lived longer in those days. Noah was himself six hundred years old, so perhaps they were not subject to the hurry-up syndrome that would develop in future generations. No matter, the longer it went on, the more people talked.

Noah tried to do everything just as God told him. Unfortunately for Noah, God didn't mention anything about how the neighbors were going to react to a construction site and a petting zoo in the neighborhood. They complained loudly when they weren't laughing at the crazy old man next door. His family was so humiliated; they finally stopped leaving the house at all during daylight hours.

Then one day it started to rain. It rained, and still it rained. It rained so much that for the second time in its history, floodwaters were about to cover the earth. Let me tell you, the water came from everywhere. It came from above, and it came from below. It poured from the sky, and it sprang up like a geyser from beneath the surface of the planet. It was a flood all right, but oddly, it was not the same kind of flood as the one Lucifer had caused before Adam.

Lucifer's flood came from Earth itself as creation retched and rebelled against the demonic hostility that had ravaged it. Lucifer's flood was a response by creation to drown itself rather than endure the onslaught of Lucifer's horde. In Lucifer's flood, the seas left their banks and became hostile and a haven for the disembodied spirits who had fallen from heaven with the rest of us.

Noah's flood was not like that at all. Lucifer's flood rendered all of Earth empty and void. Noah's flood was water, but it was just water. What it would cover would emerge again in a viable form. The flood would not destroy Earth itself, only the breathing life upon it.

I watched as Noah and the kids, the kids-in-law, and all of those animals went into the ark as God Himself closed the door behind them. More than that, I watched the other people who stood around mocking Noah. Even as the rain fell, they remained unconcerned and completely unaware of what was about to happen to them. But when the waters rose above the roofs of their houses and the ark began to float, they began to call to Noah for help. Some swam toward the ark and might have latched on to it, but they were overrun and pushed down into the water by the Nephilim, who were intent on escaping the flood.

Being part human and part angel, the Nephilim were enormous and of great strength. They swam madly for the ark and climbed its outside walls, grabbing hold of the deck with their fierce clawlike hands. Noah and his sons fought them off by pounding their hands with hammers, forcing them to let go. The Nephilim were the very reason for the destruction of life upon Earth; they could not be allowed to escape the flood.

Soon all life would succumb to the waters, which covered Earth for one hundred fifty days. I sat on my perch for every one of them watching the ark. I could not stop thinking about why or how Noah had found favor with the Lord.

"Based on what?" I asked myself. "Of all the human possibilities, why was Noah singled out for such a purpose? When did Noah come to know God so well that he would sign on to such an outlandish plan? Noah must have had some doubt as to whether two of every kind of animal in the world would simply wander up to the ark and get in. He didn't even own a dog. He didn't know the first thing about taking care of wild animals, some of which were natural enemies; some were even prone to eat the others.

As I thought about how simple Noah was, I wondered whether or not he was God's first choice for the job. I watched humans all the livelong day. I knew how many there were and where they were, and I can tell you from my careful observation, there were other candidates who had it more together than Noah did. Whether or not God had spoken to anyone else about the job opening, I could not say since that whole interview process slipped right by us. But if He had, I suspect one or two of the other humans would have interviewed pretty well.

Right off the top, I could think of several engineers I had monitored in the past who had a lot of potential. Any of them would have had some good ideas for God. Certainly they would have been able to show Him how to make the construction process more efficient. In a one-on-one tussle of know-how and corporate ambition, Noah would have lost out against any of those guys who could have done the job in half the time. As I saw it, Noah was a poor choice and barely got the thing built before the rains came. Why did God choose him? What made him righteous? God spoke, and Noah obeyed. Could it really be that simple?

"Of course," I clicked my claws together and said aloud. "It's God's soft spot."

God was a soft touch when confronted with unquestioning obedience; He always had been.

Finally, on the seventeenth day of the seventh month the ark came to rest on the mountains of Ararat, and by the first day of the first month of Noah's six hundred first birthday, the water had almost completely dried up. Noah removed the covering from the ark, and by the twenty-seventh day of the second month, Earth was completely dry. God called them out, and Noah was so glad to be off that boat, he set up an altar and sacrificed an offering to God. You might know he would lock dead-on to God's other soft spot: worshipful gratitude. This pleased God so much that He went way over the top and spoke an incredible promise over Earth, which I was sure He would come to regret.

"I'll never again curse the ground because of people. I know they have this bent toward evil from an early age, but I'll never again kill off every living thing by a flood."

"God," I wanted to cry out, "will You listen to Yourself? This human experiment of Yours has fatal flaws. Don't get sentimental now. Retain your options. You know You will never put up with the evil that man is capable of conceiving."

I was getting so worked up I was tempted to fly right out there and confront God to His face.

"Remember how You completely overreacted to that pride business when You threw us out of heaven?" I would demand. "What? Now You're going to ignore all that man is sure to do to rebel against You in the future? Listen to what You just said. How could You promise such a thing? What can You possibly be thinking?"

I was mad at and felt bad for God at the same time. I knew such an impetuous display of love and hope like what had burst forth from Him was going to be a heartbreak later on. He had to know that it would only be a matter of time until mankind fell into rebellion again. Noah was old and now too dependent on the wine to hold out much hope for further exploits. His children held no great promise that I could see. One of them, Ham, well, let's just say that apple not only fell far from the tree, but also it rolled down the street to the next block.

The cold chill crawling up my spine alerted me that Satan had come close to my perch. I wished he wouldn't do that; my nerves were bad enough.

"Is the flood over?" he asked.

"Yes," I replied. "And it looks to me that God has made a tactical error that will make it more difficult for Him to deal with Earth in the future. Maybe He has no further plans for it after this generation."

"What about Og?" Satan asked.

"Og? What about him?" I had no idea why he was asking about the Nephilim king.

Enjoying my bewilderment, Satan condescended to tell me, "Og tried to hide in the rafters of the ark. I wonder if he made it."

CHAPTER 18

I'M SURE GOD was expecting more lasting results from the flood than what He got. It wasn't long until humans played right back into Satan's hands. I suppose God did manage to clean up the gene pool in both man and the animals, but beyond that, there was very little behavioral modification in the humans. I wondered what it would finally take for God to admit that the idea of free will was going to be a continual source of trouble for Him. Unless He pulled it out of the human formula, I could not see anything changing.

If you wanted to see a man hugging trees and kissing the ground, you should have been there when Noah stepped out on terra firma. He was so glad to be off that boat, he could not wait to start planting gardens. He didn't care what he planted; he just wanted to feel dirt in his hands. One crop that grew well for him was the grape. There were grapes all over the place, so many that no one family could eat them all. So naturally, Noah went into the wine-making business. The only problem was that he sampled so much of his product that he was always passing out.

Satan had told me to keep an eye on this situation in case Noah slipped up in some way. I obeyed, but I knew better.

"Not going to happen," I said to myself. "Noah might drink too much wine and drift off to sleep wherever he happens to be, but he isn't about to do anything to affect his standing with God."

I might have known Satan didn't really have any interest in Noah anymore. It was Ham upon whom he had his glassy eye. I knew the boy was going to be bait for the demons at some point. He, of all the kids, had been the one most intrigued by the sexual perversion that had been upon Earth. Noah never knew a thing about it, of course, but Ham found some of the goings on exciting to watch. As soon as Satan saw the opening in Ham's soul, he dispatched an earthbound spirit of lust and another of voyeurism to attach themselves to Ham. The weeks Ham spent on the ark with nothing but time on his hands had allowed a craving to develop deep inside him (fueled by the evil spirits' urgings) for the kind of excitement he used to enjoy in secret. He was such an easy mark. He didn't resist the temptation at all.

It happened one afternoon when Noah was sampling the wine, as was his custom. Tasting a few too many, which was also his custom, he wandered into his tent to sleep it off, another custom. Because of the warmness of the day, Noah usually took his clothes off and slept naked on his bed. I don't know how the door was left open on that particular day. Noah might have done it, or maybe Satan caused it to blow open, but however it came about, Noah lay unconscious, totally nude, when Ham passed by.

I should have known Satan had set the whole thing up when he called us together to watch and see what would happen. Ham's disdain for his father was well known and often gossiped about in the demonic ranks. Although it had been my assignment to watch Earth, because I didn't know about Noah until God selected him to rescue the human race, I completely missed whatever happened to breach the relationship between Noah and his son. So, although I had my own ideas, I didn't know for certain what the root of the offense had been. Some of the demons claimed to have seen what happened but did not think it important enough at the time to tell me. Because demons lie so often, it's foolish to rely on any information from them anyway. So I went with my own theory for Ham's character dysfunction: middle-child syndrome. That had to be it.

When Ham entered the tent, Satan sent a slew of spirits in after him: rejection, pride, and envy—all the usual suspects. Satan's eyes burned with satisfaction as he listened to Ham curse his father and make fun of his inebriated stupor.

Shem and Japheth were outside the tent when Ham came stumbling out. "What have you done?" they shouted as they grabbed him by the arm.

"Nothing. Leave me alone," he said as he tried to push his way past them.

"Tell me what you did." Shem held tightly to Ham's arm. "Why were you in his tent?"

"None of your business," Ham struggled to break free. "It was an accident. I didn't know he was in there."

Shem and Japheth did not buy into his story for a moment. They knew full well Ham would not hesitate to embarrass his father. They shoved Ham aside as they took a cloth and walked into the tent backwards to cover their father's nakedness without looking at him. But when Noah woke up and realized how Ham had disrespected him, you could have heard him screaming and cursing from any spot in the universe.

Since none of the boys were actually in the tent when Noah woke up, I found it amusing how Noah knew exactly which one had humiliated him. Before this happened, as a dad, Noah had ignored the rumors saying there was something perverse about Ham. It was obvious now that he knew better.

Satan, as you might expect, was beside himself with joy over this one. Ham would be the father of an entire nation whose sin would be passed down for generations. God knew about the brokenness in Ham and should have put a stop to his lineage right then and there. Why allow him to propagate? Ham was not a candidate for rehabilitation. If God let the bloodline continue, things could only get worse in future generations. And, of course, that is exactly what happened.

One of Ham's children was Cush, who had a son named Nimrod. This boy was bad even by our standards. He was a hunter, but not just of animals. He became a hunter of souls for Satan through his morbid fascination with the prince of darkness. Satan himself mentored Nimrod and even found the perfect wife for him.

Her name was Semiramis, and she fancied herself to be the high priestess of the demonic realm, if you can believe it. One really had to admire Satan's ability to seduce humans into thinking he would share his power with them. The grandiose lies Satan could conjure up to entrap mankind were bizarre and completely unbelievable; yet, they nearly always worked. More bizarre than the lies themselves were the humans who believed them in spite of all reason—all done in the human quest for spiritual power.

Satan told Semiramis she would become pregnant by a sunbeam. What is it with human women? She will demand written detail of the simplest thing a man might propose. How is it she will turn around and listen to Satan make the most outlandish claims and never think once to ask for a character reference? Semiramis actually believed what Satan said. She did become pregnant all right, but believe me, there was no sunbeam involved. It was Satan himself who planted his evil seed within her. She gave birth to a son named Tammuz. I remembered what God had said in the garden that day about Satan's seed, but I never really thought it would happen.

Tammuz was a hunter also, unfortunately for him; he wasn't very good at it. He managed to get himself killed by a wild boar. Semiramis went into mourning for forty days, and when she was done, she declared that Tammuz had come back to life. Of course, he hadn't, at least not the part of him that was human. But his demonic nature made a complete recovery. By this time, he and his mother were completely in the clutches of Satan.

If it had not been for Eve and how she filled in the missing gaps in Adam's personality, Satan would probably never have thought about how much there was to be gained by having women on the team. We had certainly never had any in our ranks before. But now here she was, Semiramis, the queen of heaven and the high priestess of Satan. She and her son, Tammuz, would seduce many into the worship of themselves, which they would turn to worship of Satan. Hard to believe humans could not see right through that charade, but most did not then and many of you do not now.

As the sons of Noah spread out over the entire earth, so the worship of Semiramis and Tammuz would cover the same land. Over time, they would be known by many names. It was because of Semiramis that Nimrod built a high place of worship intended to reach into second heaven. The human shell of Semiramis kept her bound to Earth, but her spirit and soul, being lost to her, longed for second heaven to be near Satan. To keep peace in the house, Nimrod built a temple for her. Satan was positively giddy with the prospect of an earthly temple connecting the demonic realm with Earth.

I must say it did look like the old serpent had them this time, but I still remained jittery about the whole thing.

"There is no way God will look the other way while His humans march headlong into perfect demonic possession," I remarked to a few of the demons who were hanging around my perch. Of course, they couldn't wait to tattle to Satan that I was a doomsayer.

"Look," Satan growled at them. "We had a wager, and I won. Just like I told Him, given free will, His miserable little humans would choose to worship me, and they did." Satan chuckled, "I don't see there is much He can do about it this time."

As I listened to Satan boast, I caught myself chewing on my claws. It is a terrible habit I picked up. I saw some of the humans doing it with their fingernails, and it seemed to calm them, so I thought I would give it a try. I can't say that it works that well, but once you get started, it's hard to stop.

I considered reminding Satan how his bragging against God was the very reason we were exiles. If he would keep quiet for once, perhaps God might not notice the tower going up.

Too late. Thunder rolled, lightning made a direct hit on the tower, and the whole thing collapsed into rubble just that quick.

"Can He do that?" Satan bellowed at me. He had never asked my opinion on anything before, so for a moment I was stunned and didn't answer.

"Is it illegal?" he snapped at me again.

"I—I don't know," I stammered.

"It's a violation of the rules. I want to talk to Him," Satan went on.

I took a quick peak over the edge to check out the collapsed structure before speaking.

"Uh, sir," I said haltingly, "I don't think God is in the mood to negotiate."

Satan and the others stood along the rim, stunned by what had happened to the people of Earth.

"How bad is it?" Satan asked.

"It looks like a total effect. God has completely confused their language. They cannot communicate."

"What about Semiramis?" he asked.

"There she is," I pointed out, "running around babbling like the rest of them." Satan took a swipe at me.

I have never seen the humans as confused and confounded as they were that day. One minute they were able to talk to each other, and the next moment they were all talking at once, but no one could understand a word the other was saying. It was chaos.

We were caught off guard because, as far as any of us could remember, God had never created chaos. It was brilliant when you think about it. No one was killed. No massive destruction; no floods, no fires, or other calamities; just utter and complete bedlam.

Of course, the humans quickly abandoned the building project. Semiramis and Tammuz were positively livid, but since no one could understand their ranting, the people simply wandered back to their own homes. Most were trying to figure out what had happened to them but had no idea whatsoever of the extraordinary supernatural event that had just taken place.

Satan insisted that God had broken the rules of engagement when He intervened directly into the affairs of Earth. Finally, one of our former demons had endured quite enough of Satan's incessant whining, and he screamed at Satan.

"He does what He does because He is who He is, and you will never win over Him. We were fools to follow you."

I said he was one of our former colleagues because, unfortunately for him, he no longer exists. Satan ate him.

CHAPTER 19

TIME KEPT MOVING with no regard as to how chaotic heaven and Earth had become. I thought God should have stopped the clock, reassessed how things were going, and let both sides regroup. Nothing like that happened. Time marched at its measured pace, and nothing could slow it down or speed it up.

Noah's sons continued to have kids, but none of them demonstrated any real promise of usefulness to God or in redeeming the confused mess reigning on Earth. God should never have bound Himself to getting things done on Earth through human beings and human beings alone. It was not working out.

It was not as if the humans were disinterested in finding God's will. In fact, we were amazed at how spiritual humans were since they were only made of flesh and blood. They could not see God, and they could not see us either, and yet they were completely convinced that some other rank of spiritual entity, as well as God, existed. They also seemed to be aware of a power structure in the spiritual world. Most of Earth people innately "knew" there was an all-powerful God out there somewhere. Most also believed this God was inaccessible to them, and so they sought intermediaries to be advocates between themselves and this God. Satan's strategy to seize this opportunity was brilliant.

Demons were assigned to humans so when the people petitioned "the gods," the demon on duty would respond. Here's how ingenious Satan's plan was. Say a person's child became ill. A parent begged the "god of the flu" to heal his child. Well, certainly a demon couldn't do anything of the kind unless the demon had made the child sick to start with. A demon could undo whatever he had done, but he could not do a creative miracle, such as healing someone.

That's how the demons became "gods" to them. They were always begging us to do things. Ironic, isn't it? Especially when you know the only lust Satan had for their kind was to devour them.

God, on the other hand, would not do tricks to prove He existed. The demons, however, would because it was so easy to snare them once we acted on a request to curse a neighbor or cause harm to an enemy. We were still bound by the rules of engagement and could not touch a human directly, but we could manipulate circumstances to get the desired effect. For example, we could not push someone over a ledge, but we could make sure there was a reason for a person to be on the ledge to start with.

With a little help from us, mankind soon learned some plants were hallucinogenic. When people ate them and chanted themselves into a lustful frenzy, we were right there encouraging them to abandon their natural inhibitions God had placed in them for their protection. Once they lost one, it was gone forever.

What with the drugs and our quickness to make them think they were in touch with some super power, humans were crazy in their desire to worship us. Satan found it thrilling, and I found it embarrassing, especially when they started imagining what we might look like. Somehow they got the ridiculous idea that we came from rocks. The stonecutters would carve outrageously bizarre little statues and declare they were idols made in the perfect images of the gods. The people wanted to buy the idols and take them home. Satan picked up on it right away. Humans wanted a god they could hold in their hands.

God would never have stood for such an abomination, but Satan did. The truth be told, it was downright insulting that anyone would think a powerful demon could be anything like one of those pathetic idols. As frightful as we might have been, we were much better looking than the way they depicted us. Satan, who himself is normally the essence of vanity, shook it off and said, "Worship is worship; take it where you find it." What amazed us was if humans truly believed we looked like those idols, why didn't they gasp and run?

Once the stonecutters convinced the masses that worshiping ugly rocks was a sane thing for rational people to do, it wasn't long until some figured out how to make a business out of religion. The one who had the largest franchise in idol making was a fellow named Terah. He was one of Shem's grandkids. Terah had shelves of every idol known to man and available in all prices. His business was booming.

Terah had a son named Abram. One fine day, Terah went to the market and left Abram in charge of the store. I didn't think much of it when it first happened. After all, I've seen a lot of teenage humans do silly things for no good reason. At first, I thought maybe one of the demons was having sport with the boy and had unleashed a spirit of destruction on him.

Later when I offered that as an explanation to Satan as to why I had not reported it sooner, he roared at me and called me an imbecile. He also told me not to think anymore. Anyway, quite suddenly, Abram took a broom from his father's closet and went about smashing every idol in the place.

When Terah came back to the store and saw what Abram had done, he was livid.

"Why did you do such a thing?" he yelled at the boy.

"Because, Father, if they were truly gods, shouldn't they have been able to defend themselves?"

Terah ranted, "Of course they are not gods. They have no power. They are only made of stone and metal."

Abram looked his father in the eye and said, "Father, do you realize what you have said?"

Whether or not Terah understood what he said was unimportant to us. Our eyes were now locked on the boy Abram. Something entirely new in the human race had surfaced: spiritual discernment. This could not be a positive development.

Right away I figured out what, or should I say who, was behind Abram's rampage, but I was not about to say a word because I did not want the grief. Not only did I know it was Ruah Ha Kadosh who had put the idea into Abram's head, but I also knew what was going to happen next. God was going to speak to Abram, no doubt about it, and it was just a matter of time until He did.

I had become pretty good at predicting when God was about to personally invade Earth's history, but I never was able to guess how. What new scheme would He come up with to try to save the humans from themselves? It always had to begin with a specific person. When I saw God pick out one of them for destiny, I would listen intently so as not to miss a word. Though, I must tell you, the human part of the conversation changed very little from Adam to Abram. When God suddenly appeared in their circumstances, not one of them showed surprise. I was certain none had ever talked with God before, so why did they behave as if the next-door neighbor had stopped over for tea? I postulated a theory, which if I were right, Satan would be beside himself in wrath. The humans had God's spiritual DNA. When God dropped in, He felt like family. I shuttered at what this might mean if they ever figured it out.

Decades later, God did stop by. Abram was no longer the upstart teenager. He had left those years far behind. In fact, he left behind a good bit of his adult years. Middle age was a distant image in the rearview mirror of his life.

God said to the elderly Abram, "Leave your country, your people, and your father's household, and go to the land I will show you."

Just like that.

Don't ask me how I knew. Just believe me; I knew without one doubt that Abram was going to obey. I saw it in Noah, and now I saw it in Abram: the uncanny willingness to believe what God says is true.

God saw it too, and He continued, "I will make you a great nation. I will make your name great, and all Earth will be blessed by you."

Then He went quite over the edge, as He was prone to do when someone has His favor.

"I will bless those who bless you and curse those who curse you."

Abram had not the slightest idea what had just been said, but Satan did. Oh, yes, when I told him, he understood completely. If Abram obeyed, the human race was about to take a turn he had not counted on.

Satan wasted no time in sending the demon of doubt and unbelief to Earth to bombard Abram's mind with confusion.

"Ask Him for a map," the dark prince hissed in Abram's ear. "Make Him show you a deed. How long is this going to take? Ask Him for proof of performance. You are the heir of your father's fortune; you are a fool if you walk away from riches for a God whom you have never heard from before. If He is real, where has He been all this time?"

"Those are great questions," I cheered from heaven's rim. "You do it, Abram. Insist on an advance. Trust me, God doesn't have a backup candidate. Use your leverage."

But it did not work. Abram packed up the camels, the wife, and the nephew and set off as if he knew exactly where he was going. The prince went back in defeat to Satan's fury. I stayed and watched Abram's caravan disappear over the horizon.

Oh, how I wished I could have gone with him.

CHAPTER 20

I WATCHED THEM LEAVE and marveled at how unconcerned they seemed to be with how old they were. Abram was seventy-five years old, and his wife, Sarai, was sixty-five (or so she said—with women, who can be sure?) when they started off for the land of Canaan. It was as if marching off the map to an undiscovered country were a normal thing for two people to do who really ought to be thinking about retirement. Satan had made it painfully clear to me to stick close to them at all times so there would be no conversations with God without his knowing about it. When God showed up again to talk to Abram, I would hear every word of it.

It was several weeks before the Lord appeared to Abram again. I knew by now how God could show up anywhere and at any time with no warning, so I was not surprised when He encountered Abram in the middle of the day in the middle of the road. Abram, on the other hand, having talked to God only one other time in his life, was not accustomed to such a strange encounter, and neither was his camel who bleated in fear, threw Abram off, and ran away with Abram chasing behind. I suppose it was God who stopped the animal so Abram could catch up.

Abram was sweating and breathing hard as he waited to see what God would say. "Look around," He said to Abram. "To your offspring I will give this land."

Just like Noah had done when he got off the boat, Abram's first response to God was not to ask a few good *when* and *how* questions; rather, he halted the whole caravan and built an altar to God right there in the traffic lane. With gratitude for what he had not yet received, Abram worshiped as if there were no doubt about God's truthfulness.

But Abram didn't stop there. He moved on to Bethel, and he built an altar. Everywhere they stopped to spend the night, Abram built an altar. The caravan was making terrible time because of the unscheduled stops, but you can guess how it pleased God. From that point on, Abram could do no wrong in God's eyes. Not only did the altar building positively guarantee Abram's success, but it also meant bad news for Satan. Before the altars were built, he had reigned and reveled in each of those locations without the slightest resistance. Just as soon as the altars went up and Abram declared that God was

Lord over that place, the land trembled, and Satan felt his hold weaken. Although in nine million years he would never have admitted to such a thing, we knew it was so.

That was not the worst of it by far. Oh, my, no. The worst was right around the corner; a full-frontal assault on Satan's tactics in a way he had not anticipated. Abram started to pray. No one had truly prayed before.

To be sure, the demons knew that when humans get into trouble or get scared, they are likely to start crying out to some hoped-for cosmic rescuer in the sky. Begging for help is not the same thing as praying. Begging, wailing, and groveling did not constitute a petition to God. It was more yelling for help to any celestial being within earshot who might respond to the person's promises to live better in the future if only rescued from his circumstances in the now.

You humans still do this, although you still do not seriously expect anyone to answer, and generally speaking, no one does. As long as mankind confused *pleading* with *praying*, the issue of prayer was of no concern to Satan. That's why at first he seemed so disinterested in my report.

"So he's praying," Satan said without looking up from what he was doing. "So what?"

"It's not what you think, master." I tried to explain that the kind of prayer coming from Abram was different and much more serious than any version of prayer previously known to be in the spiritual skill set of humanity.

"Different? How?" Satan replied. "And don't waste my time."

"Abram is actually talking to God. He's thanking God for His mercy and protection on behalf of his family, his friends, his servants, the camels, the camel drivers, the dogs, and the cats. Abram is leaving nothing and no one uncovered." I wasn't sure I was getting through.

Satan had never before worried about the kind of whiny, wimpy prayer he was accustomed to hearing from you humans. He had often said that mankind's constant complaining to God was likely to have been more annoying to Him than helpful.

"Abram's prayer is nothing like you've heard before," I insisted.

"OK, so the old man's prayer is different. Tell me why I care." At least he was paying attention to me.

"It's…it's," I waved my hands around as if trying to pull the word I was looking for out of thin air. "It's intercession. That's what it is."

"So, it is prayer, then." He seemed annoyed. "Prayer has never helped them."

"That's because no human has ever engaged in intercession." I tried to make him see the urgency of the situation.

"Never?" Satan asked as if trying to remember if he knew of such a thing.

"We would have been the first to know if it had ever happened anywhere on Earth. Whining, begging, groveling, pleading, bargaining, trying to make a deal—all the time; but intercession? Never." I was exhausted from my attempt to warn him.

Satan's hordes were highly skilled in blocking mankind's prayer attempts, so Satan was simply not troubled by what I had to say.

"Earth people think prayer is about explaining situations to God, which He already knows and understands far better than they do." Satan responded. "You know how the demons look forward to human prayer if it's a slow day."

He was right; it was like a game to them. Desperate people released their prayerettes, void of any direction, power, or authority. The little prayers floated up toward God all right, but first the fragile petitions had to pass through second heaven, where the demons shot them down before they came close to getting to God. I didn't know exactly what the repercussions of intercession might be, but I was certain there would be nothing fun about it.

I tried to explain it better. "Human prayers are like wishes floating toward heaven. Sometimes they get there, sometimes they don't, but nobody expects an answer anyway. Intercession doesn't involve wishing. It is directive and rapid. It declares what God has promised and demands it come about. It insists God remember what He has said and act upon it."

Satan looked perplexed, so I decided to chance going further. "What is more, God likes intercession."

He still wasn't getting it, so I tried harder. "God has tried for centuries to get His people to engage Him, command Him concerning His words, so to speak. Someone is finally doing it."

Satan did not believe me until he experienced it for himself. Before he could say another word, a blast of lightning broke through the stone floor in front of him, knocked him back, and then crashed through the ceiling above.

"What happened?" he demanded as he righted himself.

"That's it! That's what I've been trying to tell you. It's Abram's intercession."

We were soon to learn how intercessory prayers could speed through second heaven so quickly and with such force, the demons would have to dance a jig to avoid being hit by one. Satan, who before had feared nothing mankind might do, hopped like a bunny right along with the rest of us to avoid getting in the path of intercession. Once intercession began, the prayers came in such a rapid-fire rhythm that they tore gaping holes in the floor and left the demons dazed and confused about where to stand to avoid being hit by the next one.

As Abram got better at intercession, it became worse for us. As fast as intercession went up, the response came hurling back even faster. I cannot tell you how many a demon could not get out of the way fast enough and was flattened by an incoming answer from heaven. While we were looking at the floor, trying to guess where the next one was likely to come through, Adonai would be up there slamming the answers back down faster, and all the better if it sideswiped one of the demons on the way. Why, sometimes a tail or a wing was cut right off. When intercession started, we couldn't get out off the way fast enough.

Then it got worse yet for Satan. When God cleaned up the seas at the restoration of Earth, the spirits who had been confined in the dank waters were evicted and had nowhere to go, so they floated aimlessly about the planet until the Fall of man in the garden. After that, if a human gave one an opening, the spirit could set up a habitation with the soul of the human. For example, Ham opened the door of his soul to a perverse spirit as a result of his preoccupation with the Nephilim. That's why a spirit of perversion plagued Ham and his descendants forever.

By Abram's time, it was commonplace for spirits to be clustered and deeply embedded in human souls. But once intercession started, the spirits could not be depended upon to hold their position. When the first prayer assault launched, the terrified spirits started flying out of the human bodies they inhabited. Like a buzzing cloud of bees, they came swarming toward second heaven, where Satan and the demons swatted madly at them, trying to shoo them back to Earth and hurling threats to destroy them if they did not return. Although the spirits knew Satan would make good on his threat for having left their human hosts, faced with a choice between the wrath of Satan and the wrath of God, the evil spirits took their chances against Satan.

Well, you can imagine the problems this meant for Satan when humans were suddenly freed from the spirits who had controlled their behavior. It became almost impossible to manipulate the people through the weakness in their natures any longer. I tell you, it was a mess. From that day till this, Satan will do almost anything to keep intercession from beginning. I would never want to be quoted, but I can tell you that I have personally known high-ranking demons to cut and run before facing a fight with intercessors.

Not trusting me to handle it myself, Satan assigned an entire contingent of demons to stand watch over Abram's progress. We kept watching and hoping for an opportunity to intervene in Abram's journey and distract him from praying. When we found none, I was the one—as was always the case when there was bad news—who had to report it to Satan.

"Solve this problem," Satan snarled at me. "Stop him."

"Sir," I stammered, "you know the rules. We cannot do it if we cannot find a human to be our agent."

I knew he didn't want me to remind him, but it was the rules of engagement thing; Satan had to get things done on Earth through human beings, just like God. If he could not enlist one, he could not interfere with the events of Earth.

"Abram must have enemies," Satan retorted.

"He does, sir, but God has made them afraid of him. He's golden. They won't challenge him."

Satan ordered me back, ignoring the problem and demanding results.

We kept watching, hoping someone would be willing to move against Abram. We thought we had a few good candidates along the way, like the time Pharaoh lusted after Sarai. Now that right there convinced me Sarai probably lied about her age. But then who can explain the chemistry of attraction? Maybe it was the older-woman thing that attracted Pharaoh; whatever, but he really seemed intent on seducing her.

It looked like this might be the human agent we needed to get to Abram, but just when we thought we had him at the crucial point, Pharaoh was like the others who had backed off in fear of Abram. Maybe it wasn't Abram himself that struck them with fear. In fact, I doubt it was. It was the holy armor God had placed around Abram in response to all that altar building. No one else could see it except for us, but it worked really well. The curses and arrows the demons shot at him simply fell to the ground. I cannot tell you how much ammunition was wasted trying to take Abram out.

Satan summoned us back to his throne room to berate us for our failure to stop Abram's advance.

"His enemies won't touch him," one of the others spoke.

"Then work through his friends," Satan snapped back.

"I tell you, there's no opening," one demon blurted out before he thought about the consequences of challenging Satan's orders. Just as Satan was about to lash out at the demon who had unwisely spoken, I had an idea.

"Wait, maybe there is someone else."

"Who?" Satan asked.

"His nephew. Remember that spat with Cain and Abel and how much trouble it created for generations? Family feuds are simply wicked. What if Lot could be stirred against his uncle? Abram would never see it coming."

"Lot is the weak link," Satan said, beginning to take credit for my idea. "We'll stir up jealousy and resentment in Lot. Abram won't see it coming."

"Isn't that what I just said?" I coughed as I swallowed the words.

Satan knew timing was everything in making this work, so he restrained himself and the demons until he decided Lot was ripe. I thought he had waited too long. He should have moved earlier, before things got so good for them. But Satan seemed to think there was an advantage to letting Abram and his nephew get richer and richer.

"Why would Lot challenge Abram now, when everything in the world is going his way and he is in need of nothing?" I asked one of the others.

I tell you, Satan is a strategist. He anticipated that Abram would be able to take wealth in stride, but Lot would not. He waited until Lot was puffed up to the max and then dispatched the demon most skilled in planting resentment right to Lot's tent. When Lot went to sleep, the demon spoke into his dreams.

"You know what they're saying about you, Lot. How you can't hold your own. You'd never make it without your uncle watching your every step. He doesn't respect you either. He let's you think you're his partner, but he doesn't trust you with one sheep. Show him what you're made of. Demand your half now. Go your own way. Show them all."

It worked like the proverbial charm. It was just a few days until I heard Lot complain to one of the camel drivers about how his flocks didn't have enough grazing room because they were crowded by Abram's animals.

Lot didn't seem to notice the quizzical look on the camel driver's face because, as everyone knew, all the flocks were Abram's.

With the demon's encouragement, Lot finally worked himself into full-blown resentment toward the man who was his benefactor. He was belligerent and rude as he approached Abram and demanded half of the herds.

"Lot is trying to negotiate a departure settlement with Abram," I breathlessly reported to Satan. "You were right. He wants to go out on his own, so he's trying to broker a deal between the animals he acquired versus the ones belonging to Abram. Can you stand it?" I was so excited.

Satan laughed at the easy target Lot had been. Satan's hordes as well as Abram's army knew Lot had no legitimate claim to anything Abram owned. Lot was a hanger-on, a wannabe who never was. His sole redeeming feature was his blood link to Abram.

In the end, Abram told Lot that he could choose the land he wanted for his flocks and herds and that Abram would take what was left. Satan was especially perplexed by Abram's actions. There was no way he could process the concept of generosity.

"Why is he doing it?" Satan asked.

"Lot has always been a drag on the family business," I offered. "Maybe it's worth it to Abram to be rid of him."

The two men parted company, and Lot chose for himself the whole plain of the Jordan and set out toward the east. Abram settled in the land of Canaan, while Lot chose to live among the cities of the plain and pitched his tents near Sodom. More good news for Satan. I couldn't wait to tell him.

"Sodom? Near Gomorrah?" he couldn't believe it. "You're kidding. Abram's nephew is moving into our backyard?"

I nodded, thrilled that now twice in a row I had reported something to Satan that didn't end with me being blamed for it. Not since the heyday of the Nephilim had there been a pit of unrestrained degradation as there was in Sodom. It was a playground for the worst of us.

Under different circumstances, the demons might have turned their attention immediately to Lot and made quick sport of him. It would have been laughable to suppose for a moment that Lot might have had the moral character to withstand what Satan had going on down in Sodom and Gomorrah. It would only be a matter of time until one way or the other Lot would be swept up into the perversion.

"Let's do it," one of the demons sneered, licking his lips at the prospect. "Let's go for Lot."

Lot would have been so easy, but Satan wouldn't give it the time of day. He wasn't interested in Lot. Lot was not worth his time, but Abram was. Only Abram had the potential to bring forth the promise God made to Satan in the garden—the one about the offspring of the woman crushing Satan's head. I couldn't imagine why Satan was still worried about that happening. Now Abram was over eighty years old, and Sarah was over seventy if she was a day. Their biological clocks stopped ticking decades ago, and surely they were too old to adopt.

Satan had a renewed interest in Lot when he figured out how to use him to lure Abram into a snare. Satan stirred up a battle between the kings of Sodom and Gomorrah and the other four kings in that region. Sodom was overrun by the invading kings who ransacked the city and carried off all the assets, including the people, who included Lot.

One of the survivors of this battle reported to Abram what had occurred, so, naturally, Abram gathered his men together and went after Lot. Abram caught up with the raiding kings, and a fierce battle ensued. If numbers meant anything at all, Abram should have lost the battle. Satan counted on it. But Abram did not lose. In fact, he won it smashingly. It was the halo effect of all that altar building, I was sure of it.

Satan stomped and grumbled at his failed plan. I tried to explain to him why Abram was never going to lose in battle, but he didn't care to hear nor did he care to stay around for Abram's victory party, so he went back to his lair to pout. I went back to my perch and continued to watch Abram. It was a good thing I did.

CHAPTER 21

I F I HAD gotten there ten seconds later, I would never have seen the stranger come from nowhere to right in front of Abram. *Poof!*

Suddenly, he was gone, I think. But where did he go? I saw him; then I could not see him.

"I know he was a man," I reasoned to myself. "But a man cannot step in and out of reality like that, can he? Of course not; but he had to be a man. What else could he have been?"

Then he was back again—a strange, mysterious sort, different from anyone I had seen on Earth before. I heard him say his name was Melchizedek and that he was the king of Salem. Then he brought out bread and wine and shared it with Abram. He told Abram he was a priest and then said, "God the Most High Creator of heaven and Earth has blessed you, Abram, and defeated your enemies by your hand."

Abram was overcome by the moment and pledged to give him a tenth of everything he owned.

"Priest of God Most High?" I asked myself as I started winging it back toward Satan's den to tell him about it. "I don't think so. No way could there be a priest of God on Earth who somehow escaped our notice. King of Salem? Where is that, and, for that matter, what is a priest?"

I no more than got the words "king of Salem" out of my mouth before Satan ran right over the top of me and raced toward the rim to take a look. I dusted myself off and went after him, but by the time we got there, this priest or king, whatever he was, had disappeared.

Satan glared at me, "What did he say to Abram?"

"Really, sir, not all that much." I tried to calm him down. "He gave Abram some bread and wine. Then he left. Nothing more to it."

"You are certain?" He moved in closer to me, causing me to shrivel up a little bit.

"No, nothing," I said before I remembered the 10 percent item. I modified my response. "Nothing of importance."

Satan continued to glare at me with those awful eyes until I blabbed out the whole story.

"He blessed Abram and gave him bread and the wine, like I said." I sucked in my breath and spoke quickly.

"Then Abram promised to give him one-tenth of everything he owned, and that was it. End of story." I ducked just in case.

I certainly did not expect such insignificant information to send the prince of darkness into such a fit, but it did. He rambled and bellowed incoherently about an illegal visit from Adonai, then he shook his clawed fist toward God's heaven and raged about economics.

"Do you understand what this means, imbecile?" He yelled at me as I tried to crawl out of his way. I knew he didn't want an answer, so I cowered there in front of him, waiting until he got over himself. He grabbed me by the wing and stood me up in front of his distorted face.

"It means Abram will get richer and more powerful," he growled.

I nodded in agreement, though I couldn't make the connection in anything he was saying. To me, it didn't seem quite the same as when Adam and Eve gave some of their produce to God as an offering. How was giving a tenth of his wealth away to another human going to make Abram richer and more powerful? If anything, it meant he would have less, but I was not about to imply that Satan didn't know basic math. When I said nothing, he threw me down and strode into the darkness.

I continued to watch Abram and his family, but unless something really noteworthy occurred, I kept the day-to-day matters to myself. Wouldn't you know something noteworthy was right around the corner?

Abram was on a twilight stroll around the campground when God showed up again. "Do not be afraid, Abram. I am your shield and your very great reward."

Unlike their other encounters in which Abram's part was to nod and build altars, this time Abram had apparently been giving some thought to what God had promised Him so long ago.

"It's about time," I thought. "Abram has a few questions."

"O sovereign Lord," he began, "what can You give me since I remain childless and the one who will inherit my estate is Eliezer of Damascus?" Abram glanced up to see if God was listening, then he continued. "You have given me no children, so a servant in my household will be my heir."

I had wondered if Abram would get the nerve to bring it up to God that he was way too old to father anything, especially a nation, like God had promised him. As for Sarai, forget about it. She lost interest long ago. I was anxious to hear how God was going to answer.

God said, "A son coming from your own body will be your heir."

Abram looked down at his body. I also looked at his body, and I can tell you that it was not an inspiring sight. The Lord's plan was for Abram to impregnate Sarai.

"Come on, God," I thought to myself. "Admit it's too late. Come up with a consolation prize."

That is exactly what I expected Abram would say, but he didn't. Instead, Abram believed God—again—and God credited it to him as righteousness.

There it was again: believing God. Noah had done it and found favor with the Lord. Abram did it, and he was credited with righteousness. I tried to reason out what this meant. How does it work?

I paced back and forth on my perch and debated with myself. "If a human tells God he believes something that cannot possibly be true, does it win favor with God?"

"No, probably not," I answered my own question.

It has to be something more, but it could not be too hard or humans would never figure it out. Maybe it is like a game.

"That's it, and I'll bet Adonai is behind it," I thought, remembering His outlandish sense of humor.

Here is how the game most likely works. God proposes the most preposterous scheme possible—something that cannot possibly happen—and asks a human to believe it is true. Now, the human must say he believes it to be true even though it is contrary to his prior experience and in the absence of verifiable evidence.

To win the game, the human must not only *say* he believes what God has said, he must also start to *behave* as if he believes it. When he takes some sort of risky action to prove he's on board, bingo, God delivers on His promise, no matter how impossible it seemed or how much ruckus He must cause to make it happen.

Then I wondered, "But what happens if God speaks to a human who ignores Him?"

I already knew the answer to that question because I had seen it happen many times. In fact, most times. God would speak, and if no one responded, He simply moved on to the next person in line until He found someone who would react to Him. No wonder it takes God so long to get anything done on Earth. He has limited Himself to working with humans. He cannot do a thing until He finds one who will believe that "He is" and that He has spoken a promise to him or her. As soon as that happens, without fail, God disappears and may not show up again for years.

Naturally, this really perplexes human beings. The person with the promise must continue to believe it will come about no matter how long it takes or how unlikely it seems. The man or woman in question must continue to believe when others have stopped.

"How many humans could there be who can trust God like that?" I wondered.

Not many, I was sure. I didn't know whether to laugh at their simplicity or admire the ones who could step out and believe God with such certainty.

"Believe the impossible from a voice you cannot audibly hear, from a person you cannot physically see, and call it God?" I mused. "Then spend your life waiting for God to prove Himself. Trust God? Believe God? There must be another word for it."

CHAPTER 22

ABRAM DIDN'T HAVE to say a thing. As soon as he came back from his evening stroll and opened the flap to the tent, Sarai knew something was up. When she looked at her husband's face, she knew he had been with God again. She had been nagging Abram for months to try to get another meeting, get a few specifics as to how and when all of His great promises were supposed to come about. Excited to see something had happened and eager to find out what God had said to her husband, she began to pry the information out of him.

Poor old Abram, so completely unaware of the havoc about to be unleashed in his life. I almost felt sorry for him. Anyone who understands women—anyone who has ever had a conversation with a woman—could have seen this problem with Sarai coming and would have run. But not Abram; he was completely clueless.

"What's for dinner?" he asked as he laid his staff aside and took off his sandals.

"And so? How did it go?" she asked while pouring out a cool drink.

"Fine," Abram answered. "What's for dinner?"

"First tell me what He said."

"He said you were going to have a baby. Are we eating out?" Abram continued as he lifted the covers off of several pots, wondering why he didn't smell anything cooking.

"And you said to Him what exactly?" Sarai was no longer pouring a drink or making any move that had to do with food.

"I didn't say anything. What's to say?" Abram, sensing this was going to be a long talk, began looking around for a scrap of bread or cheese.

"What's to say?" Temperature rising, nostrils flaring; yes, all the signs of a coming storm were clearly there. Her voice was beginning to take on that shrill sound.

"What's to say, old man? Nothing at all crossed your mind?" Sarai walked around the table and got in Abram's face.

"I don't know; maybe you could have said something like, 'Oh, Lord, how is this going to be? Have You noticed that my beloved Sarai is past the time of child-bearing?'"

Spotting a piece of bread behind the water jar, he reached for it, but she was not about to let him get away. Inserting herself between him and any type of food, she continued.

"How about something like this?" Sarai adjusted her head covering and folded her hands. "'Oh, Lord, maybe I misunderstood. My hearing isn't what it used to be with my age and all. What was that promise again?'"

Unfolding her hands and planting them firmly on her hips, she waited for Abram to respond.

"It will work out as He has said," Abram replied, reaching around her for the bread.

"Really, my husband? What a relief. I am so glad to know that you and I alone are about to defy the laws of time. A lesser person with the slightest idea about where babies come from would like a few more details about how such an extraordinary thing will come about, but not you." She was pacing back and forth in a high state of agitation by now.

"Sarai, He is God, not me. Am I to question Him? It has gone well with us because I have not doubted Him."

"Tell me exactly what He said, and don't leave anything out. You were never one for details."

"All right, already," Abram began. "He said to me, 'Your servant will not inherit your legacy, but a son coming from your own body will be your heir.' That is all there is to it."

Sarai's face looked suddenly suspicious.

"What more do you want?" Abram asked as he checked the cooking pots again to be sure he had not missed something.

"He said nothing about me?"

"Of course He said something about you. You are going to have a baby. What else do you want?" He gulped down the last of his drink.

"He said I was going to have a baby—exactly?" She pressed. "Try to remember."

"He said exactly I would have a son of my own loins. Of course you are going to have a baby. How else would I get a son?" Starving by now, Abram put on his sandals and went to the camel driver's tent in hopes that dinner was still being served.

Oh, if only Abram could have observed the behavior of human women for a few centuries as I had, he would have known never to deliver that kind of information to a woman and then leave her alone to process it. Why, the next four thousand years of human history might have been different if Abram had just a little insight into how women think. God should have warned him about how complex human women are. Personally, I think God Himself didn't always know quite what to expect from females. If the truth be known about it, God probably looked at women and wondered how one of His really clever ideas had become so much more complicated than He intended.

Nothing could have pulled me away from my perch right then; I did not want to miss the action I knew was coming. I could have written the script for what was about to take place in Sarai's mind. Women think men don't want to take the responsibility for anything, so they must take the responsibility for everything. It all started with Eve.

Remember back there in the garden when Adam told God that he had eaten of the forbidden fruit because Eve made him do it? God didn't buy his story for a minute. The words Adam spoke, pathetic excuses that they were, still had an unexpected and lasting effect on Eve and her daughters.

I don't think God anticipated how female reasoning would go askew the way it did. Remember, there were no females in heaven. There was no prototype. The whole experiment with women was an entirely new idea. Women have always been very complex.

Men, on the other hand, are not complex. Men are simply made with a standard emotional package; no frills, no fuss, nothing fancy like there is with women. Men have a basic range of emotions and a standard vocabulary through which they process life. This should have been the normal equipment in all humans, male and female, nothing more or less. Men understand up/down, left/right, good/bad, black/white, hungry/eat, itch/scratch, tired/sleep, mad/yell, hit, grunt. Like that, you see? Easy and simple, that's the way it is with men.

Adam thought there were only two possible states of time: day or night. Eve insisted on breaking time into first light, dawn, morning, noon, afternoon, dusk, evening, night, just after midnight, and just before dawn.

And let me tell you about the colors. That was worse. Adam would say black or white. But Eve would say charcoal, ebony, deep black, barely black. And of course there was not just white. There was bone, eggshell, vanilla, ivory, pale white, glossy white—I could go on and on.

See what I mean? Now take that same propensity to make things more complex than they need to be and carry it into the emotional makeup of women.

Men get mad. Women get irritated, hurt, disappointed, annoyed, miffed, piqued, ruffled, upset, enraged—like that.

Here's how God had a good idea for everybody but failed to foresee how differently it might function between men and women. He put into humans a sense of shame and guilt, intended as a safety valve for their protection, so that when they turned from Him or sinned, the valve would trigger and they would feel something inside of themselves that convicted them of their error. Smart, right?

It was a simple job to install it into the soul of men. But when He started to put it into women, He had to work around the intricate wiring of those accessories and upgrades on the female model. God simply tightened the screw too much in the shame and guilt area. So, ever since Eve, if a man suggested to a woman that something might be her fault, she immediately thought that it was.

Adam said Eve made him eat the fruit. If you could have seen the size of him and the size of her, you would see how ridiculous that was. But in Eve's mind, because of that shame and guilt screw being too tight, her natural conclusion was, "Maybe I did. It must be my fault." A case of an overdeveloped sense of responsibility resides in every female who has ever been, because as I see it, God will not own up to the miscalculation and fix it.

It's that kind of dysfunctional reasoning that has stayed in Eve's daughters all the way to the present generation. And don't think for a moment that men haven't figured it out.

Therefore, when Abram repeated to Sarai what God had said to him, she analyzed the sentence structure. As I have seen women do time after time, she came to a logical and yet completely wrong conclusion about what God meant. Abram had been promised a son from his own body, but she had not. The Lord had intentionally not said anything about her.

"That must be it," she thought. "I'm too old to be the natural mother. I bet they talked about it and Abram doesn't want to tell me. He knows it will hurt my feelings. I must sacrifice my own desires. I must do something to see that Abram has an heir as God has said."

And that is when Sarai came up with one of the worst ideas in human history. She decided on her own to save the day. She believed she was too old to have children, but she had an Egyptian maidservant named Hagar who was not.

When Abram came back to the tent later that night, Sarai was waiting for him. "My husband, we must talk."

"Must we talk now?" he asked, full of bread and wine, desiring nothing more than to lie down.

"It has to be now; your happiness depends on it."

Having never heard her say anything close to this before when he had come home late, Abram came to attention. "What do you mean—my happiness?" He tried to remember if Sarai had ever been concerned about his happiness before.

Sarai sighed and said, "The Lord has kept me from having children."

"But so, who cares? You will have a baby now. The Lord said so." Abram tried to console her. "Now, let's go to bed." He turned as if going to lie down.

"No, my husband," she sighed even deeper.

Abram knew this conversation was going to happen no matter what, so he sat down on a pillow and motioned for her to go ahead.

"He said *you* would have a son. He said nothing about me. I am too old. I've thought it over. Go and sleep with my maidservant; perhaps I can build a family through her."

Now Abram, with that basic emotion package and simple thinking feature common to man, quite naturally thought that when Sarai proposed her preposterous idea, she must actually mean it. Which, of course, she thought she did at first.

When Sarai suggested Abram have sex with Hagar in order to secure an heir "from his own body," as God had promised, there were any number of ways Abram should have responded. Any of them would have been better than what he did.

He was supposed to gasp at the thought. He was supposed to fall down on his knees in gratitude when he realized how Sarai was willing to sacrifice her own happiness for his. He was supposed to marvel at how unselfish she was and how she was willing to put aside her own desperate desire for a child to secure his happiness. The number one thing in the top ten things that Abram was supposed to have done and did not: he was supposed to say, "No. Absolutely not. Inconceivable. Wouldn't consider it. The matter is settled. Don't mention it again."

He was supposed to say that having a child with another woman was unthinkable. He was supposed to say that he would never agree to such a thing. He was supposed to say they would wait and believe God until they died rather than have Sarai displaced by someone else.

What he did say was never, ever, not in ten thousand years what he was supposed to say: "OK, if you think so, dear."

My, oh, my, and I had thought Satan's wrath was awful. I had never seen a woman turn that color before. The fury that rose in Sarai's eyes made my wings wilt. Abram had no idea what he was in for. In fact, the whole human race would pay for the wrath of that woman scorned.

Abram slept with Hagar, and she conceived. Then the trouble really started. When she learned she was pregnant, Hagar began to despise Sarai. Do you wonder why? History has it wrong about this part of the story in that it blames Hagar for something she had absolutely no control over. It was bad enough for the young woman to find herself the paramour for a man old enough to be her grandfather's grandfather. It was no secret why she was in this position. The whole caravan knew the story. Sarai had insisted upon it. Now that Hagar was pregnant, she was angry with Sarai for causing a set of circumstances from which Hagar could never escape. Hagar's future was toast. When Sarai heard that Hagar was angry, Sarai got mad that Hagar was mad about being pregnant.

Then Sarai said to Abram, "You are responsible for the wrong I am suffering. I put my servant in your arms so that you could have your promised heir, and what do I get for my trouble? Now that she knows she's pregnant, she despises me. Look at what you've done."

Abram stood there scratching his head and trying to figure out why everyone was mad at him. Being a man, he thought Sarai would get over it once she remembered how the whole thing started. Not a chance.

"What I've done?" Abram asked. "Love of my life, I only did this for you. Isn't this what you wanted? Wasn't this your idea? We're going to get a baby and a nanny to boot. Isn't it great how it's working out?"

She hurled a clay pot at his head. This went on for about an hour, and at the end of it all, Abram told Sarai to do whatever she wanted with Hagar.

"Your servant is in your hands," Abram said. "Do with her whatever you think best."

Sarai took out her frustration on Hagar, who finally ran away, out into the desert alone. Hagar was scared to death and cried like a baby as she left with barely enough sustenance to keep her alive for a few days. Hagar had not been gone long before Sarai began to think it over, and, as I could have predicted, she started moving toward that guilt thing again.

"I was too hard on her," Sarai thought to herself. "Why wouldn't she hate me? She's just a child herself. She didn't want a baby with that old goat. Hagar didn't have any say in this matter. We forced her to do it. I feel badly that her mother had plans for her to marry one of the camel drivers next year. Of course, there's no chance for that now. Poor thing, out there in the desert. Lost and alone, I know she must be scared to death. This is all Abram's fault."

I couldn't be sure what God intended to do about all of this, but I knew Him well enough to know that He wouldn't let that young girl wander around out there in the desert, especially since she was pregnant with Abram's child. I knew it was God who brought about Sara's mind change, so it was a pretty safe bet He would send one of the angels to tell Hagar everything would be OK and to return to her mistress.

Not knowing about Sarai's change of heart or God's intervention with the angel, when Abram saw Hagar returning to the camp, all he could imagine was a lot of screaming and flying objects. He was certain Sarai would come out throwing pots with both hands. Imagine his surprise when Sarai emerged from the tent, ran past him, and welcomed the girl back with outstretched arms.

Oh, the hugs, and the "I'm sorry, so am I," kiss, kiss—it was enough to make a demon nauseous.

Sarai wrapped Hagar in her shawl and shepherded the girl into her very own tent. As they passed by Abram, who had no idea what had just happened, both women snarled at him.

"What did I do?" he asked no one in particular. He shrugged and started back for the tent just in time to see his pillow and mat come flying out the door, landing in the dust in front of him. From inside the tent, he could hear the sobbing of Hagar as she poured out her heart to Sarai, who clucked about her like an old hen with an orphan chick.

Abram considered barging into the tent and ordering both women to shape up, then throwing Hagar out of his tent to regain his standing with Sarai. Doing a quick mental inventory of the number of clay pots he supposed might still be in there, he thought better of it and set off to find someone to sympathize with him.

Abram went out to the desert and sat on a rock and cried to God, "God, where are You? What has happened to me? Why am I sleeping on a rock? I was thrown out of my own tent. Sarai hates me. Hagar hates me. Why did You let this happen?"

Now, I can tell you I was dumbfounded when God answered him. He just doesn't do that. He doesn't respond to whining. Usually, He doesn't give the whiner any attention at all. I was surprised when I heard Him answer Abram, "I did not tell you to be with Hagar."

"But it was Sarai's idea. It never crossed my mind to do such a thing."

"Oh, please," God interrupted. "Remember to whom you are talking. I know your every thought before you think it."

"But what am I going to do now? They have sided against me."

"Yes, I see that. Actually, I was afraid that might happen. The sisterhood bonding mix I put into women is a very delicate formula."

"You know, Mighty One ever to be praised," Abram whimpered, "I don't want to seem ungrateful. Thank You for the camels and the flocks and for saving Lot and all that, but it looks to me like most of the misery of life could have been avoided if You had not made women so complicated. Did You not declare how man was going to rule over her? You did say that, right? When is that part supposed to kick in?"

"Of course I said it, but it was not part of My plan A," God replied. "It was simply a statement as to how men would mistreat women if Eve followed Adam. Men ruling over women is the consequence of poor choices. I meant for them to rule together. But never mind, I intend to remedy that situation a little further down the timeline."

"I appreciate that You're thinking ahead, O Mighty One, but it doesn't help me out right now. Everyone in the camp is talking about it. When do I get to rule over my wife? Nobody respects a man when his wife throws clay pots at him and tosses his mat in the dirt."

God changed the subject. "You are going to name Hagar's son Ishmael. He will be born when you are eighty-six years old. Good night." God had done all of the explaining He intended to do.

"Wait," Abram cried. "Is that it? When will I hear from You again?" The rumble of thunder and flash of lightning told Abram that this conversation was over.

CHAPTER 23

THIRTEEN YEARS WOULD pass before God would speak to Abram again.

Ishmael was born and Abram loved him. Neither Sarai nor Hagar knew it, but sometimes at night, Abram would go into the desert and argue with God about how Ishmael would do perfectly well to carry on Abram's line. I wondered why Abram kept bringing the topic up as if he had to sell God on the idea of Ishmael. Sarai had been right. God did not specifically say anything about her having a child. Abram had his son; mission accomplished.

I wondered if I might be missing something in Abram's prayers, so I decided to listen more intently. Abram seemed to want God to understand how hard it was for him to be the parent of a teenager at his age.

"Can You imagine, God," Abram would say, "how difficult it would be to have another baby as old as we are?"

"Could it be that Ishmael is *not* the heir?" I asked myself. "Abram seems to have doubts."

"But he must be," I answered my own question. "Ishmael fits the only criterion God had specifically spoken about: he was from Abram's loins."

I was sure God had never said anything definite about Sarai, so I assumed when Ishmael was born, that would be it. Sarai preempted her chance by getting ahead of God. But when I listened to Abram's pleadings, I wasn't so sure. I realized that he himself didn't believe Ishmael was the son God promised. There must be another child coming.

"Ishmael is not the heir," I reported to Satan.

"What do you mean?" Satan asked. "He's Abram's son, isn't he? You said God promised him Ishmael would be the father of a great nation. So what's your point? Don't waste my time."

"God did make that promise to Abram. But apparently, that was sort of an add-on promise, a bonus son so to speak. Abram wouldn't be trying to sell God on the idea of Ishmael being his heir in fulfillment of God's commitment unless Abram knew the boy wasn't. Although he could go on to his glory in perfect contentment with Ishmael left in charge, Abram believes there is yet another son to come. Otherwise, he wouldn't be trying to talk God out of it."

Satan thought about how he could take advantage of this turn of events. He assigned two demons to dog Hagar and Ishmael everywhere they went for weeks.

"Find out where they go, what they talk about. Most importantly, do they know another child is coming?" Satan ordered.

When the two demons reported what they had learned, the information revealed nothing. They did not go anywhere. They talked and played games. They gave no indication there would be another heir besides Ishmael.

"Start with Hagar," Satan was on top of it. "You," he pointed to one of the lesser demons, "go into her tent at night. Speak into her dreams. Remind her of why Abram lay with her to start with. She would have resisted except for Abram's reassurance that her baby would be his heir. Connect the dots for her. There is another child coming, and when he comes, she and Ishmael are out."

It worked like a charm. Hagar became fearful and defensive about everything and looked for hidden meaning in what she heard from Sarai. She also treated Ishmael differently. They no longer spent their time together playing games. She went on and on to the boy about how it wasn't fair that he would never be Abram's heir. Ishmael, who didn't know what an heir was, could tell from his mother's attitude that something unjust must be about to happen. The wedge between Ishmael and the son to come was firmly established before the heir was born.

Thirteen years later, God spoke again.

Abram was now ninety-nine years old. One hot day, as he rested on a bench near his tent, the Lord appeared to him again.

"Abram," God said.

"God?" Abram blinked hard, shielding his eyes from the light now invading his shade.

Overwhelmed, Abram fell flat on his face.

Then God said to him, "This is My covenant with you: You'll be the father of many nations. Your name will no longer be Abram, but Abraham, meaning that I'm making you the father of many nations. I'll make you a father of fathers—I'll make nations from you; kings will issue from you. I'm establishing My covenant between Me and you, a covenant that includes your descendants, a covenant that goes on and on and on, a covenant that commits Me to be your God and the God of your descendants. And I'm giving you and your descendants this land where you're now camping, this whole country of Canaan, to own forever. And I'll be their God."

Wow. I had never known God to speak more than two or three sentences at one time. "Such a generous gift," I thought. "Wasteful, really. What is he going to do with such wealth at his age?"

I was impressed but not surprised at the lavish promise God made to Abraham, because it was just like Him to do something like that. He hadn't spoken to Abram—Abraham—in thirteen years, but at the end of the silence, God went way over the top to restore him into favor. Satan hated it whenever he learned God had made a covenant promise like this to a human, and I dreaded having to tell him about it. I was about to find Satan to let him know he had trouble when I realized that God was about to speak again. I dared not miss a word.

Then God said to Abraham, "This is the covenant that you are to honor; the covenant that pulls in all your descendants: Circumcise every male. It will be the sign of the covenant between us. Every male baby will be circumcised when he is eight days old."

"Whoa," I said before I caught myself.

Abraham lifted his face up toward heaven and blinked hard again. It was as if someone had awakened him from a deep sleep by throwing ice water on his head.

"Circumcised? God, are You sure?" he muttered. Abram wiped his brow and stood up, wondering whether or not this was some sort of punishment, but for what, he was not sure.

"Even the adult males, O sovereign Lord?"

God did not respond.

Maybe repentance would soften God's stand on such an extreme symbol for faithfulness, so Abraham tried again.

"I know I have made some terrible mistakes, and I've had a lot of time to think about the Hagar thing...my fault entirely. Believe me, I've paid for it already. Living with those two women is plenty of punishment. I'm really sorry I did such a stupid thing, and it is only right that You punish me. Could we not limit the circumcision to just Ishmael and me? Must we involve anyone else?"

God went on, "Every male in the house from eight days and older, free or slave, foreigner or family, all will undergo circumcision."

Abraham knelt down again. "Of course, Mighty One ever to be praised, but I should tell You that this is going to be a very hard sell. Have You seen the camel drivers lately? You can imagine how they are going to take this news."

The thunder rolled, and I knew that God was about to change the subject.

He said to Abraham, "As for Sarai, your wife, you are no longer to call her Sarai. Her name will be Sarah. I will bless her and will surely give you a son by her. I will bless her so that she will be the mother of nations. Kings will come from her."

Abraham fell on his face again, but this time it was to hide his amusement at such a notion. He laughed and said to himself, "Will a son be born to a man one hundred years old? Will Sarah bear a child at the age of ninety?"

I was about to laugh myself when I remembered it was forbidden for me to do so. Satan had disallowed it where humans were concerned. He said laughing at them could cause me to develop affection for them. As if that were possible.

But imagine how ridiculous it was. Just look at the two of them. Unless this was going to be an immaculate conception, I did not see it happening. When Abraham realized God was not kidding around, he looked up to heaven and made a request that I could understand.

"Oh, sovereign God, if only You would have favor on Ishmael. Are You sure we can't work with him? He's already thirteen. He's a good boy. Sarah would not mind; really, she wouldn't. By now she's forgotten the whole thing anyway. I don't know if I can do the diaper duty or walking the floor with a colicky baby again, not at my age." But God didn't budge.

Then God said, "Sarah is going to have a son. I'm going to establish My covenant with him."

"That's it!" I yelled out as I prepared to wing my way back to Satan's den. "I was right. There will be another son."

I waited to see if anything else was going to happen. Except for a promise to bless Ishmael as well (God rarely refused Abraham anything), that was pretty much it.

CHAPTER 24

ABRAHAM AND SARAH were about to experience what they and many after them would find to be an annoying behavioral characteristic of God. He spoke a naturally impossible promise to them and then left town for an excruciatingly long period of time when absolutely nothing happened.

Abraham and Sarah had mostly given up on the idea of seeing their promise fulfilled. Then one day, with no warning, Adonai, the second person of the Godhead, appeared in the front yard of Abraham's tent. As far as I could recall, Adonai had not set a foot on Earth since Adam.

But there He was, as real as the desert sand, standing in front of Abraham's tent with two of His warring angels at His side. I recognized Him right away, of course, but so did Abraham, which surprised me somewhat. Abraham had talked to God, but he had never actually seen Him. And who knew whether Abraham knew about Adonai? After all, the trinitarian nature of God was a theological stretch for humanity in 2000 B.C.

Abraham wasted no time in getting the whole camp into a dither to prepare a meal for his important visitors. I wanted to get close so I could hear more of what was being said, but I did not dare chance it. Those two warring angels never sat down, never took one hand off their sabers, and never stopped looking around to see who else was there, especially someone like me, a spy from the other camp. I kept my distance and strained to hear the conversation.

"Where is your wife, Sarah?" they asked Abraham. Like they didn't know.

"There, in the tent," he said.

Then Adonai said, "I will surely return to you about this time next year, and Sarah, your wife, will have a son."

Now Sarah was listening at the entrance to the tent behind Abraham. Although she covered her head with her apron and tried to muzzle herself, she laughed. But I laughed harder, despite the rule against it. I bent over into a ball, trying my best to stop laughing when I tumbled right off my perch. My balance never did improve, no matter how many times I fell off that thing. I tried to stay upright, but I'll tell you, it was hard with wings, a tail, and claws. There was not enough room to put it all.

I might have gone on giggling at the very idea of Abraham and Sarah having a baby if I hadn't accidentally rolled right over the top of Satan's tail. I hadn't heard him come up. He snatched me up by the wing and slapped the giggles right out of me, and then he demanded to know what had caused my fit.

I pulled myself together and tried to tell him what I had seen and heard. I thought he might find the whole idea as ridiculous as I had. Not a chance. In fact, he was quite stoic, showing no emotion. He lifted me off the ground and dangled me in midair while demanding to know what else had been said.

"Nothing really, master. That's it. They came to announce the baby, which we've suspected for years now, so no surprise there. There's nothing to be concerned about, I'm sure." I was gasping for air.

"Fool," he snarled at me, tightening his grip. "Adonai would not have come down for that."

"Get back down there, and find out why He is on Earth. Miss nothing. It's your head if you do."

When I returned to my listening post, the three of them were standing, and it looked as if Adonai and the angels were on their way out—or up, I suppose, is the more correct term. As they turned to leave, they looked toward Sodom but said nothing. Abraham walked along with them to see them on their way. Then Adonai stopped abruptly and turned to one of the angels and said, "Shall I hide from Abraham what I am about to do?"

"What is this?" I asked myself. When I could stand it no longer, I moved closer. They were talking in hushed and somber tones now, so I chanced it and flew in as close as I dared. I quickly ducked behind a rock when I saw one of the warrior angels tap his sword and sniff the air.

Then Adonai said, "The cries of the victims in Sodom and Gomorrah are deafening; the sin of those cities is immense. I'm going down to see for myself if what they're doing is as bad as it sounds. Then I'll know."

The men set out for Sodom, but Abraham stood in Adonai's path, blocking His way. The men continued on their way, but Adonai lingered as if intending to talk privately with Abraham, but I couldn't wait around to find out. I had to let Satan know the angels were on the way to the cities.

I was breathless by the time I reached Satan's lair. I spilled out the words as coherently as I could. "Adonai is on Earth. He's going to destroy Sodom and Gomorrah, and the destroying angels are on the way there right now."

"He cannot do it." Satan muttered. "It's against the rules. They have to be held for the day of wrath like everyone else. He cannot change the rules. He said

He would not destroy the world again. Sodom and Gomorrah are part of the world. You heard Him."

He looked to the others for confirmation and all nodded in agreement, though I was certain they had no idea what he was talking about. Then Satan looked directly at me, waiting for me to nod along with the others. I looked hard at the floor as if having discovered something important there. I tried to pretend not to hear him speaking to me. My mind was racing for an answer.

"What shall I do? What shall I say?" My thoughts sped by. "I'll lie. I'll tell him he's right. No, that won't work. If I lie he will see it in my eyes. I have only one option. I'll tell him the truth and then run."

I looked back and forth, calculating the number of seconds I would need to quote the law for Satan then make it out the nearest hole before he could process what I said. Satan yelled at me again.

"You are the one who told me what He said to Noah," Satan yelled in my face. "God said that He would not destroy the world again." His eyes narrowed. "That is precisely what you told me, isn't it?"

I scrunched my head down as far as it would go between my wings and stood my scales on end to prevent him from grabbing me and swinging me around by the neck. Then I eked out the words, "Master, you are right to have interpreted it that way. Any reasonable person would have done the same. Any court would surely side with you on your interpretation."

Satan swung at me and cut me short. "Stop slobbering. Did He say it or not? Yes or no?"

I replied, "Technically, in a word, no."

Everyone went for cover. Satan's whole body was a weapon as he spewed the worst-looking stuff out of his mouth and came after me.

"You lie, you die." He lunged toward me. I stepped just beyond his grasp.

"No, no, let me explain. God said He would not destroy the *world* again by..." I could not finish before he cut me off.

"By what? Technically." He seethed.

"God said He would not destroy the world again by water." I exhaled deeply.

"Then I'm right." Satan turned and started away from me. "He will not destroy the world again. Sodom and Gomorrah are part of the world, so He cannot deal with their sin until the day of wrath—end of problem."

Satan was completely misinterpreting what God had said. His insistence that destroying the cities was tantamount to destroying the world did not make sense. Why didn't I just let him go on his way and think whatever he wanted? I never seemed to know when to stop talking.

"No, master, that is very close to right, but just the tiniest bit off, technically, of course. Not that you aren't right." I babbled, following behind him in the meekest of postures. "Of course, you always hear right. It was my fault. I did not speak it correctly."

Satan spun around and glared at me as I tried to explain what God had actually said. "The truth is, O awesome one, when God said, and I quote, 'I will not destroy the world again by water,' He left Himself some wiggle room."

"Wiggle room?" Satan asked as the other demons covered their mouths to disguise their smirking laughter.

"You know. Just in case."

"In case of what?"

"Like, just in case He was confronted with an unequivocal, over-the-top kind of sin and had to do something about it." I lowered my voice. "Sort of like what you've got going on down there in Sodom and Gomorrah. Technically, the cities do not represent His promise not to destroy the whole world. He can do whatever He decides to do locally. Wipe them off the planet if He wants, just so long as He doesn't destroy the whole world again by flood."

Satan paused for a moment as if thinking it over. He shrugged and said, "So let Him do it. Destroy them all." Satan threw up his claws as if the topic were no longer worth his time. "Why should I care whether He destroys them now or never? Their souls are mine." Instead of stalking off as he usually did, he paced back and forth, belying his professed unconcern with the matter.

"There's something more. God would not have gone down to Earth just to destroy people who are already lost to Him." Satan reasoned out loud. "If He's there, it's for some other reason. But what?" He paused as if expecting me to say something, but he went on with his monologue before I could get a word out.

"God doesn't have any people there anymore. They belong to me. And why would He tell Abraham His plans? What is Abraham supposed to do about it?"

I have to admit that I too had to think about that one for a moment. Then it hit me. "Master, think about it. Lot is in Sodom."

"And so? That means what to me?"

I continued, "Lot is Abraham's nephew."

"Lot?" Satan sneered. "Who cares about Lot? He is the great pretender, nothing close to the piety he espouses to his wife and kids. He is ankle-deep in the perversion, even if he only watches for now. It's just a matter of time until we have his pitiful little soul as well."

I was jumping around, so excited at how I had figured it all out.

"No, no. Don't you see?" I was breathless again. "Adonai told Abraham because He knows Abraham will bargain for Lot's life. How many things has God refused Abraham?"

"Do you think God doesn't know all about Lot? Why would he want Abraham to bargain for his sake?"

"Maybe God knows Abraham loves Lot?" I wondered.

"I don't believe it," Satan shot back. "That pitiful little whiner tried to steal Abraham blind. Abraham was glad to be rid of him. Abraham would not use up any points with God over that measly weasel."

I knew not to say anything else as Satan walked to the edge of eternity and stared at Earth below. Finally, he shrugged and said, "Go find out."

I flew like the wind back to Earth and dropped down behind the rock where I'd hidden before and listened.

Then Abraham approached Adonai and said, "Will You really sweep away the righteous with the wicked? What if there are fifty righteous people in the city? Will You really sweep it away and not spare the place for the sake of the fifty?"

Adonai turned away and looked back toward Sodom. Abraham hurried around in front of Him and continued.

"Far be it from You to do such a thing—to kill the righteous with the wicked, treating the righteous and the wicked alike. Far be it from You! Will not the Judge of all Earth do the right thing?"

"There are no righteous in Sodom," Adonai replied.

"But how can You know for sure? Suppose there *are* fifty righteous."

Adonai answered, "If I find fifty righteous people in the city of Sodom, I will spare the whole place for their sake."

Then Abraham spoke up again, "Now that I have been so bold as to speak to the Lord, what if the number of the righteous is less than fifty? Say there are only forty-five; would You spare the city for forty-five?"

"If I find forty-five there," He said, "I will not destroy it."

Abraham looked down as if thinking, then spoke once again. "What if only forty are found there?"

Adonai sighed and said, "For the sake of forty, I will not do it."

Abram lifted one hand as if to touch His robe, but thought better of it and didn't. Then he said, "May the Lord not be angry, but let me speak. What if only thirty can be found there?"

Adonai answered, "I will not do it if I find thirty there."

Abraham bowed down on his knees, "Now that I have been so bold as to speak to the Lord, what if only twenty can be found there?"

He said, "For the sake of twenty, I will not destroy it."

"May the Lord not be angry, but let me speak once more. What if only ten can be found there?"

"For the sake of ten, I will not destroy it, but that is it; no lower, so do not ask."

When the Lord had finished speaking with Abraham, He left, and Abraham returned home. I decided to fly toward Sodom to see what would happen.

It was midnight, and the humans should have been in their houses asleep. Most were, but not Lot. He had waited until the candles were out and his wife was asleep before rising quietly and leaving the house under cover of darkness. Lot sat by himself in the gates of the city, obviously waiting for someone. I can tell you two things about what Lot was not doing. He was not praying, and he was not expecting the arrival of destroying angels.

When the angels appeared, Lot jumped to his feet to greet them before he realized they were not whomever he was waiting for. When he saw their shimmering outline against the night sky, he became visibly nervous.

"My lords." He bowed low. "Your servant awaits your command."

"Do not bow down to us," the first angel said. Lot stood up but kept his head down, avoiding looking at the angel's face.

"We have come to destroy the cities," spoke the second angel.

"But...but why?" Lot stammered, now looking up.

"The stench of their sin and the cries of the victims of their debauchery has reached God's throne."

"I see." Lot continued to stammer. "I'm on that. I just need a little more time. I can be an influence for good here." Lot looked around nervously, suddenly remembering who was coming to meet him at the gate.

"Let's get away from here," Lot urged. "Come to my house where we can talk. Please, come right now."

Lot could not move fast enough to get the angels away from the gate lest they find out about his late-night rendezvous. The angels agreed to follow Lot to his house, but you have no idea how close Satan came to having Lot's soul sewn up that very night. Two hours later and all of history would have been different.

Lot unlatched the door and led the angels quickly into the darkened room, bumping into the table and stumbling over a bench in search for embers to light the candles. His wife awakened and came into the room to see what the noise was about.

"What is it, Lot?" she asked. "Who are these—men?"

"Nothing," Lot replied. "Nothing, go back to bed."

At that moment, loud and rude voices from outside of the house called for Lot. Someone pounded on Lot's door.

"Come out and play, Lot," said a drunken voice from the porch.

"What is that?" the lead angel asked. As if he needed someone to tell him.

"What is what?" Lot replied as he stumbled around trying to put a lock on the door.

The angel continued, "The men at the door, what do they want?"

"Them? Oh, nothing, I'm sure. Partiers on their way home who probably lost their way; they're knocking on my door by mistake." Lot fumbled with the locks.

Lot cracked the door and shouted, "You there, on with you now. We'll sort it out tomorrow."

But the men outside would not be silenced. They had seen Lot take the beautiful strangers into his house, and they salivated at the prospect.

"Bring your friends out to play with us," the voice continued.

Lot was sweating when he opened the door just enough to squeeze himself out. He motioned for them to be quiet, but his nervous state only served to incite them all the more. Soon the crowd surrounded the house.

They called to Lot, "Where are the men who came to you tonight? Bring them out to us so that we can have sex with them."

Well, there it was for the entire world to hear. The blood drained from Lot's face as he heard the angels open the door behind him and step out on the porch.

"Step aside," they said to him.

"No, masters. Wait," Lot pleaded. "It is not what you think. It isn't like that at all. I can handle this. Don't trouble yourselves. Go back inside. Sit down, eat, drink. I can do this."

The more Lot tried to hush the crowd, the louder they became. Then Lot did the unthinkable thing.

"Leave these men alone," he begged. "I have two virgin daughters who have never known a man. I will bring them out to you. Do with them as you wish, but do not involve these strangers."

Fire leapt from the angels' eyes when they heard Lot offering to sacrifice his daughters. For a moment the crowd drew back at the sight of their righteous anger.

"Get out of our way," the angels ordered Lot as they pushed him back inside his house.

"Please, let me talk to them," Lot pleaded. Once inside the house, the angels slammed the door.

The crowd grew bolder. "Look who wants to play the judge! What's the matter, Lot? Aren't we good enough for your new friends?" The crowd mocked him as they advanced. "We'll treat you worse than them."

Contrary to what sympathizers would later write, Lot could not have stopped the crowd if he had wanted to. He had no moral authority in that city whatsoever. Whatever he may have had, he lost long ago. Neither was he trying to protect the angels. He was trying to protect *himself* from the angels lest they figure out what kind of person he had become.

When the crowds grew larger and their threats escalated, Lot became truly afraid. Just then the angels raised their arms and struck the crowd of men with blindness so that they could not find the door.

In their terror at being suddenly blind, they cursed all the louder for Lot.

"Lot, what have you brought upon us?"

"Open the door. Let us in." They tried to find the way to the door but could not.

The angels took over the situation and told Lot to get his family together and leave the city. Lot had no idea how close he was to utter destruction. He stumbled around, trying to get the family to obey him, but they laughed, especially his daughters' fiancés. The boys were never fooled by their father-in-law-to-be's pretense. It was time to go, but the family would not obey.

When Lot hesitated, the angels grasped his hand and the hands of his wife and of his two daughters and led them forcefully outside through the blind and terrified men until they reached the gates of the city. I followed, determined to keep my eye on Lot.

The larger angel urged them to run. "Flee for your lives! Don't look back, and don't stop anywhere in the plain! Flee to the mountains, or you will be swept away!"

Truly frightened now, Lot grabbed his wife's hand to pull her along with him up the hill leading away from the city gates, but she drew back and broke loose from his grasp.

"I cannot go," she cried. "All I know is in the city."

Before Lot could grab her, she spun about and was turned into a pillar of salt right before his eyes.

Lot grabbed the hands of his daughters and pulled them along with him to a cave atop the hill overlooking the city. Lot and his daughters stood helplessly by and watched the cities burn.

Days after it was over, the girls tried to run away as well, but Lot would not let them go. It wasn't long after that Lot committed incest with his daughters and then blamed them.

I don't know why Abraham bothered with his nephew.

I pondered what this might mean. It occurred to me that none of this had a thing to do with Lot and everything to do with Abraham. The angels had not gone into Sodom to save a righteous family. They were there because of the righteousness of Abraham. But why? I began to put the pieces together.

"First, Adonai came down to announce to Abraham and Sarah that a baby was coming in a year," I outlined the events in my mind. "Next, He starts to leave but decides to tell Abraham how He is going to destroy the cities."

"But, why?" I said aloud. "To save Lot? If Adonai had wanted to save Lot because Lot was a righteous man, He could have done so in response to the prayers of Lot. Why involve Abraham in it?"

"Of course," I continued to myself. "Because, obviously, Lot had not prayed any righteous prayers." Lot was as guilty as the rest of them or would have been if he had stayed there another night. Given that certainty, why was Adonai so interested in saving a loser like Lot?"

"But wait," I was beginning to figure it out. "Maybe He never intended to save Lot. Adonai had been clear about what He planned to do: destroy the whole city— end of sentence. Adonai never mentioned Lot nor anyone else as a possible exception until He started bargaining with Abraham."

"What was the bargaining about anyway?" I wondered. "God knew there were no righteous people in any quantity in the city. Why play a game with Abraham?"

"Oh, my," I collapsed into a heap as I figured it out. "God was getting Abraham to pray for Lot so no one of Abraham's bloodline would perish in the city." I knew I had the answer, and when it proved to be right, it would change the balance of power between righteousness and evil and the consequences in the human realm forever. I got myself together and trudged off to report to Satan.

Satan towered over me, demanding to know what had happened. He would tolerate no threat to his domain. I stood trembling before him, expecting to die for what he would force me to tell. He glared at me with those menacing eyes, warning me of the consequences of giving answers he did not want to hear, while at the same time demanding to know.

"Why are you holding back?" He moved closer to me. "There is more, and you know what it is. It makes no sense for God Himself to come into this realm to destroy those cities. He has no claim to anyone in there. Why did He come?"

His breath was hot on my head. "Don't tell me it was for that worthless nephew Lot. He had another reason, and you, you scoundrel, know what it is. I command you to tell me."

By now the other demons had circled us, waiting to hear my reply. "It's because God wanted Abraham to intercede for Lot to stay His hand of judgment."

"Mercy?" Satan roared.

"Something like that," I mumbled my reply.

"Impossible. Not upon the guilty." He roared again at me.

"Yes, even upon the guilty, at least for a time."

"No," he howled, "that is against the rules."

"Technically," I continued, immediately recognizing my poor word choice. "Technically, the rules He set do not limit Him in time."

"Meaning what?" he demanded.

"Meaning that He does not have to bring destruction on the guilty within a specific time period. He can wait until the day of wrath if He chooses to do so."

"But He can make no distinctions among sinners," Satan countered. "Lot is a sinner same as the rest in Sodom and Gomorrah. If He destroyed any, He is bound to destroy all for their sin. No respecter of persons and all that mumbo jumbo. By His own mouth, He said it."

I avoided the *technically* word and continued to explain the finer points of the rules of engagement that God had declared.

"His covenant states that He will do nothing on Earth except it be done in response to the request of a human being. He may do anything He wants so long as a human asks Him to do it, provided it was in His divine will to start with. When Abraham interceded for his nephew, it fulfilled the legal grounds for God to do what He wanted in the first place."

Everyone was listening, but their vacant eyes told me they had no idea the significance of what I was trying to make Satan understand.

"It was like this. Yes, Lot was in danger of judgment, as were the rest, but the intercession of Abraham, a righteous man, made it legal for God to temporarily overlook Lot's sin—a stay of execution, so to speak, in the face of judgment falling on those round about him."

"But for what reason?"

"Can only be one thing: repentance. It gives the guilty party time to repent before judgment."

It was every bit as bad as I had thought it would be. Satan was furious at the thought. He and all the rest remembered how fierce and how fast the judgment had come for us when we were thrown out of heaven because of our rebellion. Now here I was suggesting that this inferior creature, Adam's seed, could stay the hand of God in judgment by interceding for those who were about to be cast down, who, by the way, were every bit as guilty as we had been.

I almost agreed with Satan's outrage and certainly did not blame the others for their anger. I myself wanted to yell out to God, "How is that fair? Look at me. If I had been given just a moment more in heaven, I would never have followed this lunatic." But as always, I said nothing.

We didn't know how it would happen, but we knew things would change after this. How far might this prayer thing go? Certainly it had always been available to humans, but very few of them had actually used it, and until Abraham, no one could have been called an intercessor.

What would happen if this idea were to catch on? What if the righteous learned to intercede for the souls Satan had already captured? Unless he could kill them first, the intercession could buy them enough time to repent, and all of his work would be for naught.

Some of the others went into the war room with Satan to lay plans against the possibility that intercession might become more common. But I went back to my perch and stared at the abyss far below. I thought again how different things would have been for me if I'd been given a few more minutes to reclaim my sanity on the day of our rebellion. I would have made it past Michael and crawled on my belly to God's feet to beg forgiveness.

"Why was there no one in heaven to intercede for me when I needed it?" I screamed into the blackness.

No one answered.

I T HAPPENED JUST as God said it would. Isaac was born to Sarah. At first it looked as if they might be one big, albeit unusual, family of Abraham, Sarah, Hagar, Ishmael, and Isaac. But, of course, Satan wouldn't stand for that. He sent a demon into the camp to stir up the old rivalry between Hagar and Sarah. Although the two women had more or less peacefully coexisted for many years, it was easy for the demon to agitate the bitter root between them, which had never been removed. As long as the root remained, Satan could rouse the ire between the women anytime he wanted. If he thought a fight between Sarah and Hagar might advance his plan, or if he were just bored with the whole thing, he could whip one up in a moment.

The hurt feelings between Sarah and Hagar could flare because each was offended by the other and neither could do anything but feel sorry for herself. Each woman felt she had been sinned against, and each had. The problem between them could never be resolved because of the legal nature of sin. Sin against someone else requires restitution. If there is no restitution, the sin remains.

Therefore, it should have surprised no one that by the time Isaac was two or three years old, Sarah had made up her mind that Ishmael was a threat. She ordered Abraham to send Hagar and Ishmael away.

"That woman's son will not share an inheritance with my boy," Sarah declared.

"Sarah, be reasonable," Abraham tried. "There is plenty to go around. Isaac will never miss any of it."

Sarah remained unrelenting in the matter until at last Abraham agreed. He truly loved Ishmael, and the thought of sending him away crushed him. Inconsolable, Abraham went out into the desert, looking for God.

"God," Abraham cried. "Do You see what's happening here? What about Ishmael? What is to happen to him? These women will be the death of me."

God took pity on Abraham's sorrow. "Don't be so distressed about Ishmael and Hagar. Make it easy on yourself, and do whatever Sarah tells you. It is through Isaac that all I promised you will come about. Don't worry. I will make Ishmael into a nation also, because he is your son."

Hagar and Ishmael left the next day, and Satan lost interest in them for centuries.

After Hagar and Ishmael left town, Sarah settled down, Isaac grew up, and Abraham pretty much got his domestic act together. He followed God more faithfully than ever before. For the next twenty years, nothing happened of the slightest interest to Satan where Abraham was concerned. Abraham did not sin, and God protected and blessed him in everything he did.

When he finally resigned himself to the fact that Abraham was a lost cause, Satan turned his attention to Earth people who did not know the God of Abraham. They were such easy prey that he quickly tired of them and handed them over to the other demons for their sport.

It was painful to watch. Those pitiful souls were so desperate to worship something, and not knowing the true God, they were easily trapped into worshiping Satan by the antics of his hordes. The demons could get humans to do anything they wanted. The men built temples and stone images for the evil emissaries to inhabit, and Satan received the worship he lusted for. Although he protested boredom because it posed no challenge for him, everyone knew he found it intoxicating. He thrilled to see God's little dust people groveling around in front of the images they had carved, sacrificing at times their own children, begging the demons for blessing. Pathetic, isn't it?

One might think after a few centuries, it would have occurred to the people that they never got any of the things they begged and sacrificed for. As a matter of fact, their circumstances worsened; the more they worshiped the idols, the worse the demons treated them. The pitiful humans would go to any extreme to extract a favor from their stone gods. They implored and pleaded with the demonic image to punish their enemies and save their offspring, all of whom Satan had in his clutches. There was little they would not do to get in touch with the supernatural.

I expected them to resist more, but it was no time before the demons were able to convince them to offer their children as sacrifices. After that, teaching them to self-mutilate was easy. The bizarre rituals the people were willing to perform for the entertainment of Satan came from ideas the demons deposited into their wide-open minds. No life form created in God's image could have imagined doing such horrible things on its own. That was most of their problem. Earth people had lost their collective memory of being created in the image of God. Otherwise, Satan could never have forced them to do what they were now willing to do.

Satan's hordes ravished them so completely, I thought they would surely go insane or go running back in search of the God who had so lovingly created them. That's what I would have done—what I tried to do—but they never did. All of the people of Earth were in Satan's clutches. All, that is, except for the tribe of Abraham.

Given that the odds were obviously in Satan's favor—he had hundreds of tribes, and God had one—a reasonable person would have expected God to treat Abraham very carefully, even delicately, to make sure that Isaac grew up and fulfilled his destiny. If, for any reason, Abraham were to jump the fence, God would have been left with no team. No team? Game over. No question about it. If God had any chance of saving a remnant of humanity, He could not afford to call any risky plays with Abraham.

"Hold the ball, and let the clock run out." That's what I would have advised Him. I was certain this had to be His plan. Satan was so resigned this would happen that he ignored the situation entirely and allowed the demons to turn their complete attention to torturing the peasants. I alone was left to watch and wait for Abraham to die.

Years passed before God showed up again. When I heard His voice, I quite naturally assumed He was coming personally to take Abraham to eternity, but it was nothing like that at all. I had seen God require strange things of His humans over the centuries, but nothing I had seen before prepared me for what God was about to require of Abraham.

Abraham was walking in the field when he felt God's presence. Even though it had been a long time, one never forgets what it feels like when God draws near.

God said to him, "Abraham!"

"Here I am, Lord" he replied. Abraham seemed excited to hear from God again, and to be honest, so was I. Satan came right away when he heard me shouting the news. He did not want to miss the exodus of Abraham from Earth, and neither did the others. All of the demons lined up to watch. At last, Abraham would be gone, and Satan would face no resistance. He was counting down the clock when God spoke.

God said, "Take your son, Isaac, and go to the region of Moriah. Sacrifice him there as a burnt offering to Me."

A great sucking wind pulled the oxygen out of Earth's atmosphere from the cumulative gasp of both the demons who watched and from the angels who guarded Abraham. Each side was stunned by what God said.

"Sacrifice Isaac? Command Abraham to commit murder?" The murmuring traveled like an electrical current through both heavens.

"Will God defeat His own team?" a voice exclaimed.

Satan was first bewildered, then beside himself with victory lust.

"Was I right, moron?" Satan shouted at me. "Didn't I tell you there was a side to God no one else knew about? He isn't all good, now, is He? I knew He didn't really care anything about those puny humans. It was all a game. He strung Abraham along, and now that it is nearly payoff time, He turns on him."

Then Satan went off to a chant to himself as the others joined right in shouting and howling, "Satan rules. There is no god like Satan."

I walked away and sat back on my tail, trying to figure out what was happening. "Satan is *not* right about God," I said, utterly confused. "But why—what is He thinking? What does this mean?"

I don't know why I did not join in with the revelry, keep my mouth shut, and let time tell the tale. Actually, I do know why. I had been a good angel, but I was terrible at being a demon, and I could not force myself to be jubilant about any of this. There didn't seem to be any good way out of the corner God had backed into, and I felt bad about the whole thing.

I wondered if this might not be one of those faith tests God was forever demanding of people and then decided against it. If testing had been the point, God would have left an escape route for Abraham—like He always did for people—you know, in case the one being tested can't quite measure up. But there wasn't an emergency exit anywhere for Abraham.

"What will Abraham do now?" one of the demons asked Satan.

"He has only two choices," Satan bragged. "He can obey God and kill his own son, forfeit his inheritance, destroy Sarah, lose everything he's worked for, or..." Satan paused for emphasis, "...my personal favorite, disobey God and lose everything anyway because that is the penalty for disobedience when you are a chosen one." He rolled over in glee.

The demons laid bets as to which way Abraham would go. Not that they cared. No matter what he chose, Satan won. Most were betting Abraham would call it quits and disobey. We had been witnesses to the love Abraham had for Isaac and for Sarah. God's command to sacrifice Isaac was beyond all reason. The smart money was on Abraham to rebel. Satan just wanted to see someone else turn against God.

"On the other hand," Satan waxed philosophically, "there is a bonus to be had if Abraham obeys God."

"How could it get better than if Abraham were to defy God?" a cheerful demon asked.

Satan responded, "There would be no limit to the sorrow and misery we could render on Sarah and the others who would surely turn against Abraham."

"They're sure to find a way to bring him up on charges," a demon laughed.

"Or, better yet, maybe they would kill him without a trial," another chimed in.

The possibilities for devastation and chaos in the human race were endless. What Satan feared but dared not voice was the possibility that God retained a card He had not played. That's why Satan took no chances and sent his most persuasive tempter, flying at light speed to speak into Abraham's mind.

"Abraham, you've been a fool. What kind of God is this?" the demon hissed.

Abraham looked around as if expecting to see someone.

The tempter continued, "The truth is, Abraham, you have surpassed God Himself in knowledge, wisdom, and authority, and He is jealous of you."

"That is utterly absurd," I said under my breath as I watched the whole mental assault roll out. "Abraham would never believe such a thing in ten thousand years."

I could not tell whether or not Abraham was listening.

The demon continued, "Show Him what you're made of. Stand up to Him. You know what is best for your family. When was the last time He was even here? How many times have you looked for Him and He was nowhere to be found?"

Abraham looked at the ground but said nothing.

The demon continued, "Think about it. When was the last time you heard anything at all from Him? He doesn't care about you or Isaac or how this is going to make you look. You did your best; everything was on track for His promises to be fulfilled. Now, what—murder? Besides that, what kind of father entertains thoughts of killing his son? What kind of dad considers putting a knife to his son's throat as an act of obedience? How many years did you wait for a child—a son? And now you're willing to spill his blood? How can you sleep?"

I thought I saw tears in Abraham's eyes, but I could not be sure. Maybe there were tears because the demon continued to accuse Abraham to himself.

"You failed God, you know," the demon continued. "If you do this, don't expect some dramatic rescue. You made Him look bad. He never really forgave you for that tryst with Hagar. Who did you think you were fooling?"

Abraham looked to the right and then to the left, as if thinking it over.

The demon changed tactics, "You tried, didn't you? It hasn't been easy. You did your best, and all the thanks you get is the destruction of everything that has meaning to you."

Abraham stared straight ahead as the demon pressed in.

"He's made you look like a dithering old fool time after time. Remember that ridiculous circumcision business? What did that prove? People still resent you for that. What happened to that covenant? This will never stop unless you refuse to be part of His celestial insanity."

I have to say the tempter was good at his work. We could tell by the anguish on Abraham's face that he had heard every word. The betting was heating up, and the smart money banked that Abraham's faith was about to fail him; he was sure to defy God.

The others assumed I had not bet anything because I didn't have anything to gamble with—which was true, of course. The rest had territories and spoils from devastating nations and could use them as stakes in this game. I didn't have anything of value to bet with because my job was to be a watcher. One does not play for the nations if he is just a watcher. I watched and I reported; that was it. It was not necessary for me to opine which way Abraham would go, and, frankly, I was relieved no one was interested in my opinion. Anything I might have said right then would have only meant trouble for me. I knew beyond all doubt that Abraham was going to obey God, no matter who; no matter what. I don't say that I knew why he would do such a terrible thing, but I knew that he would. And, as usual when it came to humans, I was right again.

Early the next morning Abraham got up and saddled his donkey. He took two of his servants with him, and Isaac and began the long journey to the mountain God had told him about. On the third day, Abraham looked up and saw the place in the distance. Abraham and Isaac cut wood for the fire, saying nothing to each other. When they had enough, Abraham instructed his servants, "Stay here with the donkey while Isaac and I go over there. We will worship, and then we will come back to you."

Isaac, strong and tall, picked up the heavy wood and started up the mountain with his father. Tell me, where did you humans get the idea Isaac was a child and some sort of helpless victim when this happened? He was twenty-five years old. Do the math. He could have escaped at any time.

Satan was clearly taken aback by what he saw. Then a cold and fearful look of knowing came into his eyes as he looked my way. He knew what I knew: Abraham was going to obey. Satan glared at me as if this were somehow my fault. The tempter demon had failed. Abraham's faith in a God he could not see overcame his fear of the circumstances he could see.

Satan cursed and yelled at me, "Why is he like that?"

I wisely did not respond. Satan stomped his hoof, hating that he knew what would happen if Abraham obeyed God. God would rescue Abraham and Isaac. Satan turned and slapped the tempter demon for his failure and sent him tumbling through the atmosphere to Abraham's side to try once more.

"Foolish, senile old man," he seethed into Abraham's ear. "Is there no limit to your idiotic devotion to this killer God? If you do what He asks, you will kill Isaac, and your inheritance will be lost. Isaac will be dead, and you will be blamed for it. Turn back while you still have time."

With the burden of wood, Isaac continued on ahead of Abraham, who followed with the knife in his hand.

At last, Isaac spoke up. "Father?"

"Yes, my son?"

"Where is the lamb for the burnt offering?"

Abraham answered, "God Himself will provide the lamb." He turned his eyes upward as if hoping every word he had said would be true.

Exasperated by the tempter demon's failure, Satan screamed to the spirits of fear that hovered around Earth, waiting to inhabit humans. "Go for Isaac!"

The earthbound spirits were not accustomed to hearing from Satan himself, and at first they swirled about like a whirlwind in their confusion, doing nothing more than colliding with one another. At last, they organized their attack and surrounded Isaac, looking for an entry point.

"Where is he vulnerable?" one asked another.

"Did Abraham ever abuse him?" No one could remember such a thing.

"What about lies? Abraham must have lied about something. All parents lie," said another frantically.

"Did Abraham fail him or disappoint him when he was little?" said another, grasping for anything.

They were desperate to find an emotional scar in Isaac's soul. There had to be a legal entry point before the spirits of fear could overtake him and cause him to cry for mercy.

"Better yet," one hissed. "All together, as one, let's assault him with fear. Then he is sure to turn on his father; perhaps kill him."

It could have worked out that way. Isaac was taller and heavier than Abraham. He could easily have overcome the old man.

The fear spirits continued to spin and poke, but they could not find a point of entry anywhere in Isaac.

I could have told them so, but no one would have listened to me. Satan spun on his tail in his fury at their inability to penetrate Isaac's trust in his father, but the truth was that Abraham had never given Isaac any reason to fear his father's judgment or to doubt his love. So in the face of suspicious and frightening evidence that something very bad was about to happen, Isaac continued to walk with his father up the mountain.

When they reached the place God had told him about, Abraham built an altar and arranged the wood on it. Isaac held out his arms while his father bound his son, then Isaac lay down on the stones.

"Father," Isaac began, "is there any other way?"

Abraham's eyes filled with tears as he reached out his hand and took the knife to slay his son.

Suddenly a loud voice from heaven called out to him. "Abraham! Abraham!"

"Here I am."

"Do not lay a hand on the boy," God said. "Do not do anything to him. Now I know that you fear Me, because you have not withheld from Me your only son."

Abraham looked up, and there in a thicket he saw a ram caught by its horns. He untied Isaac, and the two of them took the ram and sacrificed it as a burnt offering. God reiterated His covenant promises over Abraham and Isaac while Satan returned to his previous state of moaning, wailing, and accusing God of having broken some kind of rule.

"He told Abraham to kill Isaac," he yelled at me.

"Technically speaking," I answered, "He did not. He told Abraham to sacrifice his son, which he did. God then exercised His prerogative to provide a different sacrifice."

"You should have anticipated this," one of the frustrated demons said to Satan. Realizing his extraordinarily poor choice of words, he attempted to back up. "Not you, my lord, of course, I meant him." He pointed to me.

Needing someone to blame, they swung at me at once, but I dropped to the floor quickly, so they ended up striking one another instead. The fighting escalated into a brawl between angry demons. I was no longer important to them, so it was easy to crawl out of the den under the claw fight taking place among them. I returned to my perch and thought about what had happened.

"How long will God persist in this notion that humanity can redeem what the angels lost?" I asked myself as I paced back and forth on my branch, calculating. "How many people are on Earth now?" I wondered. "Not that it's important, because whatever the number is, Satan has more souls than God has."

Then I found myself thinking more about Abraham and this thing called faith.

"What is faith?" I mused. I failed to notice one of the other demons had tired of the fight and was standing near me.

"It is an emotion," he answered. "That is all humans know. They are governed by their feelings."

"That cannot be it," I responded, actually glad to have someone to discuss this with. "If it had been emotion, things would have gone exactly the other way. Abraham's love for Isaac would have caused him to spare his son at any cost."

"Then it is some kind of special knowledge," the demon said.

"Maybe it's like foreknowledge; the human knows in advance how things are going to turn out, so there's no risk in obeying God."

"That's probably it. Otherwise, why would Abraham have been willing to take the chance that God might really have intended for him to kill Isaac?" Then I thought some more about it.

"That can't be it either," I said, somewhat disappointed we had not figured it out.

"It's obvious God was testing something in Abraham, so if Abraham had really known in advance that nothing bad could happen, it would not have been much of a test, now, would it?"

The demon grew bored and flew away, leaving me alone to ponder the idea of faith. Whatever faith was, it had to be something Abraham clung to so strongly that he would risk his life and the life of his son.

"Faith must be more powerful than hope," I thought. "It must be more like belief."

My observations of humanity convinced me that when faced with real challenge and real consequences, you humans always act on the basis of what you believe is true, not what you hope is true. What was it Abraham believed so strongly?

"Why, of course." I finally figured it out. "Abraham believed in the character of God. Faith is as simple as believing God is who He says He is and will do what He says He will do."

"Oh, my." I exhaled slowly. "If humans ever learned they need not fear God because His character is all good and His power and His love for them are without limit and are unchanging, why, they would never fear Satan again. Earth would be lost to him forever."

I promised myself I would never think such a thought again. The very idea stirred something frightening in whatever sort of soul there might be in me. Satan was horrible. But he was all I had. If Satan lost Earth, where would I go? What would I do? God had cast me out of heaven with the rebels, and I could never return.

"God!" I screamed into the vastness of nothing. "I believe You are who You say You are. I believe You will do what You say You will do. Isn't that faith enough? Why is it enough for humans but not for me? Why don't I get a second chance?"

For the first time in my existence, I collapsed in a heap and cried.

CHAPTER 26

I CONTINUED TO OBSERVE human history for many generations. It got somewhat boring because it became absolutely predictable. After Abraham died, Satan was frantic about what Isaac might become, but the truth be told, he led a somewhat ordinary life. He married a woman named Rebekah, who had trouble conceiving, as had his mother, Sarah. Figure the odds on that, but that was the way it was. Before Abraham died, Isaac went to talk to him about the problem and to seek his advice on their childless state. Abraham was quick to tell him what was positively *not* a good course of action.

Eventually, Rebekah had twins, Esau and Jacob, who could have been poster boys for sibling rivalry. Those two never could get along, and Isaac and Rebekah did not help the matter by choosing sides. Isaac loved Esau, and Rebekah loved Jacob. Isaac and Esau were men of action while Rebekah and Jacob were schemers. In my observation of the human race, schemers win out every time.

Jacob, consistent with my theory on schemers, managed to finagle the family blessing away from Esau and married two women, Leah and Rachel. Between them, they had twelve sons and one daughter. God changed Jacob's name to Israel along the way. God was always changing names—no one knows why—but it seems important to the story to mention it.

Eventually, Israel's sons would become the leaders of twelve tribes. They would fight with the world and fight with each other. They would sin, repent, and sin again. God would punish them, and the whole cycle would start over.

Satan was unconcerned with what he saw happening since none of these boys showed any real aptitude for redeeming the fallen Earth. The most promising one was named Joseph. He made Satan nervous for a time there, but at the end of it all, the Israelites (that is what we started calling them when we weren't calling them Hebrews) found themselves in slavery to Egypt as a result of one of Joseph's ideas that seemed good in the beginning but went very bad at the end. The Hebrews were really in slavery to Satan; Egypt was just his cover story.

For four hundred years they were in bondage, and it was brutal. They were treated like animals. There were so many of them that Pharaoh was happy when some of them were killed during their labors. The truth was that he feared their great numbers, although they were no more dangerous than a flock of frightened sheep. After the first one hundred years, they stopped trying to escape altogether. The other demons had begun to complain.

"This is no fun. They don't even try to get away. There's no sport in it," the torturing prince complained. (By this time, Satan had assigned specific roles to the worst of the demons, which made it easier to know who was in charge of what.)

"I liked it better when they used to cry to God," the demon in charge of religion replied. "It was exhilarating to see their agony when they realized no one was going to answer."

In one way or another, every tribe in Egypt was in Satan's hands. The demons didn't bother chasing after the souls we already had, and the only ones we didn't have were the Hebrews. For the demons, the only fun in the whole thing was the deception and the capture. After humans were caught, the game was over as far as the rank-and-file demon was concerned. The only one who got any pleasure out of it was Satan. He received the worship he craved. None of the rest of us got anything like that.

For the demons, the world had become pretty ho-hum, except for the torture of the Hebrews, and that wasn't really any fun either—no payoff. The demons never could capture their souls. Deception loses some of its zing if there isn't a prize at the end, which with these strange humans, there was not.

The Hebrews were the only remnant of the human race God seemed to care anything about, and they had simply given up. They did not run, and they would not fight. It had been four hundred Earth years since God abandoned them, and now they were enslaved to us through the Egyptians, at least physically. I suppose I don't really know whether God abandoned them or not, but Satan insisted that He had, so all of us lesser beings, not daring to suggest that his evilness might be wrong, went right along with it. They were born slaves, and they would die slaves, and not one of them expected anything else.

Four centuries is a very long time to keep alive some vague memory of a God who is supposed to be able to rescue His people. They had no textbooks. They had no religious services. They had mud and straw to make bricks and a pitiful existence to look forward to, the same as their fathers and grandfathers and great-grandfathers had before them. They had legends of Abraham and Isaac, but did these people really exist? How could any of them know for certain?

The Israelites had become slaves and had no reason to hope for anything better. They had no cause to believe a deliverer would come to them by the hand of this same

God who had allowed their disobedient ancestors to go into captivity and whose name no one could remember. They had no reason to call to a God who had done nothing on their behalf for four hundred thirty (to be exact) years. No reason to believe any of it.

Nevertheless, they did. They continued to tell one another that somehow, some way, someday, someone was coming to free them from Egypt.

In the midst of their misery, the population of the Hebrew slave nation continued to grow until at last Satan succeeded in terrifying Pharaoh with the idea of what their great numbers could accomplish if they rallied against Egypt. Pharaoh himself ordered enforced population control.

"Throw every Hebrew boy into the Nile, but let every girl live."

Satan delighted in the slaughter of children—always has. Perhaps it was because he never forgot God's promise so long ago: the seed of the woman would crush his head. Maybe that is why he tried to kill them so many times in history.

His lust for human blood was satisfied daily as he used the Egyptians to torture the Hebrews. He desperately hated that particular breed of human more than the others.

We knew why. He could not get their souls, and he could not wipe them out. In spite of possessing the souls of all of the other people on Earth, Satan was still not satisfied, and he obsessed about the Hebrews. Of course, no one would admit it, but the demons just did not get it. Hebrews were simply not worth it.

It had to be that Satan was still fixated on God's promise to Abraham about his descendants being more numerous than the sand and the stars and all that nonsense. Maybe it wasn't nonsense at the time, but it certainly looked that way now. There was no possibility these pitiful slaves could resurrect their race to fulfill the promise God had given to Abraham. That deal was dead. No one talked about it anymore.

It wasn't hard for him to cause a great lust for the blood of babies to sweep the land. People, who normally would never have considered doing such a thing, reported the births of Hebrew boys and then assisted in their destruction.

"It's for the common good," they would say to one another. "Better to die as an infant than to grow up in slavery and unwanted." They would nod and agree that if it were the law, it must be right.

I had no expectations that things were going to change for Earth. I wondered if God might be considering conceding defeat and getting on with His next project. I was thinking that very thing the morning I was at my post to watch the Nile. The Egyptians worshiped the

Nile, so Satan wanted to be sure we always had some sort of disturbance going to keep their attention.

"Watch and report," the dispatching demon said to me every day. The extent of my worth to Satan could be summed up in those words. Never mind there had been nothing to report for years. I wasn't given access to the inner sanctum for any other reason than to report. I wondered if Satan would recognize me if I were to show up with any news.

The killing of the babies was certainly not news anymore. You may think the massacre would have been so awful no one could ever become used to it. You only think that way because you are human and don't understand demonic capacity for evil. Another problem is with how you're made. The painful, emotional suffering you experience when you see death, injustice, and mindless violence against those whom you consider innocent is incomprehensible to a demon. Why should anyone care what someone else suffers? Demons cannot relate to such silly sentimentality. I watched so many babies drown that I had long since lost interest and track of the numbers. It was always the same. Screaming women, screaming babies—after a while, they all ran together.

Now that I think of it, maybe that was the reason she caught my attention. The woman was not screaming, and neither was the baby she put in the basket. She was a Hebrew, no question about that. Her clothing gave her away. The baby had to be a boy, otherwise why would she be doing such an odd thing? She had probably been able to hide him for a few weeks, but now he was too big.

Although I was under orders to report the slightest variation in the Hebrews' behavior, I considered letting the whole thing slide. It didn't seem worth my effort. Why not let her try some feeble attempt to save her baby? In the end, her plan could not work because someone was sure to find the basket and turn the baby in for a bounty. Why should I get involved in a situation that was likely to resolve itself in a matter of hours? I'm certain I would have let the whole thing pass if I had not seen the baby's face.

Humans call a person's eyes the window to the soul through which one can look and see the essence of the individual. Big deal. Demons can do the same thing. In fact, they are better at it than people. They not only see, but they can also read the soul. How do you think Satan knows who the easy marks are? He sees the soul and all of its memories, scars, and weaknesses when he looks into the eyes of humans, and he always takes the path of least resistance. After all, if one is in the business of stealing souls, it helps to know what brand of deception is going to work best.

I knew something was different when I looked into this baby's eyes and could not read his soul. It was hidden from me. What I did see scared me. I had seen it only two other times in the hundreds of years and the millions of people who had passed upon Earth. I saw it in Noah, I saw it in Abraham, and now I saw it again in the eyes of this baby. No, it was not the human soul I saw in his eyes. It was the soul of God looking back at me. I could not believe He was going to try it again, but I was convinced He was. God was launching one more attempt to save the souls of the pitiful children of Abraham.

I made mental notes as his mother placed the baby in the basket among the reeds along the bank of the Nile. His sister stood at a distance to see what would happen to him.

It wasn't long before Pharaoh's daughter went to the Nile to bathe as she did every day. Her attendants were walking along the riverbank when one saw the basket among the reeds.

"My lady," she cried. "Look, it's a basket. Shall I bring it to you?"

"Bring it," answered Pharaoh's daughter. She opened it and saw the baby. He was crying, and she felt sorry for him.

"This is one of the Hebrew babies," she said. "Where did he come from?"

As I could have guessed, the baby's sister popped out of the papyrus grass right on cue.

"Shall I go and get one of the Hebrew women to nurse the baby?" she asked, as if one might be lingering around the next bush.

"Yes, go," Pharaoh's daughter answered.

So the girl went and got the baby's mother. Pharaoh's daughter said to her, "Take this baby and nurse him for me, and I will pay you."

Now I ask you, wouldn't you think these girls might have thought this was a little too convenient? Didn't they think something strange might be going on?

Handing the baby to his mother, Pharaoh's daughter said, "His name will be Moses because I drew him out of the water."

I leaned in a bit more to take another look at the baby's face when I realized he was looking back, and he saw me. It was not possible, but across time and space, he saw me. Then he laughed. I lurched backwards, stepped on my left wing, and fell over myself trying to get away. I struggled to hurry but I couldn't get traction. I ran, I stumbled, cracked my hoof when I fell, hopped a ways on the other one, and finally got altitude.

A million questions flooded my mind. "God, where have You been for four hundred years? What makes You show up now? What are You thinking? If it's the humans You want, You've waited way too long. They are not the way You remember them. Have You seen them lately? They won't know who You are. How could the baby see me?"

I flew with all of my might to the deepest part of second heaven, where Satan reveled on his throne, but I was stopped at the entrance by his henchmen. The ranks of demons had become so defined by now that only those of high authority—the princes, powers, and thrones—could directly access Satan. I was still just a watcher. It had been a long time since anything worth reporting had occurred, so I no longer had credentials to enter in to bring news.

"I must get in," I screamed at the guarding demons.

"What do you want?"

"I know you," the other guard interjected. "You were always the troublemaker."

"I must tell him. It is important. Please, get out of my way."

I tried to rush past them, which was extraordinarily poor judgment on my part. They lashed out at me and sent me tumbling tail over claw into the wall.

"Tell him that I'm here. He will want to see me," I whimpered to them as I picked myself up. "It will be your head next if he finds that you kept this news from him."

They whispered together, and one of them went in to where the prince of darkness hid himself. In a moment the guard reemerged from the inner chambers and snarled at me.

"He doesn't want to see you. He said you are to give me your information, and I will relay the message."

In one way I was glad to let someone else give the message and let him face the wrath that would spew from Satan when he heard it. In another way, I wished

I could see the prince's contorted face for myself when he finally realized that what I had warned him about for eons was about to land on his doorstep. I thought about asking the guards to be sure Satan knew it was me who had predicted this would happen, but my good sense returned before I got the words out.

I pulled myself up and said the words that would soon enough turn his kingdom upside down.

"Tell him," I whispered, "the deliverer is coming."

CHAPTER 27

I T DIDN'T TAKE long, and it was as bad as I guessed. The gates of the inner sanctum flung open with such force that the walls on which they were hinged cracked from the weight of Satan's appearance. I had not seen him personally for quite a long time and he seemed much worse than I remembered, if you can imagine that.

"You're looking somewhat well, sir; interesting, really," I babbled, trying to figure out what was different about him. He did not acknowledge my greeting but slapped me aside and then stepped on my tail as he stomped to the edge of second heaven. I should not have said "somewhat."

At first, he did nothing. I suppose "nothing" is subject to local interpretation. In the realm of darkness, it was nothing, but to humans it might have been quite something. He stood (levitated in place is more accurate) looking back and forth with hideous eyes at who knows what, and all the while breathing sulfa and fire into the nothingness surrounding his domain. Then he began to accuse God and demand that He appear.

"Bad move, very bad move," I muttered to the guards. "What if He should actually show up here?" I could see the guards themselves were getting the jitters at the thought. I folded my wings over my eyes and hid in the corner.

"Will You never be done with them?" Satan bellowed toward the throne room of God. "What are they that You waste Your time on them? Why are they so important to You? Deal with it. They are mine, and You cannot have them back!"

I wondered if I should point out to him that, technically, the Hebrews were not his. He did not own their souls. It was the Egyptians he owned, who in turn owned the slaves. "A minor point to be sure," I was about to say, "but an important one in a court of law." Satan's snarl and low guttural growls came from somewhere deep within him.

"Maybe not." I put my head back down. He was in no mood to discuss the fine print.

In complete frustration at the silence from third heaven, Satan lurched madly into the atmosphere, chasing something that was not there. Then he crashed back onto the ledge from where he assaulted the character of God.

I stayed cowered in the corner, completely terrorized by his words. I looked at the guards who were glaring at me as if Satan's meltdown was somehow my fault. Why one of them didn't at least try to shut him up, I do not know. They knew as well as I did that Satan's ranting against the Most High God put us all at risk. There was a limit, a point, something coming one day that would mark the end of God's tolerance for this lunatic angel. None of us dared say it, but we knew it. Someday, at some time, God will have had enough. When we did not expect it, there would be a "suddenly" with God. I gasped for breath just thinking about it.

A "suddenly" of God is the thing nightmares are made of in the demonic realm. Suddenly, He would act. And when He did, it would be the certain end of this maniac and the end of us. Perhaps this was the day. I was shaking so hard that my scales began to peel off.

Satan continued, and it got worse.

"Go away, God. Go far away. Nobody remembers You here. Give them up. Find another hobby. Cut Your losses. You are not wanted. Your creation has turned against You. They worship *me*. I will kill them before I see them turn back to You. I will die before I allow them to escape."

Oh, how I wished he had not said that. "If the guards would not do something, maybe I should try," I said in my head. "We are all going to die anyway."

If socks had existed, and if I could have found one, I am sure I would have tried to stuff it in his mouth. Maybe

Satan did not fear Tartaroo, the deepest part of hell reserved for the rebellious angels, but the rest of us did. I could see the demon guards were traumatized at this tirade as they shrunk back into the darkness, as if they could hide there. They were as frightened as I was at the hysteria and rage Satan was railing at the Creator of the universe.

"You think You can save them?" Satan bellowed. "Go ahead. Try to snatch them out of my hands. But it will cost You, God. Oh, it will cost You more than You are willing to pay."

Satan rolled in laughter at his threat against the Almighty, as if he had caught God in some terrible joke only they knew. His countenance changed again, and with yellow, hideous eyes, he roared then bleated as if he were some tortured animal. Next, he began frothing from his mouth and spinning on the floor like a captured tornado. He was completely mad; there was no other way to describe it.

Then as if nothing had happened at all, everything was still. I raised my head to see the guards peering out from the cave where they had sought refuge. A dreadful and dark silence cloaked us as Satan, having worn himself out from his fit, lay in a throbbing heap hanging over the edge of second heaven.

"Answer me, God," he moaned into the darkness as he settled into a motionless trance.

God, of course, said nothing.

CHAPTER 28

As SHE HAD done for several days, Samantha waited for the phone to ring. How many weeks had it been? She read and reread the translated scrolls so many times that she could recite much of the text from memory. The hardest part was telling no one what she had. But how could she when she didn't know herself?

She had no choice but to wait. The mysterious Wonk Eman, the man without a phone number or address, would have to call her. Where was he? He had seemed so anxious to have the scrolls translated, and now he had disappeared. Nothing added up.

She answered the phone before it could ring a second time.

"Dr. Yale?" asked the voice she recognized as the strange man who had visited her so many weeks before.

"Wonk," she tried to sound calm. "Where have you been?"

"Did you translate the scrolls?"

"Yes, I did. We must talk. When can you come here?"

"I can't come. It's not safe."

"Not safe? What are you afraid of?"

He did not respond. Only the sound of his breathing assured her he had not hung up. At last he spoke.

"Someone else may try to contact you. It's desperately important that you not mention me or the scrolls."

"Who are you talking about?"

Silence.

"Wonk?" Fearing he had hung up, Samantha said, "Are you still there?"

"Yes."

"Why are you afraid?"

Wonk barely whispered, "His plan worked; he survived the flood."

Her mind raced through its stored memory of the scrolls' text to figure out who he was talking about. No one survived the flood except for Noah and his family. Suddenly she remembered.

"You don't mean Og, the Nephilim king? That's impossible."

"I'm sorry, Dr Yale. I've said too much."

"What do you expect me to do with the translation?" Her exasperation was beginning to come through her voice.

"Where are the scrolls?" he continued.

"They're safe, I assure you. I put them in my personal safe. No one has the combination besides me. You didn't answer my question."

"Yes, I know. You want to know what to do with the translation." He repeated her words back to her as if buying time to consider his response.

"Wonk, you said you knew what the scrolls contained. Is that true?"

Haltingly, "Yes."

"I don't see how that's possible. I know every person on the planet who can read cuneiform. You are not among them. Tell me what this is all about."

"It's about redemption, Dr. Yale."

"Whose? Yours or mine?"

He did not answer.

"Do you expect me to publish what I've found? Send it for peer review? What?" Suddenly exhausted, she lowered her head into one hand as she held the phone to her ear with the other.

"Not yet, Dr. Yale." His voice had a tone of concern. "Promise me you won't tell anyone yet. You don't have the whole story."

"What do you mean by that?" She was alert again.

"There are more scrolls."

"Where? How many?"

"Wait for them." He hung up.

Holding the silent phone to her ear for another moment, Samantha finally leaned back in her comfortable office chair. After several minutes, she rose and walked to her window. The sun was setting, and the Dome of the Rock shone brilliantly with the last rays of another day.

THE DELIVERER

LINDA RIOS BROOK

REALMS
A STRANG COMPANY

Children's Bible-story books are a dime a dozen. But how about adult Bible-story books? Few and far between? No longer! Linda Rios Brook tells Bible stories like I've never heard before—and I have four graduate degrees in religion! *The Deliverer* is an intriguing and fascinating insider's view of the stories of Moses and Joshua. Trust me; this is top-drawer literature. It may be fiction, but Linda's sparkling imagination probably comes closer to the real facts than you or I have ever imagined. You'll love this book!

—C. Peter Wagner

Chancellor, Wagner Leadership Institute

CHAPTER 1

S AVE ME, SAMANTHA. I didn't mean to do it."

The disembodied spirit called out to her, begging her for help. She blinked hard and peered into what seemed like an endless sea of putrid fog.

The eerie voice cried out again.

This time she had to find him. If this was a prank, it had to stop. If it wasn't, well, she was less sure what she would do if it turned out to be real.

"Stay where you are," she cried. "Don't run away again." Her voice shook with fear.

"You know I'm innocent, Samantha. I don't deserve to be in hell. Hurry! You must help me while there's still time."

Her heart pounded so hard it seemed to catch in her throat and she couldn't breathe. Fear welled up within her. But fear of what or whom?

It didn't matter; she must pursue the desperate cries for help.

The ghostly voice cried out in anguish again as she groped her way through the gloomy maze that she already knew led to nowhere. She'd been this far before. It was always the same: a mournful voice pleading for her help, and each time the voice faded before she could reach its source. This time she wouldn't stop until she found the one calling out to her.

The foul-smelling fog thickened and concealed the path beneath her feet, and like the times before, she knew she was descending lower and lower with each erratic step forward. How far did she dare to go? She opened her mouth to call out, but her own voice failed her. An invisible hand tightened around her throat, holding her words captive.

This isn't real. I won't be stopped by something that isn't real. I must keep going.

"Where are you?" she screamed, surprised with the force of the words as they broke free.

Stumbling on through a darkness that grew denser with every step, a cold, slithering tentacle tried to wrap itself around her feet. She screamed again, kicked it away, and ran faster.

"Who…who are you?" Her breathing was becoming more labored. "How can I help you if I can't see you?" Her voice was raspy, and her throat hurt. The thickening haze was hot, and a nauseating odor assaulted her nasal passages. She paused and gagged.

"Pray for me, Samantha." The voice drifted farther away.

Gasping for clean air but finding none, she wiped her mouth on her sleeve and pushed onward toward the black hole that swallowed every glimmer of light. How much deeper could she go? What if she couldn't find her way back? She swallowed her terror and pressed downward into the darkness. He must not get away again.

"Wait!" Her throat was tightening, and her cries faded into hoarse whispers. "I'll pray for you. I'll find a way." Desperation percolated through her body as she lunged forward, her arms grabbing for someone who wasn't there.

"Stop running," she pleaded, her words barely audible. "How can I pray for you? I don't know your name."

The slithering tentacle returned and tripped her. She gasped and fell to her hands and knees on a rippled surface that had once been a river of molten lava. It had cooled and hardened but was still active below the thin crust. The steam continued to rise from beneath, and it burned her hands as she struggled to stand.

It was becoming impossible to see. Disoriented from the fall and fearful of careening into an abyss, she spun in circles, unsure of which way to go. A night bird flew near her head, pulling out strands of hair and mocking her as it sped away.

"Run away, Samantha. Run away while you still can."

"Stop it! Leave me alone!" She tried to cover her hair with her blistered hands.

"Pray for me, Samantha. Pray before it's too late." The voice faded even more.

"Wait! I don't know your name." Her desperation gave way to panic as if she were about to fail a critical mission. "Why won't you tell me your name?"

"Pray for yourself, Samantha."

"Please, don't go."

"Good-bye, Samantha."

She dropped to her knees, wailed in defeat, and sobbed.

A terrified scream.

A ringing telephone.

Samantha wasn't sure whether her own cry or the ringing BlackBerry had startled her awake, but she bolted upright, escaping the nightmare that had plagued her for weeks.

The cell phone rang again.

Still groggy, she blinked hard, sat up straight, and glanced about the room, trying to remember where she was. She rubbed her eyes and blinked again. Of course she was in her office at the University of Jerusalem. Alone.

The phone was still ringing amid the stacks of paper on her desk.

"Don't hang up." Her hands trembled as she groped for it, knocking over a cup of forgotten tea from the day before. "Just don't hang up."

Still disoriented, she fumbled with the BlackBerry as she pushed a strand of hair away from her ear with one hand.

"Yes, hello," she managed.

"Dr. Yale?" The unsteady voice on the phone was unmistakable.

Samantha Yale slumped down behind her antique desk, ignoring the spilled tea dripping onto the floor. Carefully, she cupped the telephone with both hands, afraid she might drop it and lose the connection she had been anxiously awaiting. She breathed in deeply and measured her words lest she startle her nervous caller.

"Yes, this is Samantha Yale."

"Dr. Yale, it's…"

"Yes, Wonk, I know who you are. Where are you?"

Silence.

It had been six months since the mysterious Wonk Eman, the nervous little man with no address, no telephone number, and no e-mail, had visited her and delivered the ancient scrolls to her office. His silence told her she was moving too fast. She took a deep breath, slumped back in her chair, and tried again.

"All right. You don't have to tell me where you are. Are you safe?"

"Why do you ask that?"

Before she could answer, he blurted out, "Am I in danger? I'll call back."

"Stop it, Wonk." She took another deep breath and lowered her voice. "You're in no danger."

"Then why did you ask me if I was safe?"

"No reason." She rose from her desk and walked over to the window where the Dome of the Rock could be seen in the distance against the blue Jerusalem skyline. Maybe a shift in position would make her sound less tense. "It's just that when we last talked, you were concerned about safety. Remember? You were worried someone else might try to contact me about the scrolls."

"Has anyone contacted you?"

"No, no one at all." She heard him slowly exhale.

"Have you told anyone else?"

"No one, just as you directed me."

She restrained herself from asking questions too soon. Slowly she began a silent count from one to ten. If he didn't speak again in ten seconds, she would prompt him. She only got to five.

"I have more scrolls."

"Good. When will you bring them to me?"

Another of his interminable pauses. She ran her fingers through her rumpled hair and tried to control her exasperation at how long it took him to say anything. Her ring caught the edge of the newly formed scab just above her right ear. A drop of blood smeared on her fingertip. *Now what have I done?* She turned to the wall mirror to examine the injury but gave up when she couldn't make her eyes shift far enough to see it. *OK, that's long enough.*

"Wonk?" she said, attempting to prod him back into the conversation.

"Yes. How long will it take you to translate them?" Impatience, anxiety, or both had crept into his voice.

"You know that's almost impossible to say. It's a difficult task to translate cuneiform."

"But you're an expert."

"Even for an expert, it requires a thought-for-thought translation, as opposed to a word-for-word technique. Besides, you haven't told me how many more scrolls you have."

He ignored the bait.

"Tomorrow, then," he said.

"Will you bring them yourself?"

A thud told her he had dropped the phone. She could hear him scrambling to retrieve it.

"Hello?" His fumbling sent piercing beeps into her ear. "Sorry. No, no, I...very risky...not wise at all." His voice had become shriller as he floundered to answer her question.

"That's OK." *Take a breath.* "Don't worry." *Pause; let him calm down.* "How will they be delivered?"

"By messenger; same as before. Good-bye, Dr. Yale."

"Wait—" She stopped him before he could hang up. Did she dare go any further? He was so high-strung he might flee at the slightest provocation. Maybe she should wait until she had the scrolls safely in her possession. Too late. She had to say something.

"Can I ask you something else?"

"What is it, Dr. Yale?"

"When we last talked..." She hesitated. *Do I really want to go down this road?*

"Dr. Yale?"

"Yes, sorry. When you were in my office and we talked about the Torah and other relics of antiquity, you brought up Noah's ark. Do you remember the conversation?"

"Yes."

"You were concerned about someone who might have survived Noah's flood—besides Noah's family."

"Og," he whispered.

"Yes, that's it. Og, the Nephilim king." She waited for his reaction.

There was none. She ran her fingers through her hair again. Afraid he might hang up, she preempted her ten-second rule and pressed in.

"What did you mean?"

"Why do you want to know?"

"No reason except it seemed important to you. Suppose such a thing had actually happened. Why would the idea distress you so?"

Silence.

I shouldn't have said "distress."

"Then he has contacted you." His voice *was* distressed. "You said no one..."

"What? No, of course not. Don't be ridiculous."

Seeing her reflection in the mirror on the wall, she began a silent exchange with herself.

You're having a conversation with a deeply disturbed man about someone who's been dead for five thousand years—if he ever existed at all. No wonder you can't sleep. Wonk doesn't seem capable of playing mind games, but what else can he be doing?

"I was only curious to know what you meant," she continued gently. "It's hard to understand why you would care about something that might have happened so long ago."

Silence.

One second, two seconds, three...

"He must not get the scrolls, Dr. Yale. You must promise me that will not happen. You have no idea the consequences if..."

"No, it's OK. I'm sure I can keep them safe." She glanced at her reflection again to see if she looked sincere.

"Tomorrow, Dr. Yale. Wait for them. Remember your promise." The dial tone signaled the end of the conversation.

Samantha clicked the END button on her phone, sighed with relief that the conversation was over, and sat down on the window seat as she lingered at her personal portal of the world.

"Sign here, Dr. Yale." The burly man in the brown delivery uniform handed her the electronic notebook to register her signature as the authorized recipient of a carefully packed crate. She scrawled her name in silence, not wanting to engage him in any conversation that might delay his leaving. The man was barely out the door before she found a sturdy letter opener in the desk drawer and began prying open the container. At last the lid slid off, and Styrofoam peanuts went flying as her hands carefully reached inside the box. Just as she had done with the first scrolls, she gently removed each of the twelve and laid them out in what she guessed would be a somewhat chronological order on her conference table. Her only hope was that Wonk, or whoever packed them, had some appreciation for sequence.

Selecting the first scroll, she carried it to her desk and gently unrolled it. To an untrained eye it would have looked exactly like any one of the others she had already examined and locked away. Only an expert would recognize the difference in the markings of the ancient written language of the Phoenicians, cuneiform, which predated hieroglyphics by who knew how many centuries.

"I wish I knew what this material is," Samantha said, talking to herself as she fingered the scroll kept her from rushing through the delicate process.

With magnifying glass in hand, she peered intently at the first line.

"Are you in there?" She spoke aloud as if the scroll was listening. "A fallen angel with no name; what do you want to tell me? How can I help you if I don't know your name?"

CHAPTER 2

S AMANTHA GLANCED AT the clock to make note of the time. Reaching for her pen, she took a slow, deep breath and began the meticulous translation of each symbol.

"Talk to me," she whispered to the scroll.

"Come with me, Samantha," the voice inside her head answered. "This is how it was."

If he had remembered the first thing about God, Satan could have expected this to happen eventually. God would not leave the children of Abraham in slavery forever. Granted, after four hundred thirty years of silence, a casual observer might wonder if God had finally cut His losses with the Hebrews and gone on to other things, but a person who really knew God would never indulge such a thought. A person who truly knew God, as Satan most certainly had at one point, would never come to such a conclusion no matter how bad the situation looked or how long it might take to fix it.

God promised the Hebrews that He would send a deliverer. It was certain to happen one day, and then one day it did. As soon as I knew the expected one was on the earth, I flew directly to Satan's lair to let him know. Satan ran right over the top of me as he raced to the edge of the second heaven and began yelling at God.

"Go away, God. Go far away. Nobody remembers You here. Give them up. Find another hobby. Cut Your losses. You are not wanted. Your creation has turned against You. They worship *me*. I will kill them before I see them turn back to You. I will die before I allow them to escape."

Those were his exact words as he stood on the rim and berated God. Then it got worse.

"You think You can save them?" Satan bellowed. "Go ahead. Try to snatch them out of my hands. But it will cost You, God. Oh, it will cost You more than You are willing to pay."

Satan rolled in laughter at his threat against the Almighty, as if he had caught God in some terrible joke only they knew. His countenance changed again, and with yellow, hideous eyes, he roared and then bleated as if he were some tortured animal. Next, he began frothing from his mouth and spinning on the floor like a captured tornado. He was completely mad; there was no other way to describe it. At last he collapsed in a heap; it was finally over.

It took awhile, but Satan eventually pulled himself together and made his way back to his den. The demons stepped aside, avoiding eye contact with him and pretending not to have noticed the public meltdown of their ruler. I tried to slip out quietly without being seen by His Horribleness. I hoped I could avoid the badgering I knew Satan would assail against me because of this turn of events. I had nothing to do with the arrival of the deliverer, and the last thing I wanted was to be the depository for his anger at God. So, of course, that's the very first thing that happened.

"Come with me," Satan ordered.

I braced for a tongue-lashing and followed him into his dark abode. He sat down on his granite throne, and I knelt down before him. For what seemed a long time, he said nothing at all. His silence was almost harder to bear than his tantrums. I didn't dare look up at him. I thought about the news I'd delivered and wondered whether there might have been some other way to have done it, a way that would not have triggered the rage Satan had unleashed against God. I couldn't think of any. It was what it was. The deliverer was now on the earth. I didn't cause it, but I had to tell it. That was my job, to watch and report. Finally he spoke.

"Does he have a name?"

"Yes, sir. His name is Moses."

"How many soldiers has he got?"

I didn't answer because I had no idea why he was asking me about soldiers. I dared not ask for clarity because doing so might imply that his question was vague, and Satan's interrogation skills were not subject to criticism. I continued to kneel before him, trying to figure out what he meant. When he rightly discerned I didn't have a clue what he was talking about, he grabbed me by the wing and stood me upright before him.

"The deliverer, idiot," he said as he thumped me on the head. "How many men does Moses have in his army?" He let go of my wing and then turned away, which gave me a moment to think.

"Army?" What can he mean? I'm sure I didn't I say anything about an army. I could feel Satan losing patience with my

inability to follow this line of questioning, so I answered the best I could.

"If you mean an army in the conventional sense, sir, he doesn't have an army per se."

Satan turned back and looked at me as if I had spoken some incredulous thing.

"No army?"

"No, sir."

"No soldiers at all? Don't lie to me."

"No, sir, I would never dare lie."

"How does he expect to come against the Egyptians without a militia? Does he think he can simply saunter into Pharaoh's court and walk out with the slaves without a fight?"

I felt faint when I realized that in giving my report, I'd left out an important detail.

"Oh, I see what you're asking, terrible one. My fault entirely; of course you'd expect the deliverer of the Hebrews to be a man, a mighty warrior. Why would you assume anything else?"

I might have gone on groveling all afternoon had Satan not leaned into my face and snarled, "I didn't assume anything. You said the deliverer had come. Are you tracking with me on this?"

I nodded but didn't make a sound.

"Then he must be a man. God has obligated Himself to work through humans."

"Yes, sir. I mean no, of course not. But I can see how you might think that. I should have been clearer. Of course he's a man—just not quite yet. But one day soon. You know how fast they grow." I continued to prattle on when Satan grabbed me by the tail and jerked me to attention.

"Are you anywhere close to making a point? If he's not a man, what is he?"

"Well, right now, to be completely accurate, he's a baby, sir. A little one about this long." I held my claws about two feet apart to show him. "Not very big at all. Like I said, he will grow into a man, but…" Satan cut me off with another jerk on my tail.

"You dared waste my time over a Hebrew baby? Not even a grown man?" He thumped me on the head again. "What makes you think he's the deliverer? Who told you?"

"It was like this, sir…"

Satan cut me off and began mocking me by clapping his claws together as if suddenly figuring it all out.

"Let me guess. God must have taken you into His confidence."

I was about to tell him about the baby's eyes but knew it would be a waste of time.

"I'm quite sure of my facts, my lord. There's no doubt about who he is. He's the only male baby to have survived the Egyptians' sword. He floated right down the Nile in that wicker basket, slick as you please, no leaks, no alligators, no capsizing, right under the noses of the Egyptian soldiers and right into Pharaoh's backyard. An escape like that has the fingerprints of God all over it."

Satan had a puzzled look on his face as if I had said something baffling.

"What did you say? What do you mean he went right into Pharaoh's backyard?"

"That's just how it was, sir. Pharaoh's daughter and all her girlfriends were down there splashing around in the river when this baby in a basket came floating by. You know how women are, sir. They can't resist a baby, no matter what kind of baby it is. Pharaoh's daughter laid claim to him immediately. Gave him a name right away. Instant motherhood."

"She will kill him when she figures out he's a Hebrew."

"No, I'm quite sure she plans to keep him. She's already found a nanny for him. Interesting how that happened. She sent someone to find a woman to nurse him, and wouldn't you know, the friend came back with the baby's very own mother in tow. What are the odds of that? Of course, the girls didn't know I was watching. I saw the whole thing."

By now some of the other demons had decided it was safe to come in to see what was going on. They'd heard most of my explanation. Bezel spoke first.

"Now that we know where he is, we can kill him. End of problem."

"Oh, really? You'll kill him? Just like that, will you?" Satan's sarcasm dripped with hostility as he mocked Bezel's solution. "Then why didn't you kill him when you had him? You let him get away. Wasn't I clear enough? Watch the Hebrew babies and make sure the Egyptians kill the boys. Why do I have to do everything myself?"

Satan threw his arms up in disgust while Bezel kept his head down and his mouth shut, but, oh, I knew what he wished he had the nerve to say. Satan barely took a breath before continuing his tirade.

"Your dereliction in duty has allowed things to become much more complicated. If Pharaoh's daughter has him, we won't find any Egyptian soldier brave enough to touch him."

We hadn't been dismissed, so we stood in place, avoiding eye contact and waiting to see if Satan had any plans as to what he would do with this turn of events. None of us had any ideas of our own, or if we had, we weren't about to say so. Ideas were not allowed in Satan's realm unless they were his. Finally he spoke again.

"Leave him alone." He turned to me as if daring me to say the wrong word. "You did say Pharaoh's daughter has him; you did get that part right?"

I nodded.

"Then he'll grow up in Pharaoh's court. They won't keep the nursemaid for very long. After that, they'll be careful not to let him associate with the Hebrews. They won't tell him who he is, of course. He will be raised as an Egyptian with all the wealth and religion of Egypt." Then Satan started chuckling. (Hard to imagine that, isn't it?)

"The Egyptians will do our work for us. Whatever or whoever he is now won't matter; the environment of Egypt will change him. I'm not convinced he's who you think he is, but we take no chances." He glared right at me again. "After all, why would God save him from death only to send him into

Pharaoh's court to be raised among the people who are in our camp? It's not like God to make a mistake like that. You're probably wrong about who he is."

I knew I wasn't wrong, but I also knew enough not to challenge Satan's flawed reasoning.

"Nevertheless," Satan whirled back to Bezel. "Watch him, but don't touch him. In fact, make sure he gets every indulgence in Egypt. See to it the girl spoils him. Baby him, pamper him, overprotect—keep him away from the influence of men. Make sure he's a mama's boy. If he *is* the deliverer, we can circumvent his destiny. When God calls him, he won't go. He won't leave the posh comforts of Egypt. Don't let him make any friends among the Hebrews. Visit Pharaoh's daughter in her dreams. Tell her if she lets the boy spend any time with them, the Hebrews will try to steal him away from her. Plant fear and distrust in her mind.

"And you." Satan turned back to me. "Get back out there on guard duty. If he makes any moves toward God, let me know instantly."

I went back to my perch and began my watch. Mostly I watched nothing happen for what seemed like forever. I stood guard for years, and after a while, it seemed as if Satan might have been right. Moses grew up as a brother to Ramses, Pharaoh's true son. And...oh my...yes, those boys were spoiled rotten. God never intervened as far as I could tell, and Moses never indicated any particular affinity for the Hebrews. Maybe I'd been wrong about him after all; still, I couldn't forget what I'd seen in that baby's eyes.

Then one day, something quite unexpected happened. Moses was walking along the edge of the mud pits where the Hebrews were making bricks for the new pyramid. Nearby an Egyptian soldier began savagely beating one of the Hebrew slaves for no good reason I could see. Nothing new in that; it happened all the time. But all at once, Moses was in the fight.

He caught the soldier completely off guard and killed him. Looking around to see if anyone had seen what happened (no one had except me, of course), he dragged the soldier's body behind the pits and buried it in the sand. When I say that no one saw, I mean no one of any importance. None of the Egyptians were around to see it, but wouldn't you know, the Hebrews who were working in that same pit saw the whole thing. But so what? They weren't going to tattle to anyone about a dead Egyptian; one less for them to worry about. For whatever reason Moses had done what he did, he appeared to be home free. And that is exactly what I reported to Satan.

"He knows," Satan murmured as he paced restlessly in front of his throne.

"Knows what, sir?"

"Moses knows who he is."

He seemed quite certain, which was always the case with him, so I should've known to say nothing and nod in agreement whether or not I thought he might be right. But I didn't.

"Oh, I don't think so, sir," I quipped, forgetting for a moment that no one quipped a contradiction Satan's way. I tried to explain what I meant.

"He can't know, sir. He's had no contact with the Hebrews. No close encounters of any kind—nada, zilch. Further, God hasn't yet made a move toward him. I wouldn't have missed something like that. Maybe Moses didn't like the attitude of that particular soldier. Who knows what may have motivated him to kill the Egyptian? Whatever it was, I'm quite sure it could have had nothing to do with any empathy toward the slaves."

Satan ignored my explanation. "Did anyone see him do it?"

"No one who counts. Some of the slaves saw it happen, but they're not going to tell anyone, and even if they did, who would believe them? And if someone did believe them, who would care?"

It was as if I hadn't said a thing. Satan turned from me and summoned Bezel, who was hovering outside the den listening to every word. He took Bezel by the arm and instructed him as they walked toward the door.

"Go out there and watch Moses. When he goes near the pits again, stir the Hebrews up. Cause a disturbance and see what he does."

Bezel followed me back to my perch and crowded in beside me. Together we watched the pits for several days without leaving. I tried to make small talk, but he wasn't much of a conversationalist. He seemed content to simply sit there and stare at the slaves. He was much bigger than me, and when he stretched his wings out, he knocked me right off the end. Where did he think I was supposed to sit? I was already bunched up in a knot because of his size. He never once apologized. I hoped something would happen so Bezel would go home. Finally it did.

Moses was once again walking along the rim of the pits. Bezel jumped off the perch and took off for the earth so suddenly that it flipped me right off, like what happens when a child jumps off the low end of a seesaw while someone else is on the high end. I straightened myself out and watched him hover over two of the slaves in the pit. I couldn't hear what he said, but suddenly, there they were slugging each other. Moses ran down to the edge and separated them and asked them why they were fighting. One of them began berating Moses.

"Who made you our judge when you're nothing but a murderer?"

Moses turned pale. He looked around to see if anyone had heard, and someone had. One of the Egyptian guards heard every word. At first, the guard did nothing, but then I saw Bezel whispering in his ear.

"Report it to Pharaoh; there's a reward in it for you."

The guard took off for the palace, and I followed right behind him, but Bezel got there first and seated himself on the cushion right next to Pharaoh's throne.

Pharaoh listened to the guard's report with one ear and listened to Bezel interpret it with his other ear. A fight among slaves would have been a nonevent if it hadn't been for Bezel. He told Pharaoh how Moses had found out about his heritage and was trying to start a rebellion among the slaves.

"Not only that, but look how ungrateful he is for all you've done for him, treating him like your own son."

Pharaoh was immediately offended. Offense works every time.

"Seize him," Pharaoh ordered. The palace guards took off after Moses. Bezel followed the guards, and I followed Bezel. They quickened their pace when they spotted Moses not far from the city gate. While they were still at a distance, a strange wind coming from nowhere and going nowhere begin to swirl around Moses's head.

This was trouble. I hadn't seen Him for hundreds of years, but I recognized the whirling wind that was a dead giveaway when Ruah Ha Kadosh arrived on the scene. Bad, very bad for any demon when He showed up. Seeing no convenient place to hide, I remained completely still, hoping Ruah Ha Kadosh would focus on Bezel and not notice me. His voice was unmistakable to anyone who had ever encountered Him, which Moses had not. Moses had no idea the third person of the Trinity was speaking into his mind. When he heard the words, "Flee to the desert," he was off like a flash, not giving a second thought as to who had spoken to him. He ran so fast I was sure one of the guardian angels of the earth must have been zipping him along, but I quickly realized how unnecessary such a thing would have been. Ruah Ha Kadosh had breathed on him; Moses could have outrun a team of horses on that one breath. Immediately, I flew back to Satan's den to tell him what had happened and how Moses was on the run.

I was fast but not fast enough to beat Bezel back to the lair. He sat near Satan, gloating and taking credit for running Moses out of town.

"Whether or not he was the deliverer," Bezel bragged, "he will be nothing but a bad memory in a few days."

Satan chortled, and much as I hated to agree with Bezel about anything, it looked like he was right. Moses would die in the desert, no doubt about it. The wasteland was ruthless and Moses had grown up a city boy. Out there alone with no servants to take care of him, he wouldn't stand a chance against the desert.

Even if he were able to find someone in the wilderness who might take him in, all desert people worshiped one of Satan's demon gods. They wouldn't let Moses hang around their camp unless he joined in with their worship. They'd be too afraid he'd offend one of their easily angered deities. To survive, he would have to go along to get along, if you know what I mean. Once he joined in exaltation of one of Satan's surrogates, he would have done the one thing from whence there were no do-overs with God: worship of a false deity...or real demon, same thing. Moses was toast. We didn't think about him again for forty years.

CHAPTER 3

ONE DAY, WHO knows why, Satan began to fidget. He jumped at the slightest noise and then glared at anyone he thought might have noticed. He paced back and forth near the rim of the second heaven, stopped at the edge, leaned over, sniffed the air, and paced again. We didn't know *who* he was, but he was definitely not himself, which was an improvement since himself was pretty hard to take most of the time. While the other demons pretended not to be watching Satan fidget, I used the distraction to slip away by myself to my perch.

I'd been there only a moment when I felt the air temperature change. Satan came and sat down on the other end of my perch. I tried not to hyperventilate. He'd never done such a thing before, and it made me so nervous I wasn't sure I could breathe at all.

"What's the matter with you?" he asked noticing my heaving wings.

"Nothing, sir. I wasn't expecting you, that's all."

"I sit wherever I want."

"Of course, to be sure." I tried to breathe normally.

He sat there for quite a while not saying anything, just staring at the earth, particularly the Hebrew slaves. I wondered if I should say something to try to sound empathetic, although I wasn't and didn't feel anything except stress. What does one say to an out-of-sorts ruler of iniquity? I tried out several salutations in my head.

"How is it going, sir? Can I get you anything? Can I fetch you a slave for dinner?" No, that wasn't right. I tried again.

"Oh, it's you, sir. I was just sitting here, holding my post and admiring the way you've messed up the earth again." Maybe not.

Before I could think of anything safe and clever to say, he spoke to me. Well, not *to* me exactly. It was more like *at* me, if you can picture it. He never turned his eyes toward me, just kept staring at the earth, but there was no doubt as to whether or not he was talking to me; he was. If for no other reason, it was because I was the only one there. When he spoke, I knew to listen and obey immediately, whatever he said.

"Find him."

"Right away, sir."

I was so anxious to get away from him that I jumped up, stretched my wings, and flapped off toward the earth as if I understood my assignment perfectly, when in fact, I did not. Not only did I not understand it, but also I didn't know what it was. I looked back to see if Satan was still sitting on my perch. Yep, still there. I thought about turning back to get a few more details on my mission but then changed my mind.

Best not to look tentative. I'm sure I can figure this out. I wonder who I should be looking for?

In my zeal to get away, I hadn't asked enough questions. I'd foolishly taken off unsure of where I was going or whom I was supposed to find. Now, it may seem obvious to you, a reader with the benefit of history, what "find him" meant, but try to remember that at the time, I lived under the rule and whim of a crazy person where nothing could be assumed. Besides all that, no one had said the name "Moses" in forty years. Truth be told, I'd all but forgotten about him.

I guessed I was to go to the earth because I couldn't recall he'd ever sent me anywhere else. I flew in that direction, but when it came time to veer right, I got worried I might be wrong.

Maybe whoever he wants me to find isn't even on the earth. What if he meant for me to find another demon who was somewhere else in the second heaven? I could end up looking silly. No way around it; I had to go back for clarification.

I was halfway back to ask Satan exactly who it was he wanted me to find, but I changed my mind in mid flap. I knew he wouldn't be civil about it. More than likely he would get mad and tell me to figure it out. So I banked left and resumed my original flight plan.

But since I don't know who I'm looking for, how will I know if I find him? What did Satan tell me to do with him if I do find whoever it is? I convinced myself I really *had* to go back and get better instructions, so I made a U-turn and headed toward my perch where Satan waited.

When I saw his face, I changed my mind again. *No, better not. He's in no mood for questions.*

I made another wide turn, realizing I had now flown in a complete circle. A crowd of demons had gathered near Satan and were making bets as to which way I would go next. Of course, that made me all the more nervous, so I just kept flying in a circle, trying to decide what to do.

Eventually, Satan ceased to be entertained by my predicament and dispatched one of the other demons who caught me by the tail as I flew past and then dragged me back to His Awfulness. The next thing I knew, it was Satan who was holding me by the tail, seething into my upside down face.

"I'm sorry. I didn't know who I was to find," I whimpered.

"Why do I let you live?" he snarled at me.

I know a rhetorical question when I hear one, so I didn't answer, but, oh, how I would have liked to tell him what I thought about the way he ran things. Just once I wished I could stand up to him. I wished anybody would, but nobody dared. He slammed me to the floor and continued berating me, belittling every single thing I'd ever done as if I'd never once gotten anything right. I wanted to remind him how over the centuries of human history I had an exceptional track record for being right. Not that he would have cared anyway.

"Find Moses, you idiot," he steamed. "Who else did your pitiful mind think I meant? He's living in the desert with the Midianites."

"Oh, I really doubt that, sir," my mouth uttered before my brain engaged. "Not that you could be wrong, you understand, but it's quite unlikely Moses would still be alive after forty years or we would have surely heard something from him by now. And as for living with the Midianites? Highly doubtful, if you please, sir. They don't like Egyptians, and they don't like Hebrews, so there you go. Whoever Moses thought he was or claimed to be, it wouldn't matter. No one of either race could have lasted long with the Midianites."

It was Tammuz who hissed at me and said, "If you had been doing your job, imbecile, you would know Moses is married to Zipporah, the daughter of a Midianite priest."

How could I have missed such a thing? Tammuz interacted on a regular basis with the territorial principalities over Midian, and if something strange was going on in their territory, they would be sure to know. One of those demons must have come across Moses somewhere in the desert lands and reported it to Tammuz. I needed to think of something fast.

"But what of it?" I blurted out as if Tammuz's news flash were no news at all. "If Moses married the daughter of a Midianite priest, there must have been a religious ceremony of some kind."

"And so?" Satan asked.

"And so it could not have been kosher, so to speak. Moses would be in violation of the no-god-but-Yahweh rule or at least complicit in the goings-on."

They all looked at me as if I hadn't finished a sentence, so I knew they hadn't put the obvious two and two together.

"If Moses had ritual with another god," I spoke slowly so they'd understand, "it means he abdicated, flunked the test, jumped the fence, whatever you want to call it. He's forfeited his opportunity to be the deliverer."

It was as if I hadn't said a word.

Once Satan made up his mind about something, he wouldn't change it regardless of evidence to the contrary or even if it was in his own interest to do so. Why? you ask. Well, let me just tell you it wasn't because he was always right or even usually right. The extraordinarily stupid idea of rebelling against God to start with and getting all of us tossed out of paradise into the ghetto of the second heaven ought to be proof enough of that.

No, the reason Satan never changed his mind was because God never changed His. Never mind the simple fact that God was always right, always thinking ahead, always moving the earth forward through time (though toward what I do not know), while Satan was rarely right. He spent most of his time wasting everyone else's and overreacting to the last thing that happened. This whole manhunt was a case in point. But nothing would do except for me to launch out on a pointless search for Moses.

"And if I find him?"

Satan glared, and I tried again. "*When* I find him"—*that was better*—"then what?" Which was a very good question seeing as how I couldn't do anything *with* him or *to* him. I was a watcher, end of function.

"Watch him," Tammuz growled.

"Watch him do what? Count goats?" I muttered under my breath. I'd stalled as long as I could, so I set my course and started winging it toward the desert.

You might wonder how I could have been so sure of myself when I said Moses was no longer a threat to Satan because he'd flunked the test for being the deliverer. The truth is I took a chance and lied to Satan; I thought just the opposite of what I said. Oh, I know I took a big risk because I'm not a convincing liar and Satan would devour me if he caught me lying to him, but I was highly motivated.

The truth is I disparaged the idea to Satan that Moses was still in the running to be the deliverer because I desperately did *not* want to go to the desert to look for him. Nobody did. The desert was the training ground for hell. There's no other way to describe it. The worst of our kind inhabited the hot, arid sands of the wasteland. The desert devils weren't anything like the fat and happy—at least by comparison—demons in Egypt who indulged on the spoils of the land.

No, not at all. The desert rulers were deprived of any of the booty of the earth. Although they were ravenous to gratify their demonic nature on human flesh, like all the rest of the demons, they were assigned, or sentenced, to an empty place with few humans to hunt. Their prey was limited to unsavory life forms that lived under rocks or deep in the scorching sand. If I was discovered soloing it in their territory, there would be a food fight, and I would be the food they were fighting over. Never mind that I was on a mission from Satan. No one would have bothered to ask why I was in the neighborhood.

So try to imagine my relief when I flew deep into the wilderness only to find no one at home. The spiritual realm was silent. It wasn't just a case of no demonic chatter going on; it was deadly silent. It was empty. The territorial rulers were out of town, gone, completely gone. There were no telltale signs of demonic activity or presence. How could I be sure? Sometimes you know what *is* by what is *not*.

What *was not* was the unmistakable odor that emanates from demons. Most humans still haven't learned how to interpret smell. When demons are anywhere about, the air smells bad because they smell bad. The worse they are, the worse they smell. One time in Egypt during a demonic orgy, the odor got so bad I almost threw up. When I couldn't stand it anymore, I took off for one of the gardens by the Nile and plopped myself right down in a patch of pansies. I breathed in the fragrance of flowers until I was tipsy. I didn't even bother to exhale.

Unless you have personally wallowed in a flower bed, you might not know that the perfume from flowers is an intoxicant. When the others found me, I was rocking back and forth on my tail with a snootful of pansy petals, reminiscing about the good old days before we were thrown out of heaven. Satan was in a dither because I'd left my post. He had me locked in the dungeon until the effects of the pansies wore off and then assigned me to the morning-after crew for the cleanup of the orgy. I'll spare you the details.

The only smell in the desert now was, you might say, the desert—rocks, sand, clean air, nothing else. Where were the demons? They had no place to go. Even if there had been a place to go, they would never have dared leave a whole section of ground unoccupied. There would be no excuses with Satan on that one. He was positively paranoid about unoccupied ground. If the principalities were gone, and they most definitely were, what could have happened to cause them to leave? It could only be one thing: something scarier than them. But what?

I settled down on the side of a sand dune and tried to figure out what to do next. When I heard the bleating of goats, I crawled up to the top of the dune and peered over to the other side. I didn't have to see his face to know that the man with the goats was Moses. After all those years, I still recognized his voice.

Demons brag about how they can read the human mind, an undocumented claim at best. But whether *they* can or can't, *I* can't, so I was grateful when Moses began to talk to his goats. That was the only way for me to know what was on his mind. There he stood, an old man by then, leaning on his staff and carrying on a one-sided conversation with a nanny goat. It wasn't as odd as you might think. After all, most of you humans talk to animals now and then. It doesn't seem to bother you at all that the animals never talk back.

It wasn't like that in the beginning, you know. When God first created the animals, they could speak. They chatted with Adam and Eve all the livelong day. How do you think Adam got them to line up and parade by so he could name them? He simply told them what to do. He actually made up a little song for them to sing as they marched along. Let me see if I can remember how it went. Hum along with me.

> Single file, elephant style, we went to the animal fair.
> There were lions and tigers there.
> The monkey made fun of the skunk, who sat on the
>   elephant's trunk.
> The elephant sneezed and fell to his knees and that
>   was the end of the monk, the monk, the monk.

Something like that anyway. The animals all laughed at Adam's silly song.

Not convinced about the talking animals? Have you ever wondered about why neither Adam nor Eve panicked and ran away after encountering a talking snake in Eden? They weren't the least bit surprised the serpent could talk, because in the beginning, all animals in the garden could talk. At least they could until the Fall. That knockout punch God delivered to the serpent was so powerful that the ripple effects spilled over into the whole animal kingdom, and every species lost its ability to speak the human language. I've always wondered if God really meant to do that. Anyway, now you know why all people in all cultures talk to animals, even stuffed animals. It's in that genetic code thing God put into humans. Until now, you probably never thought about how odd it really is to see a grown person talking to a dog.

Moses seemed to be looking at something over the rim of the next sand dune when he turned and asked the lead goat, "What is that?"

The goat didn't seem to know, so Moses said, "Let's go over and see this strange sight." I stayed low to the ground and followed after the last nanny, who kept turning her head and sniffing in my direction.

Moses had never seen anything like it, but I had. Well, not exactly like it. I'd never actually seen a bush burning brightly yet unconsumed by the fire, but I had witnessed enough of the creative antics of Adonai to know one when I saw it. No wonder the demons had vacated the territory. God Himself had shown up once more on the earth.

The burning spectacle was so beautiful. I was captivated myself, so I could just imagine what was going on in the mind of Moses. When the voice called out of the bush and said,

"Moses, Moses," he jumped backward with such force that half the flock panicked and headed for cover over the next hill.

The voice continued, "Do not come any closer." Judging by his trembling, I could see that going any closer was about the last thing Moses intended to do.

"Take off your sandals, for the place where you are standing is holy ground."

Moses obeyed, and the voice spoke to him again.

"I am the God of your fathers, Abraham, Isaac, and Jacob."

"I knew it," I jumped up and yelled out before I caught hold of myself. Moses didn't hear me, but the goats did, and they all began bleating like a tripped burglar alarm. If the angel of the Lord saw me, He ignored me, but just in case, I dove back to the ground and hid along with the frightened goats. Moses didn't know what was going on, so he fell to the ground also and buried his face in the sand. Whether he believed it really was God or not, it was something strange, and he was too scared to find out what.

From His long experience with His humans, God knew the goats would die of old age before Moses got it together enough to ask a few obvious questions, such as, "If You're really God, why are You pretending to be a bush?" For most people, a burning bush that wasn't burnt up would be a real conversation starter, but not for Moses, who was much more comfortable talking to goats than to humans.

Knowing He would have to make the first move, God began telling Moses what was on His mind, just as if Moses had a perfect grasp on the idea that God Almighty had dropped by.

"I have seen the misery of My people in Egypt. I have heard them crying out because of their slave drivers, and I am concerned about their suffering. So I have come down to rescue them from the hand of the Egyptians and to bring them up out of that land into a good and spacious land flowing with milk and honey."

Moses still had his head in the sand, but he pulled back slightly and opened one eye when he heard this. He didn't speak, but I knew what he was thinking.

Is this something I'm supposed to care about? I tried to help them once, and look what it got me.

"So now, go," the voice continued. "I am sending you to Pharaoh to bring My people the Israelites out of Egypt."

"You have got to be kidding, God," Moses said. No, wait. Moses didn't say that; I said that.

Moses actually said, "Who am I that I should go to Pharaoh and bring the Israelites out of Egypt?"

But it meant the same thing. As far as Moses was concerned, this was not an idea that could work at all. His window of opportunity to be a hero had long since closed, and he no longer had the desire or the will to try to open a new one.

God tried to reassure him. "I will be with you. This will be the sign to you that it is I who have sent you: when you have brought the people out of Egypt, you will worship Me on this mountain."

When I heard that, I couldn't help but feel a little bit sorry about the fate that awaited the desert demons who had abandoned their posts. They'd given it up without a fight, and now

God had it staked out as an altar to Himself. Satan would have a fit when he learned about it. Not that I would have acted differently in their circumstances. Spiritual warfare against the heavenly host is one thing, but if any one of the Trinity enters the fray, *see ya'; wouldn't want to be ya'.*

At first, Moses was tracking with me; it was all over his face that he had no appreciation for why this was a good idea. Slowly rising to his feet, he stared at the ground, shifted from one foot to another, and finally spoke to God.

"Mighty God, You know I am a murderer. My execution awaits me if I go back to Egypt."

"Those who wanted your life are now dead," God responded.

"But suppose I go to the Israelites and say to them, 'The God of your fathers has sent me to you,' and they ask me, 'What is His name?' then what shall I tell them?"

Good question; very good question, Moses.

I knew God by many names: Yahweh, Elohim, Hashem, El Shaddai, and others. His creation called His name by what it saw Him do. I wondered which of these names God would assign to Himself for the task He was proposing.

God said to Moses, "I am who I am. This is what you are to say to the Israelites: 'I AM has sent me to you.'"

Moses was still standing, but I wasn't. I was slammed to the ground by the force of God's words. I tried to get up, but I couldn't. The weight of "I AM" sat on top of me.

"Say to the Israelites, 'The God of your fathers—Abraham, Isaac, and Jacob—has sent me to you.' This is My name forever, the name by which I am to be remembered from generation to generation."

It went on like that for seven days. God would lay out the plan for Moses, and Moses would explain to God why His plan could not possibly work. Finally, God told Moses to go to the elders of Israel and tell them the cavalry was coming and Moses was leading them. Together they were to go to Pharaoh and announce the exodus of the Jews. With my face still smashed into the sand all that time and goats sniffing around my protruding backside, I found myself wondering how God thought this was going to happen.

"Surely God doesn't think Moses can just drop in unannounced on the ruler of Egypt and get past the front door. How would Moses, a goatherd, a nobody, get in front of Pharaoh?" I puzzled it for a moment.

"Of course he can," I mumbled into the sand. I tried unsuccessfully to levitate myself up out of the dirt as I answered my own question. "The old pharaoh is dead. Ramses is on the throne. He and Moses were once brothers. Of course he'll get in."

God told Moses exactly what would happen. Ramses would resist. There would be signs and wonders. Plagues would be unleashed, but at the end of the day, Moses and the Israelites would leave Egypt with the plunder. Moses found his tongue and began to negotiate with God.

"What if they don't believe me or listen to me and say, 'God did not appear to you'?"

Now God had been talking to Moses for about a week, saying the same thing over and over. When God didn't strike him dead right there on the spot for lack of belief or at least terminal thickheadedness, I couldn't stand it. It was probably a good thing for me that I was stuck in the sand, because if I could have gotten up, I would have risked my life to get in front of God just to ask Him a few questions of my own.

"God," I would have said, "just what is Your definition of *fair*? How do the humans get away with it? Why do You allow them to question You? They express serious doubts about You, and not only do You let them live, but You also answer their doubt. Take just a moment here and think about my case. I never doubted You in the least. I had one fleeting moment of uncertainty, a simple question for clarity's sake when the rebellion started. Do You think I would have followed that maniac in his self-destruction if I had been allowed just one minute to think things over? Why do You allow the humans to do what You would not allow the angels to do—question You? How is that fair?"

Not even a little put out by Moses's doubt, God said to him, "What is that in your hand?"

"A staff."

"Throw it on the ground."

Moses threw it on the ground, and it became a snake, and he ran from it, which is just what I would have done if I could have stood up.

Then God said, "Reach out your hand and take it by the tail."

So Moses reached out and took hold of the snake, and it turned back into a staff in his hand.

"This is so that they may believe that the God of their fathers has indeed appeared to you."

I thought I couldn't bear to hear another word as God went on and on as to how He was going to address Moses's every concern. When I thought Moses had gone as far as he dared, he went further.

"O Lord, I have never been eloquent. I am slow of speech, and sometimes I stutter when I'm nervous."

With my head still in the sand, I couldn't see it, but I could feel the bush flame hotter. I could tell God was just about done negotiating.

"Who gave man his mouth? Who makes him deaf or mute? Who gives him sight or makes him blind? Is it not I? Now go; I will help you speak and will teach you what to say."

If Moses had any brains, he'd get going while the getting's good. He may have been treading on holy ground, but it sounded to me like he was close to treading on God's last nerve.

When Moses spoke again, I was convinced he was addled. It must have been those years of talking to goats. Talking goats, talking bush, probably not all that different in his mind. That must have been it. Otherwise, he never would have dared say what he did.

"O Lord, please send someone else to do it."

The sand where I was planted got hotter and hotter as God's wrath burned against Moses. This had to be it. I couldn't see how God could indulge him any further. But He did. When I heard God agree to allow Aaron, Moses's brother, to accompany him and speak for him, I quit trying to get up and hoped

I would die right there in the sand. I was exhausted and frustrated at the way God let these humans get by with things that would never have been allowed in the angelic realm. The last thing I remember was the crumpling of my wing as a goat laid down on it.

The ground was cold, the night was dark, and everyone was gone when I came around and realized the weight of "I AM" had lifted from my back. Shaking my wings back into shape, I looked around and, seeing no one, wondered if Moses was still alive after challenging God the way he had. Dead or alive, he was nowhere to be seen; even the goats were gone. Finding a flat sandstone, I sat down and tried to think about what had happened.

After a while, I figured it out. The desert had not killed Moses, but it had humbled him. So much so that he was likely the humblest man on all the earth. His questioning God was not because he doubted God but because he doubted himself. Moses couldn't get over his sense of unworthiness, so he begged God to use someone like Aaron, a person he thought to be holier than himself and more worthy of being chosen by God. At least Aaron was not guilty of ever having killed someone like Moses had done. Moses believed he had failed God years ago and was now of no use to Him at all. And God, of course, could not resist that kind of humility.

If I had ever doubted, there was now no possibility Moses might fail.

As I flapped my way back to the second heaven, I thought about the contrast between the arrogance of Satan and the humility of Moses. Satan's unrestrained pride caused one-third of the angels to fall to their doom. Moses's complete lack of self would redeem a nation. I wanted to rub the irony in Satan's face when I returned to his lair, but I would never have had the nerve to do such a thing. I couldn't help but think about the Hebrews and their unrelenting belief for more than four centuries that someday, some way, a deliverer was coming for them. Even as hundreds of them died every day in the mud pits, the rest of them continued their song of hope.

"My deliverer is coming. My deliverer is standing by."

I wondered how they knew.

CHAPTER 4

Is THAT THE best you can come up with?" Satan's sarcasm was intended to minimize the importance of my report lest for one minute I might take pride in bringing him useful information. "Am I supposed to believe God came up with a ridiculous plan like this?"

I told him word for word the conversation I'd heard between God and Moses in the desert, but he wouldn't believe I hadn't left something out of the story. It sounded too simple. That's another of the countless ways in which Satan is different from God. God makes things simple, especially when it comes to humans. Satan, on the other hand, makes things as convoluted as possible.

"Let me see if I have this right. Moses will just mosey into Ramses' throne room with a stick in his hand, and Ramses will hand over the slaves. Is that what you expect to happen?"

"Something like that, sir. Of course there's going to be hail, frogs, flies, blood in the river, all that at first, but at the end of it all, Moses will leave with the slaves."

"Are you suggesting I don't have the power to stop the exodus of the Hebrews?" Satan was beginning to sizzle. Trick question. *What should I say?* My mind worked double time trying to come up with an answer with the least physical consequences for me.

"No, of course not, Your Terribleness. With the humans, you've always got a shot because of that misconceived idea of free will God programmed into them. Moses has to obey every step of the way by an act of his will. It hasn't been hard for him so far. But he's been out of town for a long time, and when he comes back and sees the grandeur of Egypt and its gods (us, of course), he might realize the absurdity of the whole idea and go home. He might begin to doubt whether the burning bush really happened; maybe it was just a mirage. That sort of thing happens in the desert a lot, you know. We could help with that. Speak confusion into his dreams; suggest to his friends that he got into a hallucinogenic weed or something. It could work."

Satan ignored my suggestions and turned to Bezel and the other chief demons.

"Station your guards in Ramses' court. Be ready when Moses arrives."

"We've had a platoon on the wall for forty years, master," Bezel answered. "Do you really think we need more guards?"

Satan didn't have to answer. All he had to do was cast those awful eyes toward the demon who thought he could question Satan's decision.

"Right away, sir," Bezel said meekly as he backed away.

Off they went in blind obedience whether they had a game plan or not. As they were leaving, I decided it would be a good time to slip out the side door and get back to my perch. Satan stepped on my tail as I crept out.

"Did I dismiss you?" he scowled. "Let me know the moment Moses steps into the city. Don't let him get past you. You will rue the day if he does. Now get back to your post."

That was exactly what I was trying to do.

I supposed God must have spoken to Aaron when I wasn't paying attention. That would explain why he was headed out to the desert to meet Moses. In any event, the two of them met with the elders, handled the protocol of leaving, and before he had a chance to rethink the whole idea, Moses, his son, and Zipporah were on their way to the city.

I couldn't wait to see the look on Moses's face when he stepped over the crest of the sand dune and beheld Egypt in all of its glory, something he hadn't seen in forty years. I left my perch and flew down to where he was standing, careful not to make any noise or do anything to let him know he wasn't alone. I wanted to see what the Temple of Karnak looked like from his perspective.

I closed my eyes tightly and tried to imagine I was a human. I do that from time to time because even after all these centuries, I'm still amazed how the human race has survived against Satan's demons. I've often wondered if God secretly regretted having made mankind of such inferior materials. He handicapped the entire race right from the beginning. Think about it. The whole mortality issue for humans is a terrible motivator when He needs them to go to war. Man knows he is finite. No matter how he lives or how he dies, at the end of it all, his death will be the same as the worst or best who ever lived. By contrast, even if a demon loses a battle with a human, he doesn't die. God should have fixed this inequity centuries ago.

Humans, on the other hand, not only die, but also many of you are *willing* to die on the basis of your perceived relationship with God. Why? You die and then what? You can't be sure what, if anything, awaits you after death. Why jeopardize the life you at least have some control over now by taking impossible orders from a God who you can't be sure exists at all. And if He does exist, He's been known to disappear for hundreds of years at a time with no explanation at all as to where He's been.

And while we're talking about it, the whole idea of the natural combating the supernatural, man against the demonic realm, is preposterous. Whose idea was that? I have a hard time imagining God came up with it on His own.

Look at the facts. Demons don't bleed. Let's start right there. You humans function as a result of your blood. Poke a hole in your feeble flesh, let the blood run out, and there you go—dead human. Demons cannot be physically hurt by man, and that's just the plain fact of the matter. Humans can swing at us all the livelong day, but you cannot actually touch us. The only warfare weapon you have against us it to entreat God to dispatch the warring heavenly angels against us on your behalf. Fortunately for us, most of you never figure it out. Demons have extraordinary strength and are cunning and invisible. You humans are weak by comparison, not all that bright in my observation, and clearly visible. What kind of contest is that? Unless God has some idea of a better line of defense for you somewhere down the road, you cannot possibly win. Tell the truth—at least some of you from time to time must have thought that God set you up for failure. Certainly Satan has tried telling you that for years.

I stood beside Moses, scrunched my eyes shut, and pretended I had no supernatural powers, could not fly, and was made of flesh and blood. Then I opened my eyes and beheld Karnak, the city of the pharaohs. I have to tell you it was impressive.

Although it was built entirely by humans, the temples, the architecture, the sheer grandeur of it all almost overwhelmed me, and I had the perspective of paradise to compare it with.

Then I looked at Moses. Five feet eight inches tall—five-nine tops—one hundred sixty pounds more or less, weathered skin of a shepherd, and long gray beard and hair of one who has fought the desert all his life. Not all that impressive. Certainly he didn't look like a man in search of a midlife career change. I wondered if he felt as small as he looked.

He stood there a long time staring at the city. At a minimum he must have been reevaluating the whole idea. I wondered if he was thinking how this would be a good time to turn back before anybody realized he was back in town. God had appeared in the earth realm as a burning bush and declared him to be the deliverer of Israel. So, what of it? No one else saw it, and no one else would ever have to know, save those few elders he talked with, and who really cared what they thought about anything?

Moses continued staring at Karnak, and I continued staring at Moses. I couldn't figure it out. Why would Moses at eighty years old, a person who had escaped death and slavery and had ended up in a desert oasis with a pretty good life, care anything at all about what happened to the humans who remained in bondage in Egypt? I don't get that about you people. Why do you humans care about the sufferings of other humans? More than that, what motivates you to try to do something about it?

Here's how I would have handled the whole situation. If I'd been Moses and God showed up to tell me how the sufferings of the slaves were of concern to Him, I would have suggested to God—very respectfully, you understand—that He go get them Himself or at least send a SWAT team of angels to do it. I would have pointed out the logistical nightmare of what He was proposing. Here's what I would've said:

"So, sovereign Lord, let me see if I heard You right. You want me to lead two million Hebrews into the desert to have a party and worship You, and Pharaoh is going to go right along with the whole idea. I can see how You are about worship and all that, but say, did You have some sort of follow-up plans for after the prayer meeting? Or were You thinking all the AWOL slaves and I would just wing it after that? Where did You say this Promised Land is, and how many demonized tribes are already living there? Of course, You're probably planning to have them surrender to us when we get to the border, right?

"That's only fair if Your idea is to send me into the middle of them with just the slaves, who, I might point out, make a lousy conquering army. Why don't we just sleep on this tonight and see how we feel about it tomorrow?"

Yes, that's what I would have said. I looked to see if Moses might be thinking the same thing, but he was gone.

He was halfway to the city gate by the time I caught up with him again. I thought about going back to Satan's lair right then to let him know where we were in the process, but then I had a reality check. When Moses got to the gate, how was he going to get in? I know what I said about him being raised as Ramses' brother, but that was a long time ago. These guards wouldn't remember him; they were too young. They wouldn't know or care who he was. They were highly unlikely to let a wandering goatherd enter the gates without any prior authorization. Maybe it wasn't worth getting Satan riled up just yet. I decided to follow Moses and see what would happen.

When we got to the gate, it was just as I thought. The Egyptian guards were posted on top of the wall over the massive doors. Beside each one of them was one of Satan's henchmen to make sure the guards did not let Moses through in case he ever showed up again. As Bezel tried to remind Satan, the demons had been stationed there since Moses fled forty years earlier just in case he ever tried to come back. Moses banged on the gate with the staff the Lord had given him. I must say it did make quite a loud noise for a piece of wood. I thought I'd better wave a wing at the demons on the wall to let them know I was with Moses in case they were planning some sort of attack. They had a habit of overlooking me, and I didn't want to end up as barbecue if there was a fight. I took a step forward to get in a better position, but when I looked back up to the place on the wall where they had been, they were gone. The human guards were still there, but every last one of the demonic horde was gone. Now, that was odd.

I stayed behind Moses, simultaneously wondering where our side went and not believing it when the gates began to open. You know how you get that funny feeling down your scales—or in your case, down your spine—when you realize you're not alone? I was getting that feeling when all at once I heard a snort and felt hot breath right down the back of my neck. I turned around and was face-to-nostril with the biggest white horse I'd ever seen. In fact, there were six of them. I had to step back to see how grand they really were. When I did, I saw on their backs the elite guard of the heavenly host.

No wonder the demon guards had fled. Moses couldn't see them and had no idea the angels were even there, much less that they had arrived to ensure he got into the city. He looked first at his staff and then at the opening gates in pure amazement, having no idea that the cavalry of heaven stood round about him. The great stallion stomped his glistening hoof and snorted at me. Time to go.

I tried to flee, but I'm not at my best under stress. Those snorting horses made me so nervous I couldn't get my hooves and wings going in the same direction. I hopped around trying to get liftoff, but my tail acted like a sack of rocks. The lead horse was now bearing down on top of me with those flaring nostrils right in my contorted face. I just knew he was going to step on me.

I decided to play dead. I whimpered and rolled up in a ball under his massive chest. I figured out right away this was not a great idea, but as I said, I'm not good under pressure. The horse sniffed at me and then tossed his head, turned, kicked with those powerful legs, and sent me flying into the vast expanse. When I stopped spinning, I began flapping for all I was worth as I beat a quick path back to the second heaven.

But I wasn't as fast as the demon guards who had already made it back to Satan's court. He was furious when he learned they had left their posts. They stood cowering before him as he blasted them for abandoning their assignment. I tried not to show it, but I enjoyed seeing someone besides me on the receiving end of his thrashing. He glanced my way, seeming surprised to see me.

"Why are you here?"

"I live here, Your Majesty." Never try to be flip with Satan. I ducked whatever it was he threw at me and went on. "What

I mean is that I'm back to report. Moses got into the city." I was going to tell him about the horses and the elite guard, but he cut me off.

"How many of you imbeciles do I need to tell me Moses got into the city? I got it, all right? And here you all are comfy at home while Moses wanders around Egypt completely unopposed." His eyes seared each of us. I knew not to say anything right then, but one of the others did not.

"What did you expect us to do when the heavenly host showed up?" he blurted out. "You were certainly no match for them when we were in heaven. Don't blame us for getting out before they saw us and turned the wrath of you-know-who on us again."

Oh, my. Bad, bad answer. No one was ever allowed to remind Satan of how Michael had thrown us out of heaven after the rebellion.

Over the centuries, I'd seen Satan throw just about every kind of fit you might imagine. I'd seen rage that melted demons' wings and violence against his own kind that in any other created species would be unimaginable. But I had never seen Satan do what he did that day to the demon who dared to say what all of us were thinking. I dare not say what happened, but suffice it to know our former comrade was no more.

"Any other comments?" he snarled to the rest of us as he wiped away the demon ooze that dribbled out of his mouth. Disgusting, I know, but it gives you a hint. Of course, not a word was spoken. No one even thought out loud. Everyone fled for his post. I was glad to be going back to my perch to resume my duties of watching the Hebrews when Satan stopped me in my attempted exit.

"Does Moses have any weapons to use against Ramses?"

"Not to speak of, sir. He has his shepherd's staff, but that's about it. Nothing to worry about, although it does have one pretty impressive add-on feature." I was remembering what I had seen in the desert. "He can turn his staff into a snake. I saw him do it back there at the bush."

For a moment, Satan didn't seem to know what to do with this information. God hadn't been all that favorably disposed toward using snakes for anything since that episode in the garden. Satan summoned one of the demon princes who specialized in magic and told him to position himself with the court magicians.

"Whatever Moses does with his staff, make sure they can duplicate it," he hissed to the prince, who did not speak but just nodded and whisked away toward Ramses' palace.

"You." Satan was speaking to me again. "Dog his steps. Watch every move. If he hears from God, I want to know about it. Do not allow Moses to leave Egypt with the Hebrews."

I took to flight in search of Moses without asking any questions, but I kept thinking about that last statement. Surely Satan was not suggesting that I might be able to keep Moses from doing anything, much less liberating the slaves. Since we were not allowed to ask follow-up questions, it was a constant battle to guess what Satan meant by what he said.

CHAPTER 5

A T FIRST THEY just stared at one another as if each had seen a ghost. Moses, weathered and leathered, a man who had battled the desert and survived, seemed out of place but oddly at ease in the opulence surrounding him. Aaron stood by his side, uncomfortable and unsure of where he was supposed to look, so he stared at the floor. Ramses sat on his throne in splendor, dressed in his royal robes, with a look of confusion and disbelief all over his face. Moses had no trouble getting in to see the pharaoh because as soon as Ramses heard that someone claiming to be his long-lost brother had arrived, he canceled the business at hand and had Moses ushered into the throne room.

Ramses spoke first. "You've returned from the grave, my brother. Have you come back to us to take your place in the royal service?"

"No, Ramses," Moses said. "We both know I have no claim to the royal lineage. I am the son of Hebrew slaves."

"Nonsense," Ramses replied. "We played together as children. We were as brothers. You're welcome here, and you will be safe. After all, those who wanted your life are now dead." He rose from his throne and walked around Moses as if seeing him from every side might reveal some hidden thing.

Ramses must be psychic, I thought to myself. *That is exactly what God said to Moses in the desert. Why else would Ramses think to say it?*

Moses turned around to face his brother. "Pharaoh knows that I am a Hebrew, a brother of the slaves you hold in bondage. Their cries have gone up to the God of heaven, who has sent me for them."

I swear the temperature in the room dropped ten degrees as Ramses' eyes iced over at the words of Moses. If you ask me, God skipped an important step in the "get ready" phase when He failed to insist that Moses brush up on his diplomatic skills before encountering the ruler of Egypt. Moses had spent too many years talking to goats. God should have provided him with a life coach for a couple of weeks. Someone to help him learn the social graces he'd long forgotten, such as how monarchs like a little polite chitchat to break the ice before jumping right down to the nonnegotiables. At least a few opening words like this, maybe:

"Hi, how are you doing, brother? What's new with the family? The castle looks great; I like what you've done with the place. Sorry I haven't written. By the way, I just dropped by to walk out with your entire labor force. Nice seeing you."

No, Moses didn't give Ramses a chance to warm up to the idea at all. No sugarcoating whatsoever. All eyes were on Pharaoh. Maybe Ramses thought Moses's comments were so ridiculous they didn't merit a response. After an uncomfortable silence, it was Moses who blinked and spoke again.

"This is what the God of Israel says: 'Let My people go so that they may hold a festival to Me for three days in the desert.'" The snickering in the court came from the palace guards who couldn't contain their giggles at the absurdity of what Moses had said.

Pharaoh laughed as well. "My brother hasn't lost his sense of humor. You were always the prankster."

Moses remained silent.

Ramses stopped smiling and sat down on his throne. "Who is this God that I should obey Him and let the slaves go?"

"He is the God of Israel and the Creator of all that is."

Moses had summed it up nicely, I thought—briefly but nicely.

"Is he greater than the gods of Egypt?" Ramses shot back.

"He is."

Again I was concerned Moses wasn't investing nearly enough words into this conversation. Ramses opened the door to dialogue, but Moses was not walking through it.

"So your God cares about the Hebrews, does He? They've been the slaves of Egypt for four hundred years. Where's He been all this time if He is so concerned?"

"Let them go, Ramses."

"Here's what I think of your God." With that, Ramses turned to the foreman of the slaves.

"Give them no more straw to make bricks. Obviously they have too much time on their hands. Now let them gather the straw themselves, and let the daily quota remain the same."

Moses didn't flinch, but Aaron looked like he might run. They should have anticipated that Pharaoh would resist the idea of a total shutdown in the brick-making business. Aaron swallowed hard but didn't say a word as he waited to see what Moses would do with this unfortunate turn of events.

"Pharaoh, for your own sake, let them go."

Ramses bristled in indignation. He rose from his throne and stormed out of the room without saying another word. Moses and Aaron were summarily dismissed and booted out the same door they'd come in. It didn't take very long for the word about the straw to get to the slave masters, who themselves were Hebrews. In one grumbling group they petitioned a meeting with Ramses and got it.

"It can't be done," they said, groveling before him. "The people can't gather straw and produce the same number of bricks. We'll fall behind. The building projects will suffer. Why has Pharaoh done this to his subjects?"

"If your people have enough time to ask for three days off to party in the desert to worship your God, then they have too much time."

The foreman looked stunned. "Did we ask my lord for any such thing? It would never cross our minds to think about a long weekend. Who brought such a request to Pharaoh's ears?"

"Moses."

Well, you can guess what happened. The slave masters went back to the brick pits and told the people what Ramses had said. When Moses and Aaron showed up a little while later, the whole Hebrew population had turned on them. The brothers were flabbergasted. God had never given the slightest warning this might happen. From their ashen look, it was clear they hadn't expected things to go quite this way. Neither said very much in the face of the verbal assaults being hurled at them by the throng, but once they got out of earshot, Moses began to cry out to God.

"O Lord, I tried to tell You I wouldn't be very good at this. I've made things worse for the very people You are trying to help."

"Tell the Israelites I will bring them out from under the yoke of the Egyptians. I will free them from being slaves, and I will bring them to the land I swore to give Abraham, Isaac, and Jacob. I will give it to them as the inheritance I promised."

Aaron was in a quaking heap on the ground in the presence of the Lord, but Moses just kept talking to the Creator of the universe as if they were old chums.

"O God, here's my idea how we can turn this around. Would You mind doing the burning bush thing one more time? I told the Hebrews about it, of course, but I could see in their eyes that they didn't believe me. But if You could just fire that bush up again right there in the middle of town where the Egyptians and the Hebrews can both see it, I'm pretty sure we can be out of here by morning."

God didn't think much of his idea, so Moses and Aaron went to the Hebrews and told them what the Lord God had said. Moses was right. They didn't believe one word of it.

Satan squealed with delight when I gave him this news. He walked over to the edge of the second heaven and looked off into the distance.

"Where are they now? Hightailing it back to the desert for sure. Who does God think He's messing with by sending two country bumpkins into my territory?" Satan swung his fist in an uppercut for effect.

The other demons were congratulating themselves on running Moses and Aaron out of town, but I just stood there saying nothing at all and looking at the floor. I just knew Satan was going to comment on my silence.

"You don't see anything here to cheer about, moron? The deliverer and his sidekick are on their way back to the sticks. It's over."

I chose my words carefully. "Did anybody actually see them leave the city gates, sir?"

Satan looked at the demons, and they looked at one another. When the heads started shaking in response, Satan dispatched one of the lower-ranking devils to scour the city streets for them. They weren't hard to find, and it was only minutes before the scout was back, reporting what I knew all along. Moses and Aaron had gone nowhere but to bed.

I spent the rest of the night perched on the ledge above the door of the house where Moses and Aaron slept.

"Dog their steps," Satan had hissed at me as he sent me out on the graveyard shift.

The next morning, God appeared to them again. "You are to say everything I command you. Tell Pharaoh to let the Israelites go. Aaron can help you."

Well, I can just tell you that Aaron's face fell like a rock when he heard that bit of news. He knew he was to stand behind whatever Moses said, but his idea was to stand about forty feet behind and under a rock if one was available. Aaron had zero plans to get in the line of fire between Moses and Ramses, much less to actually enter into the conversation.

"I will harden Pharaoh's heart, and though I multiply My miraculous signs and wonders in Egypt, he won't listen to you."

Moses didn't say a word, but I knew what he was thinking because I was thinking it myself. *What are You saying, God? Number one, Ramses' heart doesn't need to be any harder, and number two, he's not listening to me now.*

"Then I'll lay My hand on Egypt, and with mighty acts of judgment, the Egyptians will know that I am God when I stretch out My hand and bring the Israelites out of it by divisions."

Here's what I've learned about God over the eons: if you don't listen carefully to every word He speaks, you can miss something big. And that's just what happened to Moses. He missed two remarkable things. God said He was going to bring the Israelites out by divisions. Out of divisions come *soldiers*, not *slaves*. Slaves come out in a mob. I didn't know what He meant by His word choice, but I knew it meant something.

I was more than merely interested in the other thing God said. He was going to play this thing out for a while so the Egyptians would know He was God. Why? Whatever for? What good would it do? As far back as I could remember, at least since Abraham, God had never before cared one way or the other about anybody but the Hebrews. Why would He suddenly be interested in what the Egyptians knew about Him?

Unless...

I couldn't bear to think about it, but I knew I must. Why would God care what the Egyptians knew about Him unless

He intended to save some of them? Impossible. Completely out of order and not fair. The Egyptians were sold out to Satan, way beyond redemption of any kind. The idea that God might be thinking of saving the Egyptians took hold of my mind, and I completely forgot about Moses and Aaron. All I could think about was how I wanted to have a little chat with God.

"God," I cried out. Sometimes I've complained to God with great bravado, secure in the knowledge that He did not hear me. This time I wished He would hear me, although I knew I was just shaking my wing at empty space. "I'm right, aren't I? You're trying to find a loophole to save some of the Egyptians, aren't You? How could You even think about it? How could You give those who don't know You and don't care about You time to repent when You wouldn't spare me five minutes? That's all I needed to recover my sanity that awful day when the war in heaven happened. Five minutes more and I could have reached Michael's side to tell him I'd changed my mind. Five minutes more and I would never have followed that lunatic Lucifer."

In total despair at the mere thought of God counting the evil Egyptians worthier of salvation than me, I flew hard into the nearest wall and tried to kill myself. Of course, it didn't work and only made my head throb. By the time I pulled myself together, God was still talking to Moses and Aaron.

"When Pharaoh says to you, 'Perform a miracle,' then say to Aaron, 'Take your staff and throw it down before Pharaoh,' and it will become a snake."

You should have seen Aaron snap to attention at that comment. The first thing he did was throw the staff on the ground to see if it was working. Nothing. Next, he started pulling on Moses's tunic with one hand while continuing to thump his staff on the ground with the other. He tried to point out to Moses that the staff was just a common tree branch with no supernatural qualities. Moses ignored him and continued listening to God while Aaron feverishly practiced behind his back, trying to make something happen—*thump, thump.* No snake.

The next day I followed them into Pharaoh's throne room to see what would happen. Moses strode with calm confidence and walked directly to the place where Ramses was seated. Aaron followed a few steps behind, continuing to thump his staff on the floor as he went along to see if it wriggled at all. Nothing. He stopped thumping and came alongside Moses, not looking at all well.

Right on cue, Pharaoh demanded proof that the God of Moses was real. "Perform a miracle," he chided.

Everyone in the room snickered. Moses turned to Aaron and told him to do what God had said. With trembling hands and closed eyes, Aaron threw his staff to the ground and prepared to run. It was the cumulative gasp from the eunuch slaves that caused him to open his eyes and jump back in disbelief at the writhing snake on the palace floor.

With nary a raised eyebrow, Pharaoh summoned wise men, sorcerers, and the Egyptian magicians to do the very same thing by their secret arts. Each one threw down his staff, and each staff became a snake. But to everyone's amazement, Aaron's staff swallowed up their staffs. No one in the room was more surprised by this than Aaron. When Moses reached down and picked the serpent up by the tail and it turned back into a staff, there was a chorus of sighs of relief from every corner of the room. Ramses, however, pretended to be unimpressed. He ordered Moses and Aaron to leave.

I was about to fly back to Satan's lair to give him an update when it occurred to me that Moses and Aaron wouldn't go home without reporting to God. I knew I'd better follow them lest I miss something. When they got to the city's edge, they called out to God. I listened with both ears to what God told them to do next.

"Go to Pharaoh in the morning as he goes out to the water. Wait on the bank of the Nile to meet him. Take the staff that was changed into a snake, and say to him, 'The God of the Hebrews has sent me to say to you, "Let My people go so that they may worship Me in the desert."' With the staff that is in your hand, strike the water of the Nile and it will be changed into blood. The fish in the Nile will die, the river will stink, and no one will be able to drink its water.

"And you, Aaron, take your staff and stretch out your hand over the waters of Egypt, the streams, canals, ponds and all the reservoirs, and they will turn to blood. Blood will be everywhere in Egypt."

Moses seemed to be taking it in fairly well, but Aaron was getting that woozy look again.

As I flew back to the second heaven to report to Satan, I wondered how he was going to take this news that God had upped the stakes in the battle for the Hebrews. He was enabling mere humans to operate in the supernatural realm. I knew Satan would demand to know if this was legal. I wasn't sure.

He took the news much better than I thought he would.

"So what? God's losing His touch if that's the best He can come up with. I can do the same thing."

He summoned two of his demons who were specialists in black magic and sent them to the quarters of the court magicians. The next day, Satan summoned all the demons to come and stand on the edge of the second heaven to watch the show. He was very smug about how this would turn out.

There they were, Moses and Aaron, standing before a full house of spectators on the banks of the Nile. They did just as God had commanded. Aaron, with newfound confidence after the snake episode, raised his staff in the presence of Pharaoh and his officials and struck the water of the Nile, and all the water was changed into blood. The fish in the Nile died, and the river smelled so bad that the Egyptians couldn't drink its water. Blood was everywhere in Egypt.

"Well, *all right*," Aaron whispered to Moses as he nodded his head proudly at this new supernatural power he had obtained.

But his satisfaction didn't last long. The Egyptian magicians did the same things with jars of water by their secret arts. Now, right there is where Moses should have thrown down the yellow flag and yelled, "Foul." Who did the magicians think they would fool with that old parlor trick? What unbiased observer would equate changing the waters of a river into blood with changing a couple of gallons in a primed jar? Obviously, the magicians tossed a little dye into the pots with all their gyrations and hocus pocus. *Unbiased observer* is the key phrase here, which there were none of in the audience that day. I have to tell you, I was sorely disappointed with the cognitive abilities of Moses and Aaron in their failure to identify the trickery.

Pharaoh watched with a smug look on his face as if this were a perfectly legitimate contest. It appeared that his heart became harder just as God had said. He wouldn't listen to Moses and Aaron, and instead, he turned and went into his palace.

The demons laughed out loud at the puzzled expressions of Moses and Aaron. God failed to mention that part about how the magicians would appear to be able to turn water to blood as well. The crowd found better things to do and left, but Moses and Aaron stood there for a long time looking at the Nile and wondering what had gone wrong.

It was seven days before anything else happened.

CHAPTER 6

A FTER BEING PUBLICLY humiliated by Pharaoh's magicians, Moses and Aaron didn't venture out much during the next week, preferring to avoid the chiding of the Hebrews and Egyptians alike. Some of the demons thought it might soon be all over and Moses would head back to the goats. I couldn't be sure what Moses would do, but I was certain what God would do. He would up the ante again.

Just as I predicted, He summoned Moses and Aaron and said, "Go to Pharaoh and say to him, 'God says, "Let My people go so that they may worship Me. If you refuse to let them go, I will plague your whole country with frogs. The Nile will teem with frogs. They'll come up into your palace and your bedroom and onto your bed. They'll come into the houses of your officials, on your people, and into your ovens and kneading troughs. The frogs will jump up on you and your people and all your officials.""

Moses swallowed hard but didn't say a word to indicate the doubt he must have had about God's new plan. Aaron was bursting to ask the obvious question but didn't. I decided to help them along by projecting my thoughts Moses's way. Other demons were always sending thoughts into human minds and seeing immediate results; I'd never given it a try but thought now might be a good time. I stared intently into his eyes and thought hard.

Are the court magicians going to be able to do the same thing and make you look foolish again?

No response. I couldn't tell if Moses received my thought transfer or not. Since he didn't repeat my question, I presumed he must not have heard me, otherwise he would have seen the wisdom in asking God whether the court magicians were going to make him look silly by making their own frogs. I myself didn't know the answer. The ability of Satan's minions to create amphibians had never come up before, although I personally doubted they could do it. I was still stumped over how they managed the snake trick. I wondered if I should dash back to the lair and ask about our ability to do frogs, but then I realized there wasn't enough time. We were about to find out anyway because Moses and Aaron, without protesting at all, turned and walked right back to Pharaoh's court.

Pharaoh was busy with the scribes when the two entered.

"So you're back, my brother," Pharaoh waved the scribes away. "What new entertainment did you bring me today?" The court laughed.

Moses motioned for Pharaoh to follow him as he and Aaron walked across the room and stepped out on a balcony overlooking the city. No one else heard it when God whispered to Moses.

"Tell Aaron, 'Stretch out your hand with your staff over the streams and canals and ponds, and make frogs come up on the land of Egypt.'"

Moses obeyed, and so did Aaron. The frogs came up out of everywhere and covered the land. But, wouldn't you know, the magicians did the very same thing by their secret arts.

The frog-making question was settled, and it was a mess. There were frogs all over the place. They hopped out of soup kettles and salad bowls and bounced across lunch tables all over Egypt. They popped out from under the long togas of women who went screaming hysterically into the street, demanding that someone do something. Even in Ramses' throne room, the soldiers and slaves couldn't contain the frogs. Moses and Aaron walked out of the chaos without much notice from anyone because every free hand in the room was slapping at frogs. The court magicians had also tried to slink out when Pharaoh ordered the guards to stop them. The guards grabbed them by their collars and deposited them right back in front of Ramses.

"Now get rid of them," Ramses seethed just as a really big jumper landed right on top of his bald head.

The nervous magicians waved their arms and spoke in Egyptian and then in gibberish, but nothing happened. If anything, there were more frogs than ever. The more the magicians cursed the frogs, the more there were, and the more aggressive they became. The one on Ramses' head would not budge, even with all the slaves swatting at him. All at once, I knew what was happening.

I couldn't help but be impressed all over again by the cleverness of God. He allowed the magicians to call the frogs in (which must have surprised them if the truth be known), but they couldn't get rid of them. God set a hook, and the magicians swallowed it, worm and all. Ramses rose to his feet in anger, dumping a dozen or so frogs out of the folds of his robe as he moved toward the magicians and slapped the main wizard to the side.

"Where are they?" he roared.

Obviously, he meant Moses and Aaron, who were outside on the front porch, trying to decide what to do next. The guards didn't have to be told to bring them back inside. Ramses stared at them, shook his head, then sat down on his throne and waved a hand of resignation at Moses.

"Tell God to take the frogs away from me and my people, and I will let your people go to offer sacrifices to Him."

Moses was stunned. So was I. This wasn't like Ramses to give up without a fight. Satan would be furious when he found out Moses and Aaron were about to leave town with the slaves in tow without any resistance at all.

Moses composed himself. "I leave to you the honor of setting the time for me to pray for you and your officials and your people, that you and your houses may be rid of the frogs, except for those that remain in the Nile."

"Tomorrow," Pharaoh waved his hand again, signaling their dismissal.

"It will be as you say so that you may know there is no one like our God. The frogs will leave; they will remain only in the Nile."

Moses and Aaron walked out in silence, having no idea what had just happened.

The next day, just as he promised, Moses cried out to God about the frogs. God did what Moses asked, and the frogs died in the houses, the courtyards, and in the fields. They were piled into heaps, and, I tell you, the land reeked of them.

In fact, it was so bad, the smell drifted all the way to the second heaven, where even Satan held his nose at the stench. He heard the whole thing and had already dispatched one of the demons to stand beside Ramses while the frog killing was going on. When it looked like most of the frogs were gone, the demon spoke into Ramses' ear.

"You can't let them go. They've made a fool of you. The brick pits will be shut down if the Hebrews leave. Your own people will turn on you. They're laughing at you right now for letting Moses pray in the presence of the great gods of Egypt. What were you thinking?"

Pharaoh listened to the demon, and when he saw that all the frogs were dead, he reneged on his promise to Moses and Aaron.

Now, this should have been the moment when Moses and Aaron stomped off in a huff after being lied to by Ramses. But they didn't. They stood quietly as if waiting for something else to happen. Satan turned to me and jerked me up by one of my ears.

"What are they doing? Why don't they leave? Did God give them any further orders?"

"No, no, not at all. I was there the whole time. He didn't say anything else."

I was frantically trying to remember if I'd left them alone at any time when God could have spoken to them and I missed something important. No, I was there the whole time. Well, except for the brief fit when I tried to commit suicide by flying into the wall. I might have blanked out there for a moment, but, no, I was sure that wasn't it.

I found myself airborne again as Satan tossed me off the ledge of the second heaven with orders to get on the ground by Moses to find out what was about to happen. I arrived just in time to hear God speak. No one could hear Him except Moses, and me, of course.

"Tell Aaron, 'Stretch out your staff, and strike the dust of the ground,' and throughout the land of Egypt the dust will become gnats."

"Gnats?" Moses asked.

"Gnats?" I echoed. Neither of us saw the wisdom in gnats. They were common in Egypt as it was. I couldn't see Pharaoh being one bit impressed by gnats, and I knew Moses couldn't see it either, but he didn't question God.

Moses did as God said, and when Aaron stretched out his hand with the staff and struck the dust of the ground, a torrent of gnats came upon men and animals. All the dust throughout the land of Egypt became gnats. Did I ever miscall that one! You can't imagine the catastrophe it was. Millions, make that billions, of flying, biting, miniscule gnats all over everything, everywhere, including me.

Pharaoh bellowed for the court magicians to come and clean up the mess. Any idiot would have known Pharaoh meant for them to get rid of the gnats, but at first they thought they were supposed to create more, which they couldn't do. It was easy to see how a person might be confused. It didn't matter anyway; they couldn't create more, and they couldn't get rid of the ones that were there. Men, women, cats, and dogs were swarmed over by Aaron's gnats.

Miserable as it was walking around in a cloud of gnats, I found myself momentarily forgetting about them as I pondered what was going on. The magicians could not make gnats. Why not? How was it the magicians could produce frogs but not gnats? Basic biology proves that a leaping, croaking, multi-dimensional amphibian just has to be harder to conjure up than a gnat. Therefore, it could only mean one thing, which should have been obvious to me all along. The magicians never really *produced* any frogs either. For all the things we demons can destroy, we cannot create a single thing. God Himself had summoned the frogs when the magicians called for them. It was all part of His plan to make Pharaoh show his hand.

If you think the frogs might have been annoying, you should have been there for the gnats. Arms waving, everyone running for cover, the animals going crazy...there was no escape. Ramses himself grabbed the lead magician by the throat and ordered him to get rid of the gnats. The magician struggled to get free and gasped for breath.

"We can't do it. This is the finger of God."

Pharaoh threw him to the ground and set off in search of Moses and Aaron.

I flew back to Satan's lair in time to hear him giving instructions to the demon he was dispatching to Ramses.

"Do not let Ramses give in to Moses. Kill him first."

Then he turned to me. "What will God do next? What have you heard?"

"I, uh, haven't actually heard anything."

Satan threw a fireball at me. I ducked but knew there would be more and worse if I couldn't come up with something.

"I can guess if you like, Your Horribleness. I've gotten pretty good at guessing what God will do next."

I ducked the next fireball but remained ready to run at any moment.

"Then guess," he snarled through his fangs.

"He will release another plague. No doubt about it. He will throw something new into the equation. It will be something to make Pharaoh look weak in the eyes of the people."

"What would that be?"

"No idea, sir."

"What good are you?" He threw another fireball at me as I dove for the floor. I didn't have to be told to return to the earth to see what would happen next. I arrived just in time to hear God speaking to Moses.

"Get up early in the morning, and confront Pharaoh as he goes to the water. Say to him, 'This is what the Lord says: "Let My people go so that they may worship Me. If you do not let them go, I will send swarms of flies on you and your officials, on your people and into your houses. The houses of the Egyptians will be full of flies.

""But on that day, I will deal differently with the land of Goshen, where My people live; no swarms of flies will be there, so that you will know that I, the Lord, am in this land. I will make a distinction between My people and your people. This miraculous sign will occur tomorrow."""

If I had been Ramses, the gnats would have been the finisher for me. Let the people go with Moses. I would've given in while it was still an option. Make them promise to come back right after the weekend, but call for a time-out. I guess Ramses' head must have hardened right along with his heart, because once again, he defied God.

So, God did it. Dense swarms of flies poured into Pharaoh's palace and into the houses of his officials. Throughout Egypt, whatever the gnats missed before was completely ruined by the flies.

This time, it looked as if God's plan was beginning to work. As soon as the word got out that there were no flies in Goshen where the Hebrews lived, mobs of people began to gather outside of Pharaoh's court. The guards could barely keep them in line. The magicians, fearing a coup, pleaded with Ramses.

"The crowd is out of control. They're going to overrun the palace unless you do something."

"You do something," Ramses roared back, pushing the chief magician aside and storming to the window to see for himself.

"Ramses, you must listen. It's been fun, but the jig is up. Our hat tricks aren't going to help."

"What am I supposed to do?"

"Cry uncle. Here's my hankie; wave it at them—just do something."

Fearing the riots were at the boiling point and about to break out, Pharaoh summoned Moses and Aaron.

"Go! Sacrifice to your God, but stay here in this land."

I thought Moses might take that deal, but he didn't.

"No, that won't work. The sacrifices we offer our God would be detestable to the Egyptians. If we offer sacrifices in the city, they'll stone us. We must take a three-day journey into the desert to offer sacrifices to our God, as He commands us."

Pharaoh sighed and slumped back on his throne. One of his advisers leaned over and whispered in his ear.

"He's right. They cannot worship their God here."

"Why not?" Pharaoh whispered back.

"What if their God proves superior to the gods of Egypt? Then what are you going to do?"

The look on Ramses' face showed he hadn't thought about what might happen in a one-on-one between the gods of Egypt and the God of Moses.

"All right. I'll let you go offer sacrifices to your God in the desert, but you must not go very far, and you must come back in three days like you said."

Then Ramses ordered everybody out of the room except for Moses and Aaron. When the guards were gone, he turned to Moses and said, "Now pray for me."

Moses never flinched, but I was dumbfounded at Pharaoh's request. Not that I wouldn't have done the exact same thing, in case there were to be a showdown between the gods. Either he was getting over himself, or he was hedging his bets.

"As soon as I leave you, I will pray, and tomorrow the flies will leave. Only be sure that you do not act deceitfully again by not letting the people go to offer sacrifices to God."

Moses's naïveté was more than I could stand. Even though he couldn't see me, I waltzed right over and got in his face.

"Are you serious, Moses? How many times are you going through this before you catch a clue? Get over the sentimentality that this man was once your brother, if that's what your problem is. You just agreed to pray for Pharaoh, who not only worships the gods of Egypt, but he also thinks he is one. He doesn't honor our God—I mean, your God—and you know it. Don't even think about asking God to cut him some slack. Do you think God could ever overlook the fact that Ramses sacrifices the Israelites to the gods of Egypt on a regular basis? If you want to go out on a limb and ask God to bend the rules for somebody, let me tell you my story."

I dropped my wings in remorse and resignation to my fate as I watched Moses walk away. He left Pharaoh and prayed to God, and God did what Moses asked. The flies left.

Then, once again, Pharaoh hardened his heart and would not let the people go.

What a surprise.

CHAPTER 7

THINGS ON THE earth were quiet for the next few days, so I returned to my perch, continued my watch, and tried to guess what would happen next. I found myself wondering about Ramses.

"By now, he's got to know he's up against something stronger than he is. Why doesn't he give it up? The consequences can only get worse the longer he holds out. What is he thinking?"

"Not only that," I paced back and forth on my perch. "What's up with God? Why does He keep sending Moses with 'Tell Pharaoh this, and tell Pharaoh that'?" I couldn't recall God ever before engaging His enemies in conversation. This messaging back and forth to Pharaoh through Moses looked like a negotiation for the release of the Hebrews, which made no sense because God doesn't negotiate with anyone who isn't a Hebrew and about to be sent out on some impossible scheme. Abraham came to mind.

Satan instigated mandatory daily debriefings from all of his hordes for as long as Moses and Aaron were in town. When I heard the report from the demon assigned to Pharaoh's side, at least I got the answer to my first question about why Ramses didn't simply give up the slaves.

"Does Ramses know what this is all about yet?" Satan asked.

"No, sir," the demon answered. "I don't give him time to think about it. I keep telling him that it's all about him and

Moses, nothing more. I remind him how Moses would have been the prince of Egypt, not him, if it hadn't been for that murder years ago that drove Moses into hiding. I tell him that it's obvious to everyone that Moses is back to take over. He thinks it's a power struggle between two brothers with a little magic thrown in."

Soon it was my turn before the evil inquisitor.

"Now you tell me what God will do next."

I thought he was serious until I realized that the rest of the demonic corps was snickering. They were waiting for me to become flustered and say something silly as I usually did when I was nervous, and I was always nervous when Satan spoke to me. I gave what I thought was a good answer.

"He will send Pharaoh another message."

"*Ooooh*, so scary," the horde began chiding me. "Big whoopee, a message to Pharaoh; we better worry now."

They continued to make fun of me as if I were the village idiot whose sole purpose was to provide comic relief for their staff meeting. They kept on for a while until one of them realized that Satan wasn't laughing. One by one, the snickering subsided as they saw the steely look in Satan's eyes as he glared at me.

"Why did you say that?"

"Because that's what He's been doing. He sends Pharaoh a message warning him about what He'll do if Pharaoh doesn't let the Hebrews go, and then He does what He said. That's all I meant."

I desperately hoped Satan wouldn't pursue this line of questioning. I just wanted to slink back to my perch, but Satan stared me down, reading my eyes and knowing there was something more.

"It may be all you *said*, but it isn't all you *meant*, is it, imbecile?" The snickering started up again. In a rare burst of public vexation, I turned on the demonic crowd and railed at them.

"Does nothing about this look a little strange to any of you? Have you learned nothing at all about God? How many times has God ever negotiated with His enemies? Let me count them for you: none. Something big is happening under our collective noses, I tell you, and we have no idea what it is. And do you want to know why we can't figure it out? It's because He never does anything the same way twice. Do you seriously think you can outguess God? You've forgotten everything you ever knew of Him. You don't remember how He thinks, so you can't possibly know what the fight is about. You're pathetic. We're all pathetic."

It was Satan himself who held them back from attacking me. Maybe he intended to personally destroy me.

"So God will send a message to Pharaoh, and then He will do what He threatens, and therein is supposed to be some cosmic mystery that you alone have figured out. Is that it?" Satan's eyes narrowed as he glared at me.

I looked about the room at the seething demons and whispered my response for fear of triggering some celestial crisis if I actually said out loud what I now knew was true. I lowered my voice.

"It isn't just about the Hebrews anymore."

"Of course it is. It's always about the Hebrews." Satan slammed his claws down on a nearby rock and then turned toward me, daring me to tell him something about God he didn't already know.

"We've made a wrong assumption. It isn't just the Hebrews God cares about. He cares about the Egyptians as well." I ducked down in case this revelation triggered a demonic fit.

Instead, the whole lot of them broke out in body-shaking laughter. Again, Satan was the only one who didn't laugh.

"For a moment I thought you were serious," he said, dismissing me with a swipe of his claw.

"No, think about it, sir. What does He say when He sends a message to Pharaoh? He says something like this: 'Tell Pharaoh this, that, or the other *so that he will know that I am God.*' Why would God care whether or not Pharaoh knows He alone is God? Why would He care what Pharaoh or the Egyptians think about Him unless by realizing that He is God, they might repent and He would save them?"

"Impossible," Satan roared and then stormed across the lair, knocking the other demons aside as he paced back and forth. "It's only the Hebrews. It's always been about the Hebrews. He doesn't care about the rest of humanity."

I ventured a bit further. "Technically speaking, sir, it's about a people who will believe Him and obey Him. It just happens that Abraham's descendents are the only ones who have done this—so far. It isn't in the rule book that He only wants the Hebrews. It has just turned out that way. Clearly, He's trying to get the attention of the Egyptians. Nothing else makes sense. He's trying to give them a way out. And isn't that His nature?"

"No, it's not His nature," Satan bellowed at me. "He can't suddenly meddle in our strongholds just because He's had a change of heart about the rest of mankind. Their sin is too deep. Their sin demands restitution; I'm entitled to that. Even if they repent, which we will not allow, they have to be paid for by blood, innocent blood of which there is none in all the earth. Those are the rules."

Suddenly Satan stopped pacing and whirled around, facing the throng as if he had just realized some magnificent truth.

"In fact, why didn't I think of this before? He can't save the Hebrews without a blood payment. Just because they're slaves doesn't mean they're innocent." He turned to the demon who kept his records. "Check that out. I know I'm right. No blood, no restitution. Game over."

I didn't know how to answer because I'd never understood Satan's fixation with the blood issue to start with. None of us knew what he meant when he went off on a blood tangent. I nodded my head like the rest and agreed that he was probably right. By now all of the other demons were nodding and chattering about how Satan was always right and how he had it over God. I took the opportunity to crawl out of the room and sneak back to my perch.

He's not right, I thought to myself. *I don't know what it is, but God has a plan.*

I wondered if Moses knew what it was.

CHAPTER 8

I WAS BEGINNING TO think it would never end. How many ecological catastrophes could God come up with? He just kept going and going. Next, there was the plague that came upon all the livestock. With one exception, of course: none of the animals belonging to the Hebrews got sick. Pharaoh buckled a bit at the knees when this happened because nothing disrupts the economy and sends merchants into a panic like cattle, sheep, and goats dying all over the place. I thought Ramses might give it up on that one, but he didn't.

Next were the boils. Ugly, oozing sores broke out on every single man, woman, and child in Egypt, except the Hebrews. By now, all the magicians and advisers were begging Pharaoh to make a deal with Moses.

It was then God summoned Moses and Aaron and gave them a verbatim message to take to Pharaoh. When I heard it, I knew that God was getting closer to making His point.

"Get up early in the morning, confront Pharaoh, and tell him I said, 'Let My people go so that they may worship Me, or this time I will send the full force of My plagues against you so you will know that there is no one like Me in all the earth. By now, I could have stretched out My hand and struck you and your people with a plague that would have wiped you off the earth. But I have raised you up for this very purpose, that I might show you My power and that My name might be proclaimed in all the earth.'"

"I knew it! I knew it!"

I shouted as I jumped straight up in the air and missed my perch altogether, coming back down with a thud and landing on my bottom side. I got myself together and headed back to Satan's lair to tell him how I'd been right all along. God wanted Ramses to repent so the Egyptians could be saved. They would declare that God alone is God, and it would spread over the entire world. I stopped short of take-off when I realized I had no proof of anything and still had no answer for that blood-for-sin detail. I thought it better to restrain my excitement and watch and see what would happen next.

It was a good thing I waited. Otherwise I would have missed hearing the very proof I was looking for. God continued His message to Pharaoh: "'Therefore, at this time tomorrow I will send the worst hailstorm that has ever fallen on Egypt, from the day it was founded till now. Bring your livestock and everything you have in the field to a place of shelter because the hail will fall on every man and animal that has not been brought in and is still out in the field, and they will die.'"

There it was, shattering every assumption Satan held. God moved sovereignly, asked permission from no one, and offered the guilty-as-sin Egyptians a way out of judgment. God promised to save the animals belonging to the Egyptians, just like the animals belonging to the Hebrews, if only they would take one step toward Him by believing His word and hiding their livestock. Not one word about letting the Hebrews go so they could worship was in the deal.

When Moses delivered the word to Pharaoh, he did it in a loud voice so all the people in the neighborhood could hear what God was offering them. Those officials of Pharaoh who feared God couldn't move fast enough to bring their slaves and their livestock inside. Others, in misguided loyalty to Pharaoh, ignored Moses and left their slaves and livestock in the field.

Satan did not take this news well at all.

"You're making it up. I should cut your tongue out." Satan threatened me as he dragged me by the tail to the edge of the second heaven to watch for himself what was about to happen on the earth.

When Moses stretched out his staff toward the sky, God sent thunder and hail, and lightning flashed down to the ground. It was the worst storm Egypt had ever seen. Throughout the nation hail struck everything in the fields—both men and animals. It beat down everything growing in the fields and stripped every tree. The only animals that remained alive belonged to the Egyptians who had obeyed God. The only place it did not hail was the land of Goshen, where the Hebrews were.

"NGYAAAAAGH!" Satan shrieked as he jumped up and down on my tail as if I'd caused this to happen. He only stopped because he wanted to hear what Pharaoh was about to say to Moses and Aaron.

"This time I have sinned. Your God is right, and I and my people are wrong. Pray for us, for we have had enough thunder and hail. I will let you go; you don't have to stay any longer."

Moses left Pharaoh and went out of the city. He spread out his hands toward God; the thunder and hail stopped, and the rain no longer poured down on the land.

Satan whirled about and stomped right in the middle of my already sore bottom side, flattening me into the floor as he sped back to his lair of demons. He was back in a flash, dragging one of the demon princes by the collar, and then he flung him over the rim of the second heaven toward the earth.

"Get Ramses back in line," Satan yelled after the soaring demon. "Invalidate his repentance."

I didn't move a scale or a hoof. I lay there perfectly still, pretending to be unconscious, so I'm certain Satan was talking to himself and not to me when he spoke.

"No blood, no restitution. The repentance is meaning-less without the shedding of blood," he assured himself as he slouched away back to his den.

I continued to lie there thinking about what Satan had said. *No blood, no restitution.* Even though I'd never figured out what it meant, I remembered exactly how and when Satan began his obsession with blood. It went all the way back to the garden when God should have killed Adam and Eve for their sin. Instead, He killed an innocent animal and made clothes for His errant humans. Satan had never been the same since that happened. It's like he knows some terrible secret he's too afraid to share.

Satan, scared? Seems unlikely, doesn't it? Especially when one remembers there's nothing in heaven or Earth scarier than him. Of course he fears God, and he knows about the judgment that will come to him—to all of us—at some point in time. He knows he is sentenced to Tartaroo like the rest of us who rebelled; there's no question about that. But he's sort of resigned himself to the inevitable because he knows that judgment day won't come until God either redeems the earth with His puny humans or cuts His losses and starts over with a better model. The day of sentencing could be pushed out to who knows how long—at least for as long as Satan holds the souls of humans.

As I peeled myself up from the floor, I thought more about it.

"The only thing in heaven or Earth that scares Satan, really scares him, is the idea of shedding innocent blood for sin. But why? Innocent people die all the time. What does he know that the rest of us don't?"

CHAPTER 9

A s FAR AS I was concerned, the locusts and the darkness were anticlimactic, if you know what I mean. I
suppose the humans might not have seen it that way,
but from my perch, it was just one big yawn after the frogs,
gnats, boils, and hail. I figured it wouldn't be much longer
before this whole misadventure to try to save the Hebrews,
much less the Egyptians, would run out of gas. The Egyptians
were not redeemable, and it didn't look like Pharaoh was ever
going to let the Hebrews go. Not today, not tomorrow, not ever.

I wasn't surprised when God summoned Moses again, but I
was baffled by what He said.

"Moses, I will bring one more plague on Pharaoh and on
Egypt. After that, he will let you go from here. Tell the people
that men and women alike are to ask their neighbors for articles of silver and gold."

"Like that's going to happen." I shrugged. "Why would the
Egyptians give the slaves silver and gold?"

Then it hit me. The Egyptian people figured out that Moses
had been right every time about what disaster was going to
happen next. They had also seen how the Hebrews had escaped
every plague that visited Egypt. So, by now the Egyptians were
favorably disposed toward the slaves. More importantly, Moses
himself was highly regarded in Egypt by almost everyone,
including Pharaoh's officials.

After all, if it hadn't been for Moses warning the magistrates as well as the Hebrews about the hail, the Egyptians would have been eating hamburger for years from all the dead cows. The people had learned to pay attention to what Moses said, so when the Hebrews asked for silver and gold, they gave it to them. They probably thought of it as a commission, so to speak, or a down payment for future information. They weren't one bit reluctant to pay Moses for his timely advice. It seemed no one thought about the fact that slaves have no use for silver and gold. What could they do with it? The slaves weren't allowed to go anywhere but to the brick pits, and there were no boutiques or blue-light specials in that neighborhood.

This could only mean one thing: "The Israelites believe they're leaving town, and the Egyptians must think so as well," I reasoned. "They're packing up because they must know they're going somewhere."

I followed Moses as he walked straight into Ramses' throne room unannounced. He slipped right by the guards as if he'd been invisible. I slipped in right behind him because I was invisible. For several minutes, Moses stood quietly before his childhood brother and stared at him as if trying to find the words to make him listen. How could he make Pharaoh understand the irreversible consequences he was about to trigger if he resisted God one more time? Ramses stared back, and the longer he stared at Moses, the more it seemed that a cold fear rose up in his eyes, but he said not a word.

"This is what the Lord says." Moses paused, swallowed hard, and then went on. "Around midnight He will go throughout Egypt. Every firstborn son in Egypt will die, from the firstborn son of Pharaoh, who sits on the throne, to the firstborn son of the slave girl, who is at her hand mill, and all the firstborn of the cattle as well. There will be loud wailing throughout Egypt—worse than there has ever been or ever will be again.

"But among the Israelites not a dog will bark at any man or animal. Then you will know that the Lord makes a distinction between Egypt and Israel. All these officials of yours will come to me, bowing down before me and saying, 'Go. Leave quickly, and let all the people who follow you go with you!' After that I will leave."

Ramses didn't blink; he just kept staring at Moses. When Moses saw Ramses wasn't going to seize the last chance being offered him, he turned in frustration and left the room. I flew my fastest back to Satan's lair.

"Is that all He said?" Satan demanded. "You're certain?"

"I'm certain that's all Moses said."

"What about God? You're certain He said nothing more?" Although Satan grilled me as if he didn't believe me, he had a strange look in his eyes, as if he was hoping I would say, "Nothing more."

I've learned how to take a cue, so of course I answered, "No. Nothing more."

But he didn't stop there. He kept pressing as if I might be keeping something from him.

"Not even an *except for* or an *all but*—nothing like that; no qualifiers at all. You're sure?" His eyes narrowed as if probing into my mind to see if something else was there.

"No, sir. No ifs, ands, or buts. I'm certain of it."

I don't know quite how to describe what he's like when Satan thinks he's put something over on God. He danced a sort of jig and made a guttural noise in his throat that sounded something like the noise a cat makes when you try to give it a bath. He jigged all around, poking at me with his long claws as if I were supposed to giggle right along with him. I never really know how I'm supposed to respond to these antics, so I hopped around a little and tried to hum a little tune to go along with the jigging and to appear as thrilled about whatever it was as he seemed to be.

"You don't get it, do you, moron?" I didn't need to answer. The sum total of my not getting it was all over my face.

"Don't you see it? He didn't give them a way out. He's getting sloppy. He didn't exclude the Hebrews. He's bound by what He said. The firstborn of the Hebrews will die along with the Egyptians."

"Oh, I don't think so, sir." The words went right by the stop sign in my brain and out my mouth before I could rein them back in.

Satan stopped jigging not two inches from my face. I closed my eyes and tried to keep on humming like I wasn't worried. He didn't say a word. He didn't have to. He just breathed on me, daring me to tell him something he didn't want to know.

"It's like this, Your Evilness." I tried not to stutter, but I couldn't help it. "I mean, it's like, well, I don't really know what it's like, but..." I grasped for words, hoping to make a complete sentence as he bore down on me. "But I know what God is like. He will find a way to save them."

"Oh, so now you know what God is like, do you? Has *He* taken you into *His* counsel? Has *He* asked your opinion on anything at all?" He snarled and growled at me at the same time. "Or is there something you forgot to tell me? Some little detail you left out."

"No, no, sir." My voice was barely audible.

"If you're so sure He's got a plan, get out of my sight and find out what it is. You make me sick."

As soon as he turned his back, I slunk out and went in search of Moses.

I arrived just in time to hear Moses giving the people instructions to prepare a hasty supper. So hasty, in fact, they were not to use any yeast in making the bread. It was obvious they weren't going to have time to let it rise. Wherever they thought they were going, they expected to make a quick exit. I followed Moses into another room, where he gathered the men. I must tell you that I wasn't the least bit comfortable being in the middle of the Hebrews like that. I don't know what it was about them, but to be honest, I really wanted to run. But I didn't dare leave without hearing what Moses had to say.

Moses summoned all the elders of Israel.

"Go at once and select the animals for your families, and slaughter the Passover lamb. Take a bunch of hyssop, dip it into the blood in the basin, and put some of the blood on the top and on both sides of the door frame. Not one of you shall go out the door of his house until morning. When the Lord goes through the land to strike down the Egyptians, He will see the blood on the top and sides of the door frame and will pass over that doorway, and He will not permit the destroyer to enter your houses and strike you down."

When I heard the word *destroyer,* then I *really* wanted to run. I knew Satan would be livid when he heard that this new deal had blood in it, but how bad could it be? Lamb's blood would be the last thing he would care about once I told him the destroyer was about to be released into the earth realm. We knew all about him all right. He had only one job. He carried out the wrath of God. His authority transcended the realm of humans and demons alike. I flapped with all my might to get back to the den to report what I'd heard.

I tried as hard as I could to get in control of myself and stop trembling before delivering the news to Satan.

"The destroyer is coming," I blurted out, reaching as high as I could to remind him how big the destroyer was. "And there's going to be a lot of dead sheep everywhere..."

Satan stopped me short by slapping my face back and forth like a cartoon.

"Get a grip," he seethed at me. I settled down except for some minor whimpering.

"Are you telling me that the destroyer is being dispatched from the third heaven to kill sheep?"

"No, no. Well, I suppose he will kill some sheep, but only if it's the firstborn. But, no, hardly, I didn't mean that's his primary purpose. Oh, my, no..."

Satan slapped me again. "Spit it out."

"It's the Hebrews who are going to kill the sheep. Well, not all of the sheep, of course. Just some of them. The destroyer is being sent to kill the firstborn of every household, just like God said."

Satan cocked his head to one side and waved one of his claws in a circle.

"So, help me out here. God is going to kill people, and the Hebrews are going to kill sheep. This means what to me?"

"Don't you see?" I was exasperated that he couldn't see the obvious. "It's the escape clause in the whole last plague deal. They'll smear the blood of the lamb on the doorposts of their houses, and the destroyer will see it and pass right over."

I was about to point out the distinct possibility that the destroyer might not stop with the firstborn of Egypt but might step into our realm as well, but I didn't get the words out in time. The change in Satan's countenance silenced me. He stood completely still as all emotion drained from him. I wouldn't dare say so, but I'm sure he actually slumped, which he would never do in front of one of us.

"They're going to use the blood of a lamb? You're sure?"

"Well, I'm sure that's what Moses said, but who knows how well that idea will really work. It doesn't seem like much of a deterrent to the destroyer."

Satan didn't say another word. He didn't take a swipe at me as he usually did in circumstances like these. He didn't jump on my tail as he often did when I brought him bad news. He did nothing. The prince of darkness turned and quietly walked out of his lair.

Not knowing what else to do, I returned to my perch and tried to make the pieces of the puzzle mean something. It was hard to say whether Satan thought the destroyer in the earth realm was the big deal I thought it was. Why had he acted so strangely? All he seemed to care about was the part about the blood.

"What is it with the blood?" I asked myself for the millionth time. If I could just figure it out, maybe I could find a way to...never mind. I looked up toward the third heaven and called out to God.

"God, what is it? What is Satan afraid of? What does he know? Why doesn't he tell us? Why won't You tell me?"

God said nothing.

A T MIDNIGHT, JUST as Moses said, the Lord struck down all the firstborn in Egypt, from the firstborn of Pharaoh to the firstborn of the prisoner, to the first-born of all the livestock. Pharaoh, all his officials, and all the Egyptians awakened to the massacre as loud wailing broke out such as had never been heard in Egypt. Even to the demons it was chilling. There was not a house anywhere without someone dead in it—except for the houses of the Hebrews.

Pharaoh was beside himself with grief when he summoned Moses and Aaron. He slumped over the body of his dead son.

"Leave us alone. You and the Israelites go, worship the Lord as you have requested. Take your flocks and herds, but before you do also bless me."

Can you believe Ramses had the nerve to ask for a blessing after he single-handedly brought such devastation on his own people?

The Egyptians urged the Israelites to hurry and leave the country in fear that more death might be coming if they stayed. The Hebrews took their dough before the yeast was added and carried it on their shoulders in kneading troughs wrapped in cloths. Their animals were laden down with the gold and silver of Egypt, and off they went.

It was hard to tell how Satan felt about the exodus of the Hebrews. One moment he seemed depressed, then angry, and finally exasperated. He shifted his eyes to and fro over the ranks of the demons who returned from Egypt and now stood on the rim of the second heaven, awaiting further orders and staring at the parade of departing multitudes. I knew what he was doing. He was looking for someone to blame. For once, I was pretty sure it would not be me.

Finally, Satan walked behind Bezel and half whispered his instructions: "Get them back."

Bezel raised his great wings and leaned over the edge as if he were about to leap across the chasm that divided our realm from the earth. But just before he took to air, he stopped abruptly, turned back to Satan, and asked the obvious.

"How am I supposed to do that? We cannot touch Moses."

"Send Ramses after them."

"Have you seen Ramses lately? He's a sniveling wreck. Did you hear what he said to Moses? 'Pray for me.' He's so close to repentance. He's of no use to you anymore."

"Am I the only one who can think around here?" Satan roared. "*Close* doesn't cut it with God. Move in. Talk to him about his public humiliation. Turn his grief into revenge. Send the armies of Egypt after the Hebrews. If the slaves don't turn back, the armies will kill them all."

I followed Bezel as he flew straight to the bedroom where Ramses lay weeping over his dead son. Hearing loud voices from another room, he decided to check it out before speaking to Ramses. The voices belonged to the financial magistrates, who were dealing with the reality that the entire labor force of Egypt had just left town. Bezel contributed to their confusion by releasing visions of a crumbled economy into their minds. Then he flew back to Ramses' side and whispered into his dreams. Ramses saw himself publicly humiliated by Moses, removed from the throne, and Moses placed upon it. By the time the magistrates knocked on his door, he was primed. I tell you, that demon was good at his job.

It was as if Pharaoh and his finance men were waking from a shared nightmare.

"What have we done? We have let the Israelites go. Who's going to work?"

Who's going to work? Can you believe it? Never mind all the dead bodies—get that assembly line going!

Meanwhile, Moses was doing his best to get the masses of people organized and facing the same direction. Knowing God was sure to give Moses new orders, I hurried over to join him. Satan would have my head if I missed anything. When God told Moses which path to take out of Egypt, it should have been his first clue that in spite of what Moses had told Ramses, this was not going to be a weekend outing. Never having been out of town before, the ex-slaves were unaware they were about to travel the longest possible way when a much shorter route was available. Moses (who *had* been out of town before) tried to point out to God that this was the long way home.

"You must take the people this way. The Philistines are waiting for them. If the people are attacked, they will turn around and try to run back to Egypt. You won't be able to stop them. You can't let them leave Egypt along a straight path."

That's why for three days they simply wandered around in circles, having no idea they weren't really going anywhere. The reason no one noticed how many times they passed by the same rock was because their attention was fixed on the cloud by day and pillar of fire by night, which God had set in front of them to lead them on.

It wasn't till the third day when God revealed His strategy.

"Tell the Israelites to turn around and make camp at Pi Hahiroth, between Migdol and the sea. Camp on the shore of the sea opposite Baal Zephon."

"Are You sure, Lord?" Moses asked, not thinking about how utterly ridiculous the question was, although I might well have asked it myself because God couldn't have picked a more dangerous campsite. It was occupied territory.

Baal Zephon was one of Egypt's favorite gods and one of the few idols still standing after the calamity with the plagues that had toppled most of the others. I knew for sure the demon residing in the idol was still very much at home there. It was hard to see how thumbing one's nose at an entrenched principality was a good idea, considering the Israelites were skittish enough without more provocation. Why stir up a skirmish if you didn't have to? Moses couldn't see the logic either.

"Are You sure, Lord?" Moses asked the same ridiculous question again.

Thinking back to how it had been with Abraham and Noah when God told them to go somewhere they had never been, and never mind about taking along a map, I knew how God's marching orders usually didn't come with a lot of explanation. I wasn't expecting God to answer Moses at all, much less share His whole strategy, but that's just what He did.

"Pharaoh will think you're lost and confused. When he's told of your location and sees you are surrounded by the wilderness, he'll think you're vulnerable to an attack."

That was when Moses first realized that some of Pharaoh's spies had been following them the whole time. Right then I put one and one together and was sure Moses had to be doing the same math. Pharaoh was going to chase them, and God was the One who set it up that way. Moses must have figured it out, but being the man of few words he was, he said nothing.

The spies were about to hightail it back to Egypt to tell Ramses the slaves had been wandering aimlessly through the desert for three days and were now hopelessly lost, at least that's the way it looked to someone who hadn't heard God tell Moses to take the loop. From his nervous look, I was sure Moses had figured out the danger they were in. That's when God chimed in to confirm Moses's worst fear.

"Then I'll make Pharaoh's heart stubborn again, and he'll chase after you."

"Now, there's a good idea," Moses answered.

Moses didn't actually say it, but I knew he was thinking it. Or maybe it was me who was thinking it. Whichever one of us was thinking it, this would have been a dandy time for Moses to ask the Lord why He was planning such a thing. Knowing Moses wasn't much of a conversationalist and would likely never get around to holding up his end of the dialogue, God decided to tell him why without being asked.

"I'll use Pharaoh and his army to put My glory on display. Then the Egyptians will realize that I am God."

Moses shook his head in confusion, not understanding this line of thinking at all, but I did. It was just like I said when I tried to tell Satan it wasn't just about the Hebrews anymore. God wanted the Egyptians to be saved. Why else would He care whether they knew He was God or not? Satan would want to know all about this right away, so I began flapping my way back to the second heaven to give him the update.

He wasn't all that impressed with the news.

"So, let me see if I have this right," Satan began. "God caused all the hoopla with the plagues just to get Ramses to let the slaves go, who would then wander around lost in the wilderness for three days to provoke Pharaoh to chase after them again to take them back to Egypt, and somehow along the way the Egyptians figure out who God is. Is that what you're telling me?"

"Yes, yes, that's it. Just like I've been saying. It's more than the Hebrews."

I don't know why Satan never took my warnings seriously. In all the centuries I'd been assigned to watch and report what happened on the earth, I was rarely wrong when it came to predicting what God was going to do with you ill-conceived humans. Still, Satan always sent someone else to verify what I told him.

"Go find out what's really happening." He dispatched Bezel back to Pharaoh's court to check it out. I was dismissed, so I decided to follow the demon, if for no other reason than to satisfy myself that I was right. By the time we got to the throne room, the spies were already telling Ramses and the magistrates about the pitiful state of affairs with the runaway slaves.

"They've wandered in circles for three days, Your Majesty. They're lost. They don't even realize they've set up camp under the watchful eye of Baal Zephon. We can easily overtake them."

He listened, but Ramses didn't see the situation the same as the spies saw it.

"Why should we do that? Moses said they would be back in three days. They're not lost; they're just coming back to Egypt. That was always the plan."

The spies were not about to correct Pharaoh, so they stood silently, looking at the floor, each hoping the other would say something. When neither said a word, Bezel, who had been observing the whole thing, positioned himself beside the throne and whispered into Pharaoh's ear.

"Pay attention to the spies. You're getting sentimental. They know Moses has no intention of returning with the slaves. Why do you think they carried out all the gold and silver when they left? You're looking a little naïve here in front of your men."

Maybe he was addled from having to deal with the frogs, the gnats, the blood, the hail, and the deaths, but I do believe that was the first moment Pharaoh really figured out what had happened. Just as his magistrates had tried to tell him, the entire workforce had taken a hike. Of course, they weren't coming back. I watched the color drain from his face as he realized the situation he was now in. He jumped to his feet, startling the two soldiers who stepped back in fear when they saw the anger in Ramses' eyes.

"What have we done? The slaves are not coming back. There will be no one to do the work."

Can you believe he was just now figuring that out?

Chapter 11

"We have to go get them," Ramses said in a state of panic and in full command of the obvious.

"Yes, yes." The soldiers were relieved it hadn't been necessary to point out Pharaoh's failure to grasp the situation. "It will be easy. They're trapped with their backs to the sea."

"Get my chariot," Ramses commanded. "Bring six hundred of the best charioteers. The slaves will not escape."

It was amazing how quickly the Egyptian soldiers mobilized. In less than an hour, six hundred war chariots were zooming toward Moses's camp with Pharaoh himself leading the charge.

Meanwhile, back at the campfire, only Moses knew that things were about to get ugly. The ex-slaves still hadn't figured out that they literally were between the devil and the deep blue sea. They went right on congratulating themselves over having escaped Egypt and the brick pits, as if any of them had a single thing to do with it. It wasn't until one of the women noticed the cloud of dust appearing over the horizon that they realized company was coming.

"What is it?"

"Can you see anything?"

Before anyone could venture an answer, the unmistakable rumble of chariot wheels thundered toward them.

"It's the Egyptians! They're after us." They cried out to each other and to God. God didn't say anything, so they quickly turned on Moses.

"Weren't the cemeteries large enough in Egypt so that you had to take us out here in the wilderness to die?"

"Why have you done this to us? Why did you take us out of Egypt?"

"Back in Egypt, didn't we tell you this would happen?"

"Didn't we tell you, 'Leave us alone here in Egypt—we're better off as slaves in Egypt than as corpses in the wilderness'?"

Of course, not one of them had ever said anything of the sort. They were all too happy to gather the booty and leave town.

Moses tried to calm them down. "Don't be afraid. Stand firm, and watch God do His work of salvation for you. Take a good look at the Egyptians today, for you're never going to see them again. God will fight the battle for you."

Moses sounded surer than he looked. He turned from the people and ran a few yards away, where he began calling out to God.

"God, please. It's time for You to do something."

"No, it's time for *you* to do something. Why cry out to Me? Tell the Israelites to get moving. Hold your staff high, and stretch your hand out over the sea. Split the sea! The Israelites will walk through the sea on dry ground."

Split the sea? Moses looked like he might faint.

"Meanwhile, I'll make sure the Egyptians keep up their stubborn chase. I'll use Pharaoh and his entire army, his chariots and horsemen, to put My glory on display so that the Egyptians will realize that I am God."

"The Egyptians don't need any encouragement," Moses muttered under his breath as he hurried to try to get the Israelites moving again. I could hear him, so I was pretty sure God could as well.

As much as God seemed to me to be enjoying what was going on, He must have taken one look at Moses's face and realized his last nerve was about to unravel. God ordered the angel who had been leading the camp of Israel to shift and get behind the people. Then the pillar of cloud that had been in front also shifted to the rear. The cloud was now between the camp of Egypt and the camp of Israel, enshrouding one camp in darkness and flooding the other with light. Pharaoh's army screeched to a halt when the horses reared up with fear and neighed at the site of the angel. Several chariots almost overturned from the panic of the strong steeds as they attempted to run away. Let me tell you, the soldiers weren't all that gung ho to try to get around that angel either. The army was at a standstill, and it stayed that way all through the night.

Meanwhile, Moses was leading the racing Hebrews toward the sea. When he got to the edge, he paused and looked around to see if God was anywhere about. Not seeing Him, Moses cried out again in that loud whisper.

"Now what, God?"

"Do what I told you. Stretch out your staff, and split the sea."

"Right, OK. I'm about to do that very thing." Moses had no conviction in his voice whatsoever.

He didn't dare look back at the people to see if they were watching. He knew they were. Every eye that wasn't fixed on the stalled Egyptian army was on Moses. He lifted his shaky arms and extended his staff out over the foreboding water before him.

Glancing toward heaven one more time, he muttered to himself, "I hope this works."

I was nervous just watching the whole thing.

Moses took a deep breath and stretched out his hand as far as he could reach over the sea, and right on cue, God, with a terrific east wind, made the waters split. It was magnificent. The sea stood up, forming two walls of water on either side of the dry land that now lay where mud had been before. I was so excited I wanted to clap, but I wisely restrained the impulse.

"Run! Run!" Moses shouted to the people. "Cross while you can."

Well, you can just imagine how the people were temporarily paralyzed with sheer terror, not knowing which was worse—the soldiers behind them or the towering sea walls in front of them. Moses couldn't get them going, but God could. He recalled the angel and released the army to race toward the hordes of people.

"Run! Run!" I shouted at the people, getting caught up in the drama before I realized what I was doing and stuffed my claw into my mouth.

And run they did. The Israelites hurried through the sea on a narrow path of dry ground with the walls of water to the right and to the left.

The Egyptians came after them in full pursuit, every horse and chariot and driver of Pharaoh racing into the middle of the sea. God looked down from the pillar of fire and cloud on the Egyptian army and threw them into a panic. The chariots were too many to stay on the slim trail of dry ground, so they were forced into the mud, which clogged the wheels of their chariots until every last one of them was stuck in the miry clay.

Then the Egyptians began yelling at each other: "Turn around! Retreat! Run from Israel! Their God is fighting on their side against us!"

The soldiers beat the horses with their whips, but the frightened animals could not dislodge the wheels from the thick mud. Some of them abandoned their chariots and tried to run back to the sea's edge, but they sunk to their knees in the mire. The glory that had been Egypt's military elite was hopelessly trapped between the lofty walls of water on either side.

Then God said to Moses, "Stretch out your hand over the sea, and the waters will come back over the chariots and the drivers."

Moses obeyed quickly and stretched his hand out over the sea, and immediately the waters crashed down upon the entire Egyptian army. Not one of them survived.

I was worn out from the stress. Since I knew he would be watching from the second heaven, I wondered if I had time to lie down for a while before heading back to give Satan my report.

When the Hebrews turned back and looked at the Egyptian dead, some of whom were already washing up on the shore of the sea, they realized the tremendous power that God brought against their enemy. The people were in reverent awe and pledged their everlasting trust in God and in Moses. There was no mistaking the relief on Moses's face. He was as exhausted as I was and sat down to rest, thinking the worst of it was over.

I could have told him it wasn't.

CHAPTER 12

THE DEMON HORDE stood on the rim and watched the sea return to normal as if nothing unusual had happened to it, much less that the fighting glory of Egypt now lay at the bottom. I wondered how Satan was going to respond to all of this.

At first, he didn't seem to be all that worked up about what had occurred. Then I remembered that Satan could not have cared any less about what happened to the Egyptians. They were of no further use to him. In fact, Egypt was of no further use to him. There was no leadership left to manipulate, and the people themselves were just a mess what with dealing with the dead firstborn and all that.

Deciding to cut his losses, Satan ordered the demon hordes to evacuate. I naturally assumed he would send them after the Hebrews into the desert. Everybody else thought that would happen as well. When he ordered the troops into Canaan instead, we looked at each other, wondering if we had heard correctly but not daring to ask. Finally, Bezel spoke up.

"We can still catch them."

"Forget it," Satan said. "We don't have to waste our time chasing them. They are slaves. They don't know how to take care of themselves. They can't function without someone driving them. There's six hundred thousand of them and one of Moses. Moses will have a heart attack from frustration before long. They'll wander around in the desert, and most of them will die there. If any of them make it across, we'll be waiting on the other side. Besides, the Nephilim are in Canaan. If some of the Hebrews do get through the desert, the freaks we created will be all too happy to have another chance at them."

The others congratulated Satan on being a brilliant strategist and then began forming battalions to move out. I assumed I would be going along and joined up with Bezel's brigade when Satan grabbed my tail.

"Where do you think you're going?"

"Obviously, I don't know, sir. Where would you like for me to go?"

"We have unfinished business."

I didn't like the look in his yellow eye, but I followed him back to his lair and waited for him to make himself comfortable on his throne. He summoned several of the others to come and witness what I was certain would be something bad for me.

"So, moron, run this by me one more time." His voice held that tinge of sarcasm again. "I want to be sure I understand that part about how much God cared about the Egyptians."

He was making sport of me. Satan stood up and strutted back and forth in front of his throne, waving a claw in the air for effect, stroking his ugly chin with the other, mocking deep thought.

"Let me see if I remember this correctly: all the chariots got stuck in the mud."

"Yes, sir," I barely whispered.

"And all the soldiers were drowned; even Pharaoh was drowned."

I nodded.

"Like, say, a pack of rats; it was something like that, wasn't it?" His eyes narrowed, and the sinister grin that split his misbegotten face only encouraged the others who hadn't left for Canaan yet to snicker louder at my humiliation.

"Well, then." He sat down on his throne. "Help me out here. Why don't you reconcile that unfortunate event with your insistence that God cared about the Egyptians and wanted to save them?" Everybody laughed.

One look at his sneer told me there was no way for me to win, so I said nothing.

"What? No defense? No glib comeback?"

I shook my head, avoiding looking at him directly.

"Why don't you just go on with your report? God drowned all the Egyptians, and then what happened?" One last snicker came from the onlookers.

"The Jews started singing and dancing and praising God for their salvation. That's it."

"Idiots," he spewed. The mere mention of worship and praise to God ruined his mood every time. "Have they started to move toward Canaan yet?"

"Moses was working on it when I flew back to report."

"How long before they get close to Canaan? I want their welcoming committee to be ready." He laughed, and so did everyone else except me.

"It depends. If they take the direct route, a couple of weeks, maybe a little more."

Satan turned as if to give an order to one of the waiting demons when I interrupted.

"But God is unlikely to lead them along the shortest route, sir."

"And why would that be?"

"History, sir." I hoped that answer would be sufficient, but a look in his other yellow eye told me it wasn't.

"God has rarely, if ever, led His people in a straight line to anywhere. My guess is He will lead them around in the desert for a while—maybe even years."

"Why? Doesn't He know what to do with them now that He's got them?" Several snickered.

I knew I was stepping out far beyond my actual knowledge if I ventured a guess about God's strategy, but why not? After all, I'd been watching God and humanity for eons. Besides, Satan's quotient for humiliating me had reached its peak for one day. My guess would be as good as anyone's and better than most.

"He will keep them in the desert until they're ready to fight."

"Fight against what?" Satan seemed surprised.

Here's what I wanted to say: "Oh, puh-leeze. Do you for one moment think God doesn't know what you've got planned through all of those demon-possessed people you have waiting for them on the other side? You will never outmaneuver God, and He will never let you get away with a massacre."

Here's what I said instead: "God will anticipate trouble once they leave the desert, and He wants them trained to defend themselves."

Satan leaned back on his throne as if the thought had never crossed his mind. After a while he motioned my dismissal.

"Follow them."

So, that's how it happened that I went winging it across the Red Sea to catch up with the jubilant now ex-slaves.

As I watched Moses leading the throngs across the desert sand, I wondered if he had the first idea what to do next.

CHAPTER 13

IT WASN'T LONG before they moved beyond the Red Sea toward the land of Shur. By the third day when they still hadn't found any water, the people began to complain to Moses.

"What are we supposed to drink?"

"You should have thought about water before we left Egypt."

Moses resisted the urge to scold the people for their short memories. Not even three days from God having split the sea on their behalf, here they were complaining to Moses about a lack of water. I tried to imagine what it would have been like for anyone in the demonic ranks to have complained to Satan about a lack of provision when they followed him in his rebellion.

Moses might have suspected there would be water at Marah, but he didn't count on it being so bitter as to be undrinkable. Frustrated with the people whining about how they should have stayed in Egypt, Moses cried out to God for help. God pointed out a pile of sticks, which Moses could have found for himself if he had been looking instead of expecting God to do every little thing for him.

"Throw the stick into the water, and it will become sweet," God said with no enthusiasm whatsoever.

Moses should have known to do this without being told. It was one of those bits of desert-survival training he learned while herding goats. He seemed to have a lot of trouble applying his prior life skills to his present situation. I'm not sure he ever made the connection between his training in herding goats for forty years and his present job to herd people through the same desert. The difference between the two was negligible as far as I could see.

Once the people filled their vessels with water, God told Moses He was ready to establish some laws and procedures for the rest of the trip.

"If you listen obediently to how I tell you to live in My presence, obeying My commandments and keeping all My laws, then I won't strike you with all the diseases that I inflicted on the Egyptians; I am God your healer."

If I'd been Moses, I wouldn't have let that decree pass without reminding God of a few things.

"God," I would have said. "Have You forgotten what happened with Adam and Eve when they had only one law in the entire universe to uphold? Two human beings in a garden couldn't successfully obey one simple rule. Now You're thinking about imposing multiple rules to thousands of people wandering in the desert and ready to flee back to Egypt at the first inconvenience?"

Although Moses didn't challenge God's idea, he must have been concerned about how well it could work. He sighed, roused himself, and got the people moving again. On the fifteenth day of the second month after they had left Egypt, the whole company of Israel moved on from Elim to the Wilderness of Sin, which is between Elim and Sinai. As Satan predicted, the whole company complained loudly against Moses and Aaron again, and I'm sure Moses was having chest pains.

"Why didn't God let us die in comfort in Egypt where we had lamb stew and all the bread we could eat? You've brought us out into this wilderness to starve us to death."

It was true that if God didn't intervene, the people were likely to starve because they were deep in the desert and there was no readily available food source. I could have pointed out to God in the very beginning that He would regret many times His decision to make humans from flesh and blood. To make it worse, He threw emotions into the mix, including the penchant to feel sorry for yourselves over the slightest difficulty. Human beings are simply too high maintenance to be of any real use in a pinch. Sorry to say, but none of you can be counted upon in less-than-perfect circumstances. Every few hours, you have to be fed and watered, not to mention needing sleep every single day.

For a fleeting moment, I wondered if, based upon prior history, He might not just let them starve after all. He certainly had precedent to do so. In all the centuries I had watched God and His humans, I had seen Him rescue them many times, but always in response to that "faith" requirement. You know what I'm talking about—when humans face a catastrophe fully believing God will rescue them because He loves them. Oh, yes, I've seen God swing into action more than once—often at the last possible minute—to respond to the faith of one who trusts Him in times of trouble, even when there is no visible evidence whatsoever that He intends to do anything. But would God respond to whining, complaining, and self-pity? I couldn't recall ever having known God to respond well to such behavior, especially after having proven Himself as many times as He had in their exodus from Egypt.

I don't mind telling you I was a little more than perturbed when I heard how God intended to give in to their griping.

God spoke to Moses: "I've listened to the complaints of the Israelites. Now tell them that at dawn they'll eat their fill of bread."

In the morning there was a layer of dew all over the camp. When the layer of dew lifted, there on the wilderness ground was a fine, flaky, frostlike something all over the place. The Israelites, having no idea what it was, took one look and said to one another, "*Man hu.*" ("What is it?")

So Moses told them, "It's the bread God has given you to eat, and these are God's instructions: 'Gather enough for each person—about two quarts per person—enough for everyone in your tent. Eat all of it. Don't save any of it for tomorrow. If you do, you will find it spoiled and inedible.'"

Stiff-necked people that they were, a couple of them just had to try it. They saved some of the stuff overnight, but it became full of worms and smelled all the way to the second heaven. Moses lost his temper over their action, but really, what did he think was going to happen? Especially when the rules changed for the sixth day.

"Tomorrow is a day of rest, a holy Sabbath to God. Whatever you plan to bake, bake today; and whatever you plan to boil, boil today. Then set aside the leftovers until morning," Moses instructed them.

So they set aside what was left until morning as Moses had commanded, and contrary to its prior behavior, the manna didn't smell bad and there were no worms in it. Go figure.

Moses said, "Now eat it; this is the day, a Sabbath for God. You won't find any more of it on the ground today."

True to character, on the seventh day, some of the people went out to gather anyway, but they didn't find anything. Once again, Moses's temper flared.

"How long are you going to disobey my commands and not follow the instructions God has given me for you? Don't you see that God has given you the Sabbath? On the sixth day He gives you bread for two days. So, each of you, stay in your tent. Don't try to gather on the seventh day."

Whether they were afraid of God or not I can't say, but they were definitely afraid of Moses, so the people quit working on the seventh day. The phenomenon of the manna continued for forty years.

CHAPTER 14

So THEY'RE ON the way to Rephidim. What of it?" Satan seemed annoyed that I'd left my post with the Israelites to give him a location update.

"There's no water there." I paused to see if he connected with the obvious. Apparently not.

"They must have water. They're humans; they can't go three days without it."

"God will let them die of thirst? Is that your point?"

"No, no. God will lead Moses to find water somewhere, but in the meantime, Moses is tired, and the people are frustrated. They keep complaining to Moses that he should have left them in Egypt instead of leading them into the desert to die. They're in a weakened condition. If you wanted to, it's a good time for an attack."

Satan stopped polishing his claw and looked up at me for the first time. Then looking right past me, he turned to one of the other demons.

"Do we have anybody at Rephidim?"

"Um, Rephidim? Where is that exactly?" The demon stumbled over his answer, having no idea what was going on in the desert. Ever since the desert demons abandoned their posts when God showed up in the wasteland as a burning bush, Satan had never been able to quite get his tight rule back together there.

"The Amalekites are there." I interrupted the stumbling.

"You're sure?"

"Near there, anyway, and they hate the Jews. It wouldn't take much to provoke them to attack. That is, if an attack was part of your plan, Mighty One."

I didn't know what Satan had planned and neither did anyone else, maybe because he rarely made any plans. He's more of a thermometer than a thermostat. Since the Egyptian army drowned, he hadn't told any of us what his next step might be.

"Make it happen," he said, looking directly at me.

"Me?" I was suddenly queasy. "Surely, my lord is not suggesting I could provoke the Amalekite army to action? Someone else would be much better."

"You said it wouldn't take much to provoke them. Well, you're not much, so go do it."

The whole room burst out in guffaws. I didn't know what to do, so I tried to join in the laughter with them as if it were all some great big joke. As soon as I opened my mouth, everyone else became suddenly silent. I couldn't guffaw, but I was able to muster up a pretty convincing chuckle.

"You had me going there for a moment, sir."

"Get him out of here," Satan ordered one of the guard demons.

The burly demon picked me up by my wing and tail, carried me to the rim, and tossed me out over the expanse between the second heaven and the earth. I tumbled over several times through space before I could right myself and flap my way back to the desert where Moses was camped. I arrived just in time to hear God tell Moses how to get water.

"Go on out ahead of the people; take some of the elders with you. Take the staff you used to strike the Nile. I'm going to be present before you get there on the rock at Horeb. You are to strike the rock. Water will gush out of it, and the people will drink."

And that's just what happened. The people were pacified, and Moses was relieved to have quieted their grumblings for the time being.

"That went pretty much like I thought it would," I said to myself as I went in search of Israel's enemy as Satan had ordered me to do, although I didn't know what to do when I found them. How would I provoke King Amalek to attack Moses? Such a thing was way above my pay grade. As it turned out, I needn't have worried. I should have known Satan wasn't really going to trust me with an act of war. By the time I got near Rephidim, one of the other demons had already arrived and goaded the king to lay siege against Israel.

I don't know whether Moses heard the horses' hooves, or whether he saw the cloud of dust rising up over the hill, or whether it was his years of training in the desert, but somehow he knew something wasn't right. He jumped to his feet, and with one hand over his eyes to shield them from the sun, he stared straight ahead toward the hill. Then he ordered a couple of the men to go up to see what was going on. They ran up the embankment, and when they reached the top, they turned and waved their arms to signal trouble was coming.

Moses sighed and then called out for a young man named Joshua.

"Who is he?" I wondered. I couldn't recall having heard him mentioned before.

Joshua came running to Moses's side with three other young men whose names I didn't know either.

"You called for me, sir," Joshua said as he bowed his head to Moses as a sign of respect. I might not have noticed his reverent tone of voice had it not been for the pervasive tone of gripe and grumble that came from so many of the other people when things weren't going just right.

"Joshua," Moses said to him in a subdued voice. "Take some of the men with you—pick the most reliable—go up to the top of the hill. See what is coming, and be prepared to fight."

"Right away, sir." He turned to signal to his three comrades.

"Wait," Moses interrupted his departure. "It may be Amalek. If it's him, there will be a battle. You must take the front line with your men. I'll come and stand on top of the hill where I can see the whole field, and I'll signal you from there."

Joshua lowered his head again and raised it quickly to show he understood his orders and ran off toward the camp with the others following close behind. I wondered why I hadn't noticed him before. If Moses was sending him out to lead the battle, he must be important. Note to self: watch Joshua.

"Tomorrow I will take my stand on top of the hill holding God's staff," Moses said to Aaron, who had come looking for him to see what was going on. "You and Hur must go up with me."

Joshua, who seemed to have a natural sense of military maneuvers, did as Moses had instructed him in order to fight Amalek. The next morning Moses, Aaron, and Hur went to the top of the hill. He didn't show it, but Moses had to be a nervous wreck. This was the first time for the poorly organized Hebrew fighters to go up against an enemy of any kind, much less one skilled in battle like the Amalekites. Three months ago they were slaves; now they were soldiers. You can imagine how chaotic it was in spite of Joshua's precise orders to the untrained Hebrew army. In fact, the Amalekites should have been able to roll those chariot wheels right over the Hebrews, and at first, it looked like that might be the story, but then something strange happened.

Moses stood at the top of the hill, watching his troops take a beating from the Amalekite army. In a gesture of desperation, Moses raised his arms up over his head—personally, I think he was trying to get God to pay attention to the slaughter about to happen—and Israel seemed to rally. Moses lowered his arms, and the Amalekites advanced; he raised his arms, and Israel took ground. Aaron and Hur exchanged a look. This was looking like a trend.

It turned out that whenever Moses raised his hands, Israel would start winning, but whenever he lowered his hands, Amalek would start winning. It wasn't long before Moses's arms got tired. Aaron and Hur, who had definitely figured out what was going on, hurried and got a stone and set it under Moses. He sat down on it, and Aaron and Hur held up his arms, one on each side, and there they remained steady until the sun went down. By the next day, Joshua had defeated the entire Amalekite army.

I hadn't counted on that. I knew I should get right back to the second heaven to let Satan know what had happened, but I just couldn't make myself go. Instead, I flew down to the empty battlefield—empty except for the dead Amalekite soldiers—and sat down on a rock, trying to figure out where things went wrong. Not that it mattered. It was still going to be my fault. After all, I was the one who told Satan it would be an easy victory for King Amalek, one of Satan's best resources to persecute the Jews. The king might even be dead now. Oh, no, I hoped not. That would surely be my fault too.

By the time morning came, I was still sitting on my rock. No one had come to look for me, so maybe Satan had other things on his mind and had temporarily forgotten about Amalek. I decided to make one more pass through Moses's camp to see if I could find some tidbit of information I could carry back to my evil master that would lessen his ire at the failure of my idea.

By the time I got there, Jethro, Moses's father-in-law; Zipporah, Moses's wife; and Moses's two sons had arrived.

Moses went out to welcome his father-in-law, bowing to him and kissing him. Then they went into the tent, and Moses told his father-in-law the story of all that God had done to Pharaoh and Egypt in helping Israel, all the trouble they had experienced on the journey, and how God had delivered them.

Jethro was impressed. He said, "Blessed be God who has delivered you from the power of Egypt and Pharaoh and the oppression of Egypt. Now I know that your God is greater than all gods because He's done this to all those who treated Israel arrogantly."

They stood up, hugged each other, and stepped outside the tent to see more than one hundred of the people arguing among themselves as they lined up for an audience with Moses.

"What is this?" Jethro asked.

Moses sighed. "It's like this every day. From morning till night they bring their grievances before me and demand I judge between them."

"No wonder it's taking you so long to get across the desert. This can't go on; they'll wear you out, and at this rate, you'll die an old man before you reach your destination."

"Don't I know it? But what else can I do? They won't move on until I rule on their petty grievances."

"You said it yourself. Their grievances are petty. Here's what you have to do. Are there any elders here you can trust?"

"Yes. Thirty, forty, maybe more."

"Concentrate on training the elders, and then let them divide the people into groups. Let each of the elders be responsible for settling the minor issues, bringing only the big deals to you."

So, for the next few days, Moses sat about selecting and training the elders who then trained captains under themselves, and before I knew it, what had been pure chaos settled into the beginnings of organization. Satan was not going to like this. One of the telltale signs that God was in something was when the chaotic morphed into order. That had been the first signal to us long ago when the rampant waters of Lucifer's flood began to settle and clear from the middle of the sea outward as Ruah Ha Kadosh hovered over the murky seas that covered the earth.

I flew back to the second heaven to deliver my report but changed my mind and went to my perch instead of to Satan's den. If he wanted me, he could send for me. No need for me to rush over to answer questions he wasn't yet asking.

CHAPTER 15

SEVERAL WEEKS HAD passed uneventfully, so one morning I decided to sleep in. I was standing on my head practicing yoga. I picked it up during one of the rare times when I wasn't glued to the Hebrews. I was on surveillance duty around the rest of the world when I encountered a strange group of people on the other side of the earth who were practicing a different sort of religious ritual. I'd never heard anyone mention the god of yoga, nor had Satan ever said anything about a rogue demon being on the loose somewhere. It didn't seem to be the "same old, same old" of a demon pretending to be a god charade I'd seen a million other times. These particular people never claimed yoga was a god, rather that the practice itself put them in touch with a higher power, so I thought I'd give it a try. After all, if there was a mediator in the hierarchy between Satan and God, I wanted to know who it was. Maybe he/it could help me bring my case to the heavenly court. I was chanting about the unfairness of fate when God's voice rolled through the expanse between the heavens and the earth with such force that I lost my balance and tumbled right onto a hard stone below.

"Speak to the house of Jacob; tell the people of Israel," He thundered. It was so loud and so clear that for a brief moment I wondered if He might be speaking to me directly—but only for a moment. He was calling to Moses.

"This is what I want you to tell the people of Israel: 'You have seen what I did to Egypt and how I carried you on eagles' wings and brought you to Me. If you will listen obediently to what I say and keep My covenant, out of all peoples you'll be My special treasure. The whole earth is Mine to choose from, but you're special, a kingdom of priests, a holy nation.'"

I blinked hard to clear the yoga mantras from my brain as I walked over to the rim of the second heaven to take a good look at the Israelites. Granted, I hadn't been watching as carefully as I should have for a few weeks now, but I'd been terribly depressed about my lot in life and found it hard to leave my perch. I wondered if the people had undergone some remarkable change in a few short weeks to make them special and holy, because they weren't anything close to that last time I looked. I peered intently at the camp, but I didn't see any change. They were still the same unruly people as before my sabbatical. I wondered if God might be talking about some other group. No way around it; it was time for me to return to Earth and check the status of the ex-slaves. I got there just as Moses was about to address the people.

Moses called the elders of Israel together and told them all that God had commanded him to say. The people were unanimous in their response.

"Everything God says we will do."

"Oh, right. Sure you will," I said under my breath. "Don't stake your reputation on them," I wanted to call out to Moses.

Moses, ever the optimist, it seemed, took the people's unedited answer straight back to God.

Then God said, "Get ready. I'm about to come to you in a thick cloud so that the people can listen in and trust you completely when I speak with you."

Again Moses reported the people's affirmation to follow God, which, as far as I was concerned, was no more convincing the second time around.

God continued, "Go to the people. Take two days to get these people ready to meet the holy God, because on the third day I will come down on Mount Sinai and make My presence known to all the people. Post boundaries for the people all around, telling them not to climb the mountain or even touch its edge. Whoever touches the mountain dies a certain death. A long blast from the horn will signal that it's safe to climb the mountain."

For the first time in weeks I was excited. If God were actually coming down on Mount Sinai to meet with the people, maybe I could wedge my way into the crowd and at last get my audience with Him. Even if He didn't speak to me directly, perhaps if I could blend in with the throng of people, then whatever blessing He released over them might fall to me as well. After all, my exile had certainly come about from standing among a crowd in the wrong place; perhaps my redemption could come in the same way. I couldn't wait for three days to pass.

On the third day at daybreak there were loud claps of thunder, flashes of lightning, a thick cloud covering the mountain, and an ear-piercing trumpet blast. Everyone in the camp shuddered in fear, including me. Moses called the people to attention and lined them up to lead them out of the camp to meet with God.

I lined up with them, more nervous than any of them, I can tell you. We all stood at attention at the base of the mountain.

Mount Sinai was all smoke because God had come down on it as fire. Smoke poured from it like smoke from a furnace. The whole mountain shuddered in huge spasms. The trumpet blasts grew louder and louder. Moses spoke, and God answered in thunder. God descended to the peak of Mount Sinai and called Moses to come up where He was. I wondered if I should chance getting closer so I wouldn't miss anything. It was then I heard God give Moses a warning.

"Go down and warn the people not to break through the barricades to get a look at Me lest many of them die. And the priests also—warn them to prepare themselves for the holy meeting lest I break out against them."

That's when I decided against trying to get closer.

Moses said to God, "But the people can't climb Mount Sinai. You've already warned us well, telling us to post boundaries around the mountain."

"Right, I did, but I've noticed that I sometimes have to tell you more than once. Go down and bring Aaron back up with you. But make sure the priests and the people don't break through and come up to Me lest My glory break out against them."

Moses hurried back down the mountain to get Aaron, who was hiding at the back of the line, scared as could be and in no rush to go up the mountain to meet with God face-to-face. See, that's just how it is with you humans. You run around boldly declaring your search for God and how God has told you this, that, or whatever, but when God finally shows up in your neighborhood, you try to crawl under the rug until He leaves.

Moses took Aaron by the shaking hand and began leading him up the mountain to where God was waiting. I so wanted to go along, but to be honest, I was as afraid as any human. I had rationalized that if God happened to spot me in a crowd of people He intended to bless, He might just let it pass that I was there so as not to inadvertently injure one of His pet people, but in a threesome? He could take me out with just a look. Better not chance making my situation worse than it was.

I don't know how long they were up there, but when Moses and Aaron came back down the mountain, Moses's face was full of light, and Aaron's was drained of color. I've noticed that is how God seems to affect you humans—with sheer exhilaration and awe or sheer terror. Moses is the one who spoke to the people.

"The Lord your God says to you, 'I am your God, who brought you out of the land of Egypt, out of a life of slavery. Have no other gods before Me. Do not use My name in an irreverent way. Observe the Sabbath day to keep it holy. Honor your father and mother so that you'll live a long time in the land that your God is giving you. No murder. No adultery. No stealing. No lies about your neighbor. No lusting after your neighbor's house or wife or servant or maid or ox or donkey. Don't set your heart on anything that is your neighbor's.'"

If you can, try to picture it: throngs of people experiencing the thunder and lightning, the trumpet blast, and the smoking mountain, totally afraid—terrified is more like it. They pulled back and stood at a distance to rethink their bravado.

Realizing the power they were about to encounter, the Israelites developed a new humility and pleaded with Moses.

"You speak to us and we'll listen, but don't have God speak to us or we'll die."

"Don't be afraid." Moses tried to reassure them. "God has only come to test you and instill a deep and reverent awe within you so that you won't sin."

Nice try, but the people were so traumatized by the glory of God that they refused to come any closer and so kept their distance while Moses turned and approached the thick cloud where God was. I suppose God must have realized He had let too much of Himself rest upon a people who in no way were prepared for who He is. That must be why He went along with their request to speak to them through Moses.

"Give this message to the people of Israel: 'You've experienced firsthand how I spoke with you from heaven. Don't make gods of silver and gods of gold and then set them alongside Me. Make Me an earthen altar to sacrifice your offerings. Everywhere I cause My name to be honored in your worship, I'll be there Myself and will bless you.'"

If I'd been God, knowing the earth people as long as He had, I would have quit right there with the rules. Moses should have interrupted and reminded God how Adam and Eve had done with only one rule to obey; it had been a disaster. Now here He was not only giving them no less than ten absolute rules, but He was also about to pour out dozens of other regulations that no human I had ever seen could possibly keep up with. Moses could barely write fast enough to get them all down. From selling slaves to property rights to oxen in ditches to seducing virgins—He covered the gamut of every possible misdeed a human might think to do.

This seemed totally out of character for God, as I'd known Him before the fall from heaven. He never was much of a thou-shalt-not kind of ruler. I had to think awhile before I could figure out why He was going into so much detail with the Hebrews.

The people had been slaves for four hundred years. They'd never before had an option to make a decision on their own and therefore had no experience in even the most trivial of matters. God took up His valuable time to think of every possible repercussion for any misdeed the average person might get himself into and gave Moses a way to avoid it. When I thought about it, I remembered that was the only reason God ever laid down laws to start with: to keep the people out of trouble, even the rules about worshiping other gods. It's not because God is jealous the way humans understand jealousy but because He knows that worship to anything other than Himself is covert worship to Satan, and once the prince of darkness gets his hands on a human, well, let's just say there *will* be blood before he lets one go.

By the time He got to the ordinance about not boiling a kid goat in its mother's milk (as if anybody would think that was a good idea) I found myself losing interest. I knew Satan wouldn't care a thing about health and diet issues, and it looked like the law giving was going on for a good while longer, so

I decided to go back to my perch and resume my meditation about the meaning of life.

I must have succeeded in meditating my way right into a trance because the next thing I knew, one of the other demons was at my perch, shaking me by the hoof and yelling something about Satan wanting to see me. I must tell you, I was a little groggy, and I had some trouble remembering why I was standing on my head on my perch. How long had I been there? I couldn't be sure—days maybe. I just didn't remember. From the tone in the demon's voice, I knew to hotfoot it over to Satan's lair without further delay.

"Where have you been?" Satan had been standing near his portal through which he could view the earth when he whirled around to face me.

"At...at my post, sir," I stammered.

"I told you to watch Moses."

"I was watching him, sir. I was right there the whole time, well, most of the time." I knew not to lie. "God began giving him a plethora of rules I knew you wouldn't want to be bothered with, so I didn't...bother you, I mean. I assure you I didn't miss anything important." I decided not to mention my meditation.

"Then where is he?"

I looked around the room to see if any of the other demons might give me a little help. Not even a side wink. I could never count on them for any support. I thought it best to clarify the question.

"Do you mean Moses, sir?"

"Of course I mean Moses, idiot. Where is he?"

I began to sweat. *Was Moses missing? How long had I been in a trance?*

"You don't know, do you?"

"I'm sure he's right there in the camp, sir. That's where I left him—well, more like on the mountain actually—but he was right there taking down all those nitpicky rules God was dictating. I wasn't gone but a minute. He couldn't have gone anywhere else. And...I mean, really, even if he wanted to, where could he go?"

"Find him." Satan's eyes narrowed as he glared at me.

I kept my head down as I backed slowly out of the room. As soon as I was safely beyond Satan's sight, I began flapping my way back down to the earth.

That was it; no more yoga.

CHAPTER 16

SATAN WAS RIGHT. I made the rounds of the whole camp, but Moses was nowhere to be found. The people were agitated and angry as if they thought Moses had simply run off somewhere and wasn't coming back. I knew that couldn't be the case, but where was he? The last time I'd seen him he was up on the mountain with God, but that had been weeks ago. He wouldn't still be up there.

The loud voices coming from Aaron's tent caught my attention, so I flew over to see what was going on. A large contingent of mixed people was arguing with Aaron over what to do about the missing Moses. Did I mention mixed people before? I can't remember, what with so many of them to keep up with.

When the slaves followed Moses out of Egypt, a whole group of other people went along with them. They were the Egyptians who believed in the power of the God of Israel as a result of living through the devastation of the plagues. Hedging their bets that the glory days of Egypt might be over, they wagered on a future's market with Moses and joined the caravan they'd heard was on the way to a land of milk and honey. These people were nothing but trouble from the first day, and I never knew why Moses didn't throw them out of the gang early on. When there was any complaining going on with the Israelites, you could just bet it was the mixed people at the bottom of it.

For example, remember when the people started complaining about how good life had been in Egypt and how they missed the food delicacies they used to eat like onions and leeks? It was the mixed people doing the complaining. Come now, you didn't really think slaves dined on such things, did you? It didn't take long for the slaves to join right in with the entitlement grousing, but they would never have thought it up on their own. Manna and quail was quite a step above the gruel they usually had.

"What do you intend to do about it?" They badgered Aaron, who sat on the floor with his head in his hands.

"What do you expect me to do? Just give him a few more days; he'll be back." Aaron rose to his feet to take a look out the tent door as if hoping Moses might stroll up at any moment."

"No, he's gone. We must have a new leader. The crowds will panic without a leader. It could be a stampede."

"Do you want the job?" Aaron shot back.

"No, don't be ridiculous. I don't want it," said several at one time.

"Well, neither do I. Neither would anyone in his right mind."

"Then make us a god."

"That's right! Make us a god to lead us out."

"Are you insane?" Aaron was incredulous. "We can't just make up a god."

"Oh, sure you can. We used to do it all the time in Egypt."

"You made gods?" Aaron couldn't believe what he was hearing.

"Well, not really, if you mean like a *real* god who could, you know, do anything."

"He means make an idol. Who cares if it's a real god? If we say it's a god, then it's a god as far as the people are concerned. They lived in Egypt their whole lives. They're used to it. They'll follow the new god because we tell them to."

"This is crazy." Aaron wiped the sweat from his brow. "Get out of my tent."

"You better think this over, Aaron. You're in real danger of a rebellion here. The crowds are turning into mobs. They think Moses isn't coming back. If panic sets in, the people will disperse like frightened animals. Then what will you do?"

"Do it, Aaron, just till Moses gets back."

Aaron looked at one then the other then out the door one more time to be sure Moses wasn't about to walk in. He threw his hands up in the air in a sign of defeat.

"OK, you win. Bring me all your gold."

"Now you're talking." They ran out of the tent and began gathering up the gold jewelry and anything else made from the gold the Israelites brought with them from Egypt.

I was stunned. Never would I have predicted this. I didn't know what to do. I didn't know what to think. Maybe I hadn't heard right. How could Aaron be agreeing to such a thing? About that time Miriam, Aaron's sister, came running through the tent door. She had been standing outside and heard it all.

"Aaron, what are you doing?"

"That's right." I agreed with her. "What do you think you're doing?"

"I'm buying time. The people won't want to give up their gold. Maybe Moses will be back before the mixed people can get it together."

"But what if he doesn't come? What if the mixed people bring the gold? You can't go through with it."

"Miriam, do you see any other way? Look at them. There are hundreds of thousands of them, and me against them by myself? How long do you think I could last?"

Oh, my. It looked like Aaron might cave. I wondered if I should take off and tell Satan right away? No, better not. He wouldn't believe me anyway; better to wait and see what happens.

"Aaron, come out here," the men shouted.

I followed Aaron outside as the men came running back with a basketful of gold. Aaron was dumbfounded, and so was I, to see how quickly the people had turned over their treasure. It was a downward spiral after that, at least as far as God's plan was concerned. The mixed people built the fire to melt the gold while Aaron watched. I began to wonder about God; something like this wouldn't escape His notice. He must have known what was going on. And where was Moses anyway? I was so caught up wondering what God and Moses would do about the fiasco in process that I didn't actually see what happened next.

All I know is they threw the gold in the fire, and *presto*, there was a golden calf. Some said Aaron made it with a chiseling tool, but honestly, Aaron didn't have the skills to make something like that. Others said the sorcerers who were hidden among the mixed people had used their magic to bring forth the calf. Whatever. There it was for all to see: a golden idol, courtesy of Aaron, the priest of God.

That was when throngs of Israelites came running up to see what was going on. The mixed people shouted to them, "These are your gods who brought you up out of Egypt."

The looks of shock and disbelief on the faces of the true Israelites made it clear they could not have possibly been party to such a scheme and it really had been instigated by the mixed people. The Israelites looked first to the calf and then to Aaron, having no idea what to do next.

Aaron saw the confusion on their faces as well. He was quicker on his feet than I had previously given him credit for.

"Help me build an altar in front of the calf," he shouted to the crowd. "Tomorrow is a feast day to our God. We'll celebrate His goodness right here in front of the calf."

The people still looked confused, but if Aaron said it was all right, they thought it must be. They set out to build the altar and to party like all of this would work out just fine, not giving another thought to where Moses was.

I watched for a little while, but I'd seen unbridled revelry before in the name of religion, so it wasn't all that interesting to me. I knew I should probably leave right then and report to Satan, but my curiosity about where God and Moses might be was supplanting my good sense. I decided to go find them.

The last time I saw them they were on the mountain, so I flew to the base where the Israelites had gathered before to hear Moses deliver God's commands. All signs of life were gone, but the ominous clouds still hovered over the top, a sign to me that God was still there, and where God was, Moses would have to be close by. I wondered if I dared go to the top of the mountain to find them. I remembered how God had warned the people not to come close or to try to touch the mountain, and normally, that would have been quite enough to send me running back to my perch in the second heaven.

But I can go up the mountain without touching anything. I can fly.

Such courage was unusual for me, but I was compelled to find Moses and God.

I heard the rumbling before I saw Moses standing on a rock and looking toward the cloud. His face glowed from the flashes of lightning rolling over him as the voice of God spoke. I hovered within a crevice in the rocks, touching nothing, and listened.

"Go! Get down there! Your people whom you brought up from the land of Egypt have fallen to pieces."

"My people, Lord? Aren't they Your people?"

"You know the ones I'm talking about, the mixed hoards you allowed to follow you out of Egypt. You let them join with you without consulting Me."

"But, Lord, I thought that would please You, having true Egyptians deny their false gods to follow You. Granted, they've whined and complained the whole way, but no real harm has been done."

"No real harm? In no time at all they've turned away from the way I commanded them and made a molten calf and worshiped it. They've sacrificed to it and said, 'These are the gods, O Israel, that brought you up from the land of Egypt!' It's a mess down there."

Moses looked sick.

"I can't stand to look at them. What a stubborn, hardheaded people! Leave Me alone now; give My anger free rein to burst into flames and incinerate them."

"Surely You would not, Lord." Moses was nervous. "You must have a people to follow You."

"I'll start again. I'll make a great nation out of you."

That might have thrilled some people, but it was the last thing Moses wanted to do. I could see it in his eyes. Can you imagine? Starting all over with kids and more kids at eighty years old? No, thank you. Moses just wanted to get this over with as soon as possible.

"Why, God, would You lose Your temper with Your people? OK, I'll take the responsibility for the mixed people, but Your own people are at risk of Your anger. You brought them out of Egypt in a tremendous demonstration of power and strength. Why let the Egyptians say, 'He had it in for them. He brought them out so He could kill them in the mountains and wipe them right off the face of the earth'? Please reconsider bringing evil against Your people! Think of Abraham, Isaac, and Israel, Your servants to whom You gave Your word, telling them, 'I will give you many children, as many as the stars in the sky, and I'll give this land to your children as their land forever.'"

God listened to Moses and decided not to do the evil He had threatened against His people—at least not right then.

If only I could have found the courage to seize the moment to fly in front of God and demand justice. It would have been the perfect opportunity. He simply could not have justified letting these people get away with their sin while refusing to reconsider my situation.

"God," I should have said. "Listen to Yourself. You know those people have committed the unforgivable. How can You let them escape Your wrath just because Moses asked You to? What about me? My only sin was poor judgment. Why can't I have another chance?"

If only I had the nerve.

The flashes of lightning ceased, and I knew God had nothing further to say on the matter. Moses, his face still shining from the glory of God spilling out over him, bent over and picked up the tablets upon which the finger of God had been writing and started down the mountain. I hadn't noticed the tablets earlier. They were beautiful, engraved front and back in a way that no human of that day would have been able to do.

In my flight up the mountain, I was so obsessed with finding Moses and God that I completely missed Joshua, who'd been waiting beside the trail halfway up the mountain. When he saw Moses coming down with the tablets, he rushed to help him. Together they made their way down the winding path toward the camp.

They heard it before they saw it. The noise of unrestrained revelry grew louder with each step taking them nearer to the camp. When Joshua heard the sound of the people shouting noisily, he took Moses by the arm as if to warn him.

"That's the sound of war in the camp!"

"Oh, that it were only that, Joshua. Listen again. Those aren't songs of victory, and those aren't songs of defeat. I hear songs of people throwing a party."

And that's just what it was. As Moses came near to the camp and saw the calf and the people dancing, his anger flared. He threw down the tablets and smashed them to pieces at the foot of the mountain.

It was as if the people had awakened from a trance. The dancing and music stopped in mid beat. They saw the wrath and fire in Moses's eyes and panicked, running to and fro as if some horrible thing were loose in the camp and pursuing them. Moses strode into the camp with Joshua close behind, pushing the people aside as the two made their way to the golden calf.

With the strength of ten men half his age, Moses took the calf and threw it into the raging bonfire the people had built. The people were stunned at how fast the calf melted, but I wasn't. I'd seen the angel of the elite guard of heaven throw holy fire into the flames to increase the heat beyond what can occur through natural means. The primary purpose of God's fire is to consume His enemies; it works every time.

Aaron ran up to Moses and hugged him, but Moses did not hug back. Aaron stepped back and lowered his head in anticipation of what he knew was coming.

"What on earth did these people do to you that you involved them in this huge sin?" Moses demanded.

"Brother, don't be angry with me. You know the mixed people and how set on evil they are. Why did we ever let them come with us?"

Moses did not respond.

"They were spreading discontent among the Israelites, telling them that you had left and weren't coming back. Then they came to me and demanded that I make a substitute god to calm the people down and lead them out of here."

Moses did not respond.

Sweating profusely, Aaron continued. "So, I tried to buy some time, just till you got back. I ordered them to gather up the gold from the Israelites and bring it to me. Who knew the people would turn it over so easily? I thought it would take days—weeks even—to get the gold together, if they could do it at all."

Aaron paused again, but still Moses did not respond.

"So, anyway, they brought the gold to me, and I threw it in the fire, and just like that, out came this calf."

Up to that point, I think Moses might have been softening a bit toward Aaron and the impossible situation he had found himself in. I should have helped Aaron with his story before he got to sounding ridiculous. He should have told Moses how his very life was at stake or he would never have done such a terrible sin. He should have emphasized the role the sorcerers played in the whole thing. He should have added a lot more drama than he did. Otherwise, how could he possibly have thought Moses would believe such a preposterous story?

Moses shook his head and turned away from Aaron and saw that the people were simply running wild. He took up a position at the entrance to the camp. When the people saw him, the frenzy stopped as they literally froze in place under the fierce look in Moses's eyes. Finally, Moses raised his staff and bellowed at the people.

"Whoever is on God's side, join me!" All the Levites stepped up and stood behind him.

I can tell you it got ugly after that. If you ask me, Moses was out of control as he and the Levites went through the camp killing people all over the place. I don't know if they were aiming for the mixed people or not, but by the time it was said and done, more than three thousand corpses lay scattered throughout the camp. I didn't recall hearing God say the first thing about a massacre, and I wondered if Moses had done this on his own without consulting God.

Time to go; Satan would want to know all about it.

CHAPTER 17

SATAN ROARED WITH delight when I told him about the golden calf.

"It didn't take them long to get over the idea of their great deliverer, now did it?" he asked in that sarcastic way I hated. The others laughed along with him as they always did. No one would dare imply by failing to laugh that Satan wasn't clever.

"Well, to be perfectly accurate," I said, "it wasn't the Israelites who came up with the idea of making another god. It was the Egyptians who went with them. They're the ones who intimidated Aaron to do it; the people just got caught up in fervor."

"Whatever." Satan dismissed my comments entirely. "Tell me more, and don't leave anything out."

"That's about it. Moses threw the calf into the fire, and it melted immediately. That's when he lost all reason and began to behave like a madman. He called the Levites together and led them on a rampage through the camp killing about three thousand people." I paused, wondering if I should add my opinion; oh, well, why not? "I don't think God told him to do that. I would have heard it."

"Are you saying Moses disobeyed God?"

"No, no, I didn't say that. I said I didn't *hear* God tell him to kill so many people. If Moses acted on his own, technically, one could not call it disobedience in the general sense."

Satan sat back on his haunches as if pondering whether or not this meant anything to him.

"Is Moses still mad?"

"I don't know, sir."

Satan turned to one of his captains and ordered him to go to the Israelites' camp.

"Stir Moses up. Whisper in Moses's ear. Tell him Aaron betrayed him. See if you can incite him to kill more people—Aaron too."

"Wait, sir," I interrupted. "I don't think that will work." As everyone gasped I realized I had made the very foolish mistake of correcting one of Satan's ideas.

"What I meant to say, sir..." I tried to dig myself out of the hole I'd dug myself into. "Moses is a lot more like God than you know, personality-wise, I mean. His anger doesn't last. He gets aroused in righteous anger and punishes the disobedient, but right after that he always returns to loving them and seeing himself as responsible for them. He doesn't carry a grudge—nothing like you at all."

Before the words rolled off my tongue, I realized I should have swallowed them.

"Are you comparing that pseudodeliverer wannabe to me?"

"No, no, absolutely not; *cunning*, that's what I meant. Moses is not as cunning as you. Simpleminded really...doesn't have the...the chutzpah...that's it. Doesn't have the chutzpah to conduct a massacre for very long."

"Chutzpah? Am I supposed to know what that means?"

"You know, the Jews say it all the time when they want to communicate, uh, virility, sort of." I stopped mid sentence. There was no way to make this better. "Never mind, sir, all

I meant is Moses will not stay mad. He'll feel bad about the people for a little while and then feel bad that he felt bad and punished them."

"Never mind what Moses feels." He began to chuckle in that evil tone I hated. "No, never mind about Moses at all. The question is, how does God feel now that His precious people have bowed down to another god?"

"Idol, sir."

"Did the people acknowledge it as a god or not?"

"They acted like they did. Some of them probably; yes, I suppose."

"Then God will abandon them or, better yet, kill them. He has to do it. He can't break His own rules. No one can save them. We've won. Get ready to descend on the earth unopposed," he shouted to the onlookers.

Cheering broke out from the demon guards like it always did when Satan announced a victory, real or not. I stood quietly by, shuffling my hoof back and forth in front of me, never looking up and hoping I would be dismissed as no longer needed. Satan was basking in the shouts of praise from the others when he looked at me from the corner of his yellow eye and stopped in mid chuckle.

"Now, what's the matter with you? If you can't celebrate my victory, get out."

"Right away, sir. I'll just be leaving, then." I began slinking toward the door before he could change his mind.

"Stop him!" Satan yelled at one of the guards who grabbed me by the tail just as I was making my getaway.

The guard held me up and dangled me like a morsel on a string as the others roared with laughter at my predicament. When he saw the look in Satan's eyes, he knew recess was over, and he slammed me down in front of his evil ruler.

"You know something; what is it?"

"I just don't want you to get your hopes up, master," I said in the gentlest voice I could find. Was that ever a poor choice of words.

Satan himself came down on top of me and kicked me like a soccer ball. I fell to the floor and rolled up in the corner. The evil prince came and stood over me with those awful eyes. This was it; I just knew it. At last he would destroy me and only because I had tried to show a little concern for his feelings.

"I do not have hopes." He snarled as he bent down close to my face with breath that could wilt a rock. "I am not one of His pathetic humans. I have hope neither in Him nor in any other living thing in the universe. I am my own god; I decide how things will be; I do not hope. Do you understand that?" He kicked me one more time for emphasis.

"Yes, yes, of course. I misspoke."

"Get him up!" he yelled at one of the guards who promptly grabbed me by my tail again. Satan stomped across the floor and sat down on his throne, motioning for the guard to deposit me in front of him.

"Talk!"

"Yes, I was just about to..."

"Spare me the groveling."

"Right. OK, it's just that there is the possibility that God will not destroy the Hebrews as you are hoping." I couldn't believe I'd said it again. I tried to recover. "Not *hoping*, of course. What I meant to say is God may not be required to destroy the people even though they fell into idol worship."

"Because?"

"Because of intercession, sir."

The boos and hisses from the other demons didn't dissuade me. I surprised myself by spinning around to face them. "Has the past been so wasted on you that you've learned nothing from it? I said *intercession*, not praying, not begging. *Intercession!* Have you forgotten what God does in response to intercession?"

Satan motioned for them to leave me alone. I turned to face him.

"Master, if Moses intercedes for the people, God will not destroy them. I'm sure of it."

"You said Moses was so angry with the people that he killed three thousand of them. Why would he intercede for the rest of them?"

"Because humans are not like us."

The room was silent as each head turned to see how Satan would react. I couldn't imagine getting into deeper trouble than I was already in, so I risked it and continued.

"God's people get mad and do terrible things, but they don't stay mad. Eventually, they get over it. Demons never get over anything. Each offense just adds to the last offense. Therefore, we have no frame of reference for understanding human guilt or their penchant to care about other humans. They repent for their madness and plead with God to reconcile what the madness has brought about, and He usually does. Moses is going to intercede for the people, and God will forgive them. I know I'm right about this." I sat down hard on the floor and curled my tail up under me so no one could grab it again.

Satan leaned back on his throne and grasped the arms with both claws. He was obviously thinking about what I said. I tried to remember whether that had ever happened before. Finally, he stood up, walked over to me, and lifted me up by one wing. He then stood me on the floor in front of him. He walked around me as if examining me to see what foreign substance I might be made of. At last, he stopped in front of my face.

"Not about idol worship." No one said a word as we waited for his next sentence. "You may be right about other things, but not worship of other gods. His jealousy consumes Him. Have you forgotten why we were thrown out of heaven? He was jealous of me."

I bit my tongue so hard I was afraid a piece of it would fall out. I dared not respond with anything close to a true depiction of what happened in the war in heaven.

"Get back down there and follow Moses; you will see I'm right." The guarding demons began chanting ad nauseam that ridiculous ditty about how Satan rules.

I kept my head down and was able to walk out of the room under my own power instead of being heaved out by one of the other demons, which was usually the case.

"I'm not wrong," I said under my breath when I was a safe distance away.

Chapter 18

I returned to the Israelites' camp to find them struggling with what to do with three thousand corpses. The whole mood had changed. There was no singing, no partying, and, for once, no griping going on. The people were traumatized; that's the only way I can describe it. They had seen and applauded God's judgment against Egypt, but I suppose it never crossed their minds that He would exact devastating punishment on them as well if they disobeyed. It's hard to say who they were more terrified of, God or Moses. They were virtually immobilized because of their fear. So much so that Aaron and Hur were concerned they might not be able to get the people moving again. That's when Hur asked for a private meeting with Moses.

"Unless you do something, Moses, I don't think we can get them to go either forward or back."

"If we don't get them going soon," Aaron interjected, "our enemies will think we're lost or vulnerable in some way. It's just a matter of time until one of them tries an attack."

"How do you think it would make God look if all these people He rescued are killed here in the desert?" Hur asked. "Right now the people are walking around in a fog and in no condition to fight. They're afraid to make a move."

"I agree with Hur," Aaron said. "This could all end up looking like God called the people out of Egypt and then abandoned them to their enemies."

Moses bristled. "And whose fault is it that we're in this predicament?"

Aaron dropped his head. "It's mine. I let it happen. I'm not cut out for this line of work. Let somebody else be in charge if you're planning on taking off again."

Moses ignored the comment. "All right, gather the people, and in the morning I'll talk to them."

True to his word, the next day Moses addressed the people. "You have sinned an enormous sin! I don't know if it will help, but I'm going up to God on your behalf. I'm not making any promises, but maybe I'll be able to clear you of your sin."

Moses told Joshua to follow him at a distance as he trudged up the mountain in search of God. He wasn't hard to find. The mountain still manifested the glory of God as the fire and smoke billowed upward. Moses went to the last place he had been when God talked to him, sat down on a rock, and waited. It wasn't long before God revealed Himself and spoke to Moses.

"They are a rebellious people."

"Don't I know it?" Moses stood up and paced back and forth with his hands on his hips. "This is terrible. They have sinned an enormous sin! There's no excuse for it. It was the mixed people who made the god of gold for them, but Your people are responsible for their willingness to worship it."

"Aaron is also responsible."

"Yes, I know, and believe me, he feels horrible about it. He's admitted his fault and has asked for forgiveness."

God did not respond. Moses waited a few minutes and then tried to move the conversation along.

"And now, if You will only forgive their sin."

"I will not," God interrupted.

Moses dropped to his knees with desperation written all over his face as he tried to persuade God to forgive.

"If you cannot forgive them, then erase me as well out of the Book of Life You've written."

"I'll only erase from My book those who sin against Me."

"If You don't forgive them, then I have failed You. My sin is greater than theirs, for I have been with You."

God remained silent. Moses closed his eyes and rocked back and forth on his knees, determined to wait for God to speak. After five minutes, he couldn't stand it. He opened one eye and whispered.

"Are You thinking it over?"

"All right. For now, lead the people to where I told you. My angel is going ahead of you. On the day, though, when I settle accounts, their sins will certainly be part of the settlement."

Moses nodded eagerly as if in total agreement.

"Now go. Get on your way from here, you and the people you brought up from the land of Egypt. Head for the land that I promised to Abraham, Isaac, and Jacob. I will send an angel ahead of you to the land flowing with milk and honey, and I'll drive out the Canaanites and the rest of your enemies before you. But I Myself will not go with you. They are such a stubborn, hardheaded people; I might destroy them on the journey."

I was mesmerized. God spoke to Moses the way neighbors talk to each other over the backyard fence.

But Moses wouldn't quit. He kept right on pleading with God, just exactly as I'd told Satan he would.

"Lord, first You tell me, 'Lead this people,' and now You've changed Your mind and aren't going with us? You don't even let me know whom You're going to send with me. An angel? It's not the same. And it's not what we agreed to. You tell me, 'I know you well, and you are special to Me.' If I'm so special to You, let me in on Your plans. Don't send me where You won't go. How can I know You're still pleased with me if You make me go on without You? Don't forget; this is Your people, Your responsibility. I never wanted this job in the first place."

"Whoa there, Moses," I almost said out loud. "Take a good look at who you're talking to."

Moses didn't seem to be worried about pushing God too far. He paused for a moment and then kept right on going.

"If Your presence doesn't take the lead here, and if You won't go with us, let's call this trip off right now. How else will it be known that You're with me in this, with me and Your people?"

He paused again, waiting for God to respond. When He didn't, Moses just kept pushing. I wondered how far this might go before God had enough.

"Well, what's Your answer? Are You traveling with us or not? How else will we know that we're special among all other people on the earth?"

I began to get nervous when God didn't say anything. I was afraid He might have left. From the beads of sweat on his upper lip, I knew Moses feared the same thing. After another unnerving minute, God finally spoke.

"All right. Just as you say; this also I will do, for I know you well, and you are special to Me. I know you by name, and I will go with you."

Moses clasped his hands together and waved them at God.

"Thank You, O Lord, for You are great and mighty and faithful to Your word."

Doesn't that beat all? God agreed to forgive the grievous sin of the people because Moses interceded for them. Isn't that just what I told Satan would happen? I was right; I didn't think it was fair, but I was right.

From watching all the people on the earth, I'd learned a few things about doing deals. The first thing I learned was when you get a yes from the customer, quit talking. Pack up your kit, and get out before he can change his mind. I thought surely that would be what Moses would do. He'd gotten the best deal he was going to get, so he should have moved right along as quickly as possible. But he didn't.

"Please, God, before You send me away, let me see Your glory."

What? I couldn't believe it. *Moses, are you addled from all the stress? God isn't going to show you His glory. Who do you think you are?*

I wasn't expecting God to say anything to such an arrogant request. I would even have bet money that God wouldn't respond. I would have lost.

"I will make My goodness pass right in front of you; I'll proclaim My name right before you, but you may not see My face. No one can see Me and live. Look, here is a place right beside Me. Put yourself on this rock. When My glory passes by, I'll put you in the cleft of the rock and cover you with My hand until I've passed by. Then I'll take My hand away, and you'll see My back. But you won't see My face."

When I heard God say those words, an old aching began to rise up within me. Moses had never seen God, but I had. How many times in my exile had I longed to see Him just one more time? I had to get closer. I crept up to the rock where Moses stood and set myself down right beside him. When the shadow of God's hand passed over us, I panicked and jumped down and hid behind the rock instead.

I couldn't see it, but I could feel it as God passed by Moses. When I dared take a peek, Moses's face was radiant beyond anything I'd ever seen in a human. Without saying another word, Moses bowed low and backed away; then he turned and ran down the mountainside.

I knew I should have followed Moses back to the camp as he hurried down the mountain, but I was momentarily paralyzed with indecision. Why was I such a coward? I was right there near the place where God was. I might never get this close again. Since He seemed to be in a conciliatory mood, I wondered whether He might be willing to hear my case now that Moses's issues were settled. He might get angry and not hear me, but how could that be any worse than things were for me now? I decided to chance it, and with great trepidation, I climbed back on top of the rock and tried to squeeze myself into the cleft where Moses had stood.

I hadn't as much as wedged my hoof into the opening before the weight of His glory forced me down on the rock, and I could not move. I was frightened beyond what words can convey. But it didn't matter; I was near the presence of God. Even if He destroyed me right there and then, my lot would be so much better than living under the dictatorship of an insane ruler who thought he was a god.

After a while, I got a cramp in my midsection from the weight of all that glory and wished I could stand up.

"I wonder if God knows He's standing on top of me?" I asked myself. "Did He cause His glory to weigh down on me because He knew I was here, or did His glory descend and I just happened to be in the way?" Not that it mattered, unless I was actually going to be allowed to speak to Him, in which case my opening line would be important.

I didn't have to wonder much longer. Slowly His weight lifted from me, and I knew He was giving me a chance to escape. I was torn between going and staying. What should I do? If I tried to approach Him instead of fleeing, as I was sure He was allowing me to do, He might be angry, and my window to get away could suddenly close, and who knew what would happen to me then? I couldn't chance it. I raised myself up and flew as fast as I could.

I will never know what might have been if only I'd had the courage to stay.

CHAPTER 19

I WAS IN NO hurry to return to the second heaven only to tell Satan I'd been right again about the intercession. I needed something else to report so it wouldn't seem like I was gloating about being right. Satan doesn't respond well to gloating from anyone else, although he himself is in a constant state of gloat. I figured God was sure to speak to Moses again with better instructions about going forward. I didn't dare miss anything, so I hung around the camp and waited for God to show up again.

Moses was sitting outside the door of his tent, appreciating the cool of the evening and apparently not expecting God to drop by. He jumped abruptly when God spoke to him, almost knocking me off the bench I was sharing with him.

"Cut out two tablets of stone just like the first set, and engrave on them the words that were on the original tablets you smashed."

God often started a conversation in the middle of a paragraph, so it was not surprising that Moses had to think for a minute before knowing exactly what God was talking about. God paused a moment until Moses got that clear look in his eyes, which signaled he was now tracking and all systems were go for God to continue with the rest of the paragraph.

"Be ready in the morning to climb Mount Sinai, and get set to meet Me on top of the mountain. Not a soul is to go with you; the whole mountain must be clear of people, even animals. Not even sheep or oxen can be grazing in front of the mountain."

Moses stayed up half the night cutting two tablets of stone just like the originals. He got up early in the morning and climbed Mount Sinai as God had commanded him, carrying the two tablets with him. Just as He said, God descended in the cloud and took up His position there beside Moses and then did what I thought was an odd thing. God began to call out *His own name*. Don't ask me why. I'd never seen Him do anything quite like this before, and believe me, I'd seen some odd things.

God turned, and with His back to Moses, He passed in front of him and called out, "God, God, a God of mercy and grace, endlessly patient. So much love; so deeply true; loyal in love for a thousand generations; forgiving iniquity, rebellion, and sin. Still, He doesn't ignore sin. He holds sons and grandsons responsible for a father's sins to the third and even fourth generation."

Why was God talking about Himself in the third person? I looked around to see if there was anyone besides Moses and me to whom God might have been making these declarations. It didn't seem like He was talking to Moses, and He certainly wasn't talking to me. I didn't see anyone else, so when God started talking again, I had to deduce that Moses was His only intended audience. God soon stopped with the third-person talk and spoke to Moses as if nothing at all strange had happened.

"As of right now, I'm making a covenant with you. In full sight of your people I will work wonders that have never been created in all the earth, in any nation. Then all the people with whom you're living will see how tremendous the work will be that I'll do for you. Take careful note of all I command you today. I'm clearing your way by driving out all of your enemies."

Moses really perked up at that last part. I once heard him tell Aaron privately that he feared the day his ragtag militia of ex-slaves would have to face on its own a real army. Even though they'd been successful in that earlier skirmish, Moses worried what might happen if they ever came up against a foe whose defeat God had not predetermined.

As far as Moses was concerned, the conversation couldn't get any better than hearing how God intended to remove his enemies before him, so he stood up, anxious to get back down the mountain to tell Aaron the good news, but God was not finished.

"Moses, listen to Me."

Moses stopped his exit attempt as he realized God's tone had changed from exuberant to somber.

"Stay vigilant. Don't let down your guard lest you make covenant with the people who live in the land that you are entering and they trip you up."

"I don't understand, Lord." Moses seemed confused by this warning. "I thought You just said You were going to drive Your enemies—our enemies—out before us."

"I did, but I'm going to use you as the instrument in My hand to accomplish what I promised."

Moses's face fell as if such a thought had never crossed his mind.

"Oh, come now, Moses. How else did you think I would do it? You know I have limited Myself to working through these people of yours."

"I just thought that when You said *You* were going to do it, You meant *You* were going to do it; that's all."

"If I were going to do everything Myself, I wouldn't need you, now would I?"

"Can You be a little more specific about what You expect us to do to drive them out?"

"Sure. Tear down their altars, smash their phallic pillars, and chop down their fertility poles."

"Oh, well, nothing to it." Moses ventured a little sarcasm but quickly recovered. "This isn't going to be easy, is it? They're going to fight back, aren't they?"

God ignored his questions but continued with a stern warning as to what Moses must be uncompromising about.

"Don't allow My people to worship any of their gods. I, the Lord, am jealous for My children. Be careful that you don't make a covenant with the people who live in the land lest the Israelites be tempted by the sex-and-religion abomination of their worship. Don't join them in meals at their altars. Don't allow your sons to marry their women. Those women will take up with any convenient god or goddess and will get your sons to do the same thing."

"Is there anything else?" Moses asked.

"Don't make any more molten gods for yourselves."

"That wasn't me. Aaron allowed that to happen." Moses seemed to immediately regret implicating Aaron. "I shouldn't have blamed him; it was my watch."

Moses may have thought they were through with the important stuff, but God wasn't anywhere near done. He went right on listing the things the Israelites could or could not do. Moses might not have understood why God was suddenly issuing dozens of new rules, but I did. He was trying to cover every possible way those stiff-necked people could get themselves into trouble.

Moses must have thought it was never going to be over. At least that's what I was beginning to think. God kept him up there forty days and forty nights, and I had to stay for every minute of it. I didn't dare miss a word because you could just never know which one of God's words might shift the power balance in the whole universe. Moses didn't eat any food, and he didn't drink any water. And he wrote on the tablets the entire time, until the words of the covenant, the Ten Commandments, were inscribed in the stone.

It must have seemed like an eon to the waiting people back at the camp. I was sure Aaron was beginning to sweat. When Moses finally came down from Mount Sinai, carrying the two tablets of the testimony, with me following along right behind him, the elders raced to greet him. I wondered what it must feel like to have others miss you and be glad to see you when you returned from duty.

No one ever hurried to meet me when I returned to the second heaven to report to Satan. Nobody was ever happy I'd come back. No one cared what I had to report, or at least they pretended it wasn't important. Since the humans couldn't see me anyway, I hurried and got in front of Moses and pretended all those cheering people were coming to greet me. I tell you, I was almost misty-eyed there for a moment.

Not having a mirror handy, Moses didn't know that the skin of his face glowed because he had been speaking with God. When Aaron and all the Israelites got near enough to see Moses's radiant face, they pulled back, afraid to get closer to him. Moses called out to them to reassure them even though he didn't know what they were nervous about.

"Don't be afraid. God is for us, not against us.

"Come close and listen carefully to what He has said because He loves us."

Aaron and the leaders in the community came slowly back at Moses's reassurance that they weren't in more trouble. Moses talked with them and told them everything the Lord had commanded for them. Later that afternoon, the rest of the Israelites came up to him, and he passed on all the commands to them that God had told him on Mount Sinai.

And, of course, they promised to obey every last one of them.

CHAPTER 20

I s HE NEVER going to be done with them?"

Satan stood on the rim of the second heaven, staring down at the bulging camp of the Israelites far below. He had convinced himself that God would wipe them out after the golden calf affair. He refused to believe me when I tried to tell him how God would give the people a pass even for idol worship—all because of Moses's intercession. It happened just like I predicted, but I didn't dare say anything that sounded like "I told you so."

"How can He do anything else, sir? You have the rest of the people on the earth in bondage. The Israelites, pitiful as they may be, are the only team God has. If He gives up on them, game over; He has nothing."

"I can still win. I've watched these miserable humans for centuries. God has overestimated their potential. He might get them through the desert to Canaan, but they'll never be able to stand up to our forces there. How many do we have?"

"The Amorites, Canaanites, Hittites, Perizzites, Hivites, and Jebusites, sir."

"Just as I thought; my strategy is working."

"What strategy would that be, master?"

"What are you, blind? Why do you think I haven't sent forces after them in the desert? I *want* them to get across. I don't know which I look forward to the most—seeing them slaughtered at the border or seeing them seduced by the sex priestesses in my temples." He paused as if relishing both possibilities.

"I think I'll have them go lightly on the slaughter." The smirk continued. "It gives me much more pleasure to see them defile themselves with those sex perverts than to see them dead. Whatever angers God the most, that's what I want to see. He will regret the day He took me on as an enemy."

"Uh, Your Majesty..." I struggled with whether I should tell him what God had said about all those "ites." If I didn't tell him and he found out later, it could only be much worse for me than if I just told him now and gave him time to get over it. He turned and looked at me as if daring me to contradict his plan.

"What is it?"

"Well, sir, to be perfectly honest, God mentioned those people to Moses while they were up on the mountain."

"Go on."

"He told Moses that He—God—would drive them out before him—Moses. To be exact, what He said was He intended to use Moses to drive them out, but He would be behind the whole thing."

Satan did not respond right away so I thought he might need to be reminded about the rules of engagement.

"It's like this, sir: God can do anything He wants on the earth, but He has to do it through human beings."

"Really?" The sarcasm dripped from the word. "I didn't know that."

He pushed me aside as he stomped back to his den. Since he didn't order me to follow him, I didn't. Instead, I climbed upon my perch and looked at the earth. I kept an eye on the Hebrew's activities, but it didn't seem to me there was much going on there that anyone except God would care about.

Moses was still hearing from God on a daily basis with a new set of regulations to govern the lives of the people. I suppose He wanted them to have a fully functional form of government when they reached their destination so no time would be wasted in political scuffling. It would be easier for the people to fight if they knew in advance what they were fighting for. It takes a government to overthrow a government, not a band of vigilantes. That would certainly be the case once they crossed into the enemy territory where all the governments were under the reign of Satan. That had to be God's reasoning behind all the rules.

However, it did not explain the tabernacle. God ordered Moses to gather the artisans and craftsmen from among the people to begin the construction of a tabernacle, a tent of meeting, and a box. If I thought God was meticulous on the rule giving, it was nothing compared to the detail He insisted upon for this new building project. The attention to every thread, every color, and every building material that was to be used would boggle the mind of human or demon. Fascinating as it all was, what most captured my attention was the box.

God referred to the box as the ark, not to be confused with the boat Noah built by the same name. (Don't even ask. I don't know why He didn't call it something else for simplicity's sake.) God was in every detail of how it was to be constructed, how it would be carried, and what would be in it. This is where it began to get interesting. God told Moses to put the tablets of the covenant in the ark. No particular big deal; he had to keep them somewhere. But it's what God said next that thickened the plot.

"Sculpt two winged angels out of hammered gold for either end of the lid. Make them so they're one piece with the lid. Make the angels with their wings spread, hovering and facing one another but looking down on the ark. I will meet you there at set times to speak with you from between the angel figures that are on it. I will speak the commands that I have for the Israelites from that place."

Well, I was confused. What was He doing? God speaks from heaven, from the mountains, from the pillar of fire, from just about every grand thing imaginable. But God does not stand on the lid of a box to speak. Furthermore, He would certainly never get *in* the box, which was bound to be the next illogical conclusion to which the Israelites were certain to jump given enough time.

Much as I hated to do it, I needed to talk this over with someone. This was just not like anything God was known to do. Unfortunately, the only person who knew more about God than me was Satan. I supposed I'd have to tell him about the box eventually, so it may as well be sooner than later. Reluctantly, I took myself to his throne room and waited to be admitted. It didn't occur to me that Satan might outjump the Israelites en route to a wrong conclusion, but that's just what he did.

"A box? God in a box."

"Something like that, yes, sir." It was pointless to argue about whether God was on top of the box or in the box.

"And just why do you think God might do something like that?" He pretended interested in my opinion.

"I…I hoped you might know, sir." Then the tittering began among the onlooking guards.

"Well, let's see if we can figure this out. What was Moses supposed to do with the box once God got inside?"

"Only the priests were to handle the ark—the box—and even they were not permitted to touch it. They were to carry it on their shoulders on poles that would fit into rings on the sides. Once they start moving again, the priests are to get in front of the people and carry the ark."

Satan couldn't seem to get over the hilarity of visualizing God in a box, but I was figuring the whole thing out just from talking out loud. Note to self: I don't need to consult with Satan for answers; I just need to hear myself talk.

"I think I've got it, sir. God is preparing the people for war."

"By getting in a box?" Everyone roared at Satan's retort.

"Yes, yes, that's it. Don't you see? God knows what they're like. It's plain from the golden calf debacle. The people want a god they can see, one they can carry in their hands. They were willing to follow the golden calf because they could see it, handle it, and know where it was at all times."

"That has nothing to do with war."

"But it does, or it will. God knows what you've got planned with those nations lying in wait for the Israelites to cross over. He knows the Israelites will be terrified and might run away.

But when they see the priests carrying the box with God in it, they'll feel invincible and be willing to go to war."

Satan's face showed he wasn't connecting the same dots as me.

"You'll see I'm right, master." I probably shouldn't have made that boast. No one was allowed to be right except for Satan. "Shall I go down for a closer look, Mighty One?"

"Go down for a closer look," Satan commanded as if I hadn't just said the same thing.

CHAPTER 21

I FOUND MOSES IN his tent with his hands over his ears. I couldn't blame him. The people were back at their national sport, whining and complaining. It was the mixed people who had stirred them up again. They hadn't counted on the journey taking so long. Their soft life back in Egypt hadn't prepared them for an extended camping trip. It was inevitable they would fall back into loud grumbling over their hard life and lead the Israelites right into misery with them. Moses had learned to ignore the mixed bunch, but when it spread to the others, the din could not be shut out. Moses wasn't the only one who heard them; God heard them also.

From experience I knew there was a point at which God would have had enough. I didn't always guess right as to where that point might be, but it was always there eventually. On this day, the Israelites hit it dead on. When He heard their unabashed ingratitude, His anger flared, and He sent fire that blazed up and burned the outer boundaries of the camp.

The people thought they were goners for sure and went running toward Moses's tent, crying out for him to help. Moses stepped out of his tent to keep them from trying to get inside.

"Don't you care that He will destroy us?" they shouted.

"He's not going to destroy you. You've given Him plenty of opportunity and reason. If He were going to destroy you, He would have already done it."

"But how do you know? Look at that fire," they clamored.

Moses sighed and tried to ignore them, but they would not be quieted.

"Help us. Talk to God on our behalf. Save us." The crowd was growing.

"I'll try." Moses sighed and went back inside his tent.

He lifted his hands toward God as if trying to grab hold of Him. "You know You're not going to destroy them. Please, can't I have a little rest?"

God didn't answer, but the fire flickered out, and the people settled down. When Moses heard the cries of discontent fading, he peeked out the door of his tent to see what had happened.

"Thank You," he whispered to God as he rolled his eyes heavenward.

Anyone who knew humans the way I do would also know the calm wouldn't last. The mixed people were soon at it again. Now they had a craving for meat.

"Why can't we have meat? We ate meat and fish in Egypt—and got it free—to say nothing of the cucumbers and melons, the leeks and onions and garlic. Nothing tastes good out here; all we get is manna, manna, manna."

"Why can't we have meat?" the Israelites cried right along with the mixed people. Never mind that most of them had never had a bite of meat in their entire lives. Meat was not on the Egyptian menu for slaves.

Moses heard the whining of all those people moving toward his tent again. God heard it too, and Moses began to get worried about what might happen next.

Moses looked up and raised his hands. "Are You here, God?"

"Yes, I'm here."

"Where do I go to resign?"

"Don't be ridiculous. You're My chosen servant."

"Can't You choose someone else for a while?"

"This is the reason I created you."

"Then why are You treating me this way? What did I ever do to You to deserve this? Did I conceive them? Was I their mother? Why do You dump the responsibility of this people on me? Where am I supposed to get meat for all these people?" He lifted the flap of his tent door as if showing God the crowds outside.

"Give us meat; we want meat." It sounded like a lunchroom brawl.

"God, I can't do this by myself," Moses complained as he closed the tent flap. "It's too much for one person with all these people. If You're not going to help me with them, do me a favor and kill me. I've seen enough; I've had enough. Let me out of here."

"Get a grip. You know you can't go anywhere. Gather seventy men from among the leaders of Israel, men whom you know to be respected and responsible. Take them to the tent of meeting. I'll meet you there, and I'll come down and speak with you. I'll take some of the Spirit that is on you and place it on them; they'll then be able to take some of the load of this people. You won't have to carry the whole thing alone. How does that sound?"

"Well, OK, that's better than nothing." Moses himself was close to whining.

"Now go tell the people to consecrate themselves and get ready for tomorrow when they're going to eat meat."

"Really?"

"Oh, yes, really. I'm as tired of their griping as you are. 'We want meat; give us meat. We had a better life in Egypt. Whine, whine, whine.'

"I've heard their whining, and I'm going to give them meat all right. Not just meat for one day or a few days or even a week. I'm going to give them meat for thirty days. They're going to eat meat until it's coming out of their nostrils. They're going to be so sick of meat that they'll throw up at the mere mention of it. And you can tell them why. It's because they have rejected Me, who is right here among them, whining to My face, 'Oh, why did we ever have to leave Egypt?'"

Apparently Moses had never seen God's emotional side. But then Moses was a bit emotional himself; otherwise, he would have been a little more careful with his tone of voice.

"I'm standing here surrounded by six hundred thousand men on foot, and You say You'll give them meat every day for a month. So, where's it coming from? Even if all the flocks and herds in the land were butchered, would that be enough? Even if all the fish in the sea were caught, would that be enough?"

"So, do you think I can't take care of you? You'll see soon enough whether what I say happens for you or not."

"No, I didn't mean it like that. I know You've never failed me."

"Then do what I tell you."

I was flabbergasted. That's all I can say about it. I know what I said earlier about God and Moses talking as if they were friends, but this was too much. Even though it might sound like a real argument was going on, it was an argument between two people who respected and trusted one another. Moses trusted God so much he could pour out his anger and frustration and feel safe doing it. God trusted Moses so much He pulled no punches in letting him know just how He felt about things. I was pretty sure God would never have been that transparent with any of the angels.

Moses went out and told the people what God had said. He called together seventy of the leaders and told them to stand around the tent. Right on cue God came down in a cloud and spoke to Moses and took some of the Spirit that was on him and put it on the seventy leaders. When the Spirit rested on them, they prophesied.

Then Moses and the leaders of Israel went back to the camp. A wind set in motion by the breath of God swept quail in from the direction of the sea. They piled up to a depth of about three feet in the camp and as far out as a day's walk in every direction. All that day and night and into the next day the people were out gathering the quail by the bushel baskets. Quail was all over the place. Huge amounts of quail; even the slowest person among them gathered at least sixty bushels.

They ate so much quail some of them got sick and died. The mixed people said God had sent a plague on them. It didn't look that way from where I was sitting. They gorged themselves like pigs and died of gluttony. That would be the official story for sure. But I knew what had really happened; after all, I watched the whole thing.

The people insisted they knew more about what they needed than God did. Spurred on by the mixed people, they harangued God and Moses endlessly about something they didn't really need, something that, in fact, was bad for them. Their digestive systems were not suitable for an orgy of meat, and they were unrestrained in eating as much and as fast as they could.

So, why did God give in and let them have something He knew would make them sick? Because He won't make people do what they are supposed to do even though their lives would be so simple if only He would. His will is perfect for them if they would accept it. But when they won't, He'll hold out for a while to give them time to think through their impetuous nature. If they won't accept His will for them, He won't force them into compliance. It's sort of like He finally says to them, "Very well; *thy* will be done."

Many people died because they got exactly what they insisted on having.

CHAPTER 22

Ⓘ T TOOK DAYS to take care of all the people who were sick from food poisoning and to bury the many who died. If there was a good thing for Moses in all this, it was that at least there was positively no more griping about food. I followed Moses as he walked through the outer camp, where all the dead and dying had been moved. If he intended to call on God again, I didn't want to miss it. When I figured out he wasn't going to do anything but survey the damage and console the people when he could, I got bored and decided to go back to the main camp to see if anything was going on that Satan would want to know about.

I smelled him before I got close to him. As I said before, once you've smelled a demon, you can never mistake the odor for anything else. There was definitely a demon in the camp. Satan must have sent someone to check on me, not for my well-being, of course, but probably to see if I was on the job. I found him with Aaron and Miriam. They didn't know he was there, but he was right in the middle of their conversation. When the demon spotted me, he flew over to my side.

"Why are you here?" I asked him.

"Watch and see. Satan knew you would let things get too cozy for the leaders. He sent me to stir them up a bit."

Miriam and Aaron were deep in quiet conversation, but I couldn't hear without moving in closer. When I did, it was clear they were talking against Moses behind his back because of his Cushite wife, Zipporah.

"What did she tell you?" Aaron asked.

"She's unhappy. They haven't had marital relations in all this time because Moses insists on remaining chaste in order to hear God."

"It isn't good for Moses to ignore his wife. He's coming up now; let me talk to him."

Moses joined his brother and sister to give them a status report on the condition of the camp after the food epidemic. Sensing he had walked in on a private conversation, he asked Miriam.

"What's going on?"

Miriam lowered her head as if captivated by an ant crawling across her shoe. Then peeking up, she tilted her head toward Moses as if urging Aaron to speak.

"Let me ask you something," Aaron began. "Is it only through you and you alone that God speaks?"

"What?" Moses had no idea where this conversation was going.

"Doesn't God also speak through us? Aren't Miriam and I prophets as well as you? Or are you the only one who can hear from God?"

"Yes, you can hear God; I suppose so. What's this about?"

Miriam and Aaron exchanged looks with one another. Miriam gave him that "go ahead" nod.

"It's about your wife."

"Zipporah? What about her?"

Aaron looked to Miriam for encouragement before speaking again.

"She's unhappy. She told Miriam that you haven't been a husband to her in all this time."

Moses looked embarrassed. "She told you that?"

Miriam jumped in. "Why not? You said Aaron and I are also prophets. Yet we don't have to deny our spouses to hear the Lord. Where did you ever get such an idea?"

"Or is there another reason?" Aaron asked.

"Like another woman?" Miriam whispered.

Moses was the most humble man on the earth, and he simply didn't know how to reply to such an implied accusation.

None of them realized God was hearing every word. No one expected Him to break right into the middle of their conversation, but that's just what He did. At the same moment, the loud *whoosh* by my ear told me the demon menace had taken off at the first hint of God being in the neighborhood.

God said to the three of them, "Come out, you three, to the tent of meeting." The three went out, not saying a word. I can tell you Aaron was wishing he had minded his own business and stayed out of the women's talk.

When they got to the tent, God descended in a pillar of cloud and stood at the entrance to the tent. He called Aaron and Miriam to come closer to Him, which neither was eager to do. When they stepped out, God spoke.

"Listen carefully to what I'm telling you. Most of the time, if there is a prophet among you, I make Myself known to him in visions. I speak to him in dreams. That's the way I do it with you two. But I don't do it that way with My servant Moses. I speak to him intimately, in person, in plain talk without riddles. He knows Me personally. You have no way of knowing what I've said to him or what I require of Him in our relationship. So, why did you show no reverence or respect in chastising and accusing My servant?"

The anger of God blazed out against the two of them from the pillar, and then He left.

When the cloud moved off from the tent, Miriam had turned leprous; her skin was white and covered with lesions. Aaron took one look at her, rolled up his sleeves, checked himself out, and then pleaded with Moses.

"Please, my master, please don't allow God to come down so hard on her for this foolish and thoughtless sin."

"Am I greater than God that I can tell Him what He can do?" Moses was distraught, but he pleaded with God as Aaron had asked. "Please, God, heal her. Please heal her."

Aaron dropped to his knees, sweating rivers in fear of what might be about to happen to him.

God answered Moses: "Quarantine her outside the camp for seven days. She will get well, and then she can be readmitted to the camp."

So, Miriam was placed in quarantine outside the camp for the seven days. The people didn't march on until she was readmitted. Aaron had dodged a bullet, and he knew it.

I sat down on the bench outside Moses's tent and tried to remember if I'd ever seen God in a four-way conversation with humans before. I was certain it had never happened.

CHAPTER 23

OR A BRIEF moment, I almost felt like I was one of them. Of course, they didn't know it, but I planted myself right there beside Moses, Aaron, Hur, and Joshua as they stood quietly at the top of the hill and gazed long and hard at the land of Canaan spread out before them in the valley below. It was a picture-perfect moment. They'd made it. They'd survived the desert, and the Promised Land lay before them for the taking.

Suddenly, the realization of what this meant hit me.

"They made it!" I yelled as if waking myself up from a dream. "What am I doing hanging around here? I must get back to tell Satan."

Think talking on a cell phone and driving a car at ninety miles per hour and you can understand how my mind was not on my flying as I careened over the rim into the second heaven at daredevil speed (pardon the pun). In my zeal to tell the news, I forgot to adjust my speed for altitude and crashed right into the stone door that blocked my path to Satan's lair. Disheveled and stunned from my sudden stop, I must have also looked desperate because the guards didn't try to stop me or bother to laugh as I rushed passed them and entered in without any protocol at all.

"Lord Satan... " I was breathless.

Satan had plenty of breath and seemed only mildly curious as to why I'd barged in the way I had.

"So, speak," he said to me as his attendant held a mirror for him to check out his appearance. He'd developed new interest in preening himself, or, better said, having one of the lower-ranking demons do it for him. I was momentarily distracted by the primping; there wasn't a makeover artist in the universe who could make him pretty. I wondered what he saw in the mirror that kept him coming back to take a look. Maybe he still imagined himself as he used to be when he was Lucifer, the light bearer of heaven.

"Don't make me repeat myself," he said with irritation. "Why are you here?"

"Right. Why am I here?" The preening caused me to lose my train of thought. When he glared at me, my recall returned.

"They made it, sir. They're on the hill above Canaan. They actually made it."

"Have they entered in yet?" Continuing to admire himself in the mirror, he showed some interest in my report but not nearly enough for this kind of news.

"No, not yet. They won't go in all at once. If I know Moses, he'll send a scouting party in first."

He took the mirror from the attendant and held it closer to his face.

"One of the boys brought me some aloe gel from the earth. I've only used it for a week, but I think it's given me a smoother look. What do you think?"

"You're lovely, sir."

"Now, what were you saying?" He gave the mirror back to the attendant.

"The Hebrews have reached Canaan."

He snapped his claws in the direction of one of the guards. "Alert the Nephilim."

"The Nephilim?" I knew my voice cracked. "Are there Nephilim in Canaan? How? They all drowned in Noah's flood."

Satan looked at me as if I were too simpleminded to live.

"Og, the Nephilim king, survived. He has a new clan, the sons of Anak." He sneered as if telling a dirty secret. "Why do you think Canaan is so wicked? Og is serving me well; you could learn a few pointers from him. I never have to send anyone down there to be sure he's doing his job." Then, pressing his claws together and cocking his head with the prissiness of mock courtesy, he continued. "But manners do require me to alert him that lunch is about to be served."

The guard laughed right on cue.

"Tell Og they're coming," he snapped at one of the messenger demons who always hung out around his throne, waiting to do his every bidding. The messenger sped away with a mere nod of acknowledgment.

"And you." He turned to me.

"I know, I know. I'll show myself out."

I looked around the camp until I found Moses, Joshua, Caleb, and Aaron huddled around a drawing in the sand where Moses had sketched a rough layout of the land. I knelt down beside them to take a look.

"Go up through the Negev and then into the hill country. Look the land over; see what it's like. Assess the people: are they strong or weak; are there few or many?"

Joshua nodded, anxious to be off, but Moses wasn't through giving instructions.

"Observe the land: is it pleasant or harsh? Describe the towns where they live: are they open camps or fortified with walls? Pay close attention to the soil. Is it fertile or barren; are there forests?"

Joshua and Caleb rose to their feet. Moses grasped Joshua's garment before he could get away.

"And try to bring back a sample of the produce that grows there—this is the season for the first ripe grapes." With that, the twelve scouts led by Joshua and Caleb headed into the land God had promised their ancestors.

At last, they were on their way without the slightest notion as to what awaited them over the next hill. Motley crew though they were, they eagerly scouted out the land from the Desert of Zin as far as Rehob toward Lebo Hamath. Their route went through the Negev Desert to the town of Hebron.

"Pay close attention in Hebron," Joshua warned. "It is said to be a city older than the cities of Egypt. There's a legend that the descendants of Anak are there.

"Who's Anak?" several asked together.

Caleb looked sharply at Joshua and said nothing with his mouth, but his eyes said it all. "Too much information, Joshua."

"Never mind." Joshua returned Caleb's look and tried to change the subject.

"Nephilim," called out the skittish one who lingered toward the back of the group. "The sons of Anak are the Nephilim."

Uneasiness spread rapidly through the men.

"Nephilim? Impossible."

"They were drowned in the great flood."

"If there are Nephilim in there, we can't go in." Eagerness was giving way to nervousness.

"Like I said," Joshua answered, "it's a legend."

"A myth," Caleb said. "Never proven; now let's get going."

When they arrived at the Valley of Eshcol they cut off a branch with a single cluster of grapes that took two men to carry it slung on a pole. They also picked some pomegranates and figs. They named the place Valley of Eshcol ("valley of grape clusters") because of the huge cluster of grapes they had cut down there. After forty days of scouting out the land, they returned home.

Moses and all the people were waiting for them. Some boys from the camp had been on watch for the scouts, and when they saw them from a distance with the luscious produce of the land, they raced back and told the people.

There were loud cheers and slaps on the backs as the twelve arrived and presented themselves before Moses and Aaron and the whole of Israel.

"Just look," Caleb exclaimed. Everyone wanted to try one of the grapes that were as large as plums. "This is just a sample of the fruit of the land."

"Now tell us what else you found there," Moses said.

"We went to the land just like you told us to do, and, oh, it does flow with milk and honey. Just look at this fruit." Joshua held a pomegranate high above his head so people in the back of the throng could see.

"Tell him the rest," said one of the twelve.

Joshua and Caleb exchanged a look with each other and then sent a piercing glare to the one who had spoken.

"Yes, you must tell them," said another. "Tell them why we can't go back."

The crowd murmured. "What? Why can't they go back?"

Joshua glared at the frightened man who belonged to the voice.

"There is one challenge," Joshua began, "but it's only a challenge."

"How naïve would we be if we didn't expect challenges?" Aaron chimed in.

"Go ahead," Moses encouraged him. "What did you find?"

"Well," Joshua continued, "the people who live there are fierce; no doubt about it. And their cities are huge and well fortified."

"That's not all. Tell them the rest." The man whose voice had earlier quaked with fright jostled his way through the crowd to get in front of Moses. Joshua reached out as if to push the man away, but Moses stayed his hand.

"Let him speak," Moses said.

"We saw descendants of the giant Anak."

Some of the people looked puzzled.

"Nephilim, get it? There are Nephilim in the land. They didn't all drown."

The people gasped in disbelief and fear.

"That's not all," the man said. "Amalekites are spread out in the Negev; Hittites, Jebusites, and Amorites hold the hill country; and the Canaanites are established on the Mediterranean Sea and along the Jordan."

Sounds of concern and fear rose up from the crowd.

Caleb interrupted. "Silence all of you." Turning to Moses, he continued. "Let's go up and take the land—now. We can do it."

The mob roared and turned on Joshua and Caleb.

"Is Caleb crazy?"

"Does he have a death wish?"

"We can't attack those people; they're way stronger than we are."

"They're not even people. They're giants."

"That's right. It would be a massacre if we tried to fight them," the other ten scouts said, one right after the other. Then they dispersed through the crowd and spread scary rumors among the people.

"We scouted out the land from one end to the other. It's a land that swallows people whole. Everybody we saw was huge."

"Didn't you hear what we said? Why, we even saw the Nephilim giants. The Anak giants come from the Nephilim, in case you've forgotten. Alongside them we felt like grasshoppers.

"And they looked down on us as if we were grasshoppers," another added.

Satan would have loved it. Instead of cheering and praising God for safely bringing them into the land they had come all this way to subdue, ten scared voices turned the hope of thousands to paranoia with cries to go back to Egypt. As if that were even an option.

Moses was angry and sent them all back to their tents with a stern warning to keep silent lest the Lord hear their grumbling, but they were so afraid that nothing could have kept them quiet. The whole community was in an uproar and wailed the whole night long. All the people of Israel grumbled against Moses and Aaron.

"Why didn't we die in Egypt? Or in this wilderness?" voice after voice lamented.

"Why has God brought us to this country to kill us?"

"Our wives and children are about to become plunder."

"Why don't we just head back to Egypt?"

"And right now!"

Soon they were all calling for the inevitable. "Let's pick a new leader; let's turn and go back to Egypt." A crowd of men headed toward Moses's tent where Moses, Aaron, Joshua, and

Caleb had gathered in an emergency session to figure out what to do.

"We can surely do it," Caleb insisted. "We can take them."

"What about it, Joshua?" Moses asked. "Can we defeat them?"

Joshua paused for a moment and looked at Caleb's face, beet red with emotion.

"Yes, yes, we can," he answered ever so haltingly. "There will be casualties, but we can take them if the Lord is on our side."

The men of the camp arrived at the door of Moses's tent, demanding they come out.

Joshua and Caleb followed Moses and Aaron outside and then ripped their clothes and addressed the assembled people of Israel.

"What is the matter with you people? Where is your courage? The land we walked through and scouted out is a very good land—very good indeed. If God is pleased with us, He will lead us into that land, a land that flows, as they say, with milk and honey."

"He will give it to us as He promised our ancestors," Caleb shouted, raising his staff high above his head.

"Just don't rebel against God!" shouted Joshua. "Don't listen to those cowards who went with us, and don't be afraid of those people we found on the land that belongs to us if only we will take it. Why, we'll have them for lunch! They have no protection because God is on our side. Don't be afraid of them!"

"We can't lose," Caleb cried out, trying to assure them.

I was beginning to feel a little patriotic myself at the fervor of Caleb and Joshua. I believed they could do it and would have joined up with them right there on the spot if I could have. Unfortunately for them, however, the cowardly scouts had done such a good job of terrifying the people that instead of rushing to join up, the whole crowd was up in arms and talking of hurling stones at all four of the men.

Whoosh! A wind kicked up, so strong it knocked over many of the people. Moses and Aaron were leaning into their staffs for balance as Caleb and Joshua shielded their eyes from the bright light invading the night. If the people thought they were afraid before, they were about to learn what real terror was. There neither was nor is anything in the universe to compare to the wrath of God when Ruah Ha Kadosh splits the atmosphere as the glory of God Almighty descends into the earth realm and all created things bow to His presence.

They were on their knees, but I was face down in the dirt as the bright glory of the Lord appeared at the tent of meeting, and every Israelite saw it. God was in the house.

The voice of God rumbled to Moses. "How long will these people treat Me with contempt? How long will they refuse to trust Me? And with all these signs I've done among them! I've had enough."

"No, wait, Lord," Moses pleaded.

"Don't talk to Me about them anymore, and don't pray for them. I will send a plague and kill them."

"No, don't say that, my Lord." Moses struggled to stand.

"Don't fret; I'll keep the promise I made to Abraham, Isaac, and Jacob. I'll give the land to you. I'll make you into a nation bigger and stronger than they ever were."

"But You can't, my Lord. The Egyptians will hear about it. They'll say You delivered this people from Egypt with a great show of strength and then abandoned them. The Egyptians will tell everyone. They've already heard that You are God, that You are on the side of this people, that You are present among them, that they see You with their own eyes in Your cloud that hovers over them and in the pillar of cloud that leads them by day and the pillar of fire at night. If You kill this entire people, all the nations that have heard what has been going on will say, 'Since God couldn't get these people into the land that He had promised to give them, He slaughtered them out in the wilderness.'"

Whether or not the people on their knees could hear God, I couldn't say, but they could certainly hear Moses, and they knew he was pleading for their very lives. They continued to be very quiet and to listen as Moses cried out to God to spare them.

"Now, please, let the power of the Master expand, enlarge itself greatly along the lines You laid out earlier when You said You were their God. Remember who You are: slow to get angry and huge in loyal love; forgiving iniquity, rebellion, and sin; still, never just whitewashing sin. But extending the fallout of parents' sins to children into the third, even the fourth, generation."

I tried to lift my face out of the dirt to shout, but I could only manage to mumble. "So that's what He was doing back there!"

I was always excited whenever I learned something new about God. "Months ago when God began talking about Himself in the third person, He was writing the intercession Moses would need today to stay His hand of wrath against the nation. Moses probably doesn't even remember where he heard the words he's saying to describe God."

I shook my head the best I could and marveled at the cleverness of God. Who would ever have thought God's words of intercession released into the atmosphere could be snagged by an intercessor later on when the stakes were really high? I wondered if God had done this before. Satan was not going to like this at all.

Moses continued, "Please forgive the wrongdoing of this people out of the extravagance of Your loyal love just as all along, from the time they left Egypt, You have been forgiving this people."

Moses put his face down into the dirt near me and waited for God to answer.

"I forgive them, honoring your words," God said. Big surprise. "But as I live and as the glory of God fills the whole earth, not a single person of those who saw My glory, saw the miraculous signs I did in Egypt and the wilderness, and who have tested Me over and over and over again, turning a deaf ear to Me, will set eyes on the land I so solemnly promised to their ancestors. No one who has treated Me with such repeated contempt will see it."

Then God added a PS: "My servant Caleb is a different story. Both he and Joshua have a different spirit; they follow

Me passionately. I'll bring them into the land that they scouted, and their children will inherit it."

The people heard it all and began dispersing, relieved they would live to see another day. They were so glad to still be alive that they didn't even care about not being allowed to enter the Promised Land. They were in no mood to argue about the terms of the deal.

Moses and Aaron stayed behind. They knew God had more to say to them.

"Since the Amalekites and Canaanites are so well established in the valleys, for right now change course and head back into the wilderness, following the route to the Red Sea."

They nodded but still did not speak. Experience had taught them that a pause in a conversation with God did not mean the conversation was over.

"I will spare them, as you have asked," God continued. "But how long is this going to go on, all this grumbling against Me by this evil-infested community? I've had My fill of complaints from these grumbling Israelites. You can tell them again they aren't going into the land. Their corpses are going to litter the wilderness—everyone twenty years and older who was counted in the census, this whole generation of grumblers and grousers. Not one of them will enter the land and make their home there, except for Caleb and Joshua.

"You can tell them that their children, the very ones they said would be taken for plunder, I'll bring in to enjoy the land they rejected. These children will live as shepherds in the wilderness for forty years, living with the fallout of the unfaithfulness of their parents until the last of that generation lies a corpse in the wilderness. They scouted out the land for forty days; their punishment will be a year for each day, a forty-year sentence to serve for their sins."

By now, both Moses and Aaron were facedown in the dirt from the weight of God's anger. They didn't dare move, and neither did I.

"I, God, have spoken. I will most certainly carry out these things against this entire evil-infested community, which has banded together against Me. In this wilderness they will come to their end. There they will die."

Smoke filled the tent, and the light of the glory lifted. But none of the three of us could get up. I'm pretty sure I passed out right away. When I awoke, Aaron and Moses were gone.

It got bad for some of the Israelites after that. Right away God confronted the ten scouts who had come back with a bad report and sent fear through the people. He released a consuming plague on them, and they died quickly. Only Joshua and Caleb escaped His wrath.

Moses didn't want to deliver God's word to the people, but with good sense, he feared God more than he feared them. So when he told the people of Israel everything God had said against them, they mourned long and hard. But early the next morning they were up like nothing had happened and started out for the high hill country.

"We're here; we're ready. Let's go up and attack the land that God promised us. We sinned, but now we're ready."

I shook my head in disgust at them.

"A little late!" I wanted to shout out. I could have told them a few things about God's mercy and grace. There's a limit to it. Humans never think about it until it's too late. Part of the problem is God's own fault. He never should have taught Abraham about intercession. When people see how many times sincere intercession will stay the hand of God's wrath, they presume it will always be that way.

"It's not always that way!" I finally did shout, though no one could hear me. "Look at me; I'm living proof that God has a limit. It wasn't even my fault. I wasn't grousing and whining like you people. You deserve God's punishment. I didn't. I was innocent. I would never have rebelled against God. It was an accident."

When Moses heard what the people were planning, he ran to stop them.

"Why are you disobeying God's command yet again? This won't work. Don't attack. God isn't with you in this. You'll be beaten badly by your enemies. The Amalekites and Canaanites are ready for you, and they'll kill you. Because you would not obediently follow God and trust Him, God is not going to be with you in this. Don't go! I can't help you this time."

But they went anyway. Recklessly and arrogantly they climbed to the high hill country. If I had been one of them and turned around to see that neither the ark of the covenant nor Moses had budged from the camp, I would have turned around and run for cover. Not them, though. They simply didn't understand the line they had crossed with God. They were in the battlefield barely half an hour when the Amalekites and the

Canaanites came out of the hills and attacked, beat them, and chased them all the way down to Hormah.

They called out to God for help, and He did just what He said He would do—nothing.

CHAPTER 24

WHY DO YOU think this is good news?" Satan's eyes were narrow and even colder than usual as he glared at me.

The longer I was in exile with this egocentric maniac, the surer I was that I could understand humanity—and I daresay God too—better than I could understand the thought processes of this mercurial personification of everything evil. Why wouldn't I think it was good news? Moses had failed. God had failed. The Israelites who were rescued and assured they were a chosen people on the way to their Promised Land were now going to die in the desert. Even Moses wasn't going to make it across because of an insignificant (in my mind) episode when he struck the rock for water like he did the first time they hit a drought. God had clearly told him to speak to the rock the second time, not pound on it. What possible difference it made as long as the water came out was lost on me.

Satan was winning the game with God for control of the earth. He wouldn't have to deal with the Israelites for at least a generation, maybe more. There would be no challenge to the land he now ruled so effortlessly. He had every reason to celebrate; why was he so macabre? He continued to stare at me, and although I wouldn't daresay what I was thinking, I knew I'd better say something.

"I thought you would be pleased to know the ex-slaves are all going to die in the desert."

"All of them?" His tone gave him away. It was not a real question, so I needed to be careful about my answer.

"Well, uh, most of them—certainly the most important ones. The ones who had witnessed God's miracles in Egypt will not cross over. He was clear about that. Only the younger ones who were too young to know what was going on have a chance to go in sometime in the future."

"So, God is going to kill all of the first generation for angering Him?" Another trick question.

"Yes and no. Not exactly but eventually." I was beginning to get confused. "He won't kill them directly. They'll die in the desert of the usual stuff—disease, accidents, things like that."

Satan didn't respond; he just continued to stare at me.

"He'll let them wander in the desert until the first generation dies. Could be sooner, could be later," I stated with certainty.

"You have no idea how long this will take, is that right?"

I was straining now to remember the fine print of what God had said to Moses and Aaron. Suddenly I remembered.

"Now I remember. Forty years. God said they would wander in the desert for forty years—one year for each day the scouts had been gone."

Satan rose from his throne and walked over to one of the demon guards and stared at him directly in the eyes. The guard did not move or blink, but he was beginning to sweat. No one could ever be sure whom Satan was mad at or what he was mad about, so the guard was as nervous under that icy stare as I would have been. Finally, Satan turned, and his eyes locked on me again. I heard the guard exhale slowly.

"Do you think I want the slaves to die in the desert?" Another trick question; now I was sweating. My eyes darted quickly around the demonic ranks to see if anyone was going to give me a little help. Every face was expressionless. I wasn't the only one who didn't know the answer Satan was looking for.

"Don't you, sir?" I managed to get the words out.

With one claw under his chin and the other under his elbow, he rolled his eyes around the room as if searching for an answer on the ceiling.

"Why don't you tell me how it helps my cause if some of the slaves die of old age in the desert?"

Now I really forced myself to think deeply. What had caused Satan to hate the Israelites to start with? Hadn't he always tried to kill them? Yes, but why? I forced myself to remember. As the memories came rushing back, it was like being there again. Why, of course. How could I forget? It started in the garden when Satan tricked Adam and Eve. In my mind I could hear the voice of God all over again. It was that day when He cursed Satan.

"The seed of the woman shall crush your head." I wouldn't dare say it out loud, but that must be it. As long as even one of the Israelites remained alive, it didn't matter how many were dead. He hated them all but feared only one. But which one? I scrambled for words to answer him without suggesting he might be afraid of the Israelites.

"I just thought, you know, the more we eliminate, the fewer you have to worry about." I knew *worry* was the wrong word the moment it crossed my quivering lips. I tried quickly to recover.

"Not that you're worried; nothing like that. I just meant they wouldn't be crossing over into Canaan to cause any trouble."

I swear he changed colors right there in front of me. Not a different color entirely, more like a deeper shade of the color he was. Saying nothing, he turned and walked back to his throne, where he stood for a moment before turning around sharply and sitting down. He leaned toward me and motioned for me to come closer with the crooked digitlike appendage on the end of his claw.

I was so afraid I could barely move, but I forced myself to inch closer to him.

"I want you to listen to me."

"Of course, sir. I hang on your every word."

"Shut up. Just shut up and listen to me. I do not want to have this conversation again. Do you understand me?"

I nodded but dared not speak.

"Dead Jews do not help me. How long they wander in the desert or how long they live or how many there are is of no interest to me. None. Zilch. Zero. Do you understand that?"

No, I didn't, but I managed to nod that I did.

"I wanted them to cross over to Canaan; the sooner the better. I do not care about their bodies. I want their souls. I want their worship. I want them to abandon God the way a frustrated wife leaves her husband for her lover. I want God to hurt for them, long for them, pine for them as He watches them come to me in unabashed worship. I want Him to watch as I ravish them. I cannot seduce them in the desert. They must cross over into my…boudoir." He laughed wildly.

I was feeling queasy as I processed what he was saying.

"But now look what you've done," he said.

"I'VE DONE?" I screamed the words but kept them from leaving my throat by swallowing them and biting down hard on my tongue. Didn't I say if things went wrong it would be my fault? I thought things had gone right, and it was still my fault.

"If you had done your job correctly, they would be crossing over instead of turning back to the desert."

"My job is to watch and report. I don't cause anything to happen," I wanted to shout.

"What do you suppose is going to happen to them while they wander in the desert for forty years?" I knew it was rhetorical question, so I looked at the floor as if at a loss for words, which was mostly the case.

"Let me tell you what will happen. They will get stronger. God will pay more attention to detail with them. He will instruct them in every aspect of life. He will leave nothing to chance. It will give Moses time to designate a successor and to train him. When they cross over, it will be harder to seduce them."

Joshua, I thought but did not give any hint that I knew who it would be.

"Now, get out of my sight. Watch them every minute of every day for the forty years. Miss nothing, and do not come back until the time of the transfer of the mantle. You are of no value to me until that time."

My wings were limp and dragging on the floor as I trudged slowly out of the throne room. Why did I feel so dejected? Certainly Satan never had any affection for me—or anyone else—so it wasn't like I'd been suddenly spurned. Why did I care whether he thought I was of value or not? My service to him was always a matter of my existence, not my devotion. I hated him. He was the reason for all of my misery, all of my loss. He was the destroyer of my purpose. It made no sense that I felt discarded as some worthless thing. He had always treated me as worthless. What was wrong with me?

I managed to drag myself to my perch and crawl up on it, letting my limp wings dangle on either side to keep me from falling off. I didn't have the strength to hold myself erect. To have been rejected by God was more pain that I thought I could bear. But to be rejected by Satan, the sum of all that is evil, corrupt, and distorted, confirmed my worst fear.

I no longer existed.

CHAPTER 25

IT DIDN'T TAKE me long to get over myself and realize that Satan's opinion of me had nothing whatsoever to do with my value. I was glad to be exiled from his presence for the forty years the Israelites were sentenced to meander in the desert. He had been right about one thing, however. God did use the wandering as a time to have Moses give the Israelites a remedy for every eventuality of life. I watched faithfully for decades, but after a while I lost interest. Besides, once the trek was over and I would be called back in before His Awfulness to report, he wouldn't care anything about how many rules God had given them. Satan wanted to know one thing: when was the handoff coming between Moses and Joshua.

I planned to use most of the years to work on my brief to present before God and the heavenly court so I would be ready when my day came. Every year I gathered more and more evidence of the disparity between how God treated humanity versus the angels. I just knew that before an impartial court, the evidence would call for my case to be reopened. I could provide thousands of instances when humans committed grievous sin worthy of death only to have God intervene and find a way to let them off the hook. Before a heavenly court, His partiality to you people would surely work to my benefit—at least, I told myself it would.

It's amazing how fast forty years can pass by. When I realized what time it was, I knew I had to check on the earth to see how near the Israelites were to the finish line. When I saw them stopped near the border at Canaan gathering around the place where Moses was, I took off immediately. Just as I suspected, Moses was giving his farewell speech to the people.

"I command you today: Love God. Walk in His ways. Keep His commandments, regulations, and rules so that you will live blessed by Him in the land you are about to enter and possess."

"We will," the people said.

Moses didn't look convinced. "But I warn you, if you have a change of heart, refuse to listen obediently, and willfully go off to serve and worship other gods, you will most certainly die. You won't last long in the land."

"You don't have to worry about us," they assured him.

"Well, good, then." Moses was still not convinced his words were hitting home. "I call heaven and earth to witness against you today. I place before you life and death, blessing and curse. Choose life so that you and your children will live. And love God, listening obediently to Him, firmly embracing Him."

"We got it," they shouted.

"Sure you do," I added silently.

Finally, someone in the crowd realized this was not a training session but a good-bye speech.

"Wait a minute, Moses. You make it sound like you're not going in with us."

"I'm one hundred twenty years old today. I can't get around like I used to. And besides, God told me I wasn't going to cross the Jordan with you due to a misunderstanding on my part about how to get water from rocks. Anyway, God will cross the river ahead of you and destroy the nations in your path so that you may dispossess them. Joshua will lead you now."

"But Joshua is untested," another called out.

"How can you say that? Joshua's proved his mettle these forty years. He's served me faithfully, and God will be with him as He was with me."

Then Moses summoned Joshua and said to him with all Israel watching, "Be strong. Take courage. You will enter the land with this people. You will make them the proud possessors of it. God is striding ahead of you, and He won't let you down. Don't be intimidated. Don't worry."

Moses didn't look worried, but Joshua did. Promotion from within is the riskiest way up the ladder. The people watched Joshua "grow up," so to speak, and knew every mistake he ever made. Joshua, on the other hand, had watched the people and knew how likely they were to duck and run at the first sign of opposition.

Then God whispered to Moses, "You are about to die. Bring Joshua quickly to the tent of meeting so I can commission him."

"Well, that's it, then." Moses took Joshua by the arm and turned to go. "Meeting adjourned."

God was waiting for them in the tent in a pillar of cloud. In a tender voice, He said to Moses, "You're about to die and be buried with your ancestors."

Now, to my mind, this would have been the place to end the conversation. Spirit the old guy off to wherever it is you humans go when you die; let him pass in peace. Moses was ready, standing there with outstretched arms and closed eyes before the pillar of cloud. It sort of ruined the mood when God decided to keep on talking.

"You'll no sooner be in the grave than this people will be up and searching after the foreign gods of this country that they are entering. They will abandon Me and violate My covenant that I've made with them. I'll get so angry I'll walk off and leave them on their own and won't so much as look back at them. Then many calamities and disasters will devastate them because they are defenseless."

"What?" Moses asked as he dropped his arms and opened his eyes.

"What?" I echoed. Really, why was God dropping all this on Moses on his retirement day?

"Don't think I don't know what they are already scheming, and they're not even in the land yet."

"I thought we were here to commission Joshua," Moses replied.

"Right, we are."

Moses summoned Joshua to come and kneel down as God spoke His blessing over him.

"Be strong. Take courage. You will lead the people of Israel into the land I promised to give them. And I'll be right there with you."

Moses closed his eyes again and stretched out his arms in obvious expectation of taking off, but no go. No chariot swinging low, no angels singing, no heaven opening up...nothing. He opened one eye to see if God was still there. He was.

"Was there something else You wanted, Lord?" Moses opened the other eye.

"I've got a few more things to say to the children of Israel."

"Can't Joshua say it?"

"No, I want you to tell them so they'll know I'm serious."

Moses sighed, looked around for something to write with, and then plopped himself down on a pillow on the floor.

"OK, go."

God began to dictate an entire new set of warnings and admonishments and told Moses to take them to the priests to put in the ark. When Moses entered the tent where the priests were, they were startled, to say the least.

"You're back?"

"I haven't left yet. I know what rebels these people are and how stubborn and willful they can be. Even today, while I'm still alive and present with them, they're thinking rebellious thoughts against God. How much worse is it going to be when I've died?"

"Does that mean you're not leaving?" the chief priest asked.

"Don't be ridiculous; gather the leaders of the tribes and the officials here. I have something I need to say directly to them with heaven and earth as witnesses, and then I'm out of here."

So, the priests hurried out and did as Moses had commanded them. It was a little difficult to get the people to assemble again. You know how it is when a crowd disperses, but when they heard Moses had something else to say to them, they hurried up. As soon as they were gathered, Moses began speaking.

"I know that after I die you're going to make a mess of things, abandoning the way I commanded, inviting all kinds of evil consequences in the days ahead. You're determined to do evil in defiance of God, deliberately provoking His anger by what you will do."

"How can you say that?"

"It would never cross our minds to do such a thing."

"Never mind," Moses interrupted. "Pay attention; I'm going to teach you this little song."

"What?" they asked in unison.

Odd as it may sound, that is just what Moses did. All those words he was writing down as God dictated were a song the people were to learn before Moses could die. Why, you may ask. The only explanation I can offer is that your race seems to be able to remember anything you can sing. How many times have you seen a grown person singing the "ABCs" because it's the only way he can remember that *j* comes before *k*.

When Moses had finished teaching the words of the song to the people of Israel, he said, "Take to heart all these words to which I give witness today, and urgently command your children to put them into practice. This is no small matter for you; it's your life. In keeping this word you'll have a good and happy future in this land that you're crossing the Jordan to possess."

Moses rolled up the scroll and handed it to the priests, and then he turned to walk back toward the tent of meeting. I followed close behind because I knew God would be there, and I wanted to hear whether He planned a surprise ending in which He would forgive Moses's one and only sin and let him enter the Promised Land. After all, He had forgiven people for a whole lot more than what Moses did. I loved a happy ending and just knew this was going to be one. Besides, if God changed His mind about Moses's punishment, it would be more ammunition for my legal brief. Everything was hushed as God spoke from the cloud.

"Climb the Abarim Range to Mount Nebo in the land of Moab, overlooking Jericho, and view the land of Canaan that I'm giving the people of Israel to have and to hold. Die on the mountain, and join your people. This is because you broke faith with Me in the company of the people of Israel at the waters of Meribah Kadesh in the Desert of Zin. You didn't honor My holy presence in the company of the people."

"I know, sovereign Lord," Moses replied.

"You'll look at the land spread out before you, but you won't enter it."

The pillar of cloud disappeared, and all by himself, Moses, the deliverer of Israel, walked away.

I was so dejected I could have cried. If God wouldn't commute Moses's sentence after all his years of service with those rebellious people because of one little foul-up, I knew I didn't have a chance.

CHAPTER 26

ALL THE WAY back to Satan's lair, I found myself thinking about Abraham and Moses and how God had used them as both prophet and intercessor. Each of them carried so much spiritual authority that it could be said that they held both the office of prophet and the office of intercessor. In succeeding generations, things would change, and it would be rare to see one human with both offices. Prophets would be able to intercede, and intercessors would be able to prophesy now and then, but the fullness of both gifts would not normally be resident in one person. Knowing humans as I do, I find it amazing that the two groups insist on working together. The way I see it, when it's done right, the work of each cancels out the work of the other; must be horribly frustrating.

Here's what I mean: Suppose God decides to bring about a calamity to punish His disobedient people. But before He does, He tells a prophet all about the coming disaster with instructions for the prophet to proclaim it for everyone to hear. The prophet obeys and goes about warning, "Thus sayeth the Lord," to everyone.

The intercessors hear the warning, and they start repenting and praying and interceding for God's mercy to avert the disaster. God responds to the intercessors and stays His hand of judgment, and the calamity does not come about.

Who looks foolish here? The prophet. What he clearly heard God say *would* happen does *not* happen because of the intercessors; so even though he may be a *good* prophet, he will always appear to be *wrong* when it comes to judgment. It must be the worst job in town. You'd think a prophet would stay a mile away from an intercessor when he gets a word from the Lord. I know I would; believe me, I know what it's like to be thought wrong all the time. But that's not the case with these odd humans. They seek each other out even though a good intercessor will always make a good prophet look bad because right away when calamity is averted, all you humans start calling him a false prophet. It amazes me how God continues to find people willing to accept such a dead-end assignment.

As I got nearer to Satan's abode, I found myself getting nervous. After all, it had been forty years since I was allowed inside the doors of his throne room. I wondered if I should stop by my perch and spruce up a bit. What was I thinking? I have hooves, claws, and scales. No amount of sprucing was going to help that. Instead, I decided to practice my opening line.

"Lord Satan, it's good to be back. I've missed you." No, too sentimental.

"Your Majesty, I've returned victorious." Too unbelievable; I might be asked to prove it.

I was still practicing when the guards opened the heavy doors to let me pass. As I got nearer to his throne, where he perched like a vulture, I realized my tongue had tied itself in a knot. "Oh, no." I was only a few steps away. "Maybe I can swallow it," I thought in desperation. I tried—I really did—but it would not go down, and it would not untie.

"So, you're back," Satan said.

I nodded and tried to smile but did not open my mouth.

Satan leaned in toward me. "What's the matter with you? Cat got your tongue?"

"No, thir." I struggled to make a sentence, "Ith wight heah in my mout. Thee?" I opened wide to show him. He jerked back as if I'd assaulted him with bad breath.

"Is he speaking in tongues?" Satan asked one of the guards.

"It's possible, sir. We've had reports that when he's on the earth, he spends a lot of time with intercessors."

"No, no." I mumbled as Satan glared at me the way he would a common traitor. "Nofing like at." I shook my head as hard as I could and with all my might thrust my tongue out as far as it would go. It sprung undone with a snap.

"Nothing like that." I panted. "How are you, sir? I've missed you." One of the guards snickered. Satan turned a deep red, and I could have just died right there; I was so mortified.

"What's so funny?" Satan snarled at the guard who immediately tried to swallow his tongue. His natural color was coming back as the evil prince turned his attention back to me.

"This had better be about Moses."

"Well, yes, it is…sort of. Actually, Moses is probably dead by now, but—"

"Dead? Are you sure?"

"Pretty sure. I heard God tell him he would soon die, so, yes, probably."

"Where is the body?"

"I don't know, sir. God said something about his ancestors, but I wasn't really concentrating on that part."

"Fool," he yelled. He jumped from his throne, pushed me aside, and sped past the guards and out the door, headed for the rim of the second heaven. There, he stopped short and looked keenly across the hills and valleys near the land of Canaan.

"There it is. I see where He buried him." With that he was off like a rocket, headed toward the earth.

I couldn't remember the last time Satan himself had gone down to the earth. Some of the others came over to see what was causing all the commotion.

"What's happening? Where's he going?"

"What did you say to him to make him take off like that?"

"Whatever it was, say it again."

Everybody but me burst into laughter. Since none of us had a clue what had caused Satan's reaction, we remained glued in place, watching to see what would happen when he got there.

Like a lightning bolt, he flew spot-on to a place near Beth Peor, and then he came to a stop in front of a cave so hidden it was doubtful any human would have ever found it. He looked frightening—much more so than usual. He was always horrible, but now he appeared to be enraged and much larger and more powerful. Taking long, deliberate steps and clenching his claws, he marched toward the opening of the cave.

He paused and looked both ways then lunged toward the entrance. In the split of a second, a blinding light appeared before him, causing him to stumble backward as he tried to shield his eyes.

A gasp escaped from those of us who stood watching.

"Who is it?"

"It's Michael."

"Michael?" I blurted, pushing my way to the front. "It can't be Michael."

But it was. Michael, the archangel and captain of the angelic guard, blocked Satan's path into the cave where Moses's body lay buried by the hand of God. Michael's flaming sword flashed like fire as he wielded the magnificent weapon, causing Satan to stumble a few more steps back.

"Are you back for another match?" Michael chided him.

"Hand him over."

"The Lord rebuke you." Michael did not flinch from position.

"Give me the law breaker."

"Law breaker?" I said. "Moses was the law *giver*, not a law *breaker*. Why is he calling him that?"

No one answered me, but several shook their heads. Nobody knew what was going on. I tried to think. When had Moses broken any laws? Yes, there was that one thing with striking the rock, but one would have to stretch to call that law breaking. And even if that were the case, what did Satan want with a dead body, even if it was Moses?

Satan tried once more to lunge past.

"The Lord rebuke you," Michael shouted as he thrust his sword within centimeters of Satan's contorted face.

Satan pulled back in fear.

"Flee!" Michael spoke the word in a quiet voice but with such authority that Satan whimpered as he slunk back farther. Several of us also felt the power behind Michael's word and moved back a safe distance from the rim. Not knowing whether anything else might happen and not wanting to miss it if it did, we continued watching until we saw the chastened archdemon leave the earth realm.

Completely confused by what we'd seen, we were still standing there when Satan came storming back.

"What are you gawking at?" he growled. He pushed past us and headed back to his throne room.

We tried to follow him, but when we got close to the doors, at Satan's command, the guards slammed them shut and refused entry to any of us. Under normal circumstances, demons—gossips that they are—would have been a titter with speculation, but not this time. None of us had any idea what had happened or why Satan had done such a bizarre thing. Why had he tried to steal the body of Moses? Why was Michael there to defend it so fiercely? Why had God buried Moses Himself and not allowed the people to do it? We had no answers.

Till this day, we still don't.

CHAPTER 27

I WASN'T SURE WHAT I was supposed to do next, so I retired to my perch, knowing Satan would send for me when he wanted to hear my report. It wasn't long before his messenger showed up. I followed him back to the lair where Satan waited.

"Do they have a new leader?" Satan asked in a matter-of-fact tone.

Let me point out how this is an example of one of the rare ways in which God and Satan have similar speech patterns. Both of them are prone to start a conversation in the middle, assuming the other person knows what's being talked about. Fortunately, I did.

"Yes. His name is Joshua."

"Why don't I know about him?"

"I'm sure I mentioned him, sir." I wasn't sure at all, but I didn't blink and stuck to my story. "He followed Moses around for several years helping him out. Sort of like his assistant. Nothing really special about him that I've noticed."

"Keep careful tabs on him; I want no surprises." Satan motioned for two other demons to come closer to where he sat. "Moron here," he said, pointing to me, "will move out with the Israelites as they cross the Jordan. He'll keep me posted. As for you, be sure the king is ready for them. I want them stopped at Jericho, but do not allow them to be killed. I have other plans." He rubbed his claws together and licked his lips. The others laughed as though they had an inside joke and I wasn't part of it.

Satan stopped chuckling and looked sideways at me. "Why are you still here?"

I bowed quickly and backed my way out of the room. *Just once*, I thought, *I'd like to be treated with a little respect.* Was that too much to ask?

I flew toward Earth and arrived just in time to hear God speaking to Joshua, who lay prostrate on the ground before Him. God had spoken to Moses face-to-face, but let's be honest, for all he would later accomplish, Joshua never quite reached the level of intimacy with God that Moses had. Whether that was God's preference or his, I can't say, but Joshua seemed more comfortable with his head in the sand than to chance a glance at the face of God.

"Moses, my servant, is dead," God said. "Lead these people, and get ready to cross the Jordan River into the land I am about to give to them. I will give you every place where you set your foot, as I promised Moses. Your territory will extend from the desert to Lebanon, and from the great river, the Euphrates—all the Hittite country—to the Mediterranean Sea in the west. No one will be able to stand against you. As I was with Moses, so I will be with you; I will never leave you nor forsake you. Be strong and very courageous. Now stand to your feet before Me."

Joshua rose to his feet but kept his head bowed as God spoke again.

"Be careful to obey all the law My servant Moses gave you; do not turn from it to the right or to the left and you will be successful wherever you go. Keep this book of the Law always on your lips; meditate on it day and night, so that you may be careful to do everything written in it. Then you will be prosperous and successful."

"I will do as my God has said."

Then Joshua went back to the camp and called the leaders together. "Go through the camp, and tell the people to pack their bags. In three days we will cross the Jordan River to enter and take the land God is giving us."

The leaders cheered and pledged their allegiance to Joshua.

"Call the Reubenites, the Gadites, and the half tribe of Manasseh together. I want to talk to them apart from the others."

The men saluted Joshua and ran back to do as he directed them. It wasn't long before the three groups were gathered and anxious to hear Joshua's instructions.

"Remember what Moses, the servant of God, commanded you. Your wives, your children, and your livestock can stay here east of the Jordan, but the rest of you are soldiers, so you must cross the river in battle formation, leading your brothers, helping them until God gives them a place of rest just as He has done for you. They also will take possession of the land that God is giving them. Then you will be free to return to your possession, across the Jordan to the east. Am I clear?"

"Everything you commanded us, we'll do. Wherever you send us, we'll go."

"As we obeyed Moses in all his commands, so we'll also obey you."

I could tell by the look in Joshua's eyes that he wasn't sure whether this was good news or not since he'd been right there as a first-person witness to the rebellion of the people against almost everything Moses told them to do. They never obeyed the first time.

"OK. Well, good, then," Joshua said.

"We just pray that God will be with you as He was with Moses," someone called out.

"You can count on us," said another. "Anyone who questions what you say and refuses to obey whatever you command him will be put to death."

"Let's hope it doesn't come to that," Joshua said.

Joshua went back to his tent, where two men whom he had summoned from Shittim, Jehoa and Simon, were waiting for him. He motioned for them to sit down, and then he shared his plan with them.

"You know the land we are going into is occupied."

"Why should it matter if the Lord has promised it to us?" Jehoa asked.

"It does matter. He's promised it, but make no mistake, we'll have to fight for it. We need intelligence as to what's awaiting us when we get there."

"Command us, and we will serve you." They both nodded in agreement.

"Here's what I want you to do: Go secretly over to Jericho and spy out the land. How many men does the king have? What kinds of weapons are there? Tell no one where you're going."

"You sound like you're expecting trouble," Simon said.

"I'm expecting nothing but trouble. We don't want to walk into a trap."

Jehoa and Simon exchanged a quizzical look. Joshua was not a man exuding confidence and certain victory.

Simon ventured a question. "What is it, Joshua? What are you worried about?"

"Who said I was worried? We've got the word of the Lord on this, don't we?"

Jehoa and Simon knew by his eyes that Joshua was not asking a question he wanted answered. I myself was curious as to what was going on in Joshua's head. Could he be having doubts? Finally, he spoke.

"I wish Moses were here. That's all."

"Moses is dead," Jehoa quipped, obviously not thinking.

"So I've heard," Joshua shot back.

"What I mean to say is you're wearing Moses's mantle now. No one questions that."

"But I'm not Moses. I don't hear from God the same way Moses heard. What if I'm wrong? What if I'm hearing nothing but my own ambition?"

Uh-oh, I thought to myself. *This is not going to be good news for Satan.* Joshua was not a duplicate of Moses for sure. He didn't presume to know more than Moses or to be a new and improved version of Moses. This was almost unknown behavior in young successors who nearly always thought they knew more than their aged predecessors. Joshua was bringing a new element to the human equation, at least as far as mighty-men-macho-leader types go. Joshua was examining his conscience and questioning the purity of his motives. I tried to remember if any of the leaders of the Jews had ever done anything like that before; none that I could remember. Moses had been humble all right, but he never once questioned whether or not he had heard correctly from God.

Simon put his hand on Joshua's shoulder. "Be strong and very courageous. God is with you, and so are we."

"We'll leave when it gets dark so as not to draw attention," Jehoa added.

"Right, good idea." Joshua stood, shook off his moment of self-doubt, and extended his hand to each of the men as they slipped quietly out of his tent.

I wondered if I should stay with Joshua or go with the spies. "Better to go with the spies," I reasoned. "Joshua won't do anything until they come back."

It was dark when we—the spies and I—left for Jericho. It was still dark when we got near the city.

"We need a place to hide out; we could be here several days," said Jehoa.

"I may know of such a place," Simon answered.

"How could you know of a place? You've never been here before."

"I know, but I've heard of a place from some of the travelers we encountered in the desert. I've heard stories about a woman named Rahab."

"And so?"

"She owns a food market. At least that's what some people think." He lowered his voice as if not wanting anyone to hear what he said; not that there was anyone else around.

"It's only a food market during the day. At nightfall, it's a different story. Upstairs she has a brothel."

"A brothel? We're out here on a dangerous mission and your first suggestion is to find a brothel?"

"Well, look, I'm just telling you what I've heard. We have to have someplace to spend the night. I think we should try to find her."

Not having a better idea, both men agreed and set out in search of Rahab's house. I was getting kind of excited about it myself. I'd never seen a brothel. Oh, to be sure, I'd seen plenty of the temple prostitutes wherever Satan had set up idols to himself. But just a working-girl harlot? Never.

It was pitch dark on the road that night, but those two spies found the way to Rahab's house as if they'd had a map. Simon had been right about a market. Of course, it was closed up due to the hour, but right there in front were the bins where the figs and pomegranates were kept during the day and an oven where bread was baked. The boys went around to the back of the house and knocked on the door.

A young girl opened the door just wide enough to extend a candle to illuminate the faces of the men. When she didn't recognize them, she was immediately suspicious.

"What do you want?"

"We have business with Rahab."

"What kind of business?"

"Tell her we're here. She's expecting us."

"Wait here, then." The girl looked doubtful as she closed the door.

"She's expecting us?" Jehoa looked incredulous. "Is that the best you could come up with? Since she's obviously *not* expecting us, she probably won't come down."

"I didn't hear you offer any clever answer."

"Well, I might have if you hadn't jumped right in."

The disagreement ended when the door opened again and a woman early into middle age stepped out with a lantern and closed the door behind her. As I said, I'd never seen a harlot, so I didn't know what to expect, but I guess I didn't expect her. To start with, she was substantial. I don't mean that she was large, more medium sized I suppose, but her demeanor was, well, substantial. She was not timid, and she certainly was not the least bit, uh, flirty. That's it. Not flirty in the least. She looked intently into the face of each man before speaking.

"I know who you are."

"You do?"

"You do?" I said before I caught myself.

"Yes, I do. You must come with me quickly, and do just as I say. They're already looking for you." She ushered the men through the door and then stepped in front of them to lead the way. Neither of them expected such a reception, but they had no doubt they were to do just as she instructed them.

"Follow me up to the roof. Hurry."

"Come and help me, Rhoda." She nodded to the young girl who had first met them at the door. The girl dropped the basket she was carrying and scurried up to the roof behind the spies.

"Now, quickly, both of you lie down near the wall."

They hesitated only a moment before doing as she told them.

"We're going to cover you up with these bundles of flax. Do not move and do not talk until I come back for you."

Just then a warning voice from below called out to her.

"Rahab, the king's men are here. They're asking for you. Come down quickly."

"I'm coming."

Spreading the last bundle of flax over the spies, with urgency in her voice, she whispered loudly, "Not a word. Not a move."

The two soldiers were waiting inside the house when she came down. Smoothing her apron out before her and adjusting her head scarf, she bowed slightly before speaking to them.

"What do the king's men want with a widow?"

"Widow? Is that what you are now?" The captain laughed.

"Why, of course you're a widow. That explains the long line of men who visit this house," said the junior of the two.

"I'm a poor grocer. What do you want with me?"

Rahab did not twitch or display any nervousness at all as she lied through her missing teeth. I would have been a wreck seeing the swords those soldiers carried and knowing the ruthless reputation of the king of Jericho to anyone who betrayed him. But not her; not a stumble of any kind.

"Bring out the men who came to you to stay the night in your house. They're spies; they plan to lead an insurgency."

"Spies? Is that what they were? Yes, two men did come to me earlier. They looked suspicious, and since I didn't know where they'd come from, I sent them away. Why do you seek them?"

"It's none of your concern. Where did they go?"

"I don't know. When the gate was about to be shut, they left. But I have no idea where they went."

"You're sure they said nothing to indicate where they were going?"

"Wait, now I remember. They talked about getting to the river. They must have taken off down the Jordan road. If you hurry, you can still catch them!"

Without so much as a thank-you, the soldiers set chase down the Jordan road toward the fords. As soon as they were gone, Rahab closed and locked the door.

Gathering her skirts about her, she climbed back on the roof, where the spies lay motionless and quiet.

"They're gone. You can come out now."

Jehoa and Simon shook the flax off and stood up.

"We're grateful," Simon said.

"You don't know us," Jehoa interrupted. "Why did you help us?"

"I know who you are and that God has given you this land. We're all afraid. Everyone in the country is terrified of you."

Jehoa and Simon looked at each other, unsure of what to say in response.

"We've heard how God dried up the waters of the Red Sea before you when you left Egypt and what He did to the two Amorite kings east of the Jordan whom you put under a holy curse and destroyed."

She paused to gauge their reaction, which was hard because they were too dumbstruck to react.

"We heard it, and our hearts sank. Fear consumed us all because of you and your God. They say He is the God of the heavens above and God of the earth below. Is that so?"

"It is so," Jehoa said.

"Then swear to me by your God that because I showed you mercy you will show my family mercy; my father and mother, my brothers and sisters—everyone connected with my family. Promise me you will save our souls from death!"

"We'll protect you with our lives because you have risked your life to save us!" said Simon. "But don't tell anyone our business. When God turns this land over to us, we'll do right by you in loyal mercy."

"The soldiers will be back," Jehoa cautioned. "How can we get out of here?"

"I'll show you." She called for Rhoda to come and help her. Together they lowered the men through a window with a rope; as I said, Rahab was a substantial woman.

"Run for the hills so they won't find you. Hide out for three days, and give your pursuers time to return. Then get on your way."

Jehoa called back to her, "In order to keep this oath you made us swear, here is what you must do. Hang this red rope out the window through which you let us down, and gather your entire family with you in your house—father, mother, brothers, and sisters. When the fighting starts, anyone who goes out the doors of your house into the street might be killed."

"If that happens," Simon added, "it's his own fault—we aren't responsible. But for everyone within the house we take full responsibility. If anyone lays a hand on one of them, it's our fault."

"But if you tell anyone of our business here, the oath you made us swear is canceled—we're no longer responsible," Jehoa added.

"If that's what you say, that's the way it is," she answered and sent them off. They left, and she hung the red rope out the window.

With me right behind them, the spies headed for the hills and stayed there for three days until the king's men had returned to Jericho. The pursuers looked high and low but did not find them.

Jehoa and Simon returned to their camp to find Joshua waiting in anticipation for their report. They were out of breath from running the last mile in excitement to tell him what they'd found.

"You won't believe it." Simon bent over and rested on his knees to catch his breath.

"They are terrified of us!" Jehoa blurted out.

"Terrified?" Joshua asked.

"It's true," Simon interrupted. "Every word of it. They know who we are. They know where we've been, and they are convinced we are coming to take the land away from them."

"That wouldn't make them terrified unless they thought we could do it." Joshua seemed skeptical. "Why would they assume a people who has wandered in the desert for forty years could just walk in and take out a fortified city? Jericho is walled up. No one goes in or out without the permission of the king."

"They know God has promised it to us."

"How do you know all of this?"

"The harlot told us," Jehoa blurted.

"You were with a harlot?" Joshua's eyes widened.

"No, not like that," Simon interrupted. "She's not a real harlot."

"Not a real harlot?"

"No, she's sort of a grocer." Simon struggled for words to describe Rahab. "She's more like a part-time harlot, just to make ends meet, I'm sure."

"And, so, was she pretending to be a harlot or pretending to be a grocer when you went to her house?"

"I don't know. We weren't there more than thirty minutes, but I can tell you she saved our lives."

"That's right," Jehoa said. "The king of Jericho sent soldiers looking for us. We don't know how he knew about us or how he would have known that we sought refuge in the harlot's—Rahab's—house."

"A grocer harlot?" Joshua tried, but he couldn't get a visual. "Never mind; go on with the story."

"Rahab hid us on the roof and covered us up with bundles of flax. The king's soldiers came looking for us, but she told them we'd been there and gone."

Joshua's face was more perplexed than jubilant at such a development.

"I don't understand. Why?"

"It's like we told you. The news of us has gone before us, and the people fear us."

"It's more like they fear God," Jehoa corrected. "Rahab said the people near and far know that God is with us and has promised us the land."

Joshua put his hands on his hips and walked back and forth as if having received some important new revelation. I walked back and forth with him. I was also thinking how the scales might tip in Israel's favor if the people were already afraid before they got there.

"That settles it." Joshua clapped his hands together in newfound resolve. "Tomorrow we go out."

The three men slapped shoulders, gave each other a manly hug, and then each headed back to this own tent, leaving me to pace by myself.

CHAPTER 28

B Y MORNING JOSHUA's confidence in God and in himself
had returned. He energized the people and got them
moving toward the Jordan River where they set up
camp. His renewed zest for life caused me to wonder about
what had changed in his spirit and why. Just the day before,
Joshua doubted his motives, the people, and his ability to hear
from God, although he clearly had. I myself heard the promises God spoke to him. I clearly heard God say the words, "Be
bold and very courageous." Yet, Joshua was feeling anything
but that. Why? He had affirmation from the highest authority
there was on the matter.

Depressed and unsure of himself, he shared his feelings with
Jehoa and Simon, underlings in the power structure for sure.
Then Simon said to Joshua, "Be bold and very courageous," the
exact words God said (which, to be honest, hadn't produced
all that much confidence in Joshua), and look what happened.
Overnight, Joshua recovered and was squarely back in control
of the situation. Why would a human's words mimicking God's
words cause such a reversal in attitude, especially when there
was no new information contained in them? It was just a repeat
of what God had said. Do you see my perplexity? Why weren't
God's words alone good enough to keep Joshua cheered up?

I feared I was about to figure out something else about God's
strategy for humanity that Satan was not going to like the least
little bit. God's words in the mouth of a human can carry
the same authority, cause, and effect as if God Himself were

speaking. Say, for example, God speaks a prophetic word into the spirit of a person. The person may know what he heard, and he may even believe it was God, but after a while when nothing seems to be happening, doubt creeps in. He begins to say things like, "I don't know if it was God or me." I've heard you people do it thousands of times. Not being 100 percent supernatural like we are, you simply don't trust your ability to operate in the supernatural and hear God without doubting yourself. If you only knew how supernatural you really are, but I digress. To compensate for this flaw in your makeup, God causes another human to audibly speak His exact same words to the same person; it's as if God is bearing witness to Himself.

I struggled for a way to describe such a dynamic. *Encouragement*. There's no other word for it. A human speaking the words of God to another human gives him courage. I don't say I understand how such a thing *can* work, but there is no doubt that it *does* work every time.

Oh my, but this was not good news for Satan.

Encouragement combined with intercession could be a one-two punch for any scheme a demon might have. If the chosen person had one human interceding for him and another speaking God's encouragement, who knew where it could end? Joshua would prove to be a textbook case for what was possible.

After they'd been by the Jordan for three days, God said to Joshua, "This very day I will begin to make you great in the eyes of all Israel. They'll see for themselves that I'm with you in the same way that I was with Moses. Now, command the priests who are carrying the ark of the covenant to go to the edge of the Jordan's waters and stand there on the river bank."

Joshua called the leaders together and told them what to do. "Get ready to go through the camp. Tell the people that when they see the ark of the covenant, carried by the Levitical priests, to start moving. Follow it. Make sure they keep a proper distance between themselves and the ark, but don't lose sight of it, because they've never been on this road before, and we don't want any wrong turns."

Then Joshua called out a rallying cry to the people: "Sanctify yourselves. Tomorrow God will work miracles and wonders among you."

Next, Joshua turned to the priests. "Take up the ark, and step out before the people." So they took it up and paraded before the people.

Joshua turned to the people. "Look at what's before you: the ark of the covenant. God Himself will cross the Jordan as you watch."

Turning back to the priests, Joshua instructed them. "Now take the ark and step into the water. When your feet touch the Jordan's water, the flow of water will be stopped and the water coming from upstream will pile up in a heap."

That's when the honeymoon ended between Joshua and the priests. The priests carrying the ark froze, stared in disbelief at Joshua, and wouldn't take another step. They exchanged fearful looks between themselves. Then, turning his back to the people, the chief priest motioned for Joshua to come to his side. He whispered so none of the people could hear him rebuke Joshua.

"Have you lost your mind? Are you mad? Look at that river. It is far above flood stage. You can't be seriously telling us to just march into the river like there's no problem."

"We can't be sure where the bottom is," came the voice from one of the other priests.

"We could drop the ark. We could drown," another chimed in.

"How about you send a good swimmer out there first, and let's see how he does before you imperil the entire Levitical priesthood?"

"Have you no faith?" Joshua whispered back.

"I have faith, but I have eyes also, and so do the other priests."

Joshua looked at the frightened faces of the priests and could see they were in agreement and in deep fear.

"Are you refusing to obey your God?"

"No, no, it's not that, but just look at that river!"

Joshua didn't respond. The priest was visibly uncomfortable in challenging Joshua, but no one with a sense of self-preservation would have dared walk into the river. Those swirling waters even made me dizzy. Looking to the other priests, then to the people, then to Joshua, the chief priest asked what no one had dared to ask before.

"Joshua, how sure are you that you've heard from God?"

This was the first real test of Joshua's leadership apart from Moses. What if the priests wouldn't obey? If they showed no confidence in Joshua, the people would scatter like frightened sheep. Oh, I could see clearly what was really at stake here, and I wondered if God had a backup plan if the priests faltered. This particular scenario hadn't ever happened before.

In other crisis moments of obedience, God spoke to His anointed, and the anointed spoke to the people who obeyed or didn't and were rewarded or judged pretty much on the spot. But this was different. Between Joshua, the anointed, and the people was a whole new layer of management: the priests. Moses and Aaron, as well as Joshua, had spent a lot of time convincing the people to respect the priesthood. The people saw Joshua as the leader but saw the priests as their religious authority, who presumably also heard from God. What would Joshua do if the priests flatly refused to step into the water? He wouldn't dare send the people into the river unless the ark went before them as God had instructed. The rest of history would depend on that moment and what the priests did.

Right then I knew why I could never be a leader. I couldn't stand the stress. I would never have the nerve to tell people to do something with real consequences for fear that they might not do it—like what was happening right there with Joshua and the priests. If they didn't obey me, I would have no idea what to do next. I was suddenly glad that my entire role in life was to watch and report and nothing more.

Joshua stepped closer to the chief priest, nose to nose and toes to toes. He did not blink, he did not raise his voice, and he did not plead.

"Step into the water, and see the salvation of the Lord."

The priest did blink—several times, in fact—but said nothing. Signaling the other priests, he turned, and with each in position and wide eyes locked straight ahead, they stepped into the whirling waters of the Jordan. When they did, the waters began to heap up just as God had said they would.

I'm telling you, this would have never happened had it not been for the encourager. If God hadn't put His words into the mouth of Simon, I'm convinced Joshua would never have had the courage to stand up to the priests.

Those priests carrying the ark stood firmly planted on dry ground in the middle of the Jordan while all Israel crossed before them. Finally, the whole nation was across the Jordan, and not one foot was wet.

God spoke to Joshua again. "Select twelve men from the people, a man from each tribe, and tell them to take twelve stones from the center of the river where the priests are standing. Carry them across with you, and set them down in the place where you camp tonight."

Joshua called out the twelve men and said, "Cross to the middle of the Jordan, and take your place in front of the ark. Each of you heft a stone to your shoulder, one for each of the tribes of the people of Israel, so you'll have something later to mark the occasion. When your children ask you, 'What are these stones to you?' you'll say, 'The flow of the Jordan was stopped in front of the ark of the covenant as it crossed the Jordan. These stones are a permanent memorial for the people of Israel.'"

The people did exactly as Joshua commanded. They took twelve stones from the middle of the Jordan, carried them across to the camp, and set them down.

The priests carrying the ark, trembling the whole time, continued standing in the middle of the Jordan until everything God had instructed Joshua to tell the people to do was done. The people crossed quickly; no one dawdled, but it seemed like forever to the priests, who thought the crossing was never going to be complete. When every last one of the Israelites stepped out of the river, the ark of the covenant and the priests crossed over as the river closed in behind them. You have never seen a group of holy men hightailing it like those priests were as they ran out of the river.

The Reubenites, Gadites, and the half tribe of Manasseh lined up in battle formation as Joshua had told them to do. All told, about forty thousand armed soldiers crossed over before God to the plains of Jericho, ready for battle.

Just as He said He would do, God made Joshua great that day in the sight of all Israel. For the first time, they were in awe of him just as they had been in awe of Moses. This was a risky move on God's part, if you ask me. He should never allow humans to get to the "awe" state. Why would God think humans could stand up under adoration any better than Lucifer had when all the other angels were in awe of his beauty and majesty? If I'd been God, I would have gone with letting the people feel gratitude and be done with it. There was way too much danger in allowing awe.

Joshua stretched out his arms over the people and proclaimed to them, "God dried up the Jordan's waters for you until you had crossed, just as He did at the Red Sea. This is so that everybody on Earth will recognize how strong God's rescuing hand is to save you."

When all the Amorite kings west of the Jordan and the Canaanite kings along the seacoast heard how God had stopped the Jordan River before Israel until they had crossed over, their hearts sank, and just thinking about it made the courage drain from them.

Figuring Joshua would ride the momentum of the moment, I expected him to go after Jericho right away, and he probably would have except that God had another idea.

God said to Joshua, "Make stone knives, and circumcise the people of Israel a second time."

Can you imagine how that news went over? I still had nightmares from the time Abraham had to circumcise all the males and I had to watch. Certainly Joshua had seen circumcisions before leaving Egypt, but it had always involved a baby eight days old—not too much blood or kicking and screaming. But when it came to circumcising grown men by the hundreds, there's no way he could have imagined how bad it was going to get.

This was a good time for me to leave. I needed to report in to Satan, and if Joshua went through with it, the men would be laid up for three days at least. I could get to the second heaven and back before the siege against Jericho began.

By the time Joshua raised his new flint knife into the air and began explaining what he was going to do with it, I was airborne and headed for home.

CHAPTER 29

SATAN LAUGHED WHEN I told him about the circumcisions.

"Why does He keep making them do that ridiculous self-mutilation?" he asked, meaning God, of course.

"I know. It sounds more like something *you* would've come up with." That's what I wanted to say. What I did say was less inflammatory.

"I really don't know, sir. As far as I can recall, He's never said why."

"Will wonders never cease? There's *something* you don't know about God? You who are always so quick to lecture me on the what and why of God?" He raised his claws and grasped his head, feigning amazement. "At last, to find something about Him you don't know."

I did know one thing: I'd better not offer a response to such a loaded remark. If I'd had the nerve, I would have pointed out to Satan that, as a matter of fact, most of the time I was exactly right in predicting or explaining what either God or humans were apt to do. But as for the circumcision business, I have to admit I'd never quite figured that one out.

Ignoring his jab at me, I went on to tell Satan about Rahab and then about the priests carrying the ark and the Jordan River heaping up so the people could cross, but he just yawned and looked bored.

"I care nothing about harlots and priests. As for the river, is God still relying on that old trick, splitting waters in half? He should know anything after the Red Sea is passé. It's a shame He hasn't moved on by now and developed a new act."

"Well, the truth is, sir, most of the people who were alive at the time when the Red Sea split are pretty much dead now. The new generation has heard the story from their parents. Not having been there, they're pretty impressed with making the waters of a river rise up and stand at attention."

He yawned again. "So, basically, you have nothing new to report, and you're only here because you didn't want to watch the circumcisions. Is that about it?"

Why couldn't I get over the need to impress him? I loathed him. I thought I was over caring what he thought about me. Why was I here again trying to get his approval? It was impossible. Why didn't I just leave right then?

"Not exactly. I thought you might want to know that God has released another weapon into the arsenal of humanity for spiritual warfare." I turned slightly as if intending to leave. "But if you're not interested, I'll just be going."

"What do you mean?"

I swallowed hard and tried to sound foreboding. "He has released the spiritual gift of...encouragement."

Satan stared hard at me for several seconds before slapping his knee and roaring into laughter. The guards also began their obligatory snickering of agreement whenever Satan saw anything funny.

"Encouragement?" He could barely get it out for his laughing. "God has released people to say sweet things to each other?" Snort, chuckle, and snicker. "You're such an idiot."

Don't answer, don't answer, don't answer, my brain kept saying as my mouth opened and my tongue escaped.

"I'm not the idiot; you're the..." My brain forged ahead and caused my jaw to clamp down on my tongue before it could seal my absolute doom.

"I'm what?"

"You're..." My brain froze. I couldn't think of a single thing. "You're wise to see what's behind God's cunning." My brain unfroze just in time.

"I am? Of course I am. I've always known His motives."

"God can't get anything by you, sir. That's why you see right away that encouragement may seem innocent enough but is really a cover for a powerful delegation of God's power."

"Of course I see that. Nothing gets by me. He should know that by now."

"Right, so that's why you see right through what God is doing by releasing His words into the mouths of one human to speak to another human, thereby empowering him as if God Himself had spoken."

"What else do I see?"

"You can see that when you send a demon to torment and accuse a human to make him feel inadequate and rejected, God no longer has to send an angel to countermand the demonic lie. All God has to do is speak to another human who will take His word to the dejected person, and just like that—" I snapped my claws—"the person is no longer dejected. His spiritual energy is renewed, and he's able to withstand whatever the demon has released against him." I paused to see if Satan was still listening. He was, so I continued.

"Fortunately, the humans haven't yet learned how to use this new weapon. They don't even know it is a weapon. But it's just a matter of time until the intercessors will see what's going on and call the encouragers to the front lines of the battle. A human who can speak the words of God to another human can thoroughly undo any demonic word curse released to the person. It's much more efficient and conserves God's angelic resources."

Satan sat silently thinking over what I said for at least a minute before brushing it off.

"I don't get it. For human number one to carry God's word to human two would have to mean number one cared about number two to start with. Otherwise, why bother?"

Now it was my turn to look perplexed.

"You don't get it, do you, moron? Humans don't care anything about each other. They only care about themselves, or maybe their blood kin, but nothing more than that. A human isn't going to stick himself in the middle of a spiritual war between a demon and another human."

"They will do it, sir."

"Maybe those weird ones, the intercessors; they might do it. But normal humans won't."

"They will, sir."

"Why do you insist on such nonsense?"

"Because they…they love each other; whether they are related or not. They care about people they don't personally know. When they see other humans in terrible situations, they have strong feelings of compassion for them and want to help."

"Only if they are going to get something out of it."

"Regardless of whether they're going to get something out of it. You can't understand this characteristic of humans because you care about no one but yourself."

Now, you may think, knowing his temper as you do by now, that this would be the point where he would do something terrible to me for my impertinence. But you'd be wrong. Satan can't *feel* things like a human, but you humans can't *think* things like demons, although you like to tell yourself you can and that's how you outwit us. Nonsense. You interpret what I said to Satan about not caring about anyone but himself as an insult. He interpreted it as a matter of fact. Not caring about anyone except one's own self makes perfect sense to him. Caring about other beings—unless you need them—in the demonic realm is silly sentimentality.

Satan stood up, signaling the end of his interest in what I had to say.

"Go down to Jericho. Watch the battle, and then come back and report when the king has backed Israel into a corner."

I flew back toward the earth, knowing full well that Satan hadn't believed a single thing I said about the encouragers. He hadn't believed me about intercession either when it first appeared in Abraham. He would learn that the encouragers would have as much or more to do with Israel's perseverance than the intercessors and the prophets put together. Gift by spiritual gift and office by spiritual office—it was so clear to me what God was doing, what He told Satan He would do oh so long ago when the earth was restored and Adam and Eve were created. He told Satan He would redeem the earth through men and women. Satan laughed. Fool that he is, he is still laughing.

"Mark my words," I spoke into the atmosphere as I flew, "God will laugh last."

CHAPTER 30

CURIOUS TO SEE what was going on in Jericho before heading back to the Israelite's campsite, I flew over the city wall for a look but decided to take a pass when I saw the entire town was tightly shut up and locked down—no one going in; no one coming out. Fearing I'd already tarried too long trying to explain encouragement to Satan, I hurried on to find Joshua. I barely got there in time to hear God speak to him.

"I've already given Jericho to you, along with its king and its troops. Here's what you are to do: March around the city with all your soldiers. Circle the city once. Repeat this for six days. Have seven priests carry seven ram's horn trumpets in front of the ark."

"When do You want us to lay siege to the city?"

"Don't raise a sword. You won't have to do a thing."

"But You must want us to do something. You're not thinking they'll just surrender to us?"

"Just do what I tell you. On the seventh day, march around the city seven times with the priests blowing away on the trumpets. Then tell them to sound a long blast on the ram's horns. When they hear that, all the people are to shout at the top of their lungs. The city wall will collapse all at once."

"Uh-huh. Just like that? The wall will simply fall down?"

"Just like that. After that, Israel can enter right in and take the city."

I suppose if God were thinking surprise attack, this strategy was the one to go with. Whatever the king of Jericho was expecting, a parade around the city for seven days probably wasn't it.

Joshua called the priests and the people and told them what God had said. I thought they might at least have a few questions, but not so. When Joshua spoke the orders, the people moved out without so much as a raised eyebrow. After the heaping up of a river in midair, Joshua's stock was pretty high, even with the priests. He could have told them to run around the wall swinging a dead chicken over their heads, and they would have done it. No one questioned the oddness of his battle plan the least little bit.

Seven of the priests with their seven ram's horn trumpets set out before God, the ark, and the Israelites and then blew the trumpets for all they were worth.

Joshua hushed the people. "Don't shout until I tell you. In fact, don't even speak—not so much as a whisper."

Then he gave the signal and sent the whole contingency on its way around the city. It circled once, came back to camp, and stayed for the night. Joshua was up early the next morning, and the whole process began again. They did this for six days.

I couldn't stand it. I had to know what the king of Jericho was thinking when he saw the parade marching around his town. I found my way to his quarters in time to hear a debriefing from one of his captains.

"What are they doing?" The king stood on his balcony where he could see the whole thing.

"Marching around the city with a wooden box and blowing horns," the bearded officer said.

"I can see that. *Why* are they doing it?"

"No idea, sir."

The king returned to his throne, leaned his chin on one hand, and tapped the arm of his chair with the other. After a few moments, he perked up, signaling that he had figured it out.

"Perhaps we've been worried about them for no reason. They may have been fierce at one time, but obviously, by now they've gone mad. Wandering in the desert for forty years could do that to a person."

"That's as good an explanation as any, Your Majesty."

"So, what do you think they'll do next?"

"Don't know, sir. Hard to predict what crazy people will do."

When it became clear that strategy was not the long suit of either the king or the officer, I tired of their uninspired conversation and went back to Joshua's tent. The next day would be the seventh, and I was excited to see if the walls of Jericho would fall down like God had said.

Right on cue, the people got up early and marched around the city the same way as before, but this day they circled the city seven times. On the seventh time around, the priests blew the trumpets and Joshua got before the people.

"Now, pay close attention to my instructions. When I tell you to shout, do it, and the walls will come tumbling down. So, watch yourselves; don't get close until it's all on the ground."

Maybe the king was right; they were all crazy. Otherwise, surely someone would have pointed out the odds against such a thing happening.

Joshua paused and raised his hands to settle the excited people down and to let them know that what he was about to say was important.

"The city and everything in it is under a holy curse and is to be offered up to God. That means nobody keeps any of the gold or silver. Everyone is to be killed except for Rahab the harlot. She is to live—she and everyone in her house with her—because she hid the agents we sent."

The excited chitchatting stopped cold in mid chat. Lots of confused looks were exchanged among the people, but not a word was uttered.

Right there was a perfect example of how I could have helped God anticipate and avoid a problem with Joshua if He had only restored my standing. My entire existence had been reduced to watching you humans. I knew all the personality types. If only I had His ear, I could have urged God to hold up a minute and think about what He had made Joshua to be: a commander/soldier type. Joshua was constructed to take orders, give orders, lead wars, and that was pretty much it. He was not a thinker, feeler, metrosexual kind of guy. Joshua had no sensitivity skills to speak of and therefore could not process what the emotional impact was going to be on the men when they heard they were going into battle where there was to be no payoff…at all. Joshua assumed the men would just suck it up and obey like he would have done, ergo his willingness to obey God's seemingly ridiculous battle plan for taking Jericho without raising an argument.

"Have Joshua take one of the priests along with him," I would have told God. "Let the priest explain the theological implications, inspire them to greater good, bigger payoff later on for blind obedience—things like that. Soften it up some. It's bound to work better than Joshua's my-way-or-the-highway attitude."

"What do you mean everything else is under a holy curse?" shouted someone from the back of the crowd.

Was I right? I could have written the script.

The excitement of the crowd was noticeably subdued as they waited for Joshua's answer.

"I meant what I said; take nothing from the city. It's under a holy curse."

The teaspoon of sugar concept was completely unknown in Joshua's world.

"Wait just a minute," another of the men called out. "We do get the booty, don't we?"

"No, and watch yourselves. Be careful that you don't covet anything in the city or take something that's cursed. If you do, you endanger the whole camp and make trouble for everyone. All silver and gold, all vessels of bronze and iron are holy to God and going into His treasury."

Well, I can just tell you this was a deal killer for some of the men. Joshua's stock took a noticeable dip, especially with the man named Achan. When Joshua turned his back, Achan gathered a couple of the other men, spoke in low tones not to be overheard, and complained about Joshua's orders.

"Do you see what's going on here?" Achan looked over his shoulder to be sure Joshua was out of earshot. "I've seen this happen before with people who think God speaks to them personally. Before you know it they become fanatics."

"His orders don't make sense. Why does he think God needs the gold and silver more than we do?" the fat one asked.

"Right," replied the third man. "What's He going to do with it? If God wanted gold and silver, He could just make Himself some more of it."

"The way I see it," Achan said, "there's no point in attacking the city if there's no payoff. We may as well leave it alone and spend our time on something worth more."

"Oh, sure. So, which one of you is going to tell Joshua we've changed our minds about Jericho?"

"Not me."

"Never mind," Achan said. "I've got a plan. Just wait for my signal."

Just at that moment the priests blew the trumpets.

When the people heard the blast of the trumpets, they gave a thunderclap shout. The wall fell down exactly as God said it would, and the people rushed straight into the city and took it. They put everything in the city under the holy curse and then set about killing man and woman, young and old, ox and sheep and donkey.

Joshua called Jehoa and Simon to his side. "Enter the house of the harlot and rescue the woman and everyone connected with her, just as you promised her."

When I heard Joshua's orders about Rahab, I lost all interest in seeing more of the wall falling down. I had to go with Jehoa and Simon. If Joshua followed through with the promise to give shelter to a harlot, I just knew it had to be good for my case. I'd have to look it up to be sure, but I was all but certain that in those thousands of laws God dictated to Moses while they wandered in the desert, there had to be one about stoning the harlot. I'd have paid more attention if I had known it was ever going to come up.

The men made their way through the fighting to Rahab's house, finding her inside huddled together with her whole frightened family. When the men burst through the door, Rahab ran to Simon and Jehoa and bowed to them.

"You came to save us!"

"We gave you our promise."

The men got the whole family out and rushed them to safety, giving them a place outside the camp of Israel for sanctuary.

Well, there it was; sanctuary for the harlot and her kin. God was all too willing to let Joshua make an exception for a habitual sinner. Rahab wasn't a fallen woman who had fallen only once. She fell several times a week. She couldn't plead the only-once-when-I-was-young-and-foolish-thought-he'd-marry-me-never-did-it-again defense. If God let her off the hook, how could He refuse to consider my case?

Meanwhile, Joshua's army burned down the city and everything in it, except for the gold, silver, bronze, and iron vessels—they put all that aside to be placed into God's treasury. Joshua didn't see Achan stuff some of the gold and silver into a grain bag and then hide it beneath some rocks behind one of the burning houses, but God did.

Knowing you humans as I do, I can see you're bothered that the attack on Jericho was so brutal. How could God, who describes Himself as abounding in mercy and love, call for the killing of every person in the city, giving them no chance to escape or repent or at least be taken prisoner? You can never understand why God released such destruction on the people He created, until you know what the people He created had become. Satan owned their souls, and you should be terrified when I tell you how he got them.

It began when the archangels whom God set over the nations of the earth were enticed by Satan to go down to the daughters of men. The fallen angels raped and pillaged humankind and brought forth the dreaded Nephilim race on the earth. God destroyed the Nephilim—most of them, anyway—and every living thing in the polluted gene pool of the earth when He unleashed Noah's flood. I believe if God had thought about it for five minutes longer, He would have anticipated what could happen if He let the guilty angels remain alive, and He would have destroyed them right there and been done with it, no doubt saving Himself and humanity centuries of grief. Instead, He barred them from the third heaven, just as He did with Satan and the rest of us. They weren't thrown out of heaven as we were; they just weren't allowed back in. That left them with no place to go. It wasn't long until the whole host of them appeared before Satan's throne.

The rest of the rank-and-file demons, including me, hid in the shadows when the archangels kneeled before the one they had once served and known as Lucifer. Even on their knees they were huge, almost as big as Satan himself. We didn't know why they were there, but if there was going to be a fight over territory, well, I for one wanted to be out of the line of fire. Satan's sense of revenge at seeing them bow before him was unrestrained.

"How delightful to see you." He mocked them with false hospitality. "I'm so glad you dropped in." His eyes narrowed as his falsetto voice changed to an angry snarl.

"Now, get out."

"Lucifer, master," the one named Molech began. "We have no place else to go."

Satan swelled up with pride like a helium balloon to hear Molech address him as master.

"And what is that to me? Do you think I've forgotten how you traitors refused to stand with me? How you did nothing when He cast me out? Now you turn to me for sanctuary? You disgust me."

Molech's jaw tightened, but he said nothing more as he lowered his head. I was so relieved. Maybe they would leave without any trouble.

That might have happened if the demons hiding in the shadows with me, the ones who never knew when to shut up, hadn't begun to chatter among themselves so loudly anyone could have heard them.

"Yeah, who do they think they are?"

"Think they can just barge right in? Serves them right. Let them know what it's like to be banished."

"You tell them how it is, master." They egged Satan on.

I started looking for the exit.

Satan rose to his feet and turned his back on the kneeling angels. They kept their heads bowed but began exchanging side glances between themselves. I scrunched down to see what might be transpiring in the unspoken language of their eyes. When I saw the narrow baleful slits that Molech's eyes had become, I broke out in a rash right there on the spot. I spun around and tried my best to hush the heckling demons but to no avail. Was I really the only one who could see what was about to happen and how the archangels were beginning to stand up, some already tapping the handles of their swords?

I raced around to his front side to see if there was any trace of expression on Satan's face that would indicate he had a grasp on what could happen if he rejected these monstrous angels. As I feared, there was none. Never in his life had Satan been able to weigh risk and consequence. I rushed to his side and whispered to him.

"Master?"

Never startle Satan. He jumped and just about knocked me over.

"Idiot! Never do that again."

"Master, what will you do with them?" I nodded toward the angels who were beginning to whisper among themselves—not a good sign.

He looked at them as if wondering whether or not he could beat them in a fight. His fallen face said it all: not a chance. They were not rank and file like the rest of us who were forced to serve him. Seeing the wisdom in not testing their power, he dismissed them with a wave of his hand.

"Let them fend for themselves. They can't stay here, not after the way they betrayed me."

"Master, I know you've thought through the possible repercussions of sending them away."

"Of course, I have." He continued to stare at the wall before glancing my way. "But which specific repercussions do you mean?"

Brain, don't fail me now! The archangels were all standing up by now. I had only minutes to convince Satan of what he was about to unleash.

"Master, if they are not with you, they will be against you. Look at them."

He turned his head slightly until he could see the troop of them as they formed a huddle, contemplating their next move.

"If you act right now, you can avoid a rebellion. They're willing to serve you. They're disoriented and haven't tested their strength now that God has rejected them. You must move while they fear you, while they still think you're more powerful than they are."

"I am more powerful."

"Of course you are," I lied. "But just think what you can accomplish with an elite force like them; makes the rest of us look weak by comparison."

I don't know if I got through to him or if he finally noticed how really big they were, but just in time he swung about and walked toward them with outstretched arms.

"I'm nothing if I'm not magnanimous."

"What did he say he is?" whispered one of my lesser brethren.

Magnanimous wasn't a word usually found in the working vocabulary of a demon.

"I'm willing to let bygones be bygones." Satan sauntered to his throne and sat down, motioning for them to kneel again in front of him. "I've decided to overlook your offense and allow you to serve me."

I held my breath as the archangels looked at him, looked at each other, and looked confused, and then, on Molech's signal, one by one they kneeled down. I momentarily lost consciousness from holding my breath so long.

When I came to, the archangels were in counsel with Satan, who was laying out the plans to establish a new hierarchy of evil just below himself. He appointed Baal and Ashtera, the most powerful of the troop, as "gods" over the other demons.

"I will allow you to rule the entire land of Canaan," he promised.

Then Satan gave them instructions as to how they were to lure the people into bizarre and exotic worship of themselves, which would be nothing more than worship of Satan by another name. The first pyramid scheme, if you will. The idea of worship from the humans they once brutalized in their lust was irresistible to the fallen princes.

"Feeble humanity will become your harlots." Satan laughed and dispatched them to the earth.

In some ways I blame God for what happened next. He has to take the responsibility for the manufacturer's default in how you people are made. In your hierarchy of needs, though you won't find it on your man-made charts, is your need to connect with the supernatural through worship. God intended it to be a means for intimate and exclusive relationship with Him. It turned out to be a good idea gone bad because He didn't install the proper safeguards. God failed to eliminate the seductive alternatives that were sure to come about by Satan's lesser gods. He meant well, but He just didn't think it through. If He were going to allow for the possibility that you fleshly creatures might choose to worship someone other than Him, then He should have cut you some slack on His intransigent command that you worship only Him or face His total and utter rejection of you. I'm not absolving you of your own stupidity by any means, but I mean, fair is fair.

"What do you think about them now, God?" Satan yelled from the rim of the second heaven where he watched the archangels seduce the people. He roared in satisfaction at perfect demonic possession occurring in the people, intoxicated with supernatural sensuality, slipping deeper and deeper into an inevitable and inescapable abyss.

The lesser demons celebrated with Satan as they lusted after the travesty taking place on the earth, but I couldn't bear to watch. I slipped away to my perch and curled up with my tail tucked safely beneath me—my version of a fetal position. I didn't want to think about the people at all. Why should I care that they were sentencing themselves to hell? Humanity certainly cared nothing about me. I did find myself feeling sorry for God, though.

"Don't worry about them, God," I cried out to Him. "It's not all Your fault. They did it to themselves. Sure, You should have reined in that free will debacle long ago, but You meant well."

I put my claws over my ears and tried to hum to drown out the sound as the converging carnival and orgy from the earth became louder and unavoidable. The men and even the women of Canaan reveled and cavorted in the ecstasy of the carnal prostitution of themselves with their gods until their minds became reprobate and they were neither desirous of nor able to repent of their choices. Satan laid out the welcome mat, but they themselves had willingly walked into an addiction from which there was no escape.

When Satan realized I wasn't watching the show with the others, he came looking for me. It was a first and a shock to me since he always acted as if he didn't know or care whether I was around or not. I hoped he hadn't heard me talking to God.

"What's *your* problem?" he demanded

"Me? Oh, nothing at all, sir. I don't have a problem."

"Good. Just remember this was all your idea."

My idea? How could such degradation be my idea? I wasn't capable of such a thing. I said nothing, but my jaw must have dropped to my knees as Satan laughed at my dismay.

"You were the one with the idea to set the archangels up as gods and let them ravish the people."

"But I...but I...but I," were all the words I could put together. He couldn't possibly have interpreted anything I said to be an endorsement of such mayhem.

"Don't take it so hard. Sure, it was your idea, but it was God's fault. Egomaniac that He is, He's the one who put the desire in them to worship."

Satan blew on his manicure and polished his nails on his cape as if he had nothing to do with the chaos. "Of course, He never once thought they'd be unfaithful to Him." Then he raised his eyes and looked straight at me and jeered.

"Too bad for God that they found me to be a more exciting lover." He laughed until his laughing turned into howls that curled my feathers. Satisfied that he had undone me completely, he went back to his ringside seat at the rim.

I knew it wasn't my fault the people had fallen into such deadly desire, but I have to admit that I found myself thinking about what Satan said about it being God's fault. I wanted to ask God, "What were You thinking?

"God, why did You make them yearn for the exhilaration of worship? Neither the angels nor mankind can handle the intimacy and power of worship. And why does it attract You as nothing else does? It's almost as if You can't resist them when they worship. When You saw Lucifer risk his place in paradise for worship, didn't that tell You something? What did You think was going to happen with mere flesh and blood?"

God didn't answer me—big surprise—but I kept thinking about it for a long time until I figured out what God must have intended. He planned for worship to emanate from people and bridge humanity to Himself. He knew once people tasted true worship, they would no longer merely love Him—they would fall *in* love with Him. I know because that's how it was with us, the angels.

If you've ever experienced true worship, then you know a love affair with God consumes every part of your life. It's even more delightful for you humans than it ever was for us angels. Ruah Ha Kadosh enters into your body, and it becomes His temple where He abides, and you become as one with God. Nothing like that ever happened with us.

God manifests His love for you, and you experience Him as holy, pure, beautiful, and powerful as He brings you into communion with Himself as in a marriage where you are the cherished bride of a loving groom. It's the perfect love for which you were intended, for which we were intended. Yet, for all the things this union with God is like, there is one thing it is not. It is not erotic. But worship of a demon god is. Satan's gods could never have lured humans into worship by love because they don't have love, so they lured them by lust.

For most of you, the desire for sensual ritual, which is prohibited to you, never rises to consciousness because God eagerly makes Himself available to you and you are satisfied with His love for you and yours for Him and you don't place yourselves in situations where a forbidden desire can become aroused. Now, to be perfectly fair to the people of Canaan, it does seem to me that God is more accessible to you non-Jews now than He used to be.

Nevertheless, what God intended for all people was a holy longing for intimacy with Himself. For some, enticed by the seduction of the demon gods, that holy longing became warped and distorted into a perverse yearning for strange flesh, an erotic experience with the supernatural. In order to fill their escalating craving for more of the thrill, the people themselves became hunters of other human souls.

That's what the people of Jericho and Canaan were like—locked into a frenzy of unspeakable worship of their gods and ravenous to bring others into it with them. The only way God could protect Israel was to destroy the predators of human souls by the hands of His worshipers.

And that's why Achan's thievery was so odious and why God's punishment would be so severe. It was as if Achan had kept an engagement ring from the dark powers who ruled in Jericho. In his greed, Achan had taken the bait of Satan and put Israel within the devil's grasp, but through the obedience of His servant Joshua, God would snatch them right out of his hand.

The worship of the demon gods made the people one with the demon, a marriage made in hell with no retreat, no repentance, and no escape for the humans who succumbed to the seduction. Eternal, irreversible damnation, and it would remain so for many more centuries until...but no, wait. I'm getting ahead of myself; that comes later in the story.

CHAPTER 31

J OSHUA WAS BLISSFULLY unaware of the breach in his camp when he sent spies to the land of Ai. They returned and guaranteed him the city would be a piece of cake.

"You don't need to send a lot of soldiers," they assured him. "Two or three thousand men are enough to defeat Ai. There's no need to wear out the whole army when there aren't that many people there."

Joshua was feeling so confident after Jericho that he didn't bother to check in with God to get His take on the situation and, instead, relied solely on what the spies told him. He ordered three thousand men to go up and take care of business at Ai. But the army had no more than reached the edge of the city when the men of Ai attacked them and killed thirty-six of them as Israel turned and fled. Ai chased them from the city gate as far as the quarries, killing them all at the descent. When news of the slaughter reached Israel, the heart of the people sank, and all their spirit and confidence were knocked right out of them.

I could have told Joshua from personal experience how it was a big mistake to rely on somebody else's judgment and take God's approval for granted. He ripped his clothes and fell on his face before the ark of the covenant. He and the leaders threw dirt on their heads, as if that would help matters, and lay prostrate until evening.

Then Joshua cried out, "O God, why did You insist on bringing this people across the Jordan? To make us victims of the Amorites? To wipe us out? Why didn't we just settle down on the east side of the Jordan? O God, what can I say to Your people after Israel has been run off by its enemies?"

"I'm sure you'll think of something. Since you didn't think it important to ask Me before you rushed off to war, you figure it out," God answered. "And by the way, brush the dirt out of your hair. You're a mess, and I'm not impressed."

"Sorry, Lord." Joshua stood to his feet and shook out his hair with his hands. "I know I jumped ahead of You. Please tell me what to do. When the Canaanites and all the others living here learn of this, they'll gang up on us and make short work of us—and worse, Your reputation is at risk."

"My reputation?"

"Won't they say You brought us here but were unable to protect us?"

"Don't grovel, and don't patronize Me. Israel has sinned. They've broken the rules by taking the forbidden plunder from Jericho and then covering up their sin. The people of Israel can no longer look their enemies in the eye—they themselves are plunder."

"But, Lord, who did such a thing? I didn't know of such a sin. Neither did my men."

"Did you examine your men after Jericho? Did you make sure the forbidden things were untouched by them?"

"Not exactly. But I told them not to do it before we invaded the city."

"You were careless, Joshua. The stakes are too high, and I can't afford for you to be careless. I can't continue with you if you don't rid yourselves of the cursed things and start paying attention."

"O Lord, is there nothing we can do to repent of this awful sin?"

Joshua was obviously distraught and worried that he'd become lax in his leadership and let the people go too far with their freedom; maybe God would crush them all. Even though they were in real trouble, I could have saved him from his anguish. Joshua simply didn't know God the way I did. Oh, He was angry—no doubt about that—and He would bring severe punishment to the guilty parties. But there was no possibility God would refuse to go forward with Joshua. It just wasn't going to happen."

"Even money says He'll find a way to spare them." I wagered with myself. As usual, I was right.

"Here's what you must do. Tell the people to get ready for tomorrow by purifying themselves," God said. "Then tell them there are cursed things in the camp and they won't be able to face their enemies until you have gotten rid of the illegal booty."

"We will obey Your every word, O sovereign God."

"All right, then. Tomorrow morning call up the tribes whose names I will give you. They will pass by in front of you clan by clan, then family by family, and then man by man until the culprit is revealed. The person found with the cursed things will be burned, along with everything he has."

Joshua hardly slept that night and early the next morning called all the people to assemble tribe by tribe until the tribe of Judah was singled out. Then he called up the clans and singled out the Zerahites. He called up the Zerahite families and singled out Zimri. Then he called up the family members one by one and singled out Achan.

Before the sifting of the tribes was done, Achan knew he was busted. Sweat poured from his forehead when Joshua stood face-to-face with him.

"Make your confession to God. Tell me what you did. Don't keep back anything from me." There was no emotion in Joshua's eyes as he stared right through Achan.

Seeing no fire escape, Achan answered, "It's true. I sinned against God. In the plunder I spotted a beautiful Shinar robe, two hundred shekels of silver, and a fifty-shekel bar of gold, and I coveted and took them. They are buried in my tent."

Joshua's soldiers ran to the tent, and there they were, buried in the tent with the silver at the bottom. They gathered all the treasure and brought it to Joshua, and in front of all the people, Joshua spread out the contraband before God. Then Achan was led outside the camp, where he was stoned. The soldiers set fire to his body along with the robe and all the silver and gold while the stunned people watched in disbelief. It would be a long time before anything like that happened again.

After it was over, God sent Joshua back to Ai where he and his men thoroughly routed the city. After Jericho, Ai was the beginning of the wars Joshua would lead until the entire land of Canaan fell to Israel just as God had said would happen. All in all, I counted thirty-one kings who fell before Israel's sword.

Year after year, nation by nation, God gave Joshua success in everything he did because he was faithful and never sinned again against God's covenant with him. That's not to say he never made a mistake. All humans make mistakes, even the chosen and anointed—like the time Joshua made a treaty with the Gibeonites without asking God about it. It was nothing but trouble for Israel, but he learned from his error and never got ahead of God again.

As I watched the kings tumble one after another, I knew I couldn't postpone it any longer and had to report to Satan how Joshua was winning and taking away the land where Satan had enjoyed unfettered rule. I stood before him and tried to give the report in as matter-of-fact way as I knew how. At first, Satan simply sat on his throne and seemed unresponsive to the news that Israel was winning.

"So, that's it, sir; in spite of how it looked there for a few decades, Israel has finally won." I bowed my head and stepped back as I finished my report.

"Won?" Satan seemed startled at the word. I wondered if he had listened to me at all.

"Well, yes, they have the land God promised them. They've won."

"They've won nothing but land, and I care nothing about the land."

"You don't care about the land? What is it you care about, then?"

"I want their souls."

"But, sir," I said out of reflex without weighing my words as I had long ago learned to do with Satan. I'd been deployed to the earth for such a long stint that I was out of practice, so the words tumbled right out uncensored by my experience or good sense.

"I don't think you can have them."

Satan leapt from his throne and rose to his full huge stature, body writhing and smoke rising up all around him as he glared at me. By now I was on my knees, trembling so hard my wings caught the air movement I was generating and I began to levitate right there in place. Fearing Satan would view this as a challenge, I forced my wings down and rolled up in a ball in front of him.

"I can't have them?" He growled at me.

"No, no, that's not at all what I meant to say. I just meant you can't have them *now*. Of course, you'll get them eventually."

He didn't respond, but his eyes told me to keep talking.

"When Joshua dies, sir, it's just a matter of time. There's no successor to Joshua like there was with Moses. No one's waiting in the wings to take over."

Satan ordered one of the guards, "Kill Joshua." The guard jumped to attention, but I interrupted before he could leave the room.

"No, wait, sir. I know you don't want to kill Joshua." There I froze for a moment. He would expect me to tell him *why* he didn't want to kill him. I dared not say the truth: Joshua was golden with God, and neither his minions nor Satan himself could lay a glove on him. I bought a little time by struggling to stand up.

"Let them win a few wars, live in peace for a few years, things like that," I said as I tried to snap my wings back into alignment. "You know what will happen. They'll grow complacent as they always have. They won't be thinking they need a new leader after Joshua. They'll be wide open when Joshua dies."

Seeming to have no better idea of his own, Satan begrudgingly accepted what I said. I went to my perch, happy to be back to the closest thing I had as home and settled in to watch the earth. Since Satan wasn't interested in the land issue and didn't seem bothered about the conquered people either, there was no reason for me to wear myself out commuting from the earth to heaven with updates nobody cared to hear.

Waiting around for Joshua to die might take decades and wasn't much of a mental challenge, so I decided to find a hobby to pass the time. That's how I got into transcendental meditation. Yoga hadn't worked out all that well for me, but it was mostly the physical challenge with my wings and hooves. When you're trying to do a headstand and your wings keep falling down in your face, it ruins the experience.

But TM was different. I found my "ooohhmmm" right away. It wasn't long until I could chant my way right into communion with the free-floating Vedas of the universe. Little did I know the Vedas were part of a telecommunication system between Satan and the lesser gods. Wouldn't you know they tattled on me right off? Satan sent one of his henchmen to tell me to hang up and pay attention to the earth.

The army of Israel moved out, taking possession of all God had promised them. There were so many battles; after a while they began to run together in my mind. As each section of land was conquered, Joshua parceled out the property rights to the tribes by families. I tried to keep track of who got what, but after a while it became mind-numbingly tedious. I quit when I remembered Satan wouldn't care a thing about who got a deed to what.

What I did find interesting was the day God came up with the idea of sanctuary cities and told Joshua to build them.

"Why?" Joshua wanted to know.

"So that if a person accidentally kills another person, he will have a safe place to go for justice."

Joshua looked perplexed, as if he were not sure this was a good use of time, but being the good soldier he was, he built the cities without argument.

"Ask God how to tell an accidental killing from an intentional one since everyone in the area is sporting a weapon and is at war," I urged Joshua from my perch but to no avail.

I thought this might be useful information for me later on—you know, when I get my day in court. It could be helpful if I could point out a time when God insisted on different treatment for those who intentionally erred versus those who were victims of circumstances.

Finally, after many long battles, God was satisfied and gave Israel rest from war and safety from all its enemies. Then it really got boring.

I waited and watched for many more years until I saw the sign I was looking for. All of Israel was coming together at the place where Joshua lived. It must be time for Joshua to die. I took off and flew quickly to his tent.

All the chiefs, judges, and officers filled the tent and spilled over to the outside to hear the words of Joshua.

"I'm an old man, and I've lived a long time. You've seen everything that God has done to these nations because of you. He did it because He's your God and you are chosen and set apart to worship only Him."

Joshua took a deep, laboring breath, and so did the people gathered around him.

"Now, stay strong and steady. Obediently do everything written in the book of the revelation of Moses. Don't get mixed up with the nations that are still around."

"We won't mix in," they shouted.

"Don't so much as speak the names of their gods or swear by them."

"You can count on us."

"And by all means, don't worship or pray to them. Hold tight to your God, just as you've done up to now."

The crowd murmured their promise to be faithful.

"Now, hear me. Vigilantly guard your souls and love your God."

I shuddered as Joshua said those words. Did Joshua know their souls were what Satan had been waiting for all this time, or was that just a lucky guess?

"If you wander off and intermarry or take up with these remaining nations still among you, know for certain that God will not get rid of them when they become a curse for you—as they surely will—until you're the ones who will be driven out of this good land God has given you."

"We would never do such a thing," several of the priests said in unison.

"How could we disobey our God who has brought us here?"

Through his aged eyes, Joshua looked to and fro among the people gathered around him. He took his final breath and spoke the warning one more time.

"If you leave the path of the covenant of your God that He commanded and go off and serve and worship other gods, His righteous anger will blaze out against you. He will leave you to the ravages of the gods you choose. He will not save you. There'll be nothing left of you and no sign that you've ever been in this good land He gave you."

"There is no God but the God of Israel." The crowd cheered.

Joshua looked into the faces of the people gathered around him and then closed his eyes for the last time.

I closed mine as well, but for a different reason. I felt a cold chill down my spine, and I knew Satan was watching every move from the rim of the second heaven. Someone must have told him I was gone, and he put two and two together and figured out it must be time for Joshua to die. He didn't wait for my report. After all, hanging out until Joshua died was all that held him back, and it was obvious he wanted to see the action firsthand.

I wondered if I should try to warn God of what was coming. He hadn't been around that much since Israel was at peace with her enemies. He might be giving Israel far more credit for the ability to self-govern than was warranted. He must have known that last admonition from Joshua to the people about not worshiping other gods was going to be the exact place where Satan would go after them.

If I could alert Him to something He'd overlooked, He might be grateful. I decided to give it a try. I slipped away from Joshua's tent and found a big rock in the desert. I knelt down behind it and hoped Satan wouldn't be able to see me.

"Pssst, God," I whispered as loud as I dared. "This is, well, never mind who this is. I thought I'd better warn You of what's about to happen down here. I know how You sometimes have a tendency to forgive and forget, at least where the humans are concerned. But Satan never forgets anything, not even the slightest offense. He's been waiting for this chance. Your Jews don't have a leader right now. You might want to appoint some judges or a king maybe, someone with an official position who can tell them what to do. Satan's about to go after them through his demigods. I've seen this happen before—whole nations succumb in a day to Baal or Ashtera."

If God heard me, He ignored me.

I was flapping my way back to the second heaven when I felt the atmosphere tremble. Soon I was in position to see brigade after brigade as Satan unleashed his soul-starved hordes back into the earth realm to go after the people of God.

The seduction of Israel was about to begin.

CHAPTER 32

S AMANTHA WAS SILENTLY rehearsing her opening line when the voice on the phone abruptly ended the elevator music that had been playing while she was on hold.

"Jonathan Marks here," the voice said without emotion.

"Dr. Marks, this is Dr. Samantha Yale from the University of Jerusalem. Thank you for taking my call."

Samantha had wrestled with her conscience for several days before deciding to contact the highly regarded paleontologist, New Testament scholar, and expert on religious relics and objects of antiquity.

"I'm happy to speak with you, Dr. Yale. How can I help you?"

Rehearsing her opening line was proving to be of little help as she found herself searching for the right words to begin the conversation.

"Dr. Yale?"

"Yes, I'm here. Sorry." She took a deep breath. "Dr. Marks, out of respect for your time, let me come right to the point. I've come into possession of some very ancient scrolls that appear to have been written in cuneiform."

That's good, Sam. Spill the whole thing in fifteen seconds. Don't give him any time to warm up to the idea.

"I see. Well, now, that would be interesting and very unlikely since, as you know, cuneiform predates papyrus by at least a thousand years."

"Yes, I'm aware of that."

"Then, how can I help you, Dr. Yale?"

"I've been retained to translate the writing, which I've done. However, at some point, the authenticity of the scrolls themselves as genuine relics will need corroboration. I was hopeful you might be interested in taking a look at them."

Jonathan hesitated.

Don't bring up the Torah codes; don't bring up the Torah codes. She squinted and crossed her fingers.

"This wouldn't have anything to do with the Torah codes, would it?"

She opened her squinted eyes and rolled them at the ceiling. *One little request—is that too much to ask?*

"No, Dr. Marks. This is an unrelated matter."

"You said you have physical possession of the scrolls now?"

"Yes, that's right." She decided to say nothing more until he moved the conversation forward.

It's your ball, Dr. Marks. Are you going to play?

"When would you like for me to examine them?"

"Yes!" she whispered as she raised her arms in a victory pose, making sure he didn't hear her excitement.

"I'm not certain. The scrolls are privately owned. I need permission from the owner, and to be perfectly candid, I'm not sure he will agree."

"Then, why are you contacting me?"

"The owner is an eccentric who, in my opinion, may border on paranoia. If the scrolls are authentic, they are historically priceless. Should he agree to let me seek peer-level confirmation, I would need to move quickly before he could change his mind or disappear altogether. That's why I chose to speak with you first."

"How long before you can know whether he will agree or not?"

"I wish I could tell you."

Now there's a real confidence builder, Sam. Go for broke; try to explain Wonk Eman.

"This is going to sound odd, I know, but I have no way of contacting the owner. I have to wait until he gets in touch with me."

"So, you have no idea what sort of time frame we're talking about?"

"No. It could be days or weeks, but if I should be successful in getting the owner's permission to have you examine the scrolls, would you be willing to take a look at them?"

"Yes, Dr. Yale. I'll help any way I can."

The relief in her voice was audible. "Thank you so much, Dr. Marks. I'll be in touch when I have more to share. Until then, ciao."

Samantha hung up the phone and let out a long sigh. There was nothing else for her to do except wait until the elusive Wonk Eman reappeared. "I have a feeling I won't be waiting long." She leaned back in her leather chair, closed her eyes, and thought about the last words of the scroll. *The seduction of Israel was about to begin.*

Samantha answered the phone on the first ring.

"Dr. Yale?"

"Wonk?" she blurted before she could stop herself. It had been a month since her conversation with Jonathan Marks. Where had he been all this time?

"How did you know it was me?"

"Let's say I'm psychic." She waited for him to laugh, but he didn't. "Never mind. I was expecting to hear from you soon—sooner actually. That's all."

"Have you translated the scrolls?"

I'm fine. Thanks for asking, and you?

"Yes, I have." Best to overlook his lack of telephone etiquette.

Long pause.

"Do you believe what you read?"

"Believe? I'm not sure I know what you're asking."

"Do you believe things happened that way? Like it says in the scrolls."

Choose your words carefully, Sam. Remember he's a flight risk.

"Wonk, do you know the difference between a myth and something historically authentic?"

"Are you accusing me of lying, Dr. Yale?"

"You? Why, of course not. We're not talking about you. I mean the story in the scrolls—that's all."

"It's a diary."

"Yes, I remember you said that before." She paused and then decided to press on. "Anyway, a myth is something that may or may not be true but can't be proven. The scrolls contain a myth—albeit a captivating one—but it would be careless to assume the story describes actual events."

Silence.

"I expected more from you, Dr. Yale."

"I'm sorry, Wonk. I don't want to minimize what you've got because it is quite extraordinary—no doubt about that."

"Do you want to see more?"

"More scrolls? How many more are there?"

"Do you want to see more?"

"Yes, yes, of course I do."

Deep breath, reassuring voice, ready, go.

"In fact, Wonk, I wonder if you would allow a colleague of mine to examine the scrolls...to confirm my translation."

"No."

"But I assure you he would be discreet."

"No."

"Wonk, Dr. Marks is at the top of his field. If he verifies the age of the scrolls, it could easily..."

"Especially not Dr. Marks."

"How do you know Jonathan Marks?" She tried for nonchalance.

"You gave me your word, Dr. Yale."

"And I intend to abide by it. I was only thinking of your benefit...to bring additional credibility to the value of what you have."

No response. Maybe he was thinking it over.

The ticking grandfather clock in her office told her he had been silent for a full minute, far outside her ten-second rule.

"Wonk?"

"If you don't keep your word—if you don't finish the translation—I've risked everything to bring it to you." He picked up the sentence as if there hadn't been an interminably long silence.

"I told you I would keep my word."

"You don't know how important they are. They must not be destroyed before the translation is complete."

"Destroyed? Wonk, listen to me. The scrolls are safe with me. Forget what I said about Dr. Marks. Send the additional scrolls to me as soon as you can."

"Yes, all right. I have to trust you. You must be there to personally receive them."

"I'll wait for them just like before."

She knew this was a good time to end the conversation, while they had agreement and he had calmed down, but her curiosity as a Torah scholar won out over safety.

"Wonk, just one more thing. It's about Og, the Nephilim king. I researched him, and it turns out you were right that he may have survived Noah's flood, but his death is later chronicled in the Old Testament."

More silence.

"I only bring it up because you were so disturbed that he had somehow remained alive. I thought it would make you feel safer to know he's no threat to you. He died thousands of years ago."

"Demonic beings do not die. Only the human part of him died."

"I see." If she went further she knew she risked agitating him again. "I just wanted you to know I'd looked into it."

"Thank you, Dr. Yale. I know this all seems strange to you; you'd understand if I could tell you everything, but I can't. You just don't know me; you don't know who I am. That's all I can say. Good-bye, Dr. Yale."

Samantha carefully placed the black phone in its cradle, leaned back in her chair, and breathed a sigh of relief that things were on track. Glancing back to the phone, she smiled as she spoke to the disconnected caller.

"Actually, Wonk, you just don't know who I am."

CONTINUE THE ENGAGING STORY OF
SAMANTHA YALE AND THE FALLEN ANGEL
IN THE FINAL TWO BOOKS OF THE
RELUCTANT DEMON DIARIES

RELEASING
May 3, 2011

978-1-59979-914-8 / $13.99

978-1-61638-206-3 / $13.99

Experience the reign of King David from the perspective of a fallen angel in *The King*, an engaging story that demonstrates the unrelenting love, grace, mercy, and determination of a sovereign God amidst the demonic strategy to destroy His people.

As the final installment in the series that began with *Lucifer's Flood*, this book finds ancient language expert Samantha Yale translating the final batch of ancient scrolls that cover the life of Jesus. Discover the secrets that both Samantha and Mr. Wonk have been keeping!

VISIT YOUR LOCAL BOOKSTORE.

REALMS

9676B